STORMCALLER

Chris Wraight

More Space Wolves from Black Library

A WARHAMMER 40,000 NOVEL

STORMCALLER
Chris Wraight

BLACK LIBRARY

To Hannah, with love.

A BLACK LIBRARY PUBLICATION
First published in Great Britain in 2014 by
Black Library,
Games Workshop Ltd.,
Willow Road,
Nottingham,
NG7 2WS, UK

10 9 8 7 6 5 4 3 2 1

Cover by Raymond Swanland.

A CIP record for this book is available from the British Library.

UK ISBN 13: 978 1 84970 580 6
US ISBN 13: 978 1 84970 581 3

See Black Library on the internet at
blacklibrary.com

Find out more about Games Workshop
and the world of Warhammer 40,000 at
games-workshop.com

Printed and bound by CPI Group (UK) Ltd, Croydon, CR0 4YY

It is the 41st millennium. For more than a hundred centuries the Emperor has sat immobile on the Golden Throne of Earth. He is the master of mankind by the will of the gods, and master of a million worlds by the might of his inexhaustible armies. He is a rotting carcass writhing invisibly with power from the Dark Age of Technology. He is the Carrion Lord of the Imperium for whom a thousand souls are sacrificed every day, so that he may never truly die.

Yet even in his deathless state, the Emperor continues his eternal vigilance. Mighty battlefleets cross the daemon-infested miasma of the warp, the only route between distant stars, their way lit by the Astronomican, the psychic manifestation of the Emperor's will. Vast armies give battle in his name on uncounted worlds. Greatest amongst his soldiers are the Adeptus Astartes, the Space Marines, bio-engineered super-warriors. Their comrades in arms are legion: the Imperial Guard and countless planetary defence forces, the ever-vigilant Inquisition and the tech-priests of the Adeptus Mechanicus to name only a few. But for all their multitudes, they are barely enough to hold off the ever-present threat from aliens, heretics, mutants - and worse.

To be a man in such times is to be one amongst untold billions. It is to live in the cruellest and most bloody regime imaginable. These are the tales of those times. Forget the power of technology and science, for so much has been forgotten, never to be re-learned. Forget the promise of progress and understanding, for in the grim dark future there is only war. There is no peace amongst the stars, only an eternity of carnage and slaughter, and the laughter of thirsting gods.

Prologue

Always cold.

Cold at the moment of dawn when the red sun slid above the fields of ice like a clot of blood. Cold at the heart of the day when the ice cracked under grey, feathered skies. Cold in the long nights – bone-aching cold, cold that sunk under the skin and lodged fast.

Men could go mad from it, weeping as their fingers blackened and softened. When the pain grew too much, they would scream their hopelessness at the stars, and that brought beasts to the flickering circles of the fires. Screams always brought beasts, as lean and hungry as those who huddled at the flame-pits. Once you let the cold make you scream, that was the end. Fenris ended the weak quickly.

It was near the end of the long winter-spell when he was born, bloody and motley, wailing before being silenced by rags as the wind made the tent walls drum. The highlands were cracking by then, opening up like parted flesh. Faer told them change would come before the fire-summer, so they had to move, packing hide tents onto sleds and skiffs and wrapping them hard with leather twine.

Ana, his mother, was fifteen seasons as the Terrans reckoned it and as tough as knucklebones. When the dawn came she was ready, wrapped in furs, her face swathed from the blast-wind, her pale hands clutching the cords of her back-strapped cradleboard.

They walked in teams, dragging goods on long sleds, heading south towards the long, grey firth where the *hvalari* snorted and dived. The skies were low and stone-grey, blurred by fine rain that felt like ice when it hit. Mountains rose up in the north, bleak and dagger-sided, kindling thunder. Those mountains had no name, for they had stood less than a child's lifetime. Only one range on Fenris had a name. Only one range endured more than a mortal span, and the Ascurii knew of that range only through the sagas of Faer.

They went three days before the land ahead of them changed. Ice cracked underfoot, spreading like uncurling dark fingers as their leather-wound feet kicked through the slush. Ana gritted her teeth, bending against the weight of the bundle on her back. She suckled the infant on the move, pulling him round, trudging, staying silent.

He never cried. No infants on Fenris cried once the immense cold first washed over them – they kept their mouths clammed shut, their fists balled, their black eyes staring. He stayed swaddled tight on the cradle-board, limbs pressed to his body to retain heat, covered in a thick layer of deer pelt and grass, only his eyes and nose exposed.

Faer halted on the morning of the fourth day. Totems rattled under his arms, swinging from lengths of twine. The Ascurii stood in straggling groups around him, huddling under the shade of bony *furu* pines. They numbered no more than sixty by then, worn down and harrowed by the Long Winter. The men's skin was drawn tight over bone and wrinkled dry like cured fish. The women's faces were chapped from the wind, blotched red and white, their eyes narrowed. Their breath steamed in the morning mist, catching on furs and cloaks and drifting into the white sky.

Faer looked out over the firth as it stretched away towards a lowering horizon – lead-matt, crested with the froth of choppy water, studded with drifting ice. In the far west rose the sky-blue wall of a glacier, and beyond that the piled-high landmass of the Greater Island.

That land might survive for a dozen seasons, or one, or none. It looked sturdy enough, but no one could tell. The world was in constant change from one Great Year to the next, and that was the way of it. None complained, for none knew any different – you might as well complain about the bloodpox, or the golden-eyed wolves that roamed the islands like ravenous shadows, or the ravens that squatted over cooling corpses after the gore had sunk among the stones.

Faer's eyes narrowed. It wasn't far. They could rebuild and refit the boats within the week, and be over to the other side in less than a day. If the storms held, it would be no more perilous than when they'd last crossed the deep.

Jorund clumped over to stand by him. The big headman pulled his cloak tight around his burly shoulders, sending a shiver of snow rattling down his back.

'We go?' he grunted, watching what Faer was watching.

The shaman nodded, and his straggling beard pressed up against the folds of coarse fabric at his neck.

'Others will be there, too,' said Jorund, doubtfully.

Faer nodded again. 'Ice and iron,' he mumbled.

'We are weak.'

'We cannot stay here,' said Faer, turning his milky eye towards the headman. 'You want to stay? The land is fire-cursed. It will crack soon.'

Jorund's grey eyes scanned the firth. A month ago it had been solid with ice, thick enough for a heavy skiff. Making the boats ready would be backbreaking.

He looked up at the glacier. The land beyond was dark with trees, needling up against the horizon in tight rows.

It was a big island, a solid island, with deep roots. Many would contest the land – it would have prey under the branches, and predators watching the prey.

As Jorund thought and watched, the ice around him sighed and creaked. He looked down to see a fissure opening between his feet, just a finger's-breadth wide. The gap filled with water.

'We go, then,' he growled, stepping away. He turned to the others. They stared back at him, expectant. 'We go,' he told them, clapping his frozen hands together to get the blood flowing.

Ana looked up at him. Her round face was shiny with fatigue. Her trothed man, Aesgir, stood at her side, supporting her with one hand, dragging his sled with the other.

They knew the danger. The child might not survive the crossing. Ana was weak still; she might not, either.

'Have you named him?' Jorund asked Ana.

Ana shook her head.

'Name him,' he said. 'The gods must know him.'

Ana nodded, understanding.

Then she turned and began to unload tools from the sled. No one said anything more. One by one, the Ascurii got to work.

Only two boats foundered on the way over, tipped up by the crash of surf against floes; the rest scraped home against the icy gravel of the shoreline. The survivors clambered up a long incline towards higher ground. Once the boats were hauled high onto the glass-ice and stone, the men took up flat-bladed spears and throwing axes. They crept up into the rocky uplands, hanging together, their bodies crouched.

Jorund was wrong – there were no others there before them. They climbed up above the shoulder of the glacier, crouching against knife-hard winds from the open ocean. Immense forests stretched away from them, pine-dark, close like fur. The ground was the colour and density of steel.

Faer went quickly, confidently, guided by his visions. The tattoos on his withered skin looked bright blue in the hard light, like veins. He pulled on his old staff, and the bones and vision-trinkets jangled.

At the summit of the massif above the glacier's southerly flank, he paused. He lifted his wiry arms into the air, and his filthy rags fell from them, exposing skin to the ice-bite.

'New land!' he shouted. His voice echoed flatly. A broody forest line glared back at him, and the wind scoured across empty stone and milk-white ice and the obsidian shade of the deep wood.

Ana clutched her child close to her, listening for the rattle-growl of beasts. She had the keenest hearing of the Ascurii.

Nothing yet, but they would come. They would already be uncurling in the dark, sniffing, salivating, stretching.

Aesgir came to her side. 'Anything?'

Ana shook her head, but said, 'Baldr,' quietly, lest Faer hear.

'For the boy?'

Ana nodded, and Aesgir smiled, exposing the half-toothed jaw he'd carried ever since the fighting against the Gyeths.

'Yes. Baldr. He is awake?'

Ana wrenched the cradleboard around from her shoulder, exposing the infant swaddled within. Two dark eyes peered from the straw and leather, steady, unmoving, solemn.

Aesgir grinned again and ran his fingers over the boy's face. 'Always awake. Never sleeps.'

Ana pulled him away, hoisting him back onto her shoulder. 'What is there to sleep for?'

Aesgir looked at her, irritated that she'd pulled him away. He was about to speak when Jorund strode past, axe drawn.

'Further up,' he grunted, beckoning the others on. He glared at Ana for a moment. 'Night will come.'

Then they were moving again, dragging the boats with them, the sleds, the leather sacking and the spear-bundles, clattering it across scree and moss, searching.

Above them, the white sky stretched, remorseless, empty, like a void.

They did not name the place they built, for it would be gone soon enough, just like everywhere else, so it was just the settlement, the hearth, the fire, the *aett*. Jorund drove them hard. They raised a stockade, first using the wood of the boats they had brought, then trunks felled from the forest. They hammered the beams in, digging out the frost-rimed earth with picks. The women worked with the men, hauling, tying, hacking. By the time the sun set, all of them were shining with sweat.

The fire was lit on the first night. It roared with a blaze the height of a skiff-sail, throwing bloody shadows across the snow and turning it to grey puddles. The warriors stood guard, all of them, none sleeping, fingering axes watchfully.

Jorund was the tallest, his heavy grey cloak hanging stiffly, his frost-crusted beard jutting from under a low hood. Ana watched him from the fireside, where she was nursing Baldr. She couldn't see Aesgir – he must have been on the far side. Faer mumbled somewhere in the shadows, squatting and rocking in his visions.

As the sun went down, shadows crept out from the eaves of the forest. The air chilled fast, searing against sweat-cooled skin. Stars pricked into the sky, vivid like the jewel-belt of the gods.

Ana heard them first, as always – low, gurgling growls. They were a long way off, drumming along the earth from far away, deep away. The sounds echoed in the gathering dusk, making the hairs on the back of her arms rise.

Baldr stirred in her arms. He broke from her. His dark eyes glistened in the fire-glow, wide and unafraid. He listened.

Ana smiled at him. 'The wolves, Baldr,' she breathed, wiping a droplet of milk from his sombre mouth.

By then, the others had heard. The men tensed as they stood around the fire, their bodies black against the half-built stockade. Long spears swayed as their bearers peered into the night. Blades were drawn from leather-bound scabbards, each inscribed with scratch-runes by Faer.

Ana rocked the child, though he needed no comfort. 'The *wolves*,' she whispered again.

He was not looking at her. He twisted his head, trying to see where the noise was coming from.

'More fire,' ordered Jorund, his voice tight. Logs were thrown on, spitting and cracking, sending sparks spiralling into the frigid night.

Baldr didn't like the ligh; he screwed his eyes against it, smearing balled fists over his ruddy face. But the sound – the purring, damp, hot catch of clustered lupine throats – *that* made him listen.

Ana watched it, and her heart warmed.

It was a good sign. A sign of the god-marked, of the iron-hearted.

'Listen to them,' she told him. 'Listen. They will kill you, if they find you. They will tear you apart if they catch you before you are made strong. They will hunt you, run you down.'

She grabbed his head and turned it to her.

'But if you live, Baldr Ascurii, if you *live*...' She gazed at him with a hungry, desperate love. 'You will hunt *them*.'

It was a hard first year. Johana died when with child, and Beorth was gored when he got separated from Jorund's hunt-party. After, the Summer of Fire came, burning across the boiling seas like a fever, and pox ravaged the Greater Island, sending ten to the neverworld, their faces stark and staring with fear. They would not have been afraid to die with axe in hand, but a sickbed promised no glory.

Baldr lived. He thrived as the months passed, growing strong on milk and hunt-meat. Aesgir fed him blood from the meat of slain *konungur*, and he lapped it greedily, licking stringy matter from the sinew.

Ana watched him shoot upwards, tottering on his bent legs as the Summer faded, learning to hold a hilt as the Long Winter gripped the land again. She watched as he spoke the first word – *axe* – and the second – *father*. She watched him as Jorund showed him how to fish, to stalk, to handle a blade, and she watched him as Faer initiated him into the mysteries. Baldr's expression never changed: his dark eyes followed his teachers, drinking in their knowledge. His sombre face remained still. When the others ran the hunt, roaring their fear out and their fury, he stayed silent, like a shadow in daylight, grey and ephemeral.

He listened to Faer most closely. He would crouch at the man's feet, silent as the tales of old wyrds and deeds were mumbled into the flickering flames. He would watch the bones spiral on their cords, and reach out for them, as if he could pull them all to him.

'Is he marked?' Ana asked Faer once, after seeing Baldr scratch the outlines of runes in the dirt, intent and obsessive.

Faer's mouth creased equivocally, making the rings in his nose jangle. 'He is a hunter. A strong one.'

That satisfied her. She wrapped her cloak about her and felt the cold stir in the air again as the winter came in.

It was no life, to be among the runes and the knucklebones. Better to have spear in hand and run with the packs, to eat meat and drink blood and become a warrior of the *vlka*.

Baldr was quiet. He was placid. He would have to learn to be angry soon, for Fenris did not shelter calm souls.

So she watched him, and waited for the fire to come. She knew it would do, that it must do, but did not know when.

Four more Great Years passed. More were born, more died. The wolves took Aesgir one night, as they often did when hunters became too bold or were too unlucky, and so Ana kept hearth alone. The aett did not flourish. Wind blew hard across the highlands, scraping at the wood and making the hide tents shiver. Faer's vision had saved them from the cracking earth, but it had not led them to plenty. They hacked a living from the iron-tough earth, hunting the skirts of the forest, cheating what prey they could from the dripping maws of greater predators.

Baldr took his father's place in the hunting pack, adopting the axe. Faer gave him the hunt-mark on his shoulder. Baldr made no sound as the ink-needle went in, piercing flesh and giving him the icon of the *fjolnir* – the nightjar.

He went with them after that – thirty men of the Ascurii, clad in furs, each bearing spears or axes. His was the only beardless face, as smooth as a nutshell; he was brown-haired, clean-featured.

They walked in file, heading up the path of a half-frozen river into the jagged country west of the great glacier. Water had run clear for the long summer but was now steadily choking as the ice stretched down from the peaks. Baldr's fingers were stiff with cold as he clutched his axe, his breath steaming.

The air thinned as they climbed, taking them up winding paths and into the heights. The trees were old by the standards of the ever-changing world – a dozen Great Years, perhaps – and their bark was oil-dark and gnarled like rope.

Jorund paused, crouching low, sniffing, and the party waited silently. The headman's flinty beard brushed against the ground as he stooped. Eventually he got back to his feet. He was moving stiffly. Baldr watched him move, and wondered how long it would be before a challenger tested Jorund's mettle.

'Higher up,' Jorund grunted, and they set off again.

The trees rose up on either side, vast as pillars, covering the land in darkness. Snow piled high against the trunks, glowing a soft blue in the darkness, and the paths silted up with it. Baldr strode with the others, axe clutched tight.

Hours passed, marked only by the trudging steps, the brush of snow against leather, the drip and crack of the deep forest.

Then Jorund got wind of something, and beckoned the others to halt. He sniffed, holding his grizzly head high into the oncoming wind. He stayed motionless for a long time.

Baldr sniffed too, taking care to draw the air in silently.

Musk, he thought. *Tilbrád. Far off. Meagre.*

He'd got better at it, honing his senses, learning from the others.

Jorund tensed. He said nothing, but his hands began to move. The hunt-signals came fast – flickering fingers, gestures. On his final signal, the hunt-pack burst into movement.

They ran as one, softly, loping through the snow with high, silent strides. None of them spoke. Baldr kept pace easily, and the pack spread out, sweeping under the pine eaves. Soon each hunter was only visible to his counterpart on either side, and the net spread wide. The prey – tilbrád – were wary and agile, and far faster than a man if given a start.

Baldr stumbled as he ran. Swallowing a curse, he picked up his pace, veering past a giant trunk and ploughing through a deep drift that lapped up to his knees.

He was falling behind. The others were older, stronger, more used to the chase. Baldr pushed hard, hearing his breath echo inside his close-tied hood. He stumbled again, tripping on something beneath the snow, losing his footing and staggering against the curled root of another tree.

He couldn't match the speed of the pack, no matter how much he pushed himself. Flushing from shame, panting like a dog, he kept going, reeling and tripping as the hunters pulled away from him.

Baldr didn't know how long he'd been running before he heard the growl.

He froze – his head whipped round, his heart thumping. Tree trunks marched off in all directions, black like obsidian against the gloom. The terrain rose and fell in snow-covered clumps, broken by the jagged teeth of moss-clad rocks.

For a few terrible moments, he saw nothing. The echo of the growl resonated through the forest, low and quiet, like the soft crack of earth breaking. Baldr stared back and forth, peering into the dark, his axe-blade poised.

Then, slowly, as if resolving from the smoke of a fire-pit, he saw twin orbs of amber in the night. They were a long way away – thirty metres, across a tangled mass of snow-laden briars. They did not blink. They shone dully – black pupils, golden irises, fixed, steady, unmoving.

Baldr felt as if his limbs had been run through with lead. He heard the purring growl again, running along the ground, making the hair on his neck rise. He smelt it for the first time – musty, wet, dog-thick. The beast had come from upwind, just as they were doing to their prey.

Baldr squeezed his fingers on the axe-heft, terrified, his blood raging in his temples.

Why doesn't it move?

His eyes adjusted further. He saw the huge, ridgebacked spine curving over the briars' edge. He saw grey fur, claws sinking into the snow, ludicrously muscled shoulders bunching and flexing.

It was twice his height, a dozen times heavier, draped in a thick, dark mane. Long jaws pulled back into a snarl, sending beads of saliva glistening down to the snow.

It seemed to be regarding him as closely as he regarded it. Its huge nostrils flared. Its massive paws raked the ground before it. The beast was fighting against something – some pull, some drag.

Then it *roared* – a massive, throaty, throttled bellow that shook snow from the branches above it. With a twist and a thrust, it pounced, shouldering clear of the briars and bounding towards him.

Baldr held his ground, almost paralysed with fear, his axe-head clasped stiff. The beast ate up the ground between them, gaping its obscenely long jaws to reveal rows of yellowing, blood-mottled teeth.

The first spear came in from Baldr's right, hurled hard so the shaft trembled as it hit. Another whistled in from the left, *thunking* into the creature's withers.

The beast yowled and skidded to a halt, throwing up slush. More spears hurtled from the trees. They all hit – the hunters of Fenris who lived to adulthood had superlative aim.

The beast thrashed back and forth, caught in a crossfire of hurled barbs. Baldr suddenly felt the vice of fear lift, and hefted his axe.

The beast stared at him, golden eyes wide with pain and fury. Baldr threw, sending the axe head-over-heel, watching as it cracked into the creature's shoulder, biting deep, sending a fountain of wine-dark blood jetting.

Then he was running, scampering into cover again, weaponless in the face of the creature's wrath. He heard great echoing roars as the hunters loosed more spears. He heard the scrabble of claw on stone, and the crack of branches as the beast charged at its tormentors.

He kept running. His lungs burned, his muscles protested, but the thrill of danger, the stink of fear and exhilaration, kept him moving.

He slid to a halt under the lee of a felled trunk, twisting round to see if he was being pursued.

He saw men running between the trunks, some to throw spears, some to withdraw. He didn't see the beast. He heard its yowls and its barks, muffled in the snow and the trees. The noises grew fainter as the pack drove it off. They couldn't kill it – even Baldr knew that – but they could give it enough pain to lope away, slinking back to lick its sores and gashes in the hollowness of some meat-rotten den somewhere.

Baldr fell to his haunches, still breathless, feeling the burn of the cold air as he forced it into shocked lungs.

Jorund found him later. The headman laughed gruffly, grabbed him by his furs and hauled him to his feet.

'Got a shock?' he asked, smacking the snow from Baldr's shoulders and making him stand upright. 'Stumbled on a real killer?'

Jorund grabbed his chin and forced his gaze up to meet him. Baldr stared ahead blearily.

'Throw your axe first,' Jorund said, not letting him go. 'Fear will kill you quicker than the cold.'

Baldr nodded, shamed. He could still feel the pull of terror around his heart, and knew that was weak.

'Why did it wait?' asked Jorund thoughtfully, studying him hard. 'Never seen that.'

Baldr didn't know what to say. Jorund was handling him roughly, like a piece of carcass to be dragged over the fire-pit.

'Maybe you're marked,' said Jorund, lightly, shaking Baldr and slapping him on the shoulder. 'Or maybe it had eaten already.'

Jorund dropped him, then tramped over to the others. The hunters were retrieving their spears. Once they had weapons in hand again they pulled together, respectful of the shadows.

Baldr had lost his axe. For all he knew it was buried in the wolf's flank, sticking from its hide like a trophy.

He looked back into the trees, back into the depths where it had retreated. His heart-rate had slowed to something like normal.

Why did it wait?

Jorund called the hunt together. They had lost the trail and scared any prey far out of reach. Another failed trek, another hungry night.

'Back to the aett,' Jorund ordered, not looking at Baldr, not waiting to witness the looks of disappointment from the rest of the pack.

Baldr fell in with the others, keeping to himself, ignoring the mutters and glares that came his way. Once they started marching again, in line just as before, weapons kept ready, the monotony of the walk took over.

They fell silent. He remained so. The snow kicked over his boots, the blood of the wolf froze and crystallised on the ground.

Why did it wait?

Winter came in, blasting from the north as the last vestiges of health bled from the land. Prey became harder to find, and the iron pots that hung over the fires contained little more than dried tubers and boiled grass. More of the Ascurii died, and Faer spent his days in visions, trying to plot a path through the maze of the future. He emptied the last of his rattle-bags, scraping the strands of fungi from the leather and burning them, inhaling the god-smoke to make his visions true.

The days shortened, down to a few hours of grey light around noon, bordered by the long, frigid nights that forever threatened to gust out the fires and plunge them all into oblivion. Jorund showed his age, Ana showed hers. Lives were short on the death world – short and vigorous, driven by the eternal cycle of ice and fire.

It was at the nadir of the Great Year that Faer foretold the coming of others. Jorund sent scouts up to the headlands every day, watching for sails. The seas were closing up with ice, so passage by boat would soon be impossible.

Weeks passed, and nothing came. Some began to mutter against Faer – that his visions had led them nowhere, that they would starve before the next summer, that they should have stayed in the old lands.

Baldr never joined in. He sat with his mother and sharpened his new axe. He hadn't missed out on another hunt, and his young limbs had grown supple and strong. He hadn't lost his nerve again, and his axe and spear had accounted for two kills – a good tally for one of his age and stature, and much needed.

Hrom was the one to see them first. He came running to the aett, out of breath and with his hair hanging wildly around his face.

'Sails!' he blurted, panting.

'How many?' asked Jorund, standing grimly before him.

'Four,' said Hrom. 'More, maybe. Fog's heavy.'

The hunters stirred themselves. Jorund sounded his bronze horn to summon the other scouts back, and the Ascurii girded themselves for fighting. The Greater Island wasn't much of a home, but neither was anywhere else during the Long Winter, and the newcomers would not be coming to barter.

The Ascurii could muster only thirty warriors by then, more than half of them longbeards with unyielding joints and wasted muscles. No one questioned Baldr's presence among them. Aegnor was even younger, barely able to lift the throwing spear he took to battle, and no one questioned that either.

The warband marched back up to the headland where they had first landed. By the time they reached the vantage, the boats were already fighting through the swell to reach the beach. Fog rolled in from the ocean, breaking across rocks like summer sea-foam. The invaders waited until the last moment before jumping clear and hauling on the ropes.

Baldr hung back. He had never seen men of other nations. They looked almost as fearsome as the beast had done – huge, pelt-clad, covered in unfamiliar totems and war-tattoos. One of them was a bear of a man with a thick black beard that spilled down a metal breastplate. He carried a double-bladed axe in two hands, and swaggered through the icy surf. Others came after him – thickset fighters with throwing axes and blunt hammers and iron rings piercing their faces.

Jorund watched them come, gauging numbers. 'As pinched as we,' he muttered, fingering his own axe impatiently. 'We can take them.' He turned to Bolg, his cupbearer since Aesgir had been taken. 'Now. Before they clear the beaches.'

Bolg nodded curtly, thumping his own warhammer into an empty palm. 'I count twenty.'

The Ascurii broke into a run, careering down the steep path towards the shoreline. As he ran, Jorund bellowed his defiance, soon joined by the others. Baldr raised his voice with them, running as hard as they did, whirling his axe around his head. The fear left him, replaced by a growing excitement – a yearning to get into the fight, to crack the iron into flesh and bone. Together, the Ascurii tore across the stone-land, their leather boots thudding on the ice and granite.

Jorund was first among them, hurtling down onto the beach and barrelling straight into the oncoming newcomers. Bolg was next, then the others, all sprinting, whooping as the blades came to bear.

Baldr darted among them, faster and shorter. A man with long red hair lunged at him with a spiked cudgel, trying to catch him on the nape before lumbering after more serious prey.

Baldr dodged the blow. He lashed his axe-head across, not aiming, just swiping. It connected with the man's trailing wrist, and the edge cut clean through, taking the hand off at the bone.

The man screamed and collapsed, clutching at his pumping wrist, trying to staunch the torrent that sprayed from the wound. Blood splashed against Baldr's chest and face, blinding him. He staggered back, wiping his eyes, only to see his enemy slump onto his back, writhing in agony.

A fierce pleasure blazed through him. He spun his axe about and buried it in the man's chest, ending his yelps. Then Baldr whirled around, ready for the next one.

By then the stony beach was riven by cries and screams, by the clang and thud of metal blades clashing and finding their targets. Blood dotted the air like kicked chaff. Men ran at one another, shaggy locks flailing, arms pumping. Jorund had beaten his man and was grappling with another. Bolg had had his legs chopped from under him and lay twitching in a slick of gore.

The tang of blood made Baldr heady. He flung himself at the nearest newcomer – a boy not much older than him, hefting a long maul. The boy squared up, long sandy hair flying across his face. He bared his teeth like an animal, and ran at Baldr.

Baldr waited for the maul to swing in, jerking out of the way at the last moment. He darted back with his axe, hoping to catch the boy's leg, but missed by a hand's width.

The boy was as quick as he was, slippery as a worm. They circled one another, lunging and feinting. Baldr rushed him, hammering the axe down, but the boy got his maul up to parry and the weapons banged together.

Baldr pressed the attack, working the axe around to thrust it up at the boy's chest. The sandy-haired fighter fell away, retreating, keeping his weapon raised.

'Had enough?' taunted Baldr. The boy didn't respond – only then did Baldr realise he didn't speak the same tongue.

They clashed again. The boy swung his maul at Baldr's head – a wild lunge, full of venom. Baldr nearly didn't dodge it, and felt the rush of air as it swished past his face. Before he'd had time to feel the shock of the near hit, he was twisting at the waist, backhanding the axe across at chest height.

The blade bit deep, cracking bone and carving the muscle open. Baldr's opponent screamed, dropping the maul as his limbs spasmed. Baldr hacked again, severing the boy's neck and dropping him.

Before the body had even hit the stones, Baldr was roaring in delight. He could feel the heat of the blood on him. All around him, men fought desperate battles – eyes were gouged, skin was ripped, throats were throttled.

He whirled, looking for fresh kills. As he did so, his eyes suddenly caught the top of the headland, a long way off now and part-masked by drifting fog. For a moment, just a heartbeat, he thought he saw a hunched outline on the summit. He thought he saw two golden eyes, ridged fur, a long maw.

He kept moving, but the sight distracted him, so he didn't see the man bearing down on him, fresh from beating an Ascurii hunter into the bloody surf. This man was bigger than the first one he'd killed, wearing snarled furs that made him look half animal. The man rushed Baldr, giving him no time to swing his axe.

Baldr ducked, aiming to pounce clear and get space, but something hit him on the back, followed by a hot, sick rush across his head and spine. He crashed to the ground, tasting salty grit in his mouth.

He tried to rise, to get to his feet, but something heavier cracked across his back, flooring him. His vision blurred, and the pain came on – astonishing pain, radiating out from hot wounds.

Somehow, he pushed himself onto his back, axe still in hand. He tried to rise, to find some way to fight back before the lather of blood in his mouth choked him.

The man didn't come after him – he was standing, mouth open, looking up at the sky. The clouds were churning, tearing like fabric. Baldr thought he saw the shadow of some enormous bird swooping out of the emptiness, but then his eyes failed him.

He arched his ravaged back, racked in agony, feeling his heart racing out of control. Still he clutched the axe in his hand. He heard a booming roar, like the sea coming in, and heard men's voices raised in alarm and terror.

Then he was out, lost in a crimson world of pain and madness.

He slept for a long time. At times he half roused, and realised that he was not dead. The world was filled with sounds and smells he didn't know. Everything was thundering, swaying, tilting.

It was hard to open his eyes. Something had been done to them – it felt like wires across the lids.

He managed it, during one of the rare times his awareness returned, just briefly, before the pain pulled him back under.

He was in some kind of chamber, square-sided, smooth like the face of an axe. Men towered over him, draped in matted furs. They looked like giants. They smelt like wolves. They didn't look at him.

He twisted his head. He was lying on the floor, and it felt as if the earth were shaking. Far off, he saw a door, open to the white sky. The clouds seemed to be racing past it impossibly fast.

He didn't know what he was seeing. He didn't know why the floor of the chamber was vibrating and juddering like a seer in a fit, nor why the air was so painfully thin, nor where the thunder-roar came from.

His head cracked back, he felt groggy again and knew he was going under. Just as he did, the clouds ripped apart, showing him the face of a mountain through the narrow door.

He was *above* it. He was *above the mountain*.

Baldr passed out then. The rush of oblivion embraced him, dragging him down, sucking the last warmth from his battered, bloody, hacked body.

He slept.

It would be a long time before he woke, or saw that mountain again, or saw or felt anything else. In his sleep, unbeknown to him, came healing, and change, and augmentation. Whispered voices came and went like dreams.

When he woke, much later, nothing was the same. It would never be again. Only the name remained, the one he had been given on the ice-crossing so the gods would know his soul.

Baldr. Fjolnir. God-marked.

I. THE CARDINAL

Chapter One

'He will wake,' said Ingvar.

Gunnlaugur looked sceptical. 'How long?'

'A few days.'

'You're sure?'

'Olgeir says the same. Fjolnir dreams again.'

Gunnlaugur looked down at his hands. A thick cloth hung between his fingers, black with cleansing oils. His massive thunder hammer, *skul-brotsjór*, leant against one knee, its ornate gilding half swabbed. The old detail was coming through again, obscured for too long by blood and filth. Cleaning it away was cathartic – a reminder of old rhythms.

The sun beat down into a narrow courtyard. Dawn had broken less than an hour ago and already the heat was oppressive.

'If he dreams, he will wake,' agreed Gunnlaugur, resuming the painstaking cleaning of his weapon.

Ingvar was clad in a grey tunic, and his lean, muscled body glistened in the amber light. Soon his blond-grey hair would be slicked down, ready to take his battle-helm again. His armour would be hoisted and drilled into position, cladding him in the cocoon of murder, and he would take up *dausvjer*, cleaned and given rites of restoration.

The respite had been hard won, but it had given them time to breathe.

'What news of Njal?' Ingvar asked, strolling across the enclosed space like a caged animal, flexing his arms absently.

Gunnlaugur spat on the stone. 'The star-speakers here are *skítna*. They scrape at their dreams.' He shook his close-shaven head. Flecks of red lingering in his dirt-grey hair caught the sunlight. 'They don't know.'

'She wants to wait for him?' asked Ingvar, leaning against a whitewashed wall.

'She wants to fight,' said Gunnlaugur, his voice growling with approval.

Ingvar shared the Wolf Guard's sentiments. The Battle Sisters who had survived the assault on Hjec Aleja deserved their survival. They had fought hard for the walls, for the Cathedral, for the approaches to the last bridge. Even when the tide of plague-damned had threatened to overwhelm the entire city, they had kept fighting. Their devotions were strange, their manner alien, but in combat they showed their worth.

'Then everything is ready,' Ingvar said.

'Pretty much.'

Gunnlaugur held his weapon up. The sunlight caught the edges of the disruptor, sparkling like gold nuggets on the iron-grey of the hammer-head. He narrowed his eyes, scrutinising for flaws.

'I wanted to seek your counsel,' said Ingvar. 'About Bajola.'

Gunnlaugur didn't look away from the hammer. 'It can wait.'

Ingvar made to speak again, but Gunnlaugur held up a warning finger. His amber eyes never left the runes on his weapon. 'A long time, since I had to restore this myself. Feels good, to push the dirt out with my own fingers.' He looked up at Ingvar. 'Stormcaller will be here soon. We'll break bones before then, you and I. That is all that matters.' His savage face cracked into what passed with him for a smile. 'I am not ignoring it. Just not now.'

'When it is over–'

'When it is over, we'll talk. How's your own blade?'

Ingvar smiled dryly. 'The rites have been sung. It'll bite.'

Gunnlaugur ground his cloth into the thunder hammer's recesses.

'It'll need to,' he said.

De Chatelaine leaned against the balcony, high up in the hall of the Halicon. Her armoured fingers pressed against the limestone surface. She'd felt tense for a long time, and every gesture she made seemed tighter, more cramped.

Hot morning air wafted against her face. Sweat had broken out on her forehead, tiny beads that would only grow.

Below her, the city sprawled away in its unregulated, tangled messiness. The streets had always been crooked. Now they were choked with barricades, locked in a semi-ruined network of tumbled stone and half-dug pits. Smoke hung over the outer walls, distant across the wasteland beyond. The old Cathedral, Bajola's place, rose up from the debris like a spike of rusted iron, still smouldering long after the fires had exhausted themselves.

Beyond that, beyond the warren of occupied districts, the endless plain burned under a clear sky. The enemy army milled around in the heat-haze, their standards swaying drunkenly, half hidden by the clouds of filmy dust they kicked up. Other clouds roiled lazily amid that natural grime – masking clouds, sensor-defying murks.

More fallen troops had joined them since their first attempt to storm the inner walls. Augur readings indicated thousands more tramping across the deserts to swell their numbers. The entire world was wallowing in corruption, and the enemy had whole cities of ruin to draw on. If any other bastions of purity had endured, they had long since stopped transmitting signals. The planet was infected now, and only Hjec Aleja remained, a lone outpost of Imperial rule surrounded by seething shores of disease.

The canoness preceptor lifted her severe chin, scanning the ruins below her vantage. The Ighala Gate stood, just as it had throughout the entire siege. She could see the cloaks of her Sisters as they strode across the parapet below her, tiny with distance. Alongside them were the hunchbacked outlines of the big lascannon emplacements and rotary guns, most still in operation despite repeated assaults from the enemy.

Her people remained crammed inside the defences like rats trapped against rising water, pressed together and jostling in the shadow of the citadel. Food was not yet a problem, but water would become one soon. The wells were running dry. One of them now foamed green, like bubbling bile. They had somehow got to it, injecting toxins from the tankers that prowled the wasteland edges. Those who'd drunk unwarily died in excruciation, their innards turned into a fizzing slurry before the end. She'd seen the bodies afterwards, locked in contortions, drenched from the bloody voiding of every orifice. The poisons had not been designed simply to kill, but to inspire terror.

She would have hated the enemy enough without that – they didn't need to give her fresh reasons.

De Chatelaine heard a faint noise behind her then – a shuffle of silk on stone. Ermili Repoda, her Master of Astropaths, was waiting. His glassy eyes gazed unerringly at her, as if they were as sighted as hers.

'What is it?' she asked.

Repoda came to stand beside her. 'He's close. The Stormcaller. *Njal*. That's his name – the aether's alive with it.'

'You do not know when, though.'

'The art does not work in that way, canoness.'

'Do they try to speak to us?'

'They do not know whom to speak to. Perhaps they think we're already dead.'

'How many come with him?'

'More than one squad,' said Repoda. 'Maybe more than two.'

'We are honoured.'

Repoda smiled thinly, and his lined, pale face looked desiccated in the sunlight. 'You seem relaxed about his coming.'

'Should I not?'

'This is an Ecclesiarchy world.' Repoda inclined his head a fraction, perhaps in equivocation, perhaps in apology. 'The people look to you. They fear the Wolves almost as much as–'

'Then they're fools,' said de Chatelaine. 'They know. They *know* what waits for them out there.' She turned on him. 'We've worked *so hard*, the Wolf Guard and I, to clamp down on these fears. I won't have them intruding, not now.'

Repoda bowed. 'I merely report.'

De Chatelaine breathed in deep, tasting the smoke that hung over the entire city. It felt as if the lower reaches had been turned into a sacrificial offering, as charred and useless as a carcass on pagan flames. The stench was an accusation: *This is your failure. This is your defeat.*

'When the Stormcaller gets here, I will bow the knee. You will bow, all my people will bow. We don't get to choose our deliverers.'

De Chatelaine brushed her hair back from her face. The enemy never left her thoughts, even when out of eyesight. Now, thronged on the far horizon, seamy and massive, it dominated all else.

'We hold out,' she said. 'That is our only task. When the Stormcaller comes, he will find at least this: we did not submit.'

The servitors were crawling all over it like lice on a corpse, their grey flesh pulling at its innards and hauling them out onto the ground.

Jorundur watched them, wincing with every tug and wrench. *Vuokho* stood on the landing pad, half gutted, its flanks as black as *Undrider*'s had been, covered in scorch-marks and las-trails. Its huge engines loomed up into the sky, burned out, their systems fused. The armourglass on the cockpit was cracked, the undercarriage bent and twisted. Now that the gunship was hoisted on giant service racks designed for big cargo lifters, the full extent of the damage was visible.

He was rapt, lost in the detail of the work, though, like all his warrior kin, never fully off-guard.

'I can smell you, Sister,' Jorundur said out loud, sensing Callia's presence before she became visible.

The Battle Sister, de Chatelaine's deputy, emerged from the shadows. Her armour was as battle-worn as ever, and her face carried fresh scars – long raking lines down a smooth left cheek.

'You've been busy, Space Wolf,' she said, looking up at the gutted internals.

Jorundur sniffed. 'It'll fly again. That bastard didn't destroy everything on it. Just nearly everything.'

Callia's gaze ran across the blunt angles of the gunship. It was a huge machine up close – big enough for the void, and carrying weaponry enough to gut a small army.

As it had done, of course.

'When can you get it airborne again?' Callia asked.

Jorundur snorted. 'Days. Many days. If I am called to murder, then longer.'

Callia looked disappointed. 'We could use it.'

'You said that to me before. We all could.'

Jorundur liked Callia. She'd been there since the start, marshalling the long retreat, keeping her flamers raised the whole time. He'd seen her in action right at the end, when the enemy finally stormed the gates. Jorundur had been first into the vanguard, but she hadn't been far behind.

'They tell me more of your kind are coming,' Callia said.

'Don't trust star-speakers. They pipe all kinds of skítna.'

'They tell me a whole fleet's inbound.'

'*Fekke.* You thought *Undrider* was a whole fleet.'

'It was enough,' said Callia.

Jorundur shook his head sourly. 'You trust too much,' he muttered. 'It sticks in the craw.'

'Ah, but you believe in something.'

'My blade. My brothers.'

'You just give it a different name.'

'You name a thing, you control a thing. The Priests taught me that, at least.'

'So many priests,' mused Callia, her eyes bright with jibing, 'and so little faith.'

'Ever met a Rune Priest?'

Callia shook her head.

'You will do,' Jorundur said.

'Stormcaller is a Rune Priest, then.'

'It is one of his names.'

Callia shot him a curious, half-guilty look. 'I've seen psykers at work. I could sense the divine will in them. I could *feel* it. It must be the same. The same source, even with your war-shamans.'

Jorundur croaked out a harsh laugh. 'The source? *Skítja*, I don't care.' He grinned at her – an ugly, hooked grin that made the metal studs in his face clink. 'I saw a Priest rip a gunship in two, just like this one, and burn everything inside it like paper. They've slaughtered armies, they've scraped worlds clean. *God-marked.*' He looked up at the Thunderhawk again, knowing he needed to get back to the work of restoration. His fingers moved, itching to get among the entrails of the machine. 'They're just like the rest of us – butchers. That's all you need to know.'

The smoke rolled ahead of them, drifting and breaking across derelict buildings. Ahead, the street twisted away, heavy with dust, streaked with long-dried stains on what had once been white walls.

Hafloí applied pressure with his fingers, gently, smoothly. The mortal neck enclosed within them flexed, then burst. Hafloí's other hand remained clamped over the mutant's face, stifling its screams. Its legs stopped kicking, its swollen hands stopped trying to clutch at his armour. For a moment longer its body twitched, locked in muscle-rigidness. Then it flopped into torpor, leaking a mix of blood and infected fluids over his gauntlets.

'Quiet,' observed Olgeir, crouching beside the two of them. 'Nicely quiet.'

Hafloí relaxed, letting the corpse slide to the ground. He shook his hands free. 'They shouldn't be this strong.'

'Plague. Gets into the muscle.'

The big Wolf's armour was covered in blood, some of it ritual markings, some of it evidence of recent kills. His beloved bolter, *sigrún*, had been left up in the citadel – this work required silence – so he carried a long-handled, twin-bladed axe with knotwork wyrms' heads engraved on the metal faces.

Haflóí kicked the corpse away from him, and drew his short blade – a leaf-shaped dagger with the rune *hata* etched on the blade. Then he looked ahead, down the street, to where it ended in a high stone wall.

Olgeir's helm lenses whirred faintly as he ran a scan. 'Fifty metres. Stay close.'

He set off, keeping his body low. For such a giant, Olgeir could move both fast and quietly, barely stirring the grime beneath his boots. Power armour made its own distinctive grinding noise, but there were ways to dampen it.

Haflóí followed, keeping a careful watch. The lower city had been a haunt of horror ever since the first attacks. The main enemy army had withdrawn beyond the walls, but the old suburban zone was still occupied by mutants too addled or stubborn to leave. The residuals stumbled through the ruins, hunting for flesh that was now scarce, cradling bulbous stomachs and weeping scabrous tears.

Haflóí paused at an intersection, looking down a long alley running transverse before ghosting across it. The lower city was quiet, darkening slowly as the short dusk gathered pace. Brown-blue shadows crept across the dust, running up the sides of the tight-packed hab-shells.

It smelt foul. Corpses rotted in the heat, buzzing with flies. Icons had been daubed on the standing walls – three circles, picked out in dirty green. Some lettering lingered here and there: *Terminus Est*, scrawled across any heap of stones big enough to accommodate it.

The hunt had been meagre – stabs from the gloom, neck-twists, gut-kicks. Quiet killings, just enough to clear the path, to get them where they needed to be.

Olgeir reached his destination – a tower, half demolished, its metal skeleton visible where the render had come down. Haflóí caught up with him, slipping under the cover of the blown-open doorway.

'Really?' he voxed. 'Nothing better?'

'It will do,' replied Olgeir, pushing ahead.

They entered a narrow corridor built for mortals. The ceiling was low, barely above their helms. It sagged in places, stained brown, and watery gurgles came from above them. They reached a stairwell, running in zigzags up the floors. It was as dirty as everything else and strewn with the detritus of war – bloodmarks, bolt-shells in the rockcrete, scattered possessions dropped in the hurry to get out.

Haflóí sniffed for targets as he climbed. The proximity markers in his helm were of limited use – the walking dead would not show up on them until they were actually moving – so hunt-sense was superior.

They reached the top level, and the damaged floor creaked under them. Haflóí tensed as he left the stairwell, sensing something up ahead. Olgeir responded immediately, moving silently down the corridor towards a locked door at the end. Haflóí went with him, blade in hand. He reached the door first – a single push broke the lock, sending the metal panel swinging open.

Haflóí slipped inside, blade ready. The room beyond was unlit and clogged with rubbish. Fabric sacks piled high, bursting with rotting foodstuffs. Insects scuttled over every surface, bloated and glossy.

A single figure faced him, scrabbling back across the floor, eyes wide. He was emaciated and sore-ridden. It looked like he had been gnawing on something from one of the sacks, and dark fluid dribbled down his chicken-scrawn jowls.

Haflóí strode over to him, keeping his blade raised.

'Angels!' blurted the man, wedging himself up against the far wall and looking up at him, terrified. 'At *last.*'

Haflóí paused.

The man got to his knees, his face trembling with fear and emotion. 'Is it over?' he shuddered. 'Throne, say it's over. Get me out of here. Please, for the love of the Emperor, get me *out.*'

Haflóí glanced at the sacks. He kicked the nearest, and it spilt open. Joints of meat, crusted green with putrescence, tumbled out. He recognised a thigh, a calf, a hand – five-fingered and curled tight into a desperate claw.

The man panicked. 'I *had* to! You have no–'

Haflóí's blade punched through his neck, killing him instantly.

Olgeir walked past, heading for the doorway into a connecting chamber beyond. 'You hesitated,' he said. 'Don't hope. They're all long gone.'

Haflóí gazed down at the man's body. Sores had clustered around his mouth. Some of them were moving, as if tiny creatures writhed under the tight-stretched skin.

'Long gone,' he muttered.

He followed Olgeir. The chamber beyond must have once been the man's dorm-unit. A single bunk stood against the far wall, its grey sheets soiled. The walls were smeared with what looked and smelled like excrement.

Olgeir moved to a floor-to-ceiling window on the west-facing wall. The glass was cracked and daubed with grease, but still intact. He pulled a catch, released the lock and hauled the window open on to a balcony outside.

The two of them took up position behind the outer railing. Ahead of them, less than a hundred metres distant and on a level with their position, stood the upper edge of the city's walls, semi-ruined and tumbled into piles of rubble.

Haflói's helm lenses switched to magnocular vision, scrolling out over the rim of the walls and filtering the fading light beyond. Green wireframes flickered over the terrain, indicating troop formations, buildings, vehicles, all standing within a kilometre of the shattered perimeter.

He scanned from left to right, gradually extending the range out across the plain. Positioned high up on the very edge of the city, hard under the lip of the sensor-baffling clouds, the detail was better than it had been up in the citadel.

'Tell me what you're getting,' said Olgeir.

Haflói extended the reach again, letting his armour-mounted auspexes do the work.

'Infantry formations,' he said, passing over several big contingents. The soldiers were arranged in loose phalanxes, basking in the heat, mouths slack, ready for the long desert night. Fires had been started, massive ones, adding to the pall of smoke that hung over them. 'Six... seventeen chem-carriers. Big ones.'

The massive tanker-juggernauts stood in a makeshift compound behind the first of the infantry lines, towering into the murk and underlit by pale green marker lumens. Their engines were running, fuelling the chemical furnaces in the tanks behind.

'They've dug in,' added Olgeir, marking the trench patterns.

Haflói ran his augmented gaze along earthworks topped with coils of razor wire. Gun-towers had been built along the ridges, constructed from huge rockcrete blocks and carrying heavy, snub-barrelled cannons on rotating bases. Each tower was protected by dedicated units of gas mask-wearing troops in thick carapace armour. More lights blinked on and off in the gloom, tracing the outline of bigger edifices beyond.

'Prefabs,' said Olgeir, indicating points along the defence lines. 'They landed them, or looted them.'

Haflói remembered the empty depots they'd seen on the plague destroyer in orbit. He ratcheted up the scale again, and his helm zoomed in further. He swept over lines of infantry, some loosely formed up, some in deep-dug positions overlooked by more earthworks. A few rust-encrusted tanks rumbled between formations, belching smoke. Their hulls had been defaced and covered in corpse-racks, all of which buzzed with insect clouds.

'Until I saw this world,' murmured Haflói, 'I would not have believed so many flies existed.'

Beyond the tank columns, the land rose. The magnocular range reached its limit, and the images became less defined.

'That's it,' said Haflói.

More razor wire ran around the base of the incline, arranged in layers. Scaffolds were everywhere, all slung with swaying gibbets. Green marker lights peered fuzzily through the miasma, blinking on and off.

'Get a loc-reading on that,' said Olgeir.

Haflói had already done it, storing the positions of kill-zones, ingress routes, choke-points. 'They've got something big in there.'

'Wall-breakers. Focus more – you can see them.'

'We can take it,' Haflói said.

'Perhaps,' said Olgeir, his voice as deep and calm as ever. 'With Njal, certainly.'

Haflói let his vision lapse back into short-range. 'You fought with him?'

'I saw him. From a distance.'

'And?'

'And what?'

'What's he like?'

Olgeir kept up the scan. Haflói could hear the faint clicks as his helm-gear registered picts. Then, before he could reply, something broke out below them – a crash, a long way down, followed by a series of thumps. The walls of the building shook.

Olgeir clicked his lenses back into focus and took a deep breath. 'We've been detected.'

Haflói smiled inside his helm. 'Good.'

Olgeir turned and walked back into the hab-chamber, hefting his wyrm-blade axe loosely. 'Don't let your blood get hot. We clear them out, then back to the citadel.'

Haflói followed Olgeir. He hoped there were lots of them – a whole herd, something worth drawing a blade for.

'Fine,' he replied, feeling the first spikes of kill-urge stir. 'Just leave a few for me.'

Chapter Two

Baldr's nostrils drew in breath again. His eyes twitched as he dreamed. The ghostly pallor had left his skin, replaced by Fenrisian colouring – pale, like stone under winter sun.

Ingvar looked at him. Baldr lay on a metal slab under bright apothecarion lights, face up, limbs slack. Shackles grasped him at the wrists, ankles, neck and waist.

The door to the apothecarion was criss-crossed with sensors. A second blast-door had been rigged in the room beyond, primed to slam closed if anything disturbed the contents of the inner chamber. Pict-feed lenses dotted the ceiling, flickering intermittently as they shunted their feeds direct to Gunnlaugur's helm-display.

Olgeir had inscribed a rune of warding over the medicae-cot, scratching it crudely into the brushed metal of the lumen-housing. A Rune Priest would have done a better job, but it had been a long time since one had accompanied Járnhamar on the hunt. There were fewer of them now, they said. They were overstretched, burnt out, kept busy by Grimnar's remorseless war-calling.

Ingvar didn't know the truth of that. He'd seen the condition of other

Chapters, though, and knew well enough the trials that faced them all. Every Chapter Master from Terra to the Halo Stars was feeling the strain – they couldn't train new aspirants quickly enough, the rate of attrition was growing and the weight of ten thousand years of ceaseless combat was catching up.

If there is to be victory, I cannot see it.

But he had vowed not to think such things again. He drew a vial of liquid into a long syringe, watching as the dark red matter foamed. He discarded the vial and flicked the air bubbles from the syringe.

Then he moved close to Baldr. Feeling for the vein, he inserted the needle. He had to push – mortal instruments had trouble penetrating the skin of a Sky Warrior. As he depressed the plunger, he watched the tincture enter Baldr's system. His eyes flickered a little and his mouth tightened a fraction, then he relaxed.

Ingvar withdrew the needle and discarded it. He was no Apothecary, far less a Wolf Priest. It was one thing to keep a brother warrior alive on the battlefield – every Hunter knew the basics of chirurgy – another to shepherd Baldr through whatever horror had overtaken him.

At least the visible taint of corruption had faded. For a long time Baldr's saliva had retained a green hue, like algal scum at the edge of summer-hot pools. Lifting his lids had exposed bloodshot eyes, unseeing, the irises shrunk.

The breathing was more regular now. The rancid stench had gone, replaced by the healthier smells of perspiration. The Red Dream still had him, but the other sickness had retreated. Whether it was truly gone or simply dormant he had no way of knowing.

'Gyrfalkon,' came Gunnlaugur's voice over the comm. 'Anything yet?'

'No change,' Ingvar replied.

'But he will wake soon?'

'I cannot say.'

Gunnlaugur grunted. 'Re-seal the chamber, then. The canoness has news.'

'By your will.'

Ingvar severed the comm-link. He reduced the lumens, keeping the observation lamps over Baldr's body on full. He ran a final check, activated the locks, then left the chamber. The door clanged closed behind him, followed by the hiss of bolts sliding home. The metal briefly glittered as the detector-field swept over it.

Baldr was sealed again, as secure as one of Ras Shakeh's ancient gods, locked in the cool under the desert floor and waiting to be stirred once more.

He lay on the slab, breathing shallow, eyelids flickering.

'This is the moment,' said de Chatelaine, allowing a little pride to sink into her voice. That felt good – it had been a long time since she had done so. 'This is the time we have been holding out for.'

She stood in one of the marble-and-gold antechambers running clear of the Halicon's main hall. The war had hardly intruded there: ivory and ebony statues of the primarchs still stood proudly on lozenges of veined stone. Thick drapes warded the force of the sun outside, though bars of light still angled in, twisting with dust.

Callia stood by her, as did others of her Sororitas command retinue. Five Wolves faced them, making everything else in the chamber look fragile.

Gunnlaugur had scoured the worst of the combat-grime from him, and de Chatelaine had been surprised to see the extent of the glorious fine work around the edges of his armour. He seemed animated by a fierce, almost febrile energy, even when standing. Perhaps he thought he hadn't performed well enough, hadn't slaughtered quite as many as he should have. De Chatelaine couldn't share that view, but then she only had the scantiest of insights into the battle-culture of Fenris, and what counted for satisfaction with a Wolf Guard.

The other one, Ingvar, remained at one side, though some of the separateness she had detected in him at the start had ebbed – he now stood amongst his brothers at greater ease. Olgeir and Haflói had come to the chamber fresh from their scout mission to the walls. Jorundur, the darkest, had remained alone with his gunship.

'You have new tidings?' asked Gunnlaugur, looking at her sceptically.

'A flotilla, on the cusp of the veil,' said de Chatelaine. 'Your brothers.'

'Fleet markers?'

'Repoda is in no doubt.'

Gunnlaugur shared a look with his brothers. 'If Njal's bringing a pack, a large one, then this battle's already over.'

'Then, after it, we take it to the sector,' said de Chatelaine, her eyes shining. 'The beginning. This is the crusade we sought.'

The canoness activated a large hololith column. A battle schematic hovered in glowing lines over the marble face, picking out the perimeter of the city, the terrain beyond, and what they had discovered of the enemy positions.

'When your forces detect our beacon signal,' said de Chatelaine, 'they can make planetfall on the open plain, surrounding the enemy. We will break out then, and they will be caught between the two fronts. Caught, and destroyed.'

Gunnlaugur scrutinised the schematic. He sniffed sceptically. 'They won't wait.'

Olgeir nodded. 'They've not moved for a while, but this looks complete now.' He pointed to a low hill, two kilometres to the south-west of Hjec Aleja's ruined outer gates. 'They've brought wall-breakers. We ran deep augur sweeps while down at the wall's edge.'

'And Plague Marines,' added Hafloí. 'The last ones left. We've been waiting for reinforcements, and so have they.'

'Then we need to hold out,' said de Chatelaine. 'Just a little longer.'

'They have had all the time they needed,' said Gunnlaugur, shaking his head. 'They have dragged those guns halfway across a continent, and now they are ready to use them.'

Olgeir leaned over the column and gestured to the landscape immediately behind the fortified incline. 'The wall-breakers are there. Couldn't get a good look, but if they fire, we'll know all about it.'

It was de Chatelaine's turn to study the schematic. As she did so, her brow furrowed in concern. 'We can't launch a sortie that far out.'

'*You* can't,' said Ingvar.

'And you can't wait for those guns to fire,' said Gunnlaugur. 'They're ready to go. We have to move first.'

De Chatelaine pursed her lips. The Wolves always relished the reckless attack, but that didn't automatically make it the right tactic. 'The mortal troops aren't like you – they won't last long in the open desert, not against those numbers.'

'They don't have to,' said Gunnlaugur. 'You just need to retake the outer walls. Get their attention. Seize the towers by the main gate and you'll give us all the cover we need.'

'And you'll take on what's left.'

Gunnlaugur bowed. 'For as long as needed.'

Callia shook her head in disbelief. 'Even for you, that's–'

'Possible,' said Ingvar. 'We don't have to hold them forever – just hit them before they move.'

'They won't stand still,' added Gunnlaugur. 'Wait longer, and the city will be in flames before Njal makes orbit.'

De Chatelaine hesitated. She scrutinised the hololith again. 'You go out there, in plain view, and they'll rip you apart.'

Gunnlaugur snorted. 'Do it in plain view, and we'd deserve to be.'

'What's the readiness of the city garrison?' de Chatelaine asked Callia.

'Full readiness,' Callia said.

No hesitation, no shade of doubt. That gave de Chatelaine some comfort.

'And this is your only counsel?' she asked Gunnlaugur.

The Wolf Guard shrugged, making bone totems clatter against his armour. 'We'll take the guns out anyway. Better to do it with cover, but it's your city.'

De Chatelaine smiled. 'So it is.' She turned from the hololith, giving the nod to Callia. 'We will need time to prepare. I shall notify you when all is ready.' Then she looked back at Gunnlaugur. 'And *I* will give the order, Wolf Guard. As you say, it is still my city.'

Gunnlaugur inclined his head. 'We will aim to keep it that way,' he said.

Five hours later, Callia stood under the arch of the Ighala Gate as the sun set, casting deep orange shafts across the darkening sky above. Towering toxin-clouds glowed in the dusk, vivid and spectacular. The heavy twin defence-doors loomed up ahead of her, bolted and barred as they had been since the final hours of the last assault.

Around her stood the remains of Ras Shakeh's Celestian contingent. The remaining Battle Sisters of the Wounded Heart lined up behind them, their ebony armour glinting with the last rays of the dying light. Beyond that stood attack squads of Ras Shakeh Guard, arrayed in the mixed uniforms of hastily combined regiments. Some of their gear was in good condition, some of it looked barely capable of resisting a determined bayonet strike.

She didn't like to think too closely about numbers. They had mustered a few thousand, all told, with a skeleton reserve to follow them down and an even thinner defence force to man the wall-guns. Still, it was good to be on the front foot again. Huddling behind the gates waiting for the inevitable assault was not what she had been trained for.

Her comm-bead crackled.

'You have clearance, Sister,' came de Chatelaine's voice. 'Go with hate, and the Emperor guide your aim.'

Callia smiled. 'And yours, canoness preceptor.'

The bolts on the gate began to grind open, sending sparks flying from the adamantium sheaths. On the walls above, lascannons swivelled on their mounts, holding fire for now but already picking targets. A hundred sharpshooters mounted on the parapets crouched down, resting long muzzles on the hot stone.

Callia tensed, clutching the grip on her bolter. She could feel her heart-rate pick up, slipping into the pre-combat state she cherished.

Cleanse my soul.

The words came to her unbidden. Callia couldn't remember who'd taught them to her. Bajola, perhaps.

Clear my mind.

The last of the bolts powered home, sliding into the wall-mounts on immense pistons. A thin line ran up the centre of the two doors, and dust showered down the joint.

Enable my body.

With a jolt, the gate-engines kicked in and the two doors parted, grating slowly apart and exposing the bridge beyond. Las-beams whickered out into the gathering gloom, angled down from the parapets to lay a covering wall of fire. A wide, empty expanse stretched off, cleared of buildings during the first siege and home to nothing more than broken earth.

Callia advanced, the Celestians on either side of her, until they were directly under the arch. The narrow span of the bridge ran ahead of them, empty, before terminating on the far side of a deep gorge. In the distance, hidden by both gathering darkness and smog, ran the jagged outlines of the lower city, its habs now bombed-out and derelict.

'With me,' voxed Callia to her retinue. She strode out into the foetid air beyond the gate. More las-beams scythed out above her, whining into the line of buildings in the distance. The volume picked up as the gunners found their targets, aiming to give the infantry a clear run for as long as possible.

Callia glanced upwards, looking back over her shoulder. The face of the gate bore the tattered remains of Wounded Heart banners and iconography. Though scorched and ripped, the symbols of the Imperium still endured.

'Forward,' she ordered.

The vanguard broke into a run, leaving the cover of the Gate and charging out across the bridge. For a few moments they were totally exposed, running across the open span with no cover of any sort. Then they reached the far side and split into four columns, fanning out across the wasteland. Battle Sister squads headed each unit, followed by the more numerous Guard detachments, all heading straight towards the forbidding line of silhouettes ahead.

For a while, there was no return fire. The lascannons on the high wall behind them kept firing, briefly lighting the scene before them in stark flash-frames. It was eerily silent, save for the echo of breathing in their helms and the crunch of boots on gravel.

Callia ran hard, her movements boosted by her power armour, her head low and her bolter trained on the lines of cover ahead. They rapidly closed the gap between the Gate and the first ranks of ruined hab-blocks. Her column took the central path, the one cleared by the Wolves to aid the passage of arms down to the outer wall. The other groups split off, one to the left and two to the right, moving swiftly to take up positions in cover before the fight down to the perimeter.

A las-beam from the Ighala formation hit the remnants of a big tower ahead of her, scything clean through the weakened masonry and sending bricks cascading to the ground. More hit, crowning the shattered ruins with blooms of incandescence.

The lead group reached the line of buildings and kept running. Callia leapt across a tangled line of razor wire and felt her boots thud onto rockcrete on the far side. The serrated outlines of the lower city rose up on either side of her, enclosing the night sky like two walls of a canyon. The street ahead was littered with wreckage – blast-rubble from the walls above, the carcass of a Rhino transport, the cracked edges of craters where ordnance had hammered down during the worst of the previous fighting.

Her Celestians ran alongside her, sweeping their weapons two-handed as they searched for targets. Callia could hear the clatter of boots as the Guard units worked to keep pace. They would already be looking for ways to bring heavy weapons teams down to tactical points to cover the onwards advance.

Still no return fire. The Celestians tore down the main thoroughfare, hugging the shadow of the buildings on either side, their armour dark against dark and their robes fluttering about them like death-shrouds.

'Where are they?' voxed Callia's subordinate Djinate, advancing hard on her right flank.

'Watch the habs,' replied Callia, running, angling her helm up to the broken rooftops. 'It's only a matter of–'

The first stabs of light lanced out of the dark before she'd finished speaking. Callia didn't break stride, weaving across a patch of shattered brickwork as the barrage of small-arms fire came in. Her Sisters did the same, scattering across the open ground, using what cover the battlefield gave them and losing no momentum.

Callia let the targeting lines on her helm intersect, pinpointing a location ten metres up in the empty heart of a multi-storey hab-tower.

She took aim, compensating for her own movement, and loosed two shots. Then she kept running, barely hearing the crack and subsequent blast of bolt-rounds obliterating the sniper-nest. By then, other Sisters had opened up on their own targets and the air filled with the resounding roar and crack of bolter discharge.

'The flanks,' warned Callia, spotting another sniper position and dispatching it with a single bolt-round. 'They'll be coming around.'

The thoroughfare they ran down was broken up with the intersecting streets of the lower city, all overshadowed by the close-packed hab-blocks. Even as Callia spoke, enemy units broke from cover some twenty metres back from her position, streaking out of the dark and engaging the Guard units following in her wake. The enemy troops were wearing gas masks, and their bulbous eyes glowed softly in the dark. Grenades started to fly, detonating with puffs of toxic smoke.

The Guard responded, and the staccato growl of a tripod-mounted autocannon opened up from back up the street. Whisper-snaps of las-fire followed, crackling into the bands of mutants emerging from the gloom.

Callia pressed on, confident in the main Guard contingents to hold their own. Speed was the main thing – to secure the outer gates before the enemy could muster a full defence and drag them into street-to-street combat. Locator runes cycling across her helm-lens showed the positions of the other Battle Sister units – they were closing on the lower city edge, pushing rapidly, giving the enemy no time to form up before they reached the target defence points.

Callia swung her bolter and squeezed off another round, watching as the shell shot into the maw of a shadowed intersection to her left. She heard the wet grunt of impact, followed by the rip of explosion, and a bloated mutant staggered out in front of her, stomach spilling, gas mask ripped from its neck.

Still running, she launched a kick at its reeling face, breaking its neck before she'd landed. More mutants emerged in its wake, some with close-combat weapons, a few with projectile cannons.

Callia charged into them, firing from the waist with one hand, lashing out with her blade with the other. She was far too fast for them – a few seconds of fury, and they lay at her feet, coughing up blood and phlegm.

These were the outriders. The real enemy lay beyond the outer perimeter, holed up in their vast complex of tunnels, trenches and gun-towers. She knew they would be stirring now, roused by the sudden break from the inner gates, preparing their terror weapons again and priming the launchers. If the vanguard couldn't make their objectives before the enemy responded, this sortie would be very short-lived.

'Maintain pace,' she ordered, kicking away the last choking mutant and breaking back into a sprint.

It was good, thought Callia, to recover land they had given up after such heavy bloodshed. Her helm-display showed each assault column driving towards their objective, supported by Guard units that made good ground and seized strategic intersections. Some of the devotional buildings around them were half intact, showing the old emblems of the Wounded Heart amid the filth and desecration. This push might be little more than temporary, but it felt like a reclamation of sorts.

Another autocannon opened up from behind them, sending a heavy rain of shells rattling into the night and cracking into the buildings ahead. The Guard were getting faster at bringing them into position, securing the path back up to Ighala and clearing the long transit routes of the enemy.

Callia's bolter clicked empty and she slammed a new magazine in, barely pausing. The air was now falling away to perfect dark, shrouded by the ever-roiling clouds of smoke piling up from enemy positions beyond the walls. The ground became slimy with old chem-weapon discharge, glistening with ophidian dullness under the muzzle-flares of the massed bolters and lasweapons.

They tried to make a stand up ahead of her. Callia saw them massing across the width of the street, trying to haul drum-barrelled guns onto heaps of refuse and get some kind of fire-line established.

The Celestians needed no orders – they assaulted it in unison, laying down a curtain of bolter-fire before picking up the pace and charging head-on. The surviving enemy troops managed to get a volley of return las-fire clear, but it barely slowed them. Callia charged up the earth slope of the bulwark, drew her blade, then leapt into the mass of bodies beyond. Her sword flashed out, jamming under the neck of a grasping mutant before slicking away and cutting deep into the outstretched arm of another.

Then her Sisters were with her, whirling, cutting, blasting, crushing. Sororitas power armour didn't quite have the juggernaut impact of full Adeptus Astartes plate, but it was still formidable, capable of seeing off all but the most determined impacts and hugely augmenting the physical movements of its wearer. The barricade was smashed apart, its defenders crushed and bludgeoned aside and trodden into the shattered earth beyond.

Then the outer walls loomed, battered by past bombardments but partially intact. Callia located the target tower on her forward view – a squat rockcrete structure built up against the wall itself, just over two hundred metres north of the ruined outer gates.

'Objective sighted,' she voxed, firing all the while. 'Follow me in.'

The Celestians streaked across the last of the open ground, trading shots with the scattered resistance holed up in the buildings around them. More heavy weapons fire broke out from behind them, testament to the growing security of the Guard positions.

Callia reached the tower entrance on ground level – a gaping hole where doors had once stood. Bodies, fresh with hot blood, slumped over the jagged edges of metal plates. Djinate slammed against the wall on the far side of the entrance hole, priming a frag grenade and hefting it one-handed.

Callia nodded, and Djinate hurled the grenade into the dark. A second later and the interior of the tower filled with a boom of heat, light and screaming. Callia ducked inside, her helm-lens compensating for the swirl of smoke burning across her visual field. Disorientated mutants stumbled into her path, clutching at shrapnel wounds or gasping from severed chem-tubes, and she dispatched them one by one.

'Get a Guard squad at the breach,' she voxed, racing for the spiral stairway with Djinate close behind. 'I want this one secured first.'

She took the stairs two at a time, racing up around a tight spiral. The enemy defenders seemed to have clustered, foolishly, at the base of the tower, and she encountered no more living until reaching the summit. Half a dozen mutants tried to rush her then, tearing across the open-roofed platform at her as she emerged.

Callia charged straight into them, blade in hand and already spiralling. She jabbed it up, impaling a porcine maul-carrier under the chin, then pulled it round, severing the neck of a three-eyed horror with flailing jowls. The edge flashed in the night, catching the now-vivid glow from the piled-high toxin-clouds, and the savage beauty of it made her laugh out loud.

By the time Djinate caught up, the tower summit was heaped with bodies and Callia stood alone at the epicentre, her breathing heavy, her blade slick with diseased gore.

'Objective achieved,' observed Djinate.

Callia strode over to the parapet facing towards the lower city. Lines of tracer-fire scythed out from the fixed gun positions, cracking against the bulwarks where enemy warbands still hunkered down. Guard units were dragging heavy weapons down the cleared thoroughfare, and a long las-cannon barrel was being hauled along on the back of a half-track, ready for lifting up to the tower top where it would be mounted.

They were moving efficiently, going fast, taking care to clear out the remaining pockets of resistance. Other towers and bulwarks along the city's perimeter were rocked with explosions prior to being seized, cleared and occupied.

Callia turned around and walked over to the parapet's outward-facing edge. The tower she'd taken ran up the inside curve of the outer wall, cresting the upper edge by a few metres and affording a clear view of the plains outside.

Just a few dozen metres out, and the madness began. Hordes of glow-eyed mutants were advancing out of the night, roused by the clamour of combat from within the city. The front ranks looked as ramshackle as those the Sisters had already swept away, but behind them came more organised units – plate-armoured and carrying more lethal weaponry. The throttled growl of vehicle engines keying up rumbled across the plain, out of sight behind the shifting curtains of smog but not far away.

Callia leaned against the parapet edge. More Sisters emerged from the stairwell and took up position on either side of her.

The enemy encampment was vast. It was like a miniature city in itself – a huge, rambling collection of trenches, infantry detachments, tank squadrons and luminous, belching chemical works. Toxin-clouds blossomed above it all, blotting out the stars in swirling columns of virulence.

It was like kicking an ant's nest. Now the enemy was stirring, sending out its gathered strength. The defenders of Hjec Aleja had provoked it, forcing the assault early in order to buy the Wolves some breathing room, but set against the advance of such a huge, brooding mass of slaved warriors, the gamble now felt perilously fine.

'So, we've done our part,' Callia breathed, leaning against a rockcrete battlement and angling her bolter. 'Now, Sons of Fenris, do yours.'

Chapter Three

He no longer remembered his name.

For a while, after the sickness had first come, he'd remembered it. After that, when he'd torn his uniform to get at the sores and his skin had started to pucker, he'd still remembered it. During the long nights in Hjec Morva when everything seemed to be dissolving into a long, sweaty frenzy of contagion he'd repeated it to himself, over and over, together with his rank and his regiment, as if by mouthing the syllables he could stave off the horror that was already combining and multiplying within his body.

Now, much later, he remembered doing that, but he no longer remembered why. His name was long gone, as was his old military grade, as was caring about either.

He pushed at the pustules clustering across the back of his neck and smiled as they burst. Milky fluid leaked down his chest and gave off an interesting smell – like fungus, or rotten boot leather.

Orders came to him in different ways now. Sometimes the Masters sought him out in person, lumbering through the trenches in their gloriously distended battleplate, speaking to him in a language he knew wasn't Gothic but that somehow made sense. Other times his duties would just become clear to him, formulating in his mind as if crystallised from a dream.

This was one of those times. He pulled himself out of what had been a shallow, dream-filled sleep and hoisted his autogun into position. His uniform – what remained of it – was crusted with dusty mud from the trench floor. His weapon-casing was already beginning to rust. Once, that would have appalled him. Now he just didn't care and nor did it seem to have any effect on the operation of the gun.

He adjusted his helm, biting down against the rebreather that pressed against the inside of his mouth, then climbed up, grabbing hold of the wooden ladder that ran up the inside wall of the trench and out to the world of fire beyond.

Others came with him – his men, the ones who had followed him into damnation right from the start. Just like him, their movements were heavy, their reactions dulled by the mucus that seeped from their ears and nostrils. Some carried autoguns like him, others had resorted to meat-hooks and rusty spikes laced with the special nerve-toxins the Masters gave them.

In his more lucid moments, he wondered why the Plaguefather had afflicted them in so many different ways. He wondered why, if the gods of decay desired his service, they hadn't made him faster, more deadly, more skilful. To lace his body with such gurgling rottenness seemed like a strange choice. But then the Father's ways were hardly likely to be transparent to him. All things considered, it wasn't worth worrying about overmuch.

He reached the lip of the trench wall and heaved himself over the top, and the full vista of war stretched out and away, glimpsed through bleary gas mask-lenses. The whole camp was moving. The charred desert ahead of him, thrown into perpetual twilight by the churning smog, crawled with a steadily growing carpet of advancing men. It was a strangely awesome sight – like the planet itself stirring to excise the last remnant of those who opposed the Father. He dimly felt his small role in that, and a swell of something like satisfaction grew in his rheumy chest.

Far away, he saw the outer walls of the city. He saw bright flashes of weaponry igniting along the parapets, tiny and blurred in the distance. He saw the army of the Masters marching to respond. He saw thousands of warriors, all like him, picking themselves up, dragging themselves out of the earth, falling into loose assault formations. He saw the big tanks grind into motion, gouging up desiccated earth under their tracks. He saw artillery pieces crank into firing angles, and gun-crews working to deliver the payloads of chem-bombs and incendiary canisters.

Then he was marching himself, shambling like the others over the broken, dusty ground. His men fell in around him, dozens of them, faces hidden behind their black rebreathers. They did not follow the infantry heading for the city. They had their *own* duty, up on the earthworks guarding the Masters and their glorious Machines. They would not be hurled up against the inferno of the wall assault. They would stay amid the gun-towers and trenches, forming the final line of defence that would keep the Machines guarded.

They were needed, those Machines. They had been hauled across the pitiless sands by a hundred thousand blessed drone-slaves, their barrels anointed with pungent oils, their innards infected with the most virulent scrapcodes, their mechanisms augmented with the living sinews of sacrificial thralls, their kill-range extended through the occult rites of the Masters' red-robed, half-metal servants.

As he marched, dragging his newly bulging body up the incline towards the earthworks' summit, he envisioned the blessed slaughter to come. The barrels would be winched onto scaffolds and the breeches would be filled with flesh-burners and stone-breakers. Then, finally, when the blood of the sacrificed boiled on the iron shells and the hooded ones had doused the fire-pits with fresh spoors, the thunder would begin.

He reached his designated place in the defence lines, high on the earthworks, facing south, away from the desperate battles already breaking out across the city walls. The attention of the entire host was turned to the east, towards the fragile battlements, the slender lines of defence that dared to oppose the inevitable.

He reached his assigned trench and dropped down beyond the leading parapet, landing on the firing step and turning to take up his fire position. All along the defensive bulwark his fellow warriors did the same, dropping heavily into the protective earth-bank and slotting autoguns and lasguns into targeting grooves.

He looked out into the night, and wondered why he'd been stationed so far back from where the fighting would come. Defensive duties were surely no longer required.

The first clue came with a low growl, running along the earth like a tremor. He stiffened, looking back and forth, seeing nothing.

He pondered voxing a warning, but couldn't quite remember how to use the comm-bead. His mind was sluggish, as if in a fever.

Another growl, closer this time, emerging from the smog-filled night – everywhere, nowhere.

From further down the trench, he saw las-beams flicker out soundlessly, followed by the clatter of projectile fire. He heard short, strangled cries, like animals having their necks wrenched.

He stood back from his fire-point. To the north was the inner defence cordon guarding the blessed machines. The earthwork ran around it, manned by hundreds of gunners, each protected by hard-packed walls and backed up by gun-towers every hundred metres.

As he peered into the gloom, some vestige of fear stirred in his sluggish soul. Marker lights were going out along the length of the trench, one by one. He saw a gun-tower open fire just a hundred metres away, spraying a curtain of explosive shells into the dark, before a dull explosion took that out, too.

He couldn't see what was doing it. He couldn't see where the noises were coming from.

More growls, closer now, snickering in the air, punctuated by savage-sounding cracks and crackles. The remaining hairs on his neck stood up stiffly, as if an old race-memory lurked at the base of his brain-stem, not quite driven into abeyance by the plague.

He stood down from the firing step and advanced slowly along the trench floor. Others came with him, sharing his caution. For a moment longer, he saw nothing solid – just toxic dust swirls spilling into the trench shaft, spiralling away in the night, lit red from chem-fires.

Then something burst along the trench towards them – a grey ghost, massive and blurred by speed. He only had time for the briefest of impressions – the dull boom of machine-armour moving, a blade snarling in the dark, two red eyes blazing like afterburners. It was *huge*, it was *fast*.

The ghost bounded across the packed space of the inner trench, slaying as it came. Its victims died so quickly they had no time to scream, no time to react, just to be spliced open as an energy-spitting blade ripped them into meat-chunks.

He aimed his autogun. He even managed to get a shot away. He saw it splinter from the creature's shoulder – a burst of ice-white against the roiling dark.

Then it was on him – a hurricane of movement, a deafening snarl, a jackhammer impact. He didn't feel the bite of the blade, just a smash of a huge iron-bound fist, hurling him high into the air. His head cracked back, shattering his helm.

He landed with a snap of bone. Something burst, and hot liquid sprayed across his hands. He tried to get up, but his legs would no longer work. The air was filled with bestial noises – growls, tears, bellows of rage. He half saw more bodies flung across his field of vision, trailing gobbets of blood like gruesome mortar-trails.

Then it was on him again. He stared up at something he vaguely recognised from old devotional vids – a warrior-god towering over him, a grey-clad titan, a force of winter elements hurled out of the night and made into hellish, feral reality.

Just then, in a blaze of clarity and terror, he knew what it was. He remembered his humanity. He remembered what had happened to him. He remembered his old name.

I was Jevold.

Then the sword plunged down, slicing clean at the neck, and the misery of existence was ended.

Ingvar leapt away from the headless corpse, swaying clear of a row of incoming las-impacts and tearing down the earthwork's boundary trench. *Dausvjer* whirled around him, lacerating flesh and ripping through armour plates. The trench defenders charged at him in clumps of bodies, moving slowly as if in some dreadful dream.

He tore through them. He kicked out, pulverising torsos and breaking limbs. He punched, smashing skulls and cracking atrophied ribs. He hacked with the blade, biting into tumours and organs and spilling their contents out across the earth. The hordes clustered around him, swarming him with weight of numbers, before being broken and hurled away, tumbling through the air in a ballet of spiralling limbs. The carnage was voluminous, remorseless, implacable.

Ingvar wanted to *roar* – to open his throat and declaim the name of the Allfather, of Russ, of Fenris. He wanted to bellow at them as he slaughtered, relishing every splash of blood against his armour.

For now, though, he was silent. The Sisters had done their work, drawing the attention of the enemy towards Hjec Aleja's walls, and the need for stealth was still acute.

The Wolves, all five of them capable of bearing an axe, had sprinted out of the city just as the assault on the outer walls began, breaking clear of the Ighala Gate and ghosting through the deserted suburbs, heading down and away from the growing fighting and finding passage through the dark. Once beyond the city's southern limits they'd pulled around, running fast through empty lands before angling back up towards the enemy encampment. The few scouts they'd come across had been murdered swiftly. Like a deadly riptide, the Wolves had swept up out of the gloom and into the maze of trenches, spreading out across a wide front and kindling blade-weapons as they came. By the time they hit the main defence-lines, their momentum was unstoppable.

Ingvar heard a muffled *crump* as one of the pack – Gunnlaugur, he guessed – took out another gun-tower. Ingvar kept moving, barrelling down the jagged line of the trench, cleansing it, harrowing it, purging it. A big mutant swayed into his path, its fists crowned with grafted spikes, its heavy helm bleeding marshlight from nine iron-ringed lenses. It lunged at him, gurgling through a clutch of breathing tubes and going for his throat.

Ingvar severed the tubes with a tight swipe of his blade, spinning out of range of the spike-thrust before backhanding the mutant with the heel of his sword, breaking the creature's neck and driving its jawbone up into its skull. As the creature toppled into the dust, Ingvar spun to face three more warriors. They lumbered towards him numbly, firing a mix of las-beams and bullets from corroded weaponry. Ingvar charged straight into them, arms wide as if in an embrace. He bore them down with him, crushing ribcages and smashing limbs. Then he was up again, grinding the remains into the bloody mire at his feet, sword crackling, helm scanning for more targets.

'Target located,' came Olgeir's heavy voice over the squad-comm.

Ingvar switched to Olgeir's loc-reading – forty metres to the north, up amid the big tank formations and heading into the heart of the encampment.

He smashed aside a grasping claw, ducked under a hastily aimed thicket of green-tainted las-beams, and started running again. He leapt up the far side of the trench wall, boosted by his armour, and sprinted across open ground.

Enemy troops swarmed at him from the poison-clouds, throwing themselves at his feet, hurling spiked grenades into his path, trying to land a shot, do some damage.

It barely troubled him. Ingvar raced through it all, speeding like a loosed cannon, veering and swerving out of danger and annihilating all that remained in his path. His armour ran with blood – it slopped away from him as he moved, thick and glistening. He went noiselessly, quietly ratcheting up the kill-tally as he burned towards the hunt's focus.

The ground rose up steeply towards a crater-edge summit, laced with lines of razor wire and broken by the shafts of more concentric trenches. Each defence-line was stuffed with mutant soldiers, all now aiming at him as he came.

If he'd moved like a mortal moved, they'd have hit him – even power armour could be cracked by sufficient concentrations of incoming fire – but Ingvar moved like no human mortal had ever moved. He accelerated far too fast, then displaced himself, then checked back and loped back to full charge. It was impossible to track, to latch on to, to cope with. By the time he reached the crater's lip he was attracting whole webs of incoming shots, criss-crossing over one another in a desperate attempt to bring him down.

'Whelp – faster,' Ingvar voxed to Haflói, who wasn't closing in at the rate of the others. Haflói was a natural slayer, but he was decades younger and still had things to learn.

Then Ingvar reached the summit and vaulted through the final defences before hurtling down the far side of the ridge, down to where the objects of the hunt had been dragged.

They rose up, ruinous and magnificent, each one the size of a War-hound Titan and angled steeply into the toxin-boiling night. The four wall-breakers stood at the crater's wide, flat base, each surrounded by vast throngs of attendant slave-workers. Long telescopic barrels glinted in the light of explosions, stained dark green and bearing the ornate livery of blasphemy. Furnaces growled away at their bases. Tubes slung and bubbled, conveying skin-melting compounds to the delivery shells. Plague-burst corpses hung from the lips of the gun-muzzles, twisting in the hot smoke from exhaust vents.

The guns were nearly ready. Segmented belts churned towards snarl-mawed entry points, carrying payloads of ruination to the firing chambers. Gangs of shackled and blinded slaves hauled on chains, each link the size of a man's torso, cranking the firing angles a little higher.

Ingvar sped towards the nearest. The time for secrecy had passed – he heard Gunnlaugur's blood-chilling war-cry echoing out into the darkness. Frag explosions suddenly kicked out, and the night erupted into a ripple of pyrotechnics.

Ingvar grabbed his bolter from its mag-locked hold and opened fire. He heard Olgeir's heavy bolter breaking out on the far side of the compound. The pack was converging, bursting through the defences en masse, hitting them all at once and overwhelming them.

Ingvar cleared a whole swathe before him. It was all about speed now – sudden, overwhelming force applied to a single point. The whole enclosure held thousands of mutant warriors, and sooner or later those numbers would wear down even a Space Marine. Járnhamar had to achieve the immediate task quickly, then cut their way back to a more defensible position and hope Callia was still keeping the larger part of the huge army busy.

Ingvar neared the first of the artillery pieces, and its huge shadow fell across him. The breech section loomed out of the smoke, as tall as a Rhino, clad in thick blast-armour and vomiting palls of ink-black fumes.

He mag-locked his blade and pivoted on his heel, firing all the while to keep the enemy from him. His magazine clunked empty, and he leapt up, latching on to the jagged edge of the breech casing. He climbed fast, ignoring the rain of las-beams that pinged and snapped around him. Once he reached the top of the armour-casing, he flung himself onto an angled roof. The metal beneath him rocked and shook, boiling away like some infernal oven. Just ahead of him, the barrel-base itself soared up into the night, five metres in diameter and ringed with chains.

'They're good to fire,' voxed Gunnlaugur. 'Gut them. Now.'

Ingvar glanced up, seeing the Wolf Guard clambering across the breech-chamber on the wall-breaker across from him, less than twenty metres distant and barely ahead of a pursuing horde of screaming mutants.

Ingvar reached for melta charges and clamped them to the sides of the huge barrel, fixing six of them in quick succession, before hearing the first clang of mutants scrambling up after him onto the armour-casing.

He placed the last charge and whirled to face them, slamming a fresh magazine home just as the first of the enemy hauled itself up onto the roof of the breech section.

'Fenrys!' Ingvar thundered – the sacred word felt like catharsis as it flew from his fanged mouth. He let loose with his bolter, blasting the way clear of bodies, then raced along the spine of the breech-chamber housing. As he went, he mentally counted down the timer.

Ten seconds.

Just as he was about to leap clear, a horrific shape dragged itself clear of the metal grille in front of him. It seemed to emerge from the bowels of the machine itself, and its metal limbs pulled stickily out of a morass of boiling, glowing putrefaction. Six eyes flared at him, pulled back from a noseless, fang-lined face.

Ingvar kept firing, sending bolts thudding into the creature's emerging chest. The rounds went off, popping dully as if doused in magma. The creature dragged the last of its flame-licked body free of the machine, and flung itself at him.

The mech-mutant was as big as he was, multi-limbed, clad in oxidised armour plates and glistening with bio-augmetics. It carried twin power mauls, semi-enclosed in iron gauntlets. It charged him, skittering across the roof of the breech-chamber and screaming in overlapping vox-channels.

'Get *clear*,' warned Gunnlaugur over the vox.

Ingvar grabbed his sword, activated it and slung it wide – all in one movement – and the strike severed the thing's armour plates. Its momentum carried it forwards, though, and both mauls slammed down against Ingvar's shoulder-guards.

Five seconds.

The impact was heavy, forcing him back towards the steep-sloped chamber roof. The creature swung again wildly and pressed on towards him, but Ingvar punched his blade out point-first, snaking it between the two oncoming mauls and embedding it directly between the horror's snapping iron jaws.

Dausvjer's energy field exploded into life, lashing tendrils of disruptor-force against the mech-mutant's mottled skin. Ingvar grabbed the hilt two-handed and heaved the impaled creature over the edge. Then he whip-snapped the sword away, cleaving the creature's head in two and sending its body plummeting to the dust. Hearing the final *tick-tick* of the charges, he switched back to a sprint and tore back down the length of the breech-chamber roof. With a powerful lunge, he catapulted himself free of the armour-housing, only to hear the *whoomp* of the meltas going off behind him.

The blast was horrific – a maelstrom of heat and noise and kinetic force that snatched him up like a leaf in a storm and flung him hard through the air. Other charges on the other guns went off in tandem, cracking open all four artillery pieces in an orgy of rippling flame and spinning shrapnel.

Ingvar crashed to the ground some twenty metres from the gun-chassis he'd blown open. His head slammed forwards against the inner curve of his helm, and he felt the hot burst of blood spraying across his face.

Ignoring it, he pushed himself to his feet, and was hauling his armoured body up from the trench he'd carved in landing when an armoured fist grabbed him by his forearm and dragged him higher.

He tensed to strike, fingers tight on *dausvjer*'s hilt, before Gunnlaugur's familiar voice crackled over the comm.

'That was too close,' the Wolf Guard growled, yanking Ingvar upright before turning to face the mutants still on their feet and already coming at them.

Ingvar shook his head to clear it. 'Plenty of time.'

All four of the massive artillery pieces were cracked open and burning, riven asunder by the power of the massed meltas. Four vast columns of smoke churned up into the tortured sky, glowing angrily from within like nebulae. Sparks whirled and danced across the face of the inferno, thrown up from chain-exploding ammunition. The entire crater floor was in ruins, its defenders scattered, maimed or dazed, its war machines reduced to tilting shards of flaring metal.

Ingvar stood back to back with Gunnlaugur, his blade spitting defiant energy-stars. Those mutants not killed by the explosions began to gather again, dragging themselves up from the dust and searching for the source of their pain.

'What now?' asked Ingvar, watching them come.

Gunnlaugur nodded towards the crater's northern edge, where the concentration of enemy troops was thickest. 'They're not alone.'

The horde moving down the broken terrain towards them was not just composed of mortals. Ingvar saw flame-glints reflecting from the curved shoulder-guards of power armour. He saw single-horned helms, and pale green lenses, and reapers lifted high.

A cold rage burned instantly. 'Plague Marines.'

'I see six.'

Ingvar scanned across the compound, assessing distances, judging numbers. Olgeir, Jorundur and Hafloí were scattered across the crater floor among the corpses of the guns, out of position, isolated. More mutants were spilling into the crater from the north, adding to the horde already coming at them.

'We should pull back,' Ingvar said, pointing to a jagged outcrop of sandstone high up on the southern slopes, close to where he'd broken in. 'We could hold that.'

He fully expected to hear Gunnlaugur's growl of disdain then, followed by the command to charge into the heart of the horde, to cut a bloody swathe towards the Traitors before weight of numbers finally bogged them down.

'So be it,' said Gunnlaugur, defying expectation. 'We hold the ridge.'

Both of them started to move. A host of mutants was already racing towards their position, opening fire again in a ragged wave of las-beams. Ingvar lowered his boltgun, picking the first targets amid a sea of warped faces.

Before he could fire, though, a new roar kindled across the cloud-cover, louder than the residual furnaces of the ruined artillery or the yowls of mutant voices. It was thunderous, like main-drive starship engines gunning to full thrust. A crimson bruise spread out across the boiling brume of toxic smog, glowing angrily. Above it all came a familiar machine-howl – the whine of drop pod engines straining to break precipitous descent velocities.

Gunnlaugur laughed then, staring up at the heavens and lifting his arms wide.

'He's *here*,' he snarled, infusing the words with hunt-fervour. 'The sky cracks!'

All eyes looked up then, buffeted by the sudden storm of massed thruster down-force. The clouds split open, speared in a dozen places. Massive, fist-shaped transports lanced down from the skies, trailing smog and flame in their wake.

Ingvar watched the nearest pod make planetfall. The impact was horrendous – an earth-breaking smash that sent dust flying in a bow-wave. Cracks shot out from the epicentre, hitting the damaged foundations of the nearest wall-breaker and shivering what remained. Every mortal within fifty metres of that collision was ripped from their feet by the blast-radius and slammed hard against the churning earth.

Gunnlaugur kept laughing – the harsh laughter of impending slaughter. 'The wrath of Fenris!'

Ingvar kept watching. As the dust cleared, the shape of the pod became clearer. It was huge, far bigger than a typical Adeptus Astartes lander. Its flanks were not the slate-grey used by the Wolves, but arterial red and banded with black. Ornate gold and bronze chasing enclosed panels bearing baroque skull-icons.

'That's not Njal,' said Ingvar.

As the pall of fire and debris cleared around the drop pod, its door-bolts blew. Vivid red light bled out from the interior, wreathed in exhaust fumes, part masking a hulking shape within.

Only when it moved did the truth emerge. A towering walker stomped clear of the pod, limping out into the open on awkward, switch-backed, pistoned limbs. Heavy arms swung round, each capped with a flamer slung over a chainblade. It was more than three times the height of a man, a nightmare fusion of mortal flesh and machine artifice. Its engine shrieked like a caged ghost, its smokestacks vomited gouts of flaming gas-vapour, and its enormous segmented feet trod down the dust of Ras Shakeh, crushing the carpet of roasted limbs that surrounded the landing site.

By then more drop pods were coming down, dozens of them, slamming into the ground and opening up with halos of flamer-discharge. More bizarre war-machines streamed out from them – quadrupedal walkers with underslung flame-cannons and swollen vox-emitters screaming war-curses; half-tracked cannons with gun-servitors lurching in escort; hovering gun-drones bristling with trailing hook-lines and segmented chain-flails. Crimson-armoured mortal troops marched in the war machines' wake, all bearing the same black skull devices on their closed-face helms.

Gunnlaugur looked on, his battle-joy quickly turning to shocked disgust. 'The Church,' he snarled. 'The *Church*.'

Ingvar scanned for the Plague Marines they'd sighted earlier. This changed everything – with allies crashing into the heart of the enemy army, the odds were evening up rapidly. 'I think they're on our side,' he said.

'*Who* is?' demanded Gunnlaugur, outraged. 'Who commands?'

Ingvar activated *dausvjer*'s energy field.

'Find out later, brother,' he said, starting to move again. 'For now, be glad they hunt with us.'

Chapter Four

De Chatelaine stood at the summit of the Ighala Gate, watching as the sea of flame lapped up against the walls of her city. The platform on which she stood was broad and open, containing only her and twenty ceremonial Guard soldiers, and it felt like being isolated on a pinnacle over a universe of blood and torment.

She'd watched her Battle Sisters spearheading the assault down to the perimeter, noting with pride how swiftly and how skilfully they had retaken lost ground. She'd watched as the big guns had been hoisted into position, remounted on the old defence towers and angled at the huge mobs outside the walls. She'd watched as the enemy had responded, stirring lazily at first, then hurling its vast resources at the fragile barrier, hammering at the gates, surging up against the defiant line of defenders.

It had been difficult to witness from a distance, condemned by her rank to remain an overseer of the carnage rather than a participant in it. One of the towers had been overwhelmed less than an hour after being retaken. Waves of mutants clambered up the walls, poured through the demolished sections and surrounded the pockets of reclaimed defiance. De Chatelaine had been tempted to order a fighting retreat back to the inner walls. She could see her meagre troops being surrounded, and it felt like throwing away everything they had worked so hard to win.

She held firm. Most of the bulwarks survived, reinforced by a constant stream of troops and materiel sent down from the upper city. They were besieged and isolated, but fought on defiantly. As time went on, the precarious salient drew yet more troops out from the sprawling enemy encampment, dragging them across the poisoned desert and into the meat grinder of combat.

When the four gigantic explosions rocked the foundations under her and sent intertwined columns of burning smoke rearing high over the entire battlefield, she knew the Wolves had done what they had promised – the enemy had been blooded, its fangs drawn.

'Come back now,' she breathed, leaning out into the night air. 'No pride, no glory – you've done what was needful and now we need you here.'

But then everything changed. The sky above her burned. The roar and clamour of the battle was replaced by the thunderous crescendo of landers coming into range.

She looked up, gazing at the film of lurid pollution that had overarched them since the first days of the siege, and saw it glowing from above, lit vividly by starbursts of crimson and silver. Then drop pods broke through, hurtling down into the wastes beyond the broken walls.

As she watched them fall, de Chatelaine's sudden joy gave way to unease – they were not Space Wolves drop pods. Though hard to make out in the particulate fog, the war machines looked blood-red, their death's-head insignias surmounted by baroque crests of gold.

'Canoness,' murmured one of her guards, hovering at her side. 'Please, now, you must withdraw.'

Her bodyguards had been trying to persuade her to retreat to some-where more secure for over an hour, but now, for the first time since taking position on the Gate, she felt suddenly exposed.

'Captain, I do not–' she started, but her voice was immediately drowned out by a fresh clamour.

Six columns of actinic energy shot down around her, surrounding her and making the platform blaze wildly as if in full daylight. She reached for her sidearm, just as the eddying distortion guttered out and threw the platform back into fire-flecked gloom.

Standing before her, glistening from the residue of warp-translation, were six figures, each looking at her dryly as if they owned the planet and she were some kind of interloper.

'Put your weapon away please, canoness preceptor,' said one of them, a slender man wearing sable robes and holding a tall, aquila-tipped staff. His voice was soft, and his skin was as pale as milk. 'If we were here to harm you, by the Emperor's will you would already be dead.'

De Chatelaine stared back at him for a moment, her heart thumping. She kept her bolt pistol raised, holding it two-handed. 'This is my domain,' she said. 'I would know who treads here.'

Another of the newcomers shuffled forwards then, pulling at the robe of the speaker and gesturing for him to make way.

This one was different, his skin oil-slicked and golden. Voluminous robes swaddled a corpulent frame, picked out in brocade of gold and red and black. Armour glinted from under gaps in the robes, itself richly decorated and studded with rococo flourishes. He too carried a staff, but it was far grander, carved from gold and studded with garnets, emeralds and carnadines.

His eyes were dark, almost white-less, and had the dead-stare certainty of a man who routinely controlled the fate of worlds. When he smiled, his thick lips pursing fleshily, it was with the awareness of what honour the gesture bestowed on the beholder. There was no joy in that smile, just a smooth, practised command of indulgence. He lifted a limp hand, heavy with bands of gold, and glided towards her.

'Of course you would,' he said, extending the hand in her direction. 'But I trust you know me now?'

De Chatelaine dropped to one knee.

'Lord Cardinal,' she said, grasping his hand. She kissed the golden ring of his middle finger – a weighty band of gold surmounted by a ruby in the shape of a skull. 'Forgive me, I did not–'

'Rise, my daughter.' He gazed down at her tolerantly. 'This is war, and you were cautious. Now it is over, and the Church comes to reclaim its own.'

De Chatelaine did as she was bid, and holstered her pistol. Drop pods were falling from the skies, lancing down into the thick of the fighting beyond the walls. She could hear the crescendo of intensifying combat, pocked with the familiar rush of flame-weapons being deployed.

'We had no idea,' she said. Repoda had given her no warning, no *inkling*, that Ecclesiarchy forces had come into range of Ras Shakeh.

The Cardinal nodded. His every movement was feline.

'We can move carefully when we wish to,' he said. 'But you were clearly expecting help from somewhere. A rash assault to make, I think, if you were not.'

'The Wolves of Fenris,' said de Chatelaine. 'A pack of them fights with us, and more are due.'

At the mention of Space Wolves, the man in the sable robes stiffened. The Cardinal sniffed, as if a minor foul aroma had just wafted into his otherwise perfumed presence.

'They have an old claim on this place,' he said. 'Like half the worlds in this sector.'

As he spoke, a heavy troop lifter emerged from the clouds, far out over the plains. It was immediately strafed with flickering lines of las-fire, while labouring on a throbbing cushion of engine down-blast. The ship was huge, far larger than the drop pods, and must have carried hundreds of troops within its swollen crew bays.

'What strength do you bring?' asked de Chatelaine, observing the lifter fighting its way down.

'Enough.'

'My lord, they have Traitor Marines. The Wolves–'

'Space Marines are not the Emperor's only weapons.'

'No. No, they are not. Even so…' She trailed off.

The Cardinal gave de Chatelaine a disapproving look. 'This is *our* world. We can use the Wolves if we must, but when this filth is cleared away, they will stay or leave by our command.' He shot a glance at the sable-cloaked man, who nodded fervently in agreement. 'I may have been remiss in fortifying this sector, but there are so many for us to ward, all with mouths to feed and souls to shrive. You must forgive me, canoness, for leaving you to the mercy of savages.'

'They have died for us.'

'Which is the least of the many services a man may render. And, for them, who are not even men in the true sense, what else is there?' He reached into a deep pocket in his robes and withdrew a small ivory box. He flicked it open, retrieved a pinch of what looked like coal-dust, placed two dabs of it against his nostrils, inhaled, then replaced the box. 'There is a reckoning for all things. We are all held accountable for our service, one way or another.'

The Cardinal behaved as if the warfare thundering around them all were somehow a trifling affair, the business of others. By now, the lifter had made planetfall and was busily disgorging its contents onto the plains around it. De Chatelaine saw battle engines striding amid the carnage, blessed instruments of the Adeptus Militorum. Most were Sentinel-class walkers, adorned with Ecclesiarchy colours and bearing flamers slung under their chassis, but there were other assault machines among them, some with a darker genesis.

It had been a long time since she'd witnessed a Penitent Engine at war. The memory of the first time was still raw in her mind.

'So this is deliverance,' she said quietly. 'I had assumed it would be them. Better that it be my own kind.'

'It matters not who wields the blade,' the Cardinal said, sniffing again, 'so long as it finds a neck to bite.' He looked around him, casting dead eyes across the carnage. 'Perhaps you will show me to the Halicon now. I wish to instruct you on what is to come.'

De Chatelaine hesitated. 'My forces are engaged.'

The Cardinal smiled coldly. 'Do not concern yourself with that. You have laboured for long enough, and your service will be recognised.' The fleshy lips twitched. 'We are here now. That is all that matters.'

Down on the battlefield, the volume of fire was incredible. Penitent Engines hurled out vicious streamers of flame, catching on the enemy and exploding in promethium-laced clouds. Phalanxes of closed-helm troopers in red segmented armour stalked through the carnage, laying waste to everything before them. Most destructive of all were the Battle Sisters, hurled into the thick of the fighting by precision drop-strikes. They, too, were clad in deep crimson battleplate and bore the sigil of a teardrop surmounted by flames. Like their counterparts of the Wounded Heart, they fought with brutal commitment, charging in close before unleashing a torrent of flamer weapons.

The entire battle-plain was now a furnace of brutality. The enemy remained as stubborn as ever, fighting with the sullen, semi-conscious violence they were known for. Tides of mutant soldiers charged into hurricanes of incoming fire, overwhelming oncoming troops with weight of numbers. Twisted horrors limped out of the depths of the army, swollen with stimm-enhanced grotesquery and laying waste with chem-weapons or poison-tipped flails.

Out of all of them, though, the most formidable were the Masters – the Plague Marines, centuries old and hardened into instruments of destruction. They strode through the clogged battlefield, reaping as they came and leaving ditches of severed limbs in their wake. Las-fire glanced harmlessly from their crusted armour, blades turned from their rust-pocked breastplates, and flames coursed over them leaving nothing but surface charring. While they lived and fought, the battle remained in the balance.

'For the Allfather!' bellowed Gunnlaugur, charging to be the first into contact. Ingvar, Olgeir, Jorundur and Hafloí charged with him, howling and bellowing death-curses as they cut their way towards their fallen brothers.

The Plague Marines lumbered to meet them, striding across the flame-laced battlefield in grim silence. They carried thick-bladed power scythes, their twisted blades running with filth. Their immense armour power-packs had distended, fusing into the plague-pale flesh beneath and latching on to coils of bunched cabling.

When the two forces clashed, the impact cracked out across the battlefield. The pure fury of Fenris thundered into the pure corruption of Barbarus, shivering the earth and blasting away any combatants foolish enough to dare to intervene.

Every blow was perfectly aimed, lashed out with crushing weight and infinite hatred. Hammer and axes thudded into the curved blades of the scythes, exploding in showers of disruptor-sparks. Boltguns blazed, blasting shards from power armour.

The Wolves were faster. Up against real opposition for the first time, their speed became truly phenomenal – they hacked and shot, roaring and snarling, totems flying about them like satellites. *Skulbrotsjór* arced wildly, cracking into corroded armour with deadening force. *Dausvjer* thrust, catching the light of bloody flames on its rune-carved length.

The Plague Marines responded with equal fervour. Eerily silent, their movements were suffused with a wearing power of eternity, absorbing impacts and turning them back on the bearer. They thrust and parried with their scythes, meeting the hammer blows and blade strikes and hammering back. Green-edged energies rippled down their corrupted blades, flaring as they hit and sending webs of aetheric power dancing like ghosts.

One of them, a monster with one bulging eye-lens and a bursting abdominal armour-plate, was smashed bodily to the ground by Gunnlaugur, his death mask driven in to reveal a bloody mass of flesh beneath. Jorundur was mauled by another, his axe slammed away by a power scythe before the hilt cracked into his gorget-plating. The Old Dog hit the earth, cursing even as Olgeir raced to support him. Hafloí became locked in a frenzied duel with a tusked adversary covered in clanking skulls. Ingvar took on two at once, working his sacred blade with preternatural speed and dexterity.

Each warrior, Traitor and Loyalist alike, remained so focused on the fight, so locked into the pure state of combat, that none noticed the wind picking up around them. The blows continued to land, the boltguns continued to drum. They fought on as the earth at their feet shook and electric arcs crackled around them. They were fighting even as lances of power shot down from above, outshining the crackling roar of the flames and sending shadows leaping across the battlefield.

Only when the Plague Marines were encased in fields of writhing ball-lightning and lifted clear of the battlefield did the pack finally pull clear. Gunnlaugur checked a hammer swipe, seeing his opponent held rigid within a vice of rippling translucent force. The six Traitors were transfixed, locked in midair by snaking bolts of silver fire.

Gunnlaugur withdrew along with his brothers, hackles rising, primed for the next assault. As soon as he saw the origin of the battle-lightning, though, he let the head of *skulbrotsjór* fall. The rest of the pack, free from the grip of combat, fell back, their ragged pelts rippling in the howl of wind and dust.

More drop pods had come down, this time in grey livery with yellow-and-black chevrons. They studded the battlefield like granite monoliths, steaming from their atmospheric plummet. Two dozen Grey Hunters surrounded the pods, bolters lowered, their rune-daubed armour limned red by the fires. They remained motionless, every barrel of every gun aimed at the stricken Plague Marines.

The Hunters were not alone. Before them stood the living legend.

He towered over all else, clad in hulking Terminator plate that made him look like some storm-giant of Fenrisian myth. Runes glowed on its surface, throbbing like open wounds, and the air around him ran with static. A heavy red-mane wolf-pelt hung over the curve of his thick psychic hood, pulled by the unnatural wind that eddied around him. His staff, a thick stave of ebony, snarled and shimmered as if alive, crowned by a bleached skull whose eyes flared with pooled aetheric matter. His flame-red beard, unfaded to grey despite hundreds of years in service, spilled out across a huge barrel chest. Two frost-blue eyes stared out, perfect in their clarity, fearsome in their intensity.

He said nothing. Lines of force lashed and snaked from his staff, swept up by the circling winds and feeding the coronae that enclosed the locked Plague Marines. The very stuff of the elements seemed drawn to him, and the dust drummed and rippled around his boots.

He raised his left gauntlet, encrusted in ice-rimed ceramite, and a black shape flapped down out of the tortured air. A sleek raven, half the size of a mortal man, its night-black plumage laced with the cables and iron bands of the Iron Priest's trade, alighted on his wrist, folding semi-metal wings, cawing once, then glaring out at the battlefield.

Njal Stormcaller issued no war-cry. He lifted his immense staff, and lightning forked out, bounding across the earth before snapping into the Traitors suspended in their auras of psychic fire. Tempests howled around him, whipping up blood and smoke and grime and hurling them into vortices of destruction. The *noise* of it was incredible, as if the planet's soul were being harrowed before their eyes and remade anew.

One by one, life was strangled out of the suspended Traitors. Their limbs twitched, then flailed, then spasmed, as if invisible hands had reached up to their throats to choke them. Their armour cracked, splitting with snaps of silver brilliance, revealing pox-thick flesh within, as pale as bone and puffed up with lesions. Layer by layer, their fallen magnificence was stripped away, scorched and consumed, withering in waves of coruscation. They screamed, but the sound was snatched away by the scream of the wind. When nothing was left of them but husks, as black and fragile as coiled paper, their carcasses thudded back to the ground. Remnants of their ceramite shells rolled away, held together by inky strands of tar-like residue.

All but one. The largest of the Plague Marines, the monster Gunnlaugur had felled, still hung intact, immobile, locked by the esoteric forces that played across his armour. He fought against the coils and spiked webs of aether-force, but the dazzling lattice clamped him tight, shrinking onto his tortured frame like throttle-wire.

Njal walked slowly up to his captive, his boots crunching across the bones of the battlefield. As he moved, the raven at his wrist issued a harsh vox-caw of denunciation. Crackles of lightning continued to dance and flicker around the Rune Priest's colossal frame, as if leaking out from the furnace of power contained within.

'You,' Njal rasped, gazing up at his prey. His voice was ice-sheer, as raw and jagged as the wyrd-storm that raged around him. 'You will live. For now.'

Gunnlaugur, until then held rapt by Njal's imperious presence, remembered himself and raised his thunder hammer in salute. The rest of the pack did likewise with their blades.

'*Hjá, gothi!*' they cried.

Njal turned to look at them, maintaining the force-aegis over the Traitor with ease. It was hard, even for Gunnlaugur, to meet the stare of those eyes, laced as they were with flickers of deep aether-fire. Something about the way they burned – the inflexibility, the *acuity* – was impossible to endure.

'Grimnar sent seven to this world,' said Njal.

'He did, *jarl*,' replied Gunnlaugur. 'Váltyr's thread was cut.'

'The sixth?'

'The Red Dream.'

Njal's gaze moved towards Ingvar, as if he knew, instinctively, who was responsible for Apothecary duties. 'He will recover?'

'He will,' said Ingvar.

Njal nodded curtly, then looked out beyond the protective circle of Grey Hunters. Ecclesiarchy battle engines were by then running rampant, driving out into the reeling heart of the enemy horde. More forces were being landed all the time, hammering down into the battlefield on roiling columns of thruster-burn. With every crash-landing came the slam and recoil of lander-ramps, followed by the charge of booted feet. The air was filled with the whine of mortars, the rush of flamers, the roar and crack of bolter weapons.

In the distance, the enemy was already falling back from the city's outer walls, and Battle Sisters clad in both black and red were leading the counter-offensive. Penitent Engines swayed and burned among them, many carrying the tattered banners of the Ministorum above the carapace-shells of their agonised occupants.

'No honour in allies like these,' Njal murmured, watching a squad of what looked like men with metal flails in place of arms and thick iron plates bolted over their faces.

His raven watched it all with dark, reflecting eyes. It cawed again – a harsh vox-scrape – then turned its long-beaked head away.

'Know this!' cried Njal then, whipping up more stormwind as his huge voice boomed out into the night. 'The Rout is among you now! *Fear* us! *Flee* from us! We come only to slay, and before the red dawn rises, our axes will be black with your blood!' His pelts flared out from his shoulders, buoyed by unnatural wind and crowned with the thorn-pattern of light-ning shards. 'Run while you may! Plead to your gods! Nothing remains for you but *death!*'

Njal's raging aura exploded into a sunburst of raw light, streaming out into the gloom with eye-burning intensity. Given their cue, the Grey Hunters of his retinue broke out of the cordon and charged down the retreating mutant hordes. Járnhamar charged with them, spurred into fresh combat-fury by the arrival of their battle-brothers. With a massed howl that cut through all else on the battlefield, the Wolves of Fenris tore back into combat, driving the enemy back into the desert and breaking the grip they had exerted on the city for so long.

Birthed in fire and fury, the final deliverance of Hjec Aleja had begun.

Chapter Five

When dawn came, the sun rose over a bleak scene of devastation. The city remained enclosed in a pall of rising smoke, part chem-filth from the enemy's ample reservoirs, part smog from the broken tanks and fuel depots. A sprawl of tangled metal and armour ran out from the ravaged walls far into the desert, marred by deep gouges where the drop pods and bulk lifters had come down. Bulbous lander-craft squatted amid the ruins, some hollowed out by gunfire, some intact and operating. Reclamator machines crawled down the long embarkation ramps equipped with lifting gear and purge-flamers. Those who still walked amid the wreckage went warily, their faces covered and their environment suits tightly sealed.

The fighting had raged through the night, gradually moving away from the city's edge and further out into the wilds. The Traitor forces had been eviscerated by the initial assaults but had not yielded easily. There was no break, no panic, just a grim, futile resistance that had lasted for hours. Even as the sun climbed into the sky there were pockets of defiance – knots of mutants too steeped in mind-breaking corruption to recognise the impossibility of victory and who just kept on doing what their combat-implants told them to.

The Ecclesiarchy troops, once landed in sufficient numbers, had been horrifyingly efficient. They had swept across the battlefield in ordered zones, burning everything, responding to the terror-weapons of the Traitors with terror-weapons of their own. Fear meant little or nothing to them – it had been bled out by psycho-conditioning or neural extraction. They were reinforced by their arcane bestiary of biomechanical creations – every conceivable combination of human–weapon interface seemed to have found a home in the forces of the Cardinal.

None of them, though, had quite matched the bolstered forces of the Wolves, who had pushed deep into the heart of the enemy formations and ripped out the command centres. Caught between the fury of the Space Marines and the systematic advance of the Ecclesiarchy, the contest descended into industrial-scale slaughter. The dust of the desert thickened with blood, turning black-brown and curdling underfoot. Flames were poured across every conquered metre, sanctifying the corpses of the faithful fallen and atomising the bodies of the stricken traitors.

When the first rays of sunlight angled through the miasma, they revealed a vast circlet of ruins around a tiny epicentre of survival. Above it all, spear-leaved trees still grew in the sheltered courtyards, and the citizens still breathed untainted air behind the atmosphere-sealed chambers, but they were alone amid a swathe of destruction.

Ingvar stood in the ornate great hall of the Halicon. He remembered the first time he'd laid eyes on it, fresh from the destruction of *Undrider* and with the situation on the ground unknown. It looked little different – the real fighting hadn't reached this far up. Gaudy monuments to the Immortal Church stood in the alcoves, carved from alabaster and marble and bearing golden crowns above penitent faces. The heroes of the Adeptus Ministorum always seemed to be penitent. The edifice was *built* on penitence – an entire species held in thrall by it, locked into fear of error, transfixed by the guilt of crimes committed, planned or imagined.

Perhaps that was necessary. Halliafiore, the inquisitor who had commanded Onyx, would have agreed readily: mortal humans were wayward, prone to congenital weakness, and only their sanctioned guardians, those given the most rigorous psycho-conditioning ever devised, could hope to face up to the universe without stricture.

'My Lords of Fenris,' came the Cardinal's voice, ringing out from the throne he'd occupied. He was used to the grand occasion. 'Welcome, in the name of the Deified Master of Mankind, to the delivered shrine world of Ras Shakeh.'

The Cardinal had decreed that the deliverance of the city required immediate ceremony. His acolytes had laid on all the trappings of a celebratory service – a triumph, overseen by the servants of the Ministorum and accompanied by all the gilt-edged finery he could muster. They had done well in a short time – the Halicon chamber had scarce looked, or smelt, more opulent.

Such ostentation could almost have been calculated to antagonise the Wolves, who wished for nothing more than to capitalise on the tactical advantage and drive the remains of the enemy further into the desert. Still, Njal had ordered them all to attend, even if only for a few moments while Delvaux said his piece. The two forces would have to work together to cleanse the world, and so would have to find ways to accommodate each other's idiosyncrasies.

Njal himself stood in the very centre of the capacious chamber, his Terminator armour flecked with the muck of the battlefield. He dominated the entire hall – a man-mountain of ceramite and animal-hides, crowned with graven imagery and draped with bone icons. In the blistering sunlight, refracted through the lenses of a dozen crystalflex chandeliers, the scarce-contained brutality of his heritage was even more evident than it had been during the night. His every gesture dripped with an almost unconscious menace, underpinned and reinforced by the constant hard hum of his armour's power units.

By comparison, to Ingvar's eyes, the Cardinal looked ludicrous. Delvaux had been smoothed and primped with aggressive rejuvenat, making his sleek jowls shine. His finery was extravagant beyond reason, a level of splendour that seemed calculated to amaze or offend, depending on the audience. He spoke casually of the Emperor's godhood despite knowing Njal would not share that belief. His voice was soft and smooth, though it carried well enough throughout the hall. A vox-distributor, perhaps, lodged somewhere in the man's throat.

When Njal spoke, the contrast was stark – his unfiltered voice was like the low crack of thunder, tempered by an extended lifetime of constant warfare. He had communed with Traitors, xenos, the vilest of the neverborn, and had lived to perform rites of destruction over their corpses. Alone among the occupants of that hall, Njal could most closely claim to have experienced the terrible scope of true divine power, and the knowledge of it lent his every gesture the grim weight of innate dignity.

When the Stormcaller spoke, all listened.

'This is just the start,' Njal rasped, looking with poorly disguised contempt at the Cardinal's sumptuous throne. 'We must take the war back to the enemy.'

The Wolves of both Járnhamar and Njal's retinue stood around the Rune Priest in a semicircular honour guard. De Chatelaine stood at the right hand of the Cardinal, decked in what ceremonial finery she could lay hands on. Sister Callia, the most senior of her command still alive, remained at her side, as did forty of the Sororitas of the Wounded Heart.

Ras Shakeh's Guard regiments took up most of the rest of the space. Many had come straight from the field and bore the grime of the fighting openly. For all their fatigue, they stood as firmly to attention as they could. They were devout men, and to witness the Cardinal in their midst was more than most would have hoped for in their brutally short lifetimes.

The rest of the assembled throng came from the Cardinal's forces: storm troopers and assault troops in crimson armour, flanked by Battle Sisters of the Order of the Fiery Tear. The Cardinal's command group was the most striking. Standing at the prelate's shoulder was a thin man in black robes. A couple of cherubs hovered around him, grinning inanely and belching incense. The man's eyes flickered back and forth, searching through the throngs before him. He looked nervous.

Beside him stood a menagerie of warped biomechanics. A Battle Sister lurked imposingly among them, her entire left arm refashioned into a bronze-clad flamer housing. Cables looped up and around it, hung with devotional icons. Her face was similarly augmetic, clustered with arcane sensor bundles that obscured her otherwise alabaster-pale features.

The Cardinal sniffed. He did that a lot, Ingvar noticed.

'Of course, you are correct,' Delvaux said. 'We must fight again soon. But for now, let us remember the source of our salvation.' He smiled thinly. His flesh looked unusually supple, flexing like fat slopped over gauze. 'We are all servants of the same power. It was by His will that we found ourselves brought here.'

Njal grunted noncommittally. Ingvar could sense the impatience coursing through every muscle of his lethal body.

'And you are to be thanked, my lord,' the Cardinal went on. 'Without the assistance of your fine warriors, this world would have been lost before we arrived, and we would have taken orbit over a dead city. So on behalf of the Diocese of Hvar Primus, please take my gratitude back to your Great Wolf. Their – and your – service shall not go unrecorded.'

The psyber-raven perched on Njal's shoulder extended its wings, as if itching to rake at the Cardinal's eyes. 'Record what you wish,' said Njal. 'I care not, and nor will Grimnar. We must speak of battle.'

'So we shall. I have already ordered the pursuit. There are other cities – dens of corruption, gripped by the dead hand of contagion. They can be recovered.'

'Recovered?'

'Purged. Cleansed. Whatever word does the labour justice.'

Njal's scarred lips tightened in irritation. 'This whole *sector* is at war. Pause now, even for an hour, and they will recover.'

The Cardinal bowed. 'Correct, and my strategos are already at work planning further deployments.'

'So you have more forces inbound.'

'We do,' confirmed Delvaux, 'though they will be in the aether for months. What of your brothers?'

'When they can be spared. For now, no.'

The Cardinal extended his arms wide then, exposing more fabulous detail on his brocade robes. 'Then let us – please – take this brief hiatus to rest in a little thankfulness. Let us dwell, for a *moment*, on the deliverance of this place. The Emperor does not abandon the faithful. He will *never* abandon the faithful.'

At that, members of his command group stepped forwards. Cherubs emerged from somewhere behind the throne, pumping incense into the Halicon's upper reaches. Clanging started up, a rhythm beaten out by hooded acolytes with sutured cymbals for hands. It was smoothly orchestrated, drawn straight from the Ministorum's millennia-old patterns of devotion.

The crowd responded instantly, almost involuntarily. Ingvar turned to see fighting men, their features drawn with fatigue, suddenly spark with a kind of desperate gratitude. The Sisters bowed their heads, their lips moving in prayer. The entire place began to sway with the dull rhythm of devotion. Soldiers who had endured terror for weeks suddenly began to break down, tears streaming down grimy faces.

Njal remained where he was for a moment, his frosty eyes locked with the Cardinal's. The prelate gazed back at him, a touch of defiance, laced with impudent trepidation, playing across his bland features.

'You may join us, if you wish,' Delvaux said. 'None are refused.'

Njal snorted a short, acerbic laugh. 'Not for us,' he said, and gestured towards the chamber doors. His Fenrisian honour guard immediately turned and headed for the grand doors. Before he joined the exodus,

Ingvar caught a small look of amusement the Cardinal shared with his black-robed deputy.

'As you wish it,' called out Delvaux, as robed menials in gold masks shuffled up to attend him. They brought ewers full of boiling water, and braziers glowing with hot embers, and ritual scrolls filled with tight-curled sacred scripts. The clanging cymbals grew in volume, filling the chamber with a cacophonic dirge. 'Though we shall remember your souls.'

By then Njal was striding down the aisle towards the daylight beyond, bristling with irascibility, his staff striking the marble heavily. 'That's good to know,' he muttered.

Ingvar, Gunnlaugur and the others fell in behind the Rune Priest.

'This is going to be interesting,' remarked Ingvar, under his breath.

Gunnlaugur nodded sourly. 'Very.'

The Wolves convened as far away from the Halicon edifice as they could. The bulk of Njal's warriors were still engaged in the final stages of Hjec Aleja's cleansing, so only the pack leaders met with their master to plan the next stage of the hunt.

Njal had brought three packs of ten with him on his Gladius-class frigate, *Heimdall*, each one headed by a veteran Grey Hunter. The first was Steinn Fellblade, a sharp-faced, sleek-eyed killer with a jagged, wolf's-head-engraved broadsword strapped across his armour. The second was Hauki Long-axe, whose favoured twin-headed blade hung from his belt on iron-studded straps. The third was Kjarl Bloodhame, who bore a blackened flamer under the blood-red, age-hardened pelt that gave him his moniker.

Alongside them stood Álfar the Cold, Njal's Wolf Guard and shield-bearer. His armour was ancient and gunmetal-dark, marked with icons of Morkai. He carried a storm shield with a wolf's fanged skull set at the centre, as well as a massive chainsword marked with the ice-rune *hjarz*. He glared out at the world with heavy-lidded eyes under a frame of long, slush-grey hair. His tattooed face looked liable to crack if it smiled.

They had gathered away from the sun, deep in the shadowed chambers of the city where the air was cooler and the stone rough hewn. Only Gunnlaugur had been summoned from Járnhamar. He took his place alongside the others, his armour even more battle-ravaged than theirs, his features darkened by the pitiless Ras Shakeh sun, his restored thunder hammer freshly marked with evidence of kills.

Each one of those warriors was a truly deadly practitioner of Fenris's murderous arts of combat. Each one of them was capable of rendering whole regiments of mortals to waste, of tearing down cities and stripping starships clean of life. And each one of them, without hesitation or rancour, bowed his head in submission as Njal entered.

The Rune Priest came among them, ducking under the low stone archway. The runes on his heavy Terminator plate remained dark, but power hummed from them like heat-wash over an engine. His eyes glittered as if lit by an inner flame, blue as the seas in the Season of Fire. The psyberraven, Nightwing, perched atop his left wrist. As the Rune Priest took his place, it hopped from his hand and into the shadow of a stone alcove, where it stared out, silent and watchful.

Njal didn't speak for some time. He rested his chin on his armour's gorget, and his flame-red beard fell across the ceramite in matted snarls.

'They know what they're doing,' he said at last, his deep voice echoing from the stone. 'They will build a new Cathedral on the ashes of the old. They will drag pilgrims to their shrine and fill them with new fears.'

Álfar nodded slowly in agreement, but said nothing. No others dared speak. Njal seemed lost in his own deliberations, and none were going to interrupt those.

Eventually, the Rune Priest lifted his head and bared long fangs in a cynical half-smile. 'Loathsome. But they are here, as are we.' He turned to Gunnlaugur. 'So, Wolf Guard. This is the time for tales. Tell me what happened here.'

Gunnlaugur did, leaving nothing out. He told of the landing, the destruction of *Undrider*, the arrival in Hjec Aleja and the defence of the citadel. He spoke quickly, covering the ground with no embellishment. Váltyr's death was reported just as it would be in the annals of the Fang. 'He died with blade in hand.'

Njal nodded in satisfaction. 'And the other one?'

'Baldr. He was...' Gunnlaugur hesitated. 'Changed. A madness took him. He slew the enemy champion, tore him apart, then we lost him. Ingvar brought him back, but the Dream has him now.'

Njal looked at him sceptically. 'Madness? The Wolf?'

'He used... the way of the storm.'

'And you didn't cut his thread.'

'No.' Gunnlaugur looked defiant. 'There is no taint now, not that we can sense.'

Nightwing turned its half-steel head to face Gunnlaugur and stared at him inquisitorially.

'That is not your judgement to make, Skullhewer,' said Njal.

'I judged when there were no others to do it.'

Njal considered that. 'And now I am here,' he said. 'Which may be a sign, or it may not. In either case, you will bring him to me for examination.'

Gunnlaugur bowed.

'And what of the canoness?' Njal asked.

'Brave. I trust her.'

'Good. We have to work with these people. Fenris will not be sending more strength here, not soon. Battle has come to a hundred systems at once and the Great Companies are all engaged. They are even pulling out of Armageddon. We are just the start, the arrowhead before the shaft.'

'To what end?'

'That is what we must discover.' Njal turned to his shieldbearer. 'Álfar, tell him what we know.'

'The Cardinal is named Giorgias Delvaux,' said Álfar, in a voice as cadaverous as his appearance. 'His power comes from the hive worlds of the Hvar Belt, bordering this subsector. He has issued edicts calling for a crusade and started drawing together what he needs. He commands a Grand Cruiser, the *Vindicatus*, in orbit above us.'

'Reputation?' asked Gunnlaugur.

'Brutal. Orthodox. Fiercely ambitious, and he has the ear of those at the top of the Church.'

'That's encouraging.'

Álfar's face didn't so much as twitch. 'They were unprepared for this. They don't know what brought plague here, and they can't fight it alone.'

Njal snorted derisively. 'That won't stop them wishing they were. They number thousands, we less than forty, so we must find a means to drive this our way.'

'What of the Plague Marine?' asked Gunnlaugur. 'The one you took from the battle?'

'He lives,' said Njal. 'Just. We have him on *Heimdall*, and secrets will be wrung from him. We need more, though. The Cardinal will purge this place before taking up arms again, and we need to be faster.'

'There were deep-void listening stations on the system edge,' said Álfar. 'Dead to augur-sweeps, but they might have picked something up before being overrun.'

Njal turned to Gunnlaugur. 'You still have your Thunderhawk?'

'Just about.'

'Use it,' said the Rune Priest. 'Anything we can find before they do will give us an edge.'

'It'll barely get off the ground,' said Gunnlaugur.

'We can fix that for you,' said Álfar.

'I'll speak to Jorundur,' said Gunnlaugur, looking like he didn't relish it.

'For now, though, we have prey to run down,' said Njal. 'The Cardinal has this right – this city will not be secure until we've purged every settlement, and we can do it as fast as they.' He reached out to Nightwing, smoothing its feathers absently. The psyber-familiar half closed its eyes and angled its head back. 'But I don't want to stay here longer than I have to – the sea of stars calls.'

He looked around him, at the hot, dusty stone, as far removed from the icy wastes of Fenris as it was possible to be.

'And I already dislike this place,' he said.

Ingvar picked up Gunnlaugur's summons soon after the war council had concluded, and headed in from the wasteland to the upper city, passing through streets where reconstruction was already under way. During the first phase of fighting, the Wolves' very presence had been enough to provoke terrified gapes from the populace, but after witnessing so many horrors in turn, the packs' power to shock had diminished. Citizens and soldiery bowed as Ingvar passed them, respectful but no longer overawed.

Ingvar preferred that. It was wearying to be treated like a god.

'Is he as you expected?' he asked Gunnlaugur once they'd met up at a heavily guarded and blast-shielded entrance to the lower Halicon levels.

Gunnlaugur passed inside, and Ingvar followed him into the long corridor that led to the apothecarion. 'He is a Priest. What should I expect?'

'I don't know. That's why I asked.'

They went down, heading deeper into an underworld of old, musty tunnels. Ceiling lumens were replaced by flickering torches, set deep into the bare stone walls.

'His anger already burns hot,' said Gunnlaugur. 'He does not like to be beaten by anyone, let alone a man like the Cardinal.'

Ingvar smiled dryly. 'De Chatelaine will flay her astropaths.'

They reached the apothecarion's outer doors. Gunnlaugur pressed the entry rune, and held his face up to the scanner. A red line ran down across his right eye, before clicking off.

Heavy bolts clunked free, then slid open with a hiss. Lumens flickered on in the chamber beyond, illuminating banks of medicae supplies. Most of the shelves were bare – testament to how low materials had run.

'What would Njal have done if Delvaux hadn't turned up?' asked Ingvar, as they entered.

Gunnlaugur made straight for the inner door, disabling the proximity alarms as he went. 'Killed them all himself.' He threw a hard glance in Ingvar's direction. 'Doubt he could?'

Gunnlaugur repeated the entry procedure on the inner doors, unlocking the medicae chamber beyond. Baldr lay where he had been left – on his back, bound tight to the metal bunk, his forehead clustered with wires and probes. His eyes were closed.

'I never like to see this,' said Ingvar.

They moved closer. Just as before, no taint remained on Baldr's face. He was breathing more deeply now. The cogitator systems, all of them designed for mortal physiology, beeped and clicked around him.

'What do you think?' asked Gunnlaugur.

'That we need a Wolf Priest.' Ingvar reached for a handheld bio-scanner. He ran a series of tests, checking the results off against what he'd expect to see. 'He's just cycling now, held under by sedatives.'

Gunnlaugur rested his knuckles on the bunk-edge. 'Any advantage to keeping him under?'

Ingvar shook his head. 'His body's recovered. He's as he was.' He stared at Baldr's face, intently this time, scouring for more than the faint flicker of eyelids. 'As far as I can see.'

'He should go to Njal awake,' said Gunnlaugur grimly. 'If he's going to be judged, he should face it standing.'

'And what if the judgement goes against him?'

Gunnlaugur drew in a long breath, then looked at Ingvar. There was rare uncertainty in his warrior's eyes. 'He's one of us,' he said eventually. 'He's Járnhamar.'

'That's what I meant.'

'Just do it.'

Ingvar reached for the vial of clear liquid hanging over Baldr's forearm. He cut off the flow, then pulled the tube from the flesh. It withdrew with a faint pop, followed by an upwelling of blood, quickly clotted.

Then he reached for one of the last of the syringes, drew a stimulant into it, and found a vein. He depressed the plunger, then discarded it.

Nothing happened. Baldr's breathing stayed the same, his eyes stayed shut.

'You think–' started Gunnlaugur.

'Wait,' said Ingvar, his eyes narrowing. 'He wakes.'

Baldr's finger twitched. Then his whole hand moved. His mouth opened a fraction, exposing his fangs. He breathed more deeply, making his chest rise.

Then his eyes snapped open – two orbs of amber, marked by the black pupil in the centre, as dilated as a Space Wolf's eye ever got.

Baldr stared up at the ceiling. Neither Ingvar nor Gunnlaugur said anything – it wasn't clear whether Baldr could even see them.

Suddenly his hands clenched, pulling at his bonds. His head snapped up, the blood vessels in his neck sticking out. The metal shackles flexed, but held. Baldr stared at them, his gaze wild.

Gunnlaugur took a step back, his hand straying to the grip of his bolter. Ingvar remained where he was.

'Do you know us, brother?' Ingvar asked.

Baldr gaped at him. A flash of panic ran across his face. He thrashed against his bonds again, making the bunk rattle in its brackets.

'Then know yourself,' said Ingvar, calmly but firmly. 'You are Baldr Fjolnir, of Járnhamar pack. Of Blackmane's Great Company. Of Fenris.'

Baldr stopped moving. He looked down at himself awkwardly, as if surprised to see he had a body at all. His head fell back against the metal. He licked dry lips, and swallowed painfully.

'Why am I shackled?' he croaked.

The voice was just as it had been, only roughened from lack of use.

'You don't remember?' asked Gunnlaugur, still ready to draw.

Baldr's forehead creased. He shifted his body in its bonds, and a bone pendant secured at his neck slipped across his chest.

'This is… Ras Shakeh,' he said, slowly.

Ingvar looked at Gunnlaugur. 'Anything else?'

Baldr looked groggy and exhausted. 'What happened?'

Gunnlaugur's hand left his weapon. 'You killed a lot of people.'

Baldr closed his eyes again. 'Better tell me everything.'

'You should try to remember,' said Gunnlaugur. 'There is someone you need to meet. He will have a lot of questions, too.'

Chapter Six

This time, the repairs were made properly. *Vuokho* was covered in dozens of servitors and kaerls, most brought down from *Heimdall* following Njal's return there. The gunship was hoisted on massive cantilevered struts, exposing damage even Jorundur hadn't discovered. Pipework-encrusted hunks of the engine train were pulled clear, cleaned and restored, before being slotted back in by whole gangs of tech-crew.

'Pointless,' Jorundur muttered, watching the progress like a hawk. 'No need to replace half of this.'

Hafloí snorted, standing beside Olgeir and Jorundur and picking gobbets of blood-clumped dust from his armour. The respite from the work of clearing the wasteland beyond the city was brief, but in the punishing heat of Ras Shakeh's sun it was welcome enough, even for a Space Marine. 'You should be pleased they're doing it.'

'*Heimdall* has its own gunships,' said Jorundur. 'They could use one of those.'

'*Vuokho*'s fast,' said Olgeir in his even, low-rumbling voice.

'Do we have a location yet?'

'The system edge.'

Jorundur spat messily. 'It'll be dead, just like everything else out there. Waste of time.'

'It'll be hunting,' said Olgeir.

'So we're always promised,' said Jorundur.

'Skítja,' said Haflói. 'Don't you ever stop?'

Jorundur ignored him and looked over towards the edge of the apron, to where the first buildings clustered. Troops were moving all around the perimeter, some in Guard uniform, most bearing the signs of the Cardinal's entourage.

'This won't end well,' he said in a low voice, watching them march to their stations. Repair work had already started in the inner walls, and dozens of purge-teams prowled the lower city, flushing out infected zones, reducing anything living to ashes before moving on.

'What won't?' asked Olgeir.

'The Sisters are one thing. These... people. They're another.'

Haflói followed Jorundur's gaze. 'They can fight.'

'You know what those bastards would do if they had the stomach for it.' Jorundur looked at the whelp darkly. 'We're *devils* to them. They'd haul Grimnar up before the Lords of Terra and mind-wipe every kaerl in the Fang.'

Haflói looked derisive. '*If* they had the stomach.'

'They've tried.'

'And failed.'

Jorundur shook his head wearily. 'You look at that cardinal. What do you see?'

'Fat,' observed Olgeir.

'Weapons. A Grand Cruiser. They got here quickly. Very quickly.'

'When's that damned gunship going to be ready?' asked Haflói, shaking himself down and preparing to leave. 'If I have to listen to any more of this–'

But Jorundur was no longer listening. He walked over to the Thunderhawk's carcass, his attention caught by some minor infraction committed by one of *Heimdall*'s service crew. 'No. *No.* Have you ever *seen* inside a power train?'

Haflói watched him go. 'Is he getting worse?' he asked.

'Not that I've noticed,' said Olgeir.

Haflói drew his axe and turned it in his hands. The blade shone in the heat, flashing as it rotated. 'He needs to fight again.'

'We all do.' Olgeir drew his own blade – a shortsword with a sickle-hilt.

'You won't have to wait long. *Vuokho* will be ready in a few hours. We should spend the time well – improving your aim.'

Hafloí bristled. 'There's nothing wrong with–'

Olgeir's blade moved like a scorpion strike, snapping out and latching under the hooked edge of Hafloí's axe. The axe ripped from his fingers and clattered on the stone two metres away.

'Always room for improvement,' said Olgeir, smiling. 'There are chambers in the citadel that would serve.'

Hafloí retrieved his axe. 'So be it,' he said, a dangerous look on his ruddy face. 'Let's work on my aim.'

The Plague Marine hung in a holding cell deep within *Heimdall*'s hull.

Stripped of his armour, he looked like a side of rotten meat. His stomach was grotesquely split, glistening with entrails under a glossy sac. The skin of his pinned limbs was saggy and wrinkled, as if age had sunk deep into the bone. His head lolled against its bonds, marked by a single weeping eye, and his broken jaw dangled loosely, exposing the sinews of his facial musculature.

Njal stood over him, towering in the dark. Álfar was to one side, reaching for another drill. The cell was pooled in darkness, lit only by red lumens set in a distant ceiling. The walls trembled with the close grind of engines.

'You are resilient,' said Njal, lifting the Plague Marine's bloodied chin with a single armoured finger. 'I could admire that, in a different cause.'

The Plague Marine gazed up at him groggily. His lone eye rotated in a chafed socket, and blood ran down from the torn edges of his mouth. 'Endurance,' he rasped.

'For what?' asked Njal.

'Not a means.' The Plague Marine attempted to smile, and more flesh cracked. 'An end.'

Njal took the drill from Álfar and looked at it bleakly. He depressed the trigger, watching the spiked bit whirr. 'So how long are we going to have to do this?' he asked, the weariness in his voice perfectly genuine. 'Hours? Days?'

The Plague Marine coughed up a glut of blood. 'It's just pain.'

Njal nodded. 'That it is.' He primed the drill to the slowest setting, and moved towards the Plague Marine's pinned fingers. 'We'll start with the name *Thorslax*.'

Despite himself, the captive tensed, his breath becoming rapid and

shallow. Just as the blades were about to bite, a chime sounded. Njal
held steady.

'What is it?' he voxed to Derroth, *Heimdall*'s mortal shipmaster.

'The Cardinal, lord,' came the reply. 'You wished to be notified as soon
as he arrived.'

Njal shut the drill off. 'Send him down.'

'By your will.'

Álfar shot Njal a quizzical look. 'You permitted him to come here?'

Njal shrugged, putting the drill back amongst the other instruments.
'He's entitled. Hel, he's welcome to take over.' He reached for a cloth to
wipe his gauntlets. 'I did not come here to butcher rotten meat.'

The Plague Marine didn't seem to hear. Exhausted, his body slumped
against its bonds. A few moments later, and a second chime sounded, this
time just outside the doors.

'Come,' said Njal.

The doors slid back, revealing Delvaux and his black-robed deputy. The
Cardinal stepped carefully into the cell, pulling his robes above his ankles
to stop the hem trailing through the muck running across the floor.

'My lord Rune Priest,' he said, bowing.

'Cardinal,' replied Njal, not bowing. 'I do not know your shadow.'

In the confines of the cell, the physical disparity between Njal and the
Cardinal was even more pronounced than it had been before. Delvaux,
next to three huge, grisly, blood-spattered figures in power armour, looked
both diminutive and flabbily corpulent.

'This is my confessor,' Delvaux said. 'He is called Klaive. Bow to the
Wolf, Klaive – this is his domain.'

The sable-robed man inclined his head gracefully. By contrast with his
master, the cell seemed to suit him. His pale flesh and neat, precise movement made him the image of an excruciator, and he balked at neither the
stench nor the sights.

'Have you learned much from the subject?' asked Delvaux, searching
around gingerly for the least besmirched place to stand. Álfar watched
him with a cool mix of interest and contempt.

'He calls himself Falvo,' said Njal. 'He is of the Death Guard. All of
which we could have taken from the armour pieces before they went to
the furnace. Aside from that, he doesn't even scream.'

Delvaux regarded the prisoner with eager appreciation. 'Then this will
be a long and messy business. Klaive? What do you think?'

Klaive glided up to the Plague Marine, running violet eyes over the contours of his broken flesh. 'I think there are things we could do,' he said.

'What do you mean?' demanded Njal.

Klaive withdrew a long casket from his robes – a slender wooden case the length of his forearm, inlaid with silver. 'May I?' he asked.

Álfar looked at Njal, who nodded, and Klaive opened the box. Inside was a dagger with an iron hilt. A script ran down the blade, etched in miniscule and swaying across the metal like a serpent. Klaive discarded the box and held the blade up before the Plague Marine. It glinted dully in the red light.

'Cutting won't hasten this,' said Álfar. 'We tried it.'

'I do not intend to cut him,' said Klaive, running his finger along the edge of the blade. 'But he knows what this is – look at his eye.'

The Plague Marine stared at the blade as it neared him, going rigid in his bonds. Sweat broke out over his bone-pale hide. 'Where did you get that?' he slurred, bloody saliva foaming over his split lower lip.

Klaive drew closer, reaching up to hold the blade just over the Plague Marine's forehead. 'It is a rather fine story,' he whispered. 'I could tell it to you, if you wished, but I would rather hear yours.'

Then he pressed the flat of the blade against the Plague Marine's skin. Immediately the prisoner writhed in agony, shrieking with pain. The smell of burning filled the chamber, curling up from the crisping edges of skin. The Plague Marine spasmed against his bonds, jerking and kicking out, opening up fresh wounds where iron coils bit into his wrists and ankles.

Then Klaive withdrew the blade, letting the Plague Marine recover. The confessor had a strange, eager light in his violet eyes, and his breathing was a little faster than it had been.

'Tell us, Falvo, what was your task on Ras Shakeh?' Klaive asked.

The Plague Marine regained his breath, still sweating in rivers. He shot a look of pure hatred from his single eye, his nostrils flaring. Pus, mingled with blood, dribbled down from the open weal on his forehead.

When no words were forthcoming, Klaive smiled and took up the blade again.

'Very well, if you will not–'

'I was under the Mycelite,' blurted the Plague Marine, staring at the blade with undisguised anguish. He panted heavily. A thick look of self-loathing rippled across his ruined features.

Klaive gave the two Wolves an assured look of triumph. 'Well then. I think we may make progress now.'

Njal looked down at the dagger with distaste. Everything in the cell made him feel sullied, and that wasn't the worst of it. 'What is on that blade?'

Klaive held it up to the light, turning it slowly. 'Words,' he said. 'Ancient words. We have discovered, in our researches, that words may be used for all sorts of purposes.'

Silently, Álfar's hand had strayed to his weapon, something neither Klaive nor Delvaux had noticed.

Njal had. In an instant, sickened by what surrounded him, he was tempted to let the shieldbearer use the chainsword, and damn the consequences.

Then, wearily, he shook his shaggy head.

+Time is against us,+ he sent, implanting the words into Álfar's mind. +A warrior cannot always choose his weapons.+

As Álfar relaxed, Njal turned back to the Plague Marine, who now looked up at him with real terror. 'I do not wish to see that thing used again,' said the Rune Priest, his voice a low growl. 'Neither do you.'

Njal leaned forwards, until his beard was almost brushing against the captive's face.

'So we will start where you did,' he said. 'Who is the Mycelite?'

The lander from *Heimdall* came down on the plains south of the city, far from the main deployment zones for Delvaux's forces. Ingvar, Gunnlaugur and Baldr slipped out of the city to meet it, hardly noticed by the crowds of menials and reclamators still at work.

Baldr walked haltingly, as if remembering how to use his muscles from scratch. The bright sunlight made his eyes water, just as the ice-glare had once done before the Helix. He felt heat rising from the packed earth, making him sweat under his loose robes.

In time, such things would cease to register with him – his physiology would return to its chameleonic adaptability, his strength would return, his animal spirits would roar back into immediacy. For the time being, though, he felt as frail as a mortal.

You killed a lot of people.

He remembered so little of it. Every so often, flashes of memory would return – a leering, joyful face burning amid a corona of green fire, a bone pendant spinning in the dark. His hands were still sore from where his skin had burned. Scars puckered the flesh, marring the smoothness of his old skin.

Ingvar and Gunnlaugur said nothing. The antagonism that had needled away between them on the journey out to Ras Shakeh seemed to have abated, replaced by uncertainty over how to deal with this new problem.

I have become the poison at the heart of the pack. Baldr smiled to himself wryly. *They fear me now.*

In truth, he feared himself. Though he detected no trace of the madness, there could be no denying what had happened. On the balance of probabilities, death waited for him on *Heimdall*. Stormcaller was not a sentimental soul, and had cut the thread of more heretics and witches than most inquisitors.

So be it. Better to end now than face corruption.

The grey-sided lander waited for them on the desiccated earth, surrounded by drifting clouds of dust, its ramp down. Two dozen kaerls stood before it, all in blast armour and with their helms on. The squad leader slammed his fist against his chest in salute.

Baldr looked at them. 'Surprised he didn't send more,' he said.

He turned, looking over his shoulder. The desert wind skipped and eddied across the plains. The air was clearer than it had been. A charred smell of burning flesh lingered from the pyres, and there was an undertow of plague-sweetness that hadn't quite been eradicated. The spires of Hjec Aleja glinted in the sun, though the blackened shell of the old Cathedral spoke of the tremendous destruction that still had to be cleared away.

All in all, the place had a stark beauty to it now. He could understand why pilgrims had come here. The pious always sought deserts, the pagan the ice.

'Until we fight again, brother,' said Gunnlaugur.

Baldr nodded, at him and at Ingvar, then turned and walked up the ramp into the lander's crew bay. Once he'd taken his place, the kaerls piled in after him, averting their eyes as they filled the vacant spaces. The lifter engines started to whine, and the ramp lifted noisily.

It slammed closed, locking him within a shaking metal shell. For a moment, he remembered how it had been the first time, dragged from battle and spirited away to Asaheim. He remembered how he'd felt the steel panels tremble, and how he'd been unable to work out where he was or what had happened or whether he was even alive at all.

Then the main thrusters fired, and the lander swayed up into the air.

Ingvar watched it go. The craft's atmospheric drives angled round on thick ball-and-socket housings, and it gained loft quickly, cushioned on a white-blue cushion of engine-wash. Once high above the city, the orbital thrusters kicked in, hurling it up into a fast-dwindling ascent. After only a few moments it was lost amid the relentless blue of Ras Shakeh's open sky.

'So what do you think?' asked Ingvar.

'Didn't sense a thing,' said Gunnlaugur. He ran his hands over his bald pate, wiping sweat from the tattooed skin. 'You can *smell* it, normally.'

Ingvar knew what he meant. The plague-mutants all had it – that faint stench of rotting fruit, lodged deep in their being, hovering over the human stink of illness. You couldn't disguise it, couldn't scrub it clean.

'He is free of it,' Ingvar said.

'You trust him, then?'

'It is not up to me.'

They turned away from the landing site and started to walk back towards the city perimeter. Over to their left, a few kilometres distant in a haze of heat and kicked-up dust, an army of labourers was working to clear and secure the battlefield. The acrid smell of promethium laced the air, the after-effect of fuel-spills and burn-teams at work.

'We could not have kept it secret,' said Gunnlaugur, striding out with his swaying, belligerent gait.

'I know.'

'But you think we should have tried.'

Ingvar felt a spike of annoyance, and pushed it down. Gunnlaugur had done the right thing, *was* doing the right thing. 'I'll say it again – what if the judgement goes against him?' he asked.

'It won't. You said it yourself – he is restored.'

'Njal may think different.'

Gunnlaugur stopped walking. 'He's gothi, brother. He carries the Law engraved on his staff. If we tried to keep Baldr from him–'

'I know,' insisted Ingvar. 'Still, if he is to be damned...'

He stopped before saying the words. There was no point, not until they knew the outcome.

Gunnlaugur sighed, screwing his eyes up against the glare. By now the lander had passed out of view, leaving the sky empty and trackless.

'You wanted to speak to me,' he said. 'About Hjortur.'

'You need to know.'

Gunnlaugur nodded. 'I have kept you waiting long enough.' He started to walk again. 'But not here. Come with me to the city. When we are back under shadow, you can tell me everything.'

De Chatelaine had to admit that the reconstruction, its speed and its completeness, had been remarkable. The Cardinal's troops had swamped the ruins with earth-moving crawlers and atmospheric lifters. Walls had been shored up, hab-blocks purged and made fit for reoccupation, defence towers restored and crowned with fresh ranks of operational weaponry. Temples had been cleansed of filth, their icons scrubbed clean and their statues replaced. Fresh images of the Blessed Primarchs and the Saints of the Ministorum were carted in, drilled into place and unveiled before the populace.

The people flocked back to the altars, falling prostrate before them. The scars of the conflict were close, and they wept openly during the ceremonies giving thanks to the Emperor. Thousands had died, perhaps three out of every four citizens according to some estimates, and those who remained were still in a kind of mass shock, plucked from the brink of annihilation just as all hope had faded.

For the survivors, it was a simple fact – He had delivered them. The faith that had sustained them through the worst of the long night flourished like a plant bursting into flower after drought.

The Cardinal's agents were everywhere, scouring the ruins of the Cathedral, pulling material out of every last remaining chapel, working their way through the Halicon undercroft. Their attention to detail was phenomenal – they worked as if in perpetual fear of some flaw in their labours being discovered. If some agents took certain liberties, and extended their control into areas where they had no strict right to, then few of the survivors were going to make any kind of complaint. They were too busy praying, and working, and weeping.

De Chatelaine glanced at her chrono. She had lost track of time. The marble surface of her pedestal desk was piled high with papers and dataslates, all of it bearing the skull-invested 'I' of the Ministorum. Delvaux's servants were assiduous, recording everything they did with almost compulsive completeness.

She rose, adjusting her robes over her armour and reaching for her ceremonial sword.

'Sister Callia,' she voxed, setting off for the short walk that would take her to the audience chamber where Delvaux had set himself up since returning from *Heimdall*. 'It is time.'

Callia joined her just as she reached her destination.

'Canoness,' Callia said, bowing. 'If I may, what is this about?'

'The restoration of authority,' said de Chatelaine, smiling. 'The Cardinal wishes to update us on progress. We should consider ourselves fortunate. Have you ever seen the city in such blessed fervour?'

Callia looked at her uneasily. 'No. Never.'

De Chatelaine gestured to the guards standing on either side of the two gilt doors, then strode through as they opened.

Inside, incense billowed across the polished floor, carried by servo-skulls trailing lengths of clanking chains. The sun had been filtered out by heavy fabrics, making the hall within glow with a dull, suffused light. Crimson-armoured Battle Sisters stood motionless amid the twin ranks of pillars running down each aisle. The air felt humid, fuelled by glowing brazier-pans.

The Cardinal was seated at the far end of the hall atop a towering throne, crusted with gold-leaf and flanked by helical columns. Cherubim buzzed lazily over an elaborate dome, dusting it with more incense, squabbling and blundering into the stonework. A low dirge of devotional chanting came from vox-emitters set in the high roof.

The Cardinal waited for the two of them to approach. He looked somehow larger than he had on their first meeting. His heavy robes flowed in thick folds over a substantial belly. He slumped in the golden seat, his eyes heavy-lidded, his fleshy fingers drumming on lion's-head armrests.

'My lord Cardinal,' said de Chatelaine, bowing.

Delvaux gazed down at her disinterestedly. 'Canoness,' he replied, his voice flat.

'You have been busy, I see.'

'These things?' Delvaux said, looking around absently at the finery. 'Brought down from *Vindicatus*. You had nothing suitable here.'

As he spoke, de Chatelaine noticed a Battle Sister move to his elbow, leaning up from the throne's stepped edges to whisper something in his ear. With a twinge of distaste, de Chatelaine saw the extent of the Sister's augmetic alterations – the entire left-hand side of her body was encased in bronze plating. Her half-concealed arm was bulky and stiff, ending in a blunt metal clump under a fabric glove. It looked like a flamer.

'You do not approve of Sister Nuriyah, canoness?' Delvaux asked, as the Sister withdrew again.

'Not at all,' said de Chatelaine, wondering at the Cardinal's changed tone with her. 'I commend her diligence.'

'She is most diligent. She performs every task I set her, even to the gravest extremity. The galaxy is not a forgiving place. It asks sacrifices of us all.'

A servo-skull swooped in from the aisles then, bearing a gold platter. It hovered over the Cardinal's lap, and he took a piece of peeled fruit from the platter before it swayed away.

'My lord, did you–' started de Chatelaine.

'I return from interrogating the fallen,' Delvaux said, still studying the fruit. 'Judgement comes to all. Or did you not preach that doctrine on this world?'

'We preach the Imperial Truth,' de Chatelaine said, stiffly.

'But there is more to our task than the truth, is there not? There is guidance. There is discipline.'

De Chatelaine bristled. 'My lord, if there is anything you find remiss, then I trust you will speak of it.'

Delvaux took a bite of the fruit, and red-purple juice ran down his chins. He chewed, dabbing at the runnel with a silk napkin. 'You were in command throughout the invasion?'

'I was.'

'Then you bear responsibility for what happened here.'

'I do.'

Delvaux nodded, taking another bite. 'Investigations continue. My people have spoken to many of those who served. We hear things.'

De Chatelaine's impatience began to get the better of her. 'Things,' she said, coldly. 'Perhaps you will elaborate?'

Delvaux lifted a finger. From the shadows of the aisles, masked by the rows of pillars, de Chatelaine heard a shuffle. A second later, two Battle Sisters of Nuriyah's contingent emerged, their faces hidden behind white masks. They dragged a bundle of rags between them. Only as they emerged into the pool of dusty light before the throne did de Chatelaine see that the bundle was a man, pulled by slack arms, his head hanging between his shoulders.

The Sisters threw him to the floor. He lay prostrate, as limp as sackcloth.

'Tell us your name,' said the Cardinal, chewing the last of his fruit.

At the sound of Delvaux's voice, the man's head snapped up. Two wide eyes glared in terror from sunken cheeks. De Chatelaine saw the unmistakable signs of agony in his bearing.

'Velash, lord,' he said, his voice panicky. 'Velash! You asked me this.'

De Chatelaine looked at Delvaux stonily. 'By what right was this man put to the trials?'

Delvaux ignored her. 'Tell us what you told Sister Nuriyah, Velash.'

The man stared around him, though it wasn't clear if he was able to focus any more. 'They let them in! They let them in. They came across the desert, and they let them in.'

Delvaux nodded sympathetically. 'That is what you told us, yes. Who gave the order?'

'The canoness.'

De Chatelaine felt a chill run through her heart. This was a distortion – a grave one. 'Some mistakes were made,' she said. 'We had regiments returning from the front. Quarantine was not perfect.'

'What happened next, Velash?' asked Delvaux.

The man grinned. It was a manic, deranged grin – the grin of a man whose mind has turned. 'They came for us. The plagued. The flesh-eaters.'

'This is in my report,' said de Chatelaine, feeling as if she were hardly there.

'How many died?' Delvaux asked Velash.

Velash smiled wider. 'Thousands,' he said, gleefully. '*Thousands.*'

'Thank you, that is–'

'They kept coming!' Velash shouted, dragging himself up to his knees. De Chatelaine saw the way his legs bent under the fabric, and winced. 'They could not be stopped! The dead! The dead were eating the living!'

Delvaux motioned to his Sisters again. One of them cuffed Velash across the forehead, silencing him, before they both dragged him away. A trail of something liquid remained on the marble where he'd been.

'You had no right,' said de Chatelaine, her voice tight with anger.

'Did he speak the truth?' asked Delvaux.

'He is a citizen under my protection. Under the protection of the Church.'

'Did he speak the truth?'

'How many others have been questioned?'

'Did he speak the truth?'

The Cardinal's face was a slack mask of superiority.

'You know he did,' said de Chatelaine, quietly.

Delvaux rubbed his stained fingers on his napkin. 'This planet was nigh consumed. The Wolves were needed to save it. The *Wolves*. I have just spent time with this Stormcaller, and I have seen the way he behaves. I have seen how his trained beasts fawn over him. They believe in nothing. Their souls are the souls of animals. You should have done better.'

De Chatelaine looked about her, finding it difficult to believe such things were being said in her citadel. The red-armoured Battle Sisters of

Delvaux's entourage gazed back at her from the margins, their faces blank with steady hostility.

'We… *fought*,' said de Chatelaine, struggling to find the words. 'We fought. My Sisters died. My… people died.'

Delvaux considered her as if she were something he had found lurking in the salty dregs of a ritual goblet. 'You were appointed to make hard choices, canoness. The reward for success is a record of glory, the price of failure is penance. What would you say happened on this world? Did you succeed? Is that what you think happened?'

De Chatelaine could sense Callia on the cusp of intervening then, and spoke quickly to prevent that.

'My lord, you were not here,' she said, speaking as steadily as she was able. 'If you had been, you would know that we did everything in our mortal power.' She pushed her shoulders back, feeling her armour flex as she stood straight before the throne. 'None could have worked harder. We were alone. We resisted, right until the end. We would have done so for as long as our bodies drew breath. You may conduct whatever investigations you wish. My conscience is clear.'

The Cardinal regarded her for a while longer, masticating. A thin trail of juice lingered on the pulpy underhang of his lower chin.

Then he stirred himself, reaching for a casket secreted within his robes. Just as before, he withdrew a pinch of powder and dabbed it under his nostrils.

'So you say, canoness,' he said. 'And your word counts for much, even with me.' He sniffed heavily, causing his eyes to water. He replaced the casket, adjusting his position on the throne, and a deep flush came to his cheeks. 'Our investigations will continue. Those who remain faithful receive the benedictions of the Ecclesiarchy, those who fall short receive its castigation. You know to what I refer.'

De Chatelaine remained defiant. 'I do,' she said calmly.

'Then let us hope that the testimony we uncover reveals a favourable truth.'

'There can be no doubt.'

'That is all, then. We understand one another. You may go.'

De Chatelaine stayed where she was for a moment longer. Then she turned to Callia, whose face was a tight mask of fury. 'Come,' she said.

The two of them walked back down the long nave, observed in silence by Nuriyah's Sisters. The doors closed behind them with an echoing clang that took several seconds to die away.

'He *dares*–' Callia started, but de Chatelaine held up a warning finger.

'He is the Hand of the Emperor,' she warned. 'Say nothing that will damn you.' She looked up to the ceiling, her eyes roving for vox-detectors. Callia took the hint, and fell silent.

De Chatelaine sighed then, and smiled – a forced smile, but it was important to maintain appearances. 'Have faith, Sister,' she said. 'This will be resolved.'

Then they started walking again, back along the corridors to their own chambers. As they went, de Chatelaine's mind worked furiously, gauging how many of her troops would remain faithful, how many would speak against her, how many would be taken for the trials.

She remembered the last words she'd shared with Gunnlaugur.

It is still my city.

Back then, it had been.

Chapter Seven

The void was lit virulent green, like a spiralling glut of ink poured into the dark. The dust-cloud towered through the well of space, sending fronds arching in a slew of vivid translucency. Asteroids cycled past it in procession, ink-black against the swathe of colour, held in place by the distant pull of Ras Shakeh's young star.

Vuokho ghosted in close, engines working on low burn. Jorundur steered it deftly, angling under a mammoth ball of tumbling rock before applying a little more power, sending the gunship skimming towards the central mass of asteroids beyond.

'Getting anything?' asked Olgeir, voxing from the forward hold below the cockpit.

'Just as they said,' replied Jorundur, tilting the Thunderhawk to starboard to dip below the field-plane. 'Coordinates were perfect.'

Amid the stellar rubble, one asteroid loomed closer – a mid-sized rock, ten kilometres in diameter, as black and cratered as the others. Jorundur locked on to it, running a brief scan to confirm the target.

'How does it look?' asked Hafloí, also from the hold.

'Like the rest,' said Jorundur, noting the results of the auspex run and checking it against what he'd been told to expect. The asteroid showed no power readings and no more than a trace heat signature. If he had not been given the precise location by de Chatelaine's strategos then he would have skimmed right on past. It was perhaps too much to hope that the enemy had done likewise.

He nudged *Vuokho* nearer, drifting to fifty metres over the asteroid's pitted surface. Retro exhausts fired, and the gunship came to a semi-stop, pulled along for the final few metres by residual momentum.

'I've got some damage on the outside,' said Jorundur, peering down at the gently scrolling landscape. 'Blast marks? Probably. Faint power readings. You might have gravity, might not.'

'Understood,' voxed Olgeir. 'Just get us there.'

Jorundur angled the Thunderhawk to the left, dipping the nose. *Vuokho* skimmed a few metres above the ash-grey outer crust before coming to rest just above a jagged pit, five metres across and ringed with black. Metal glinted down in its maw, charred and broken.

'This is it,' voxed Jorundur. 'Opening doors.'

The forward hold ramp bolts clanged back and the heavy armoured bow of the gunship swung open. Jorundur held *Vuokho* steady, making use of the retro thrusters to hold it in position.

He switched to the external viewers and watched Olgeir push himself down the ramp, still shackled to the gunship's interior by a length of metal cabling. Hafloí edged down after him. It was impossible to look graceful in zero gravity, even with the reactions and poise of a Space Wolf, and they looked like lumbering giants.

Olgeir reached the lip of the ramp and ran a scan of the pit below. 'Blast damage,' he voxed. 'Melta charges. All armour doors blown. You're right – no power.' He chuckled dryly over the comm. 'Done much zero gravity work, whelp?'

Hafloí held the anchor cable loosely, balancing casually further up the gunship's lowered ramp. 'How hard can it be?'

Jorundur rolled his eyes. 'Move faster,' he voxed, watching the incoming patterns of space-rubble on the scanner. 'I need to pull up.'

Olgeir pushed himself out into the void, unlatching the cable as he drifted clear of the hold. Hafloí followed, going a fraction too fast and nearly hitting the edge of the ramp. Olgeir touched down ahead of him, just on the lip of the pit, bending his knees to absorb the impact and grabbing hold of a twisted-up sheet of adamantium to gain purchase.

Jorundur deftly pulled *Vuokho* higher, taking care not to blast the two Space Wolves with his thruster-fire. Then he powered further away from the rock, adopting a position away from the rolling clouds of debris. He ran a quick check on the gunship's bolters, just in case, for all the help they would be. As soon as Olgeir and Haflói dipped below the surface, they would be on their own.

'Good hunting,' voxed Jorundur, watching on the real-viewer as Olgeir dragged himself down into the shadow of the pit, followed by the jerkier movements of Haflói.

Then he pulled *Vuokho*'s prow around, hovering above the asteroid like a jealous raptor over its nest, and stood guard.

'Sister Bajola told me,' said Ingvar. 'She knew about Hjortur. His name was on a kill-list, and she claimed she'd seen it.'

Ingvar and Gunnlaugur were back in the apothecarion, one of the few rooms in the Halicon still off-limits to the Ecclesiarchy staff. The place looked oddly empty without Baldr lying on the slab.

'Hjortur was killed by greenskins,' said Gunnlaugur. 'We were *there*, brother.'

'None of us saw him die.'

'What did she say killed him?'

'She mentioned a group: the Fulcrum. Then she died.'

Gunnlaugur winced. 'De Chatelaine told me she was strange. She was mortal. Dying does strange things to mortal minds.'

'She said they were coming after the Chapter. She said there were others, powerful figures, targeting more of us.'

'Any names?'

'No, though she gave me this.' Ingvar produced the golden cherub-face Bajola had given him, still spotted with her blood. 'Some kind of icon.'

Gunnlaugur took the cherub from Ingvar and held it up to the light. He studied it for a while, then handed it back. 'I've seen this before.'

'Where?'

'On every Cathedral, every Navigator house, on every inquisitor, and everywhere I've ever been.'

Ingvar smiled wryly, and stowed it back away. 'I see.'

Gunnlaugur sighed. 'Are you taking this seriously, brother?' he asked.

'We have a blood-debt.'

'*If* she was speaking the truth.'

'She had no reason to lie.'

Gunnlaugur's expression became serious. 'Give me a *name*,' he said. 'Just one name, and I'll pursue it with you to the limits of the galaxy. Until then, we have war snapping on our heels.'

'There is more hidden here,' insisted Ingvar. 'On this world. Bajola knew it, and she destroyed the archives in the Cathedral to hide it. Did you not wonder why the Church was so quick to get here? We were told there were no other defenders in this sector, but the Cardinal got here soon enough.'

'So what are you going to do? Interrogate them?'

'They're lifting kill-teams out into the desert, moving ahead of Álfar's packs. They say they're taking back overrun outposts.'

'They are.'

'Yes, but what else? I could run with them. It would be good hunting.'

Gunnlaugur looked at him sceptically. 'We will be moving off-world as soon as we have a spoor. Njal is itching to leave.'

'Not until *Vuokho* returns. There is time.'

'What are you going to find, brother? It is a wasteland.'

'It can't all have been destroyed. In any case, it will keep my blade sharp.'

Gunnlaugur drew in a weary breath, exposing his long fangs. 'What if I said no?' he asked. 'What would you do then?'

Ingvar stiffened. The tension between them, almost dissipated since the last days of the siege, still lurked, ready to flare up again. 'You are *vaerangi*.'

Gunnlaugur snorted out a harsh laugh. 'True enough, but you'd defy me. I'd have to floor you myself to keep you leashed.' Then he looked at Ingvar levelly. 'Tell me you are certain. Tell me this is blood-debt.'

Ingvar returned the look, his face intent. 'Hjortur was killed, and not by greenskins. Someone here knows why.'

Gunnlaugur studied him for a long time, then nodded. 'So be it. Just find me a name.'

Ingvar looked fiercely grateful. 'I will do it. The Ecclesiarchy is a den of secrets, but they can't hide them all.'

'And go *quietly*,' urged Gunnlaugur. 'They disgust me as much as you, but we need them. Njal wants the peace kept – he'll need that Grand Cruiser, if nothing else. So we tell no one.'

'And you?'

'My duty is here. De Chatelaine and I need to speak again. Of all of them, I'd fight by her side again.'

Gunnlaugur was about to move away then, when Ingvar grabbed him by the arm. 'They have struck at the heart of us,' Ingvar said. 'Whatever happens, once we have a name, we move.'

His tone was fervent. There was a fire there, one that had been missing for too long.

'You have my word,' said Gunnlaugur.

'And Baldr?'

Gunnlaugur's expression darkened. Baldr's fate remained in the balance, and there were some paths even a Wolf Guard could not travel.

'We are all Járnhamar, brother,' Gunnlaugur said, shaking loose the hold. 'When the time comes, the decision will be mine.'

The chamber was metal-lined, hammered with runes and bitter with the stink of ash. Animal skins hung from hooks in the flickering dark, some from the old ice, some from worlds as far-flung as the curve of the galaxy. Tall, narrow windows let in only a little artificial light, angled through iron lattices onto a floor of rough stone.

Baldr breathed deeply as he entered, drawing in the familiar aromas, the familiar sights. After Ras Shakeh, *Heimdall*'s air felt almost frigid, and he liked that. His grey shift, cloak and bound leggings did little to keep out the chill, just as his meagre furs had once done on Fenris itself.

He walked into the centre of the chamber, pausing before the great fire-pit at its heart. Embers glowed like angry stars, heaped high and raked with iron tongs. Each of the lining stones had a rune picked out on it – *sfar, zhaz, rhozan*. All of them, he knew, were wards against *maleficarum*, powerful symbols that dampened and dispersed the corruption of the underverse. Everywhere he looked he could see more spiky, angular etchings, half glimpsed amid the heavy shadows.

It was like being back in the Fang. When the Space Wolves took to the sea of stars they took their home world with them, carved out of the shell of their iron-boned ships and hammered into every surface.

Baldr rolled his shoulders, trying to relax. His muscles ached from the final stages of the Dream, as tight and wound hard as weather-stiffened leather. Spikes of pain still ran down his spine, his eyes still smarted and the flesh of his hands was raw and covered in scabs.

All things considered, though, he felt more *himself* now. Time would only heal further. He stood, alone, watching the coals crack and darken in the fire-pit. Old flames licked across them. The rest of the chamber, filled with instruments and items even his acute sight could not pick out, was shrouded in frigid darkness.

He considered his position.

Would I have permitted it, he wondered, *if it had been another one of us? Would I have let him in, or cut his thread? I do not know.*

The doors hissed open again, throwing a thin bar of yellow light across the stone. Baldr turned to face it, and for an instant saw the same pair of eyes staring at him as so long ago – twin globes of amber, crouching in the snow-thick briars, slavering but not moving. With a lurch, he was straight back there, alone and unarmed, facing the wolf in the darkness of the primeval woods, and his hearts picked up in an involuntary threat-response.

Then the doors slipped closed, and the illusion faded, though the eyes remained. They were not the amber of most *Fenryka*, but ice-blue, like mortal eyes.

Njal stepped into the glow of the fire-pit. Baldr's sense of raw intimidation didn't fade. He was a seasoned warrior, used to facing every horror on the battlefield, but facing the Stormcaller in his own lair was something else. Njal wasn't just *a* Rune Priest, he was *the* Rune Priest, custodian of the deepest lore of the Chapter and confidante of the Lords of Fenris. The air around him seemed to drop in temperature, as if ice were always on the cusp of forming across his thick runic armour. Every inch of his ancient battleplate was engraved in esoteric sigils, each one etched over decades by the finest loresmiths of the Hammerhold.

They said Njal was the greatest gothi of the Fenryka since Odain Sturmhjart. They said he had more sagas sung of him in the Aett than any but Grimnar himself, and that each told of the destruction of such maleficent foes that the skjalds struggled to find words to describe them. They said that he knew secrets dating back to the Age of Wonder, and that his own vaults in the Valgard contained artefacts carved in the childhood of the Imperium when the Allfather yet walked alongside Russ and the ways of the void were pure.

Looking up at him for the first time, Baldr could believe all those things. In the semi-dark, lit from below by the angry glow of brazier coals, Njal loomed like a shadow of a half-forgotten past, vast, mythic, and potent.

The Rune Priest took his place on the far side of the fire-pit. He stood there, studying Baldr silently. That scrutiny felt like knives pressed against flesh.

'So,' he said, finally. 'You are the one. Here to be judged.'

Baldr lifted his chin. 'I am, jarl,' he said.

'Then we begin,' said Njal.

Olgeir drew his bolter. *Sigrún* had been left behind for this mission, replaced by a more practical standard-sized Asaheim-pattern weapon. He activated his helm's night-vision, and it picked out a long circular shaft below him, a few metres in diameter, running straight down into the heart of the rock.

Olgeir felt the impact of Hafloí touching down behind him on the aster-oid surface, scuffing a little as his boots scrabbled for purchase. Olgeir leaned down and grabbed a metal hoop embedded in the shaft's wall. He pulled himself down into the shadow of the pit, moving hand over hand. As he went, he scanned the surface around him.

'Las-fire damage,' he voxed to Hafloí. 'Lots of it. Approaching inner doors now.'

The inner doors had once been adamantium and half a metre thick. Now all that remained were bulbous metallic outcrops of melta damage. The interior curve of the shaft was dented back into the rock by the force of explosions.

Hafloí followed Olgeir down more slowly. He collided with the wall, rebounding awkwardly before steadying his descent.

Olgeir smiled to himself, nudging himself further towards the base of the shaft. His helm-display showed no targets, no movements. The interior was utterly lightless, too cold even for infrared, so the way forward was picked out by his helm-lumens.

'I'm getting nothing,' voxed Hafloí from above him.

Olgeir coasted down into what must once have been the main entry chamber – a spherical capsule about ten metres across, accessed by a hatch at the top and exited via a pair of standard blast-doors on his right-hand side. He arrested his fall and touched down lightly on the bottom of the chamber, sweeping his bolter-muzzle up at the empty open doorway in front of him.

'Nothing here either,' he replied.

There was evidence of fighting – las-marks on the metal interior walls, blown hatch controls, scratches on the bulkheads, but there were no bod-ies. Aside from the sound of his own breathing and the interior hum of his power armour, the capsule was vacuum-silent.

Hafloí touched down beside him. 'How big is this place?'

Olgeir recalled the schematics taken from the archives in Hjec Aleja. 'Twenty crew. Twenty-nine rooms, augur-chamber, power plant, shield generator. This won't take long.'

He pushed off, gliding through the open doorway. He skimmed down a long circular connective tube beyond, filling it out and grazing the edges with his armour. The spaces narrowed down, small even by mortal stand-ards, claustrophobic for Space Marine bulk. His lumen-gaze moved over everyday remnants of the station's working life – devotional imagery set into the walls, prayer-beads, duty rosters. The further in he went, the more signs of violence emerged. Long, dark trails ran across the concave floor. Olgeir sniffed by instinct, as if somehow the smell of corruption could penetrate sealed battleplate.

He passed an open hatchway to his left, blasted open like the outer doors had been, and ran a lens-scan. The chamber was big, more than ten metres cubic, dominated by a floating cluster of ruined machinery – brass spheres, metal coils, crystal transistors stamped with the icons of the Ecclesiarchy. Winged iron angels drifted amid the wreckage, gazing up at the roof with empty eyes.

'Comms array,' said Olgeir. 'Still no bodies.'

Hafloí pushed past, taking point and tumbling further down the corridor. 'They've stripped it clean,' he muttered. 'There's nothing here.'

Olgeir followed him. The walls bore down on them, tight and clad in thick shadow. It felt like they were being dragged deep into the heart of the asteroid. More blood-smears appeared on the walls, thick and mottled with desperate handprints.

Suddenly, Olgeir felt the hairs on the back on his neck prick up, pressing against the inner seal of his gorget. 'Sense anything, whelp?' he voxed, watching Hafloí's boots disappear around the corner ahead.

'Another shaft,' Hafloí reported. 'No targets. I'm going further down.'

By the time Olgeir had followed him round, pushing against the corridor walls and roof to propel him along, Hafloí had gone ahead through another hatch opening, diving in headfirst. Olgeir did the same, squeezing his bulk carefully through the aperture. This shaft was smaller than the first, the space limited by a metal-ring ladder running down one side, and he grabbed the rungs to haul himself downwards. His breathing felt close and rapid inside his helm.

The chamber at the bottom was carved from bare rock, no more than five metres across. Smashed equipment rotated gently in the cramped space around them, rolling away when pushed.

Olgeir emerged through the ceiling and twisted awkwardly to right himself.

'Nothing,' Hafloí voxed, arresting his spin against the rough wall. 'Nothing at all.'

Olgeir let himself rotate, studying the chamber carefully. It looked like a storage area lodged down at the bottom of the station. The skull device of the Ecclesiarchy had been stamped over the entrance, though since gouged out with thick claw-marks.

He wished he could use his sense of smell.

'Might be right,' Olgeir voxed, scanning for heat-sources just to be sure. Nothing came back from the blank, crudely cut chamber edges.

'We should go,' said Hafloí, kicking back towards the shaft entrance.

Olgeir paused. He shoved himself over to the far wall of the chamber and pressed his gauntlet up against it. For a moment, there was nothing.

Then, fainter than breath against the wind, he felt it – vibration, like a faint breath, brushing against the far side. His pupils immediately narrowed.

'This is sensor-shielded,' he said. 'Hold position.'

Hafloí halted at the base of the exit shaft, twisting around and training his bolt pistol.

Olgeir ran his hands along the rock. He found a small change in texture, almost undetectable – a strip of stone that felt marginally different from that around it. He called up the schematics given to them by the Ecclesiarchy. There were no rooms marked beyond their position.

'Secretive bastards,' he muttered. He pulled a krak charge from his belt, clicked the countdown and clamped it to the stone strip. Then he pushed himself away, drifting back to the far wall. Hafloí drifted over to join him.

'Ready yourself,' Olgeir said, bracing himself against the wall and training his bolter on the clicking krak charge. 'Fire through the detonation.'

Hafloí locked position, wedging himself into the corner of the chamber to secure a firebase. Then the charge exploded in a stark, silent bloom of light, driving in the wall and filling the chamber with a blaze of swiftly extinguished flame. The far wall dissolved into dust and rock fragments, raining against the two Wolves' armour.

They opened fire in unison, pumping bolt-shells into the breach. As the rounds went off, the loosened wall section crashed away, breaking free from the bolts holding it in place. A howl of escaping air rushed past them, making the debris in the grav-free chamber rock and slam into the walls.

'Now!' ordered Olgeir, thrusting powerfully against the stone behind him.

Hafloí did the same, and they crashed through the disintegrating wall section, bolters firing. With the escaping atmosphere came the high-pitched scream of semi-human throats on the far side, suddenly roused in throttled fury.

They were no longer alone.

There were many wolves on Fenris, just as many as there were warriors in the Halls of the Fang. Most snarled and roared with feral abandon, given over to the frenzy of the hunt. They slavered with the scent of prey in flared nostrils, they crashed through the snow in pursuit of agile prey.

The Dark Wolf was different. It curled around the shadows, back arched, head low, hugging the frigid depths of the eternal pine-woods. It padded through the dream world of the underverse, following the spirits of the dead, escorting them deeper into the cold, cold tombs that waited prior to the battle at the end of the world. It never roared, and its soul was silent.

The Dark Wolf knew many secrets. It had seen the galaxy decay, turning from magnificence into atrophy. It had seen the fires go out, one by one, snuffed into oblivion by the crawling march of the Annihilator. The Dark Wolf had watched the compromises being made and had listened to the lies being told. It knew the sources of those lies, and where they sprang from, and upon what date the untruths would catch up with their utterers.

Njal had felt the Dark Wolf on his trail from the earliest of times. He remembered listening to its panting while still on the ice. Even in the Fang, the mightiest of fortresses, he had sensed it treading around the walls. In the utter night, when the vaults and tunnels of the Mountain were drenched in sleep, he had heard it snuffling in the outer twilight.

The Dark Wolf had always been his companion, and they both shared the secrets of aeons. One day, Njal knew, they would meet. He would look up, and see the eyes of his mirror-self staring back, and know that the hour had come.

There were times when he dreaded that meeting. There were times when he yearned for it. Neither dread nor yearning would hasten the day, though – it would come at the appointed moment, when his wyrd was accomplished and there were no more deeds ahead of him.

Grimnar was the joy of the hunt, the roar of triumph and the tang of blood in the air. Ulric was the fury of the kill, the shake and rip of flesh breaking. Njal was the echo of death, the aftermath of murder. That was his lot, and it was as sacred and unbreakable as the Annulus itself. Such was the way of the universe. There was no pity in it, just the tight grip of fate.

'I am the Law of Fenris,' said Njal, feeling the eyes of the Wolf resting on him, as always, when he spoke. 'You are bound by it, just as you were when you took the Helix.'

Standing before him, the Grey Hunter Baldr nodded in response. Given what he had endured, he looked ready enough to fight – his eyes were clear, his stance solid. If he had not been told of what had happened, Njal would not have guessed he'd been under the curve of Morkai's claws for so long.

'This is a test of corruption,' said Njal. 'You know what that means.'

'I do.'

'You are Baldr, called Fjolnir, of Blackmane's Great Company.'

'I am.'

'Fjolnir. The nightjar. What does that signify?'

'It is a hunt-mark, from the ice. The mark no longer exists, not since the Rite, but the name I kept.'

'Who gave it to you?'

'The gothi of my tribe.'

Baldr spoke clearly. As the words left his mouth, Njal listened for the faint stirrings of falsehood under them. A traitor had a thousand ways to give himself away, and the Rune Priest was a master of detecting them all. His psychic sense extended gently across the chamber, alert to the harmonics of *maleficarum*. The words spoken were a part of the examination, but there were other tests as well, hidden ones that only he would be aware of.

'Did this gothi have you marked out?' asked Njal. 'To follow him?'

'I do not know.'

'Did he ever speak to you of the way of the storm?'

'No.'

'What age were you taken by the Priests?'

'Five, of the home world.'

Nightwing, who had remained hidden up until then, stretched out its pinions. It was perched high up above the fire. Njal, if he chose, could use the creature's artificial eyes to see with, just as he did on the battlefield. The psyber-raven was a shrewd judge of souls, though, and seemed content enough. Had Baldr been obviously tainted, the raven would surely have gone for his eyes already.

'Do you remember what happened to you on this world?' Njal asked.

'No.'

'Nothing?'

'I remember sickness, during the crossing. It lingered after we landed. I put it out of my mind.'

'Describe the sickness.'

Baldr paused. 'Like a fever. I did not sleep. I had pain, often, here.' He pointed to his right temple. 'I performed battle-rites to remain of service. I thought it was warp-sickness.'

'You suffered before?'

'A few times. Never as bad.'

'You never raised this with a Priest?'

Baldr smiled faintly at that. Njal could understand why – he was a Sky Warrior, a member of the Rout of Fenris. What was he supposed to have complained of? Headaches?

'Tell me your last memory, before the sickness took you.'

'We were in a gorge, out from the city,' said Baldr. 'We attacked an enemy convoy. Hafloí, a battle-brother, was in combat with a Traitor. A witch. I charged it. After that, nothing.'

'Nothing.'

'My next memory was waking here.'

Njal nodded. The fire-pit spat as a coal rolled from the heap. He considered all the answers. He considered the way they had been given. He considered the psychic resonances within the chamber, the echoes of a deeper reality under the one his mortal senses picked out.

The Wolf made its presence felt again, like the aroma of bloody breath hanging over a kill.

'Listen to me, Baldr,' said Njal. 'When you arrived at the Fang, when you were five Great Years of age and your body was as fragile as a twig, you were tested. You were under the eyes of the Priests for a long time. We rebuilt your body, we peered deep into your mind. We took it apart. We stripped it down, scoured it clean. We were looking for a sign – any sign – of aptitude. None was found. I say this with certainty. If it had been, you would have been given instruction. You would be a Rune Priest under me, or you would be dead. There are no alternatives.'

Baldr listened carefully, taking it in.

'And yet, here we are,' Njal went on. 'If you were the only one, then I might leap to one conclusion. But you are not. Some secrets are not talked about openly, not outside the Annulus. Tell me this: do you know the word "awakening"?'

Baldr shook his head.

'For a long time,' said Njal, 'it meant nothing to me. I do not willingly keep the company of inquisitors, but on occasion I am forced to suffer their presence. When they talk, I listen, and so a thousand stories reach my ears. Some talk of awakening, some of veil-cleaving, some of soul-latching. They all mean the same thing.

'The galaxy grows old, Baldr Fjolnir. It withers, and it cools. Barriers that have existed for ten thousand years wear thin, like skin stretched too tight over bone. Things are leaking into the realm of the senses that never did before. I see it on every battlefield – men going mad, or bursting into flame, or rising into the air. Some hail these things as miracles. I do not share that kind of faith.'

Njal grimaced a little as he spoke that word. *Faith* had always been a painful concept for him, too redolent of the fanaticism of allies, and nothing like the warrior fatalism of the Fenrisian creed.

'There have been visions on Fenris,' Njal said. 'Ulric tells me the years are racing towards their conclusion. He thinks the End Times are here. We hear names whispered that have not been so much as thought of since the Fell-Handed fought alongside Russ. These are not idle fears, just as every mortal dreams of in the dark, but the visions of the Lords of Men.

'We have come to recognise that some things long accepted as true may no longer be. We have been forced to see that some old protections have lost their power. We have no new ones. All that remains is the strength of our blades, and even they grow blunt.'

For the first time, Baldr looked uneasy, as if those words hurt him. 'Then, lord, do you–'

'I said listen. These are possibilities, no more. You may be awakened. I do not know. From what you say, from what I see, from what I sense, I still do not know. There are ways of delving deeper. If we were in the Mountain, I would submit you to the trials, and Ulric and I would strip your soul bare before our eyes. That, at least, would bring certainty, if you survived it.'

Nightwing emitted a thin vox-caw then, as if the creature somehow objected to that.

'What I can do here is limited,' said Njal. 'It would be safer to end you now, just to be sure, but to throw away a warrior on the eve of battle… In these times, in this place, that is a hard choice to make.'

Baldr drew in a deep breath. 'Anything, lord,' he said firmly. 'I will sub-mit to any test. If you find fault, I will do the deed myself – my blade is sharp enough.'

Njal maintained the gaze of scrutiny, his eyes boring out into the dark-ness. 'What do you *feel*?' he asked. 'What does your blood tell you?'

Baldr thought for a long time before answering.

'It tells me I am restored,' he said. 'I would say I am cured. I would fight again, with my pack, just as I did before. But if you discovered any taint – *any* taint – better to end it now, and not to linger with a curse hanging over me.'

Njal nodded. They were good words. He could understand why Gunn-laugur wanted Baldr back in his pack.

'Well said,' he responded.

He raised his staff then, kindling fresh fire from the skull-tip. The shadows of the chamber lifted, shrinking back from the fire-pit like oil sliding from steel. Shapes were revealed – metal framed cages, stone thrones, brass orbs hung from the chamber roof and wrapped in a filigree of needle-thin wires.

'There are tests we can perform here,' said Njal, walking over to the nearest of the devices and beckoning Baldr to join him. 'You recognise these things? They are like those used when we first brought you inside the Mountain. Sit.'

Baldr took up position on a long stone bench. Above him hovered a spidery collection of probes suspended from a looped coil of cabling. As he pulled himself onto the stone, the tips of the probes glowed into life, glistening like tiny jewels in the dark. A machine began to work close by, gurgling and thrumming.

Njal moved to the far side. Nightwing flapped awkwardly over to the other end of the chamber, taking position atop the heavy stone doorframe and observing intently. Baldr lay back.

'Prepare yourself,' said Njal, resting one hand on the housing of the machine, using the other to hold his staff.

A faint crackle ran down the ebony shaft, like static discharging. Soon the veil around them would thin, and matter would run perilously close to non-matter. The entire chamber would be dangerous.

Other visions would come, then. Other times, places. Two amber eyes would be trained on him, lost in an ancient world of dreams, stalking through the void for eternity.

'This will hurt,' he warned, then threw the first switch.

Chapter Eight

'Hjolda!' roared Olgeir, firing hard as his momentum propelled him into a disintegrating storm of rock and racing, churning oxygen.

The chamber's wall had cracked and broken into a cloud of debris, blasted outwards by the explosive force of the released atmosphere behind it. The station's unnatural silence rushed back into a whirl of howling sound, punctuated by the massed screams of mutant throats.

Olgeir was first through the breach, and slammed straight into a spinning crowd of them. They clawed at his armour, piling on top of one another, scrabbling at the battleplate to get their teeth at the flesh beneath. They were everywhere, like locusts, flailing and jostling in the pitch-black zero gravity. Despite the rapidly depressurising chamber, they kept up their shrieks of bloodlust, lost to anything but the sudden prospect of slaughter.

Haflói piled through the gap next, careering into a knot of writhing bodies. He fired his bolt pistol as he came, punching into the solid glut ahead of him. Olgeir kept up his volleys but the detonations were muffled, clamped down by the pressure of skin and limbs around them. Blood speckled out from the impacts, spinning in glutinous droplets and spiralling in the whooshing air.

111

'Blades!' roared Olgeir over the vox, struggling to free himself from the dozens of claws scrabbling for his throat. The space was pitch black, confined and clogged with bodies, and gaining orientation while weightless was a nightmare – every push sent him spinning into fresh tangles of mutant legs and arms.

Hafloí somehow hauled his axe from his belt and lashed out wildly, rolling headfirst and clung to by scores of screaming mutants. Fresh blood-slicks rolled out, slapping incongruously into the bodies around them.

Olgeir resorted to his fists, punching blindly into the mass of the plague-damned. He cracked the first skull clean through, shattering the fragile bone amid a cloud of pulpy, red-blotched matter. He swung again, bursting the ribcage of another, then jabbed his elbow back, feeling the crack and snap of more bones.

More mutants came to replace those, hands swimming up out of the gloom like shoals of diseased fish, lashing out in a frenzy of claustrophobic hatred. The attacks came from every direction, all in a confused welter of jerky movements. Olgeir felt a blade scrape across the armour-joint at his knee, cutting into cabling, and kicked out against it.

Both Space Wolves were entirely smothered by then, covered in a ball of raging, calloused, desperate bodies. Olgeir felt himself driven back into the nearside wall. Able to brace against something at last, he lashed out harder with his punches, ripping a narrow space just ahead of him. The mutants' screams were the worst he had ever heard – amplified and fractured by the rushing howl of fast-escaping air.

Hafloí was dragged down, his axe pressed against him. Even as Olgeir kicked off from the wall to aid him, he was hauled back by a dozen hands. He twisted, using his bulk to crush a few more against the chamber's edge. He kicked again, feeling his boot drag through muscle. It was like fighting a single, amorphous mass of decaying meat, albeit one with a hundred biting maws and stabbing blades.

In the end, the vacuum tipped the balance. The last of the air ripped away, dissipating out into the breached station. The mutants began to gag, coughing on the thinning air as it whistled out of reach. Their eyeballs swelled, the cords of their necks strained.

'*Heidur Rus!*' roared Hafloí with real rage, sensing the change.

Then the sounds around them shredded away into the eerily silent dance of void-combat. Olgeir saw the jaws of the mutants screaming at him soundlessly. He smashed into them with greater freedom, using his gauntlets and bolter-grip. Gasping in oxygen-starved panic, their bodies were slammed away, cracking against the walls with back-breaking force.

'Further in,' growled Olgeir, angrily discarding the last of the clutching mutant hands around him and pushing on towards the chamber's far end.

Hafloí finished off the mutants around him, and followed, pushing aside the final choking, tumbling bodies. The chamber terminated in a circular hatch at the lower end, two metres in diameter, still sealed and powered. Faulty lights flickered around its edge. The metal rim was a mess of gouges, all full of blood, as if the mutants had mutilated themselves in their frenzy to get through the final barrier.

Olgeir scanned it. There was another air-pocket on the far side, and light, and some heat. 'This is where they ended up,' he said, looking for some kind of vox-unit to use.

Hafloí stared at the portal. 'Really think there's anything beyond that?'

'*They* did.' Olgeir pulled open a panel next to the hatch-rim, his armoured fingers clumsy in the zero gravity. He punched some buttons, and connected a vox-cable to his helm. 'Respond,' he said. 'Any survivors?'

A crackle came back over the comm, seething with static. Then it cleared.

'Thank the Throne,' came a trembling human voice.

The sun was high, a white hole in the sky, burning away with pitiless strength. The land extended in all directions under it, nearly flat, broken only by rust-coloured ridges of stone on the far northern horizon. There was no shade, nowhere to hide, just an endless expanse of shimmering, shaking heat.

Ingvar crouched down behind the low rise. Fifty storm troopers of Delvaux's command crouched with him. Their colonel, a man called Rigal, who wore the full crimson carapace armour of his order, lay on the earth next to him, magnoculars pressed to his visor.

Two hundred metres away rose the ruins of Hjec Falama, one of the satellite settlements that had once guarded the long road to the capital. The burned-out shells of troop transports littered the landscape around them, rising like carbonised skeletons from the topsoil. A few thin columns of smoke rose from the cover of the buildings, though with less intensity than other enemy positions they'd already purged. The defensive line started with a long, low earthwork, crowned by razor wire. Behind that rose the sawtooth lines of hollow, roofless buildings.

'Tell me what you see,' said Ingvar.

Rigal initially hadn't wanted the Space Wolf to join the kill-team, though Ingvar hadn't given him much choice. After the first few assaults, the colonel had changed his mind. Ingvar alone killed more than the rest of the team combined, and such strike-ratios went a long way towards changing attitudes. For his part, Ingvar studiously deferred to the colonel's authority during operations. He'd served with storm troopers before, and knew how their minds worked.

'They're dug in beyond that first line,' Rigal replied. 'A few hundred. Three artillery pieces, some heavy weapons. After that, the usual rabble. They know we're here.'

Ingvar knew all that, but it did no harm to let the colonel tell him. 'It's your command,' he said.

Rigal stowed the magnoculars. 'I'll take any guidance, lord.'

Ingvar studied the approach, using his helm-lenses to zoom in and pan across the hardscrabble vista ahead. Rigal might have been too conservative in his estimates – there were plenty of defenders in position. Behind them, though, there was movement. Fresh plumes of smoke were blooming from some way back into what remained of the settlement. He thought he caught the outlines of troops running across patches of open ground between the carcasses of shelled-out habs.

'Any other forces in this zone?' he asked Rigal.

'Just us.'

Ingvar nodded. 'I can break the line. Once they've started panicking, begin your advance.'

'With pleasure.'

'Begin your bombardment,' said Ingvar, unholstering his boltgun.

Rigal gave the signal and his two mortar-squads prepared to launch. Ingvar hoisted himself up onto his knees and crouched for the sprint.

'We'll be right on your heels,' said Rigal, shuffling further up the rise and resting his bolt pistol on the earth ridge.

Seconds later, mortar trails arced high into the air before thudding down behind the enemy positions. The crews had aimed them well, and explosions burst out all along the line. Reloading took place quickly, and more trails streaked out above the enemy.

Ingvar burst into motion, kicking out into the open and running hard. He was a big, bulky target and his grey armour gave him no camouflage. Las-fire started to flicker in his direction immediately, skittering across the open desert like flashes of sunlight off glass.

He kept low, zigzagging across the open terrain, picking up speed and twisting unpredictably. A few sharpshooters had taken position up in the habs, though most were clustered at ground level, hunkered down behind the barricades. Rigal's troops opened up a covering barrage from the flanks, pinning some of the bolder defenders behind the earthwork.

Ingvar selected the point to strike. Las-beams pinged from his shoulder-guards and drilled into his breastplate, doing little damage. Solid rounds puffed up the dust at his feet, fruitlessly trying to catch him as he raced into contact.

He fired as he ran – a short brace of pinpoint shots, each aimed from instinct, each one finding its mark with a wet pop, followed by the messy slap of bodies being ripped apart. He seized a frag grenade from his waist and hurled it ahead of him. It bounced over the barricades and into the semi-walled space beyond, exploding in a messy, spiralling boom.

Then he was at the barricades and smashing through the razor wire. Those still on their feet raced away from him, firing steadily.

'Fenrys!' roared Ingvar, laughing with savage pleasure. He unsheathed *dausvjer* with his right hand, firing his bolter with his left, then charged them.

They kept their lasguns levelled and their mauls and flails in hand. Ingvar swept through them like a desert wind, ripping down the length of the barricade and bringing terror with him. Even the plague-damned fell back in the face of the furious assault, limping away from their posts and shambling back into the blasted townscape beyond.

That was the cue for Rigal to advance. His storm troopers moved from cover and charged across the open ground. The last of the mortars, angled for long range, whistled overhead and crashed into the ruins, blowing up amid cohorts of retreating enemy soldiers.

Ingvar went after them, saving bolts in favour of cutting their legs from under them. Rigal's forces were quick to catch up. They split into two squads, spreading out along either flank of the barricade and coming at the remaining defenders in a pincer movement. Their carapace armour – superior to the flak-plates worn by Ras Shakeh's Guard regiments – gave them good protection from return fire, and their hellguns sent better-aimed, more focused beams into their targets.

Caught between Ingvar's lone devastation and the disciplined push of Rigal's forces, the enemy line shattered entirely, breaking into bands of retreating warriors. Once they lost their shape, the storm troopers went after them remorselessly.

Ingvar pulled ahead. Like a grey ghost he flitted through the dust-kicked sunlight, pouncing on his prey before tearing it to pieces. Soon he had penetrated into the heart of the old settlement. A few big buildings still stood, blackened by fire and windowless, but with their walls largely intact. A wide courtyard ran away ahead of him, bordered on one side by a large municipal edifice with granite columns and a domed belltower. A huge Imperial aquila lay on the ground before it, broken in pieces.

Ingvar skidded into the open, catching a retreating mutant by the neck and lashing him against the stone. Dozens more fled ahead of him, stumbling over the shattered rockcrete.

His instinct was to race after them, taking down as many as he could reach before they dispersed into the ruins. Just as he was about to sprint after the nearest, though, he caught the snap and fizz of las-fire coming from the far side of the square. Some of it hit the fleeing mutants, causing them to crash to earth.

Ingvar's helm picked up multiple targets hidden in the buildings on the far side, some positioned higher up amid the hollowed windows. He raised his bolter, training it on the first such position. His finger slipped over the trigger, and he lined up the shot.

It never came. More las-fire scythed down from the cover of the buildings, cutting down more plague-mutants. The aim was good – professional, not wasteful.

As Ingvar hesitated, Rigal's troops caught up. The storm troopers pushed on, making cover and aiming their hellguns at the buildings beyond.

'No!' roared Ingvar, holding his blade up.

Rigal gave the order, and the entire square fell into echoing silence, the dust settling slowly over the corpses.

Ingvar strode ahead, looking up at the windows ahead of him. As he emerged into the open, a cry broke out from the far side. The language wasn't native to Ras Shakeh.

'*Fenrys Hjolda!*' came the cry, repeated over and over from hoarse throats.

Soldiers emerged from cover, encrusted with grime and bearing a motley assortment of lasguns and improvised weaponry. All of them wore grey uniforms, though covered in thick layers of caked dust and dried blood. Their hair was long and shaggy, many of them blond or redheaded. They laughed raucously as they advanced, saluting Ingvar with the fist-against-chest gesture.

Ingvar watched them come, dumbfounded for a moment. Only when their leader approached, pushing those around him to one side, did he realise the truth.

'Bjargborn,' Ingvar said. 'How, in the name of–'

Torek Bjargborn laughed. All of them laughed. The sound was one of relief, the release of long-coiled tension.

'We waited, lord,' said the old master of the *Undrider*, grinning. 'We held on.' He fell to one knee then, as did all those around him. There must have been more than eighty of them, all in grey Fenrisian garb.

Rigal joined Ingvar. He, like the other storm troopers, regarded the newcomers with suspicion, and kept his weapon levelled.

'Is all well, lord?' Rigal asked.

Ingvar reached down to Bjargborn and pulled him back to his feet. His fanged mouth broke into a smile.

'Better than well, colonel.' He looked up, gauging how much of the settlement remained infested, then turned back to Bjargborn. 'First, we fight,' he said. 'Then, when this place is clean again, you can tell me how in the name of Hel you're still alive.'

When Baldr came round, his vision remained blurred for a long time. For a few moments he had no idea where he was. Grey shadows loomed over him, shifting like candlelight. He heard a metallic cawing, and boots scuffing on stone.

Recollection came back slowly, along with the pain. It ran down his back like cold fire. He reached up to his forehead, feeling bloody scabs on his temples.

'Welcome back,' came a familiar deep voice from the shadows.

Baldr lifted his head, blinking thickly.

Njal was still there, towering over him. The smell of burning filled the chamber, as if he'd been cooking meat.

Baldr pushed himself up into a seated position. His head hammered as he moved. He was desperate to ask, but the words wouldn't come.

Njal prolonged the agony for a few more moments.

'Nothing,' he said at last, putting his instruments away and coming to stand by his side. 'Nothing at all.'

Baldr swallowed thickly, tasting his own blood in the bile. He wasn't sure whether he fully believed it. 'No corruption?'

'None.' Njal fixed him with his frost-clear gaze. 'I sense nothing, I see nothing. If I had, you would not have awoken.'

The Rune Priest reached for a ceramic cup and filled it with water from a ewer. He handed it to Baldr. 'When you return to the city, restart your training. Work hard. You have lost muscle mass, and I want you fighting again as soon as possible.'

Baldr nodded, draining the cup. His throat remained parched and sore.

'I have done nothing but interrogate since I got here,' said Njal irritably, turning back to his instruments. One by one, he cleaned them and put them away, treating the devices reverently, like an Iron Priest with his tools. 'First the Plague Marine, now you. This must be the end of it.'

At the mention of the Traitor, the pain burning at the base of Baldr's neck briefly flared, as if in sympathy with old memories. 'Did you discover anything from the Traitor?' he asked, before remembering it was not his place to ask.

To his surprise, Njal merely nodded, and carried on with his work. 'We have names now. The Mycelite. This one is new to me, but there is another which is not: *Festerax*.'

Baldr flexed his fingers gingerly, feeling the blood slowly flow back into the arteries. 'Another Traitor?'

'A ship. A hulk. It has been in the annals of the damned for millennia.' Njal smiled grimly. 'This is the enemy. Once this world is purged of the last dregs, we will hunt it down.'

'Where is it?'

'We do not know. Not yet.' Njal put the last of the devices away in leather-lined caskets, clicking the locks closed firmly and making the sign of warding across the lids. 'We'll know more if the deep-void stations can be trawled. If not, we're in the dark over their movements. I don't think our prisoner knew more than he told us. At least, while he still had a tongue.'

'Does he live?'

'I killed him.' Njal opened a heavy iron door in the chamber walls. 'The Cardinal seemed happy to keep going indefinitely. I was not.' He retrieved something from behind the door, and closed it again. 'Not good for the soul, that kind of work. Ulric has more stomach for it, but even he takes no pleasure. We were made for the clean kill.'

Njal returned, carrying what looked like a torc. It was white, carved from ivory or bone, and covered with lines of tiny runic script. Baldr found his eyes drawn towards it uncomfortably. As the torc emerged into the light, Nightwing became agitated, hopping from one foot to the other.

'To the fight in the open, blade to blade,' Njal said. 'That is what we aspire to, yes?'

Baldr nodded. 'Where possible.'

'Yes, where possible.' Njal turned the torc in his gauntlets, studying the script carefully. 'You still present me with a problem, Baldr Fjolnir. From the stories I've heard, a mortal would already have been burned for less. Do I risk you living? All for an extra claw in the pack? Gunnlaugur kept it secret, but will it stay that way?'

Baldr found it difficult to look away from the torc. The collar seemed to suck in the meagre light around it, making the runes blacker than night.

'If the Cardinal finds out, he'll come after you,' said Njal. 'Once this is over we can go back to loathing one another, but for the time being we need him.' He held the torc up, looking through its hollow interior at Baldr. 'So this is a precaution. It won't kill you. It won't dull your instincts. Physically, it won't affect you at all.'

Baldr felt an almost overwhelming urge to pull away from it, and resisted. 'What is it?'

'A dampener. A null-collar. If you have any aptitude at all, even something undetectable by my devices here, it will quash it.'

A sick feeling curdled at the back of Baldr's throat. He'd been surrounded by warding runes ever since entering the Mountain, but something about those on the collar appalled him.

'Is it permanent?' he asked.

'I can remove it. No others can – it is bound to my soul-pattern.'

'If they tried?'

'It would end you.'

The collar was slender – a few centimetres thick and perfectly smooth. It would slot between the armour-plates of his gorget and helm, hidden away from view.

'I thought...' started Baldr, then trailed off.

'Say it.'

'I thought that the power came from Fenris,' he said. 'From the soul of the world.'

Njal raised an eyebrow. 'And?'

'I had always believed... If a warrior had it... I believed that nothing could interfere with it.'

'All strength is finite. Everything can be countered.'

'So, where does it come from?'

Njal looked at him. 'Runecraft? Where does it come from?' His icy irises glittered in the dark. 'You think you are ready for those secrets?' He let slip a grim laugh. 'You are inches from damnation, Grey Hunter. This is not the time to be asking.'

He held the null-collar up high, rotating it as if it were a crown of conquerors. Baldr tensed as it was lowered over his head. Njal rotated it so that the open section of the torc was at the front. Two dragon's mouths, intricately carved from what looked like iron, gaped at one another across the narrow gap.

'So you are bounded,' said Njal applying pressure to either side.

There was a faint sound of hissing, and the two dragon's mouths clamped together. A ripple of heat ran across his skin, quickly dissipating. Baldr felt his breathing speeding up, and quelled it. He remained unmoving, his mind working to detect any change.

'You will not feel anything,' said Njal. 'If your pack-mates ask, it is a rune-ward. For luck. I see you already carry one.' He reached for his staff again, taking it up. 'And that is the end of this. You may go. But you know, of course, that it is not the end. I'll be watching you. Your pack will be watching you.'

Baldr felt other eyes on him, and caught sight of Nightwing staring at him from a lone obsidian ocular implant. The raven's head was eerily still.

The Rune Priest reached for his staff again, and the wolf-skull shadow fell over Baldr.

'You will never be out of our gaze again, Fjolnir,' said Njal. 'Best you get used it.'

Chapter Nine

Hafloí watched Olgeir fumbling with the airlock release controls, but the danger had passed. Behind him, open-mouthed mutant corpses twisted in the zero gravity, bumping up against the chamber's sides.

That fight had been closer than he was ever likely to admit. In such a dark, confined space, with no room to bring his superior agility to bear, the odds had been too tight. For a long time after his solo kill on Hjec Aleja, he'd gloried in his unrestrained way of war, and looked with some scorn on the older warriors of the pack. Since then, things had become steadily harder. His pack-mates took it all in their stride, but it was becoming slowly clear to Hafloí that there was still much to learn. There were other ways of fighting, not all involving pure speed and strength. Already he found himself wishing to fight in the void again, knowing that his movements would be quicker and smoother the next time.

For now, he let his breathing recover and watched Olgeir try to gain entry.

'You have air in there?' Olgeir asked, using the vox-cable again.

More static from the other side. 'The what?'

Hafloí snorted his impatience. 'Just open it.'

Olgeir persevered. 'There is a vacuum on this side,' he explained to the occupant of the chamber beyond. 'You have breathing gear?'

'Breathing gear, yes,' came the response. 'I'm wearing it. Are you of the Church? What is your ident? What diocese?'

Olgeir pushed back and raised his bolter towards the door's locking mechanism. Hafloí, seeing what he intended, moved out of range.

'Get back,' said Olgeir. 'We're coming in.'

'Wait,' came the voice. 'What is your–'

Olgeir fired, blowing up the lock-panel in a blaze of light. Crackles of electricity ran around the hatch rim, quickly snaking out.

Then he drifted in close again and seized the edge of the hatch door. Gripping with both hands, he pulled. For a moment, the door-bolts resisted.

'A bit harder?' said Hafloí, enjoying watching the big warrior struggle.

Olgeir heaved, his power armour servos geared up, and the bolts sheared. The hatch sprang open, blown out by air pressure on the other side. Olgeir shoved the hatch door aside and hauled himself through the gap, working against the rush of escaping oxygen. Hafloí followed him in.

The chamber was lit by a single lumen lodged in the ceiling. It was less than four metres square and lined with banks of flickering cogitator equipment. Three bodies hovered at the rear, their uniforms ripped and bloodstained. One of them teetered on his feet, swaying uneasily in the zero gravity, wearing a sealed helm and a red voidsuit. He levelled a lasgun at them, backing away and rising as they came in. Olgeir scanned for the man's vox-caster, and locked on to it with his helm's counterpart.

'Come no further!' the man shrieked over the vox-link. 'I will fire!'

Hafloí ignored him and moved to study the cogitators, most of which looked operational. 'Might get something out of this after all,' he mused.

Olgeir floated over to the mortal, his hand held open, his boltgun lowered. 'Are you the only one?'

The man backed up against the rear wall, his weapon still raised. The bodies of his companions bumped away from him. 'Get out!' he screamed. The muzzle shook as he gripped it. 'Get *out!*'

'We're not your enemy,' said Olgeir, keeping his distance.

'These are augur records,' Hafloí murmured, running his finger down the tall, boxy cogitator units.

'Leave now,' the man blurted, 'or, or, by the Emperor's will, I *will* end you!' As he spoke, he switched the aim of his lasgun between the two of them.

'That is unlikely,' said Olgeir. 'Just tell me–'

The man opened fire. A tangle of poorly aimed las-beams hissed into

Olgeir's breastplate, scoring the ceramite and making the chamber flash with freeze-frame light-bursts.

Olgeir shrugged off the impacts, pushed himself closer to the terrified man and grabbed his lasgun. With a twist of his armoured fingers he cracked the barrel and pushed it aside. The ruined weapon tumbled across the room, ricocheting from the walls before finally lodging up against the ceiling.

'Your mind has been damaged,' said Olgeir, speaking steadily. 'Hel, how could it not be? Remain calm. We need to know what happened.'

For a moment the man stared up at him, trembling, hovering halfway up the chamber wall with his boots twitching. Then he reached for the mouthpiece of his helm and wrenched it off. Olgeir lunged for it, but the survivor ripped it clear and threw it away.

His face went red, instantly bloodshot as the air in his lungs burst out. Olgeir tried to grab him but the man somehow scrambled away, gagging and retching, coughing up blood from a ruptured windpipe. By the time Olgeir had seized him there was no way back. The man looked up at the Space Wolf with anguished triumph in his staring eyes.

Then his body spasmed, and went limp. Disgusted, Olgeir let it float free, turning gently amid floating dots of blood.

Hafloí looked on, unimpressed. 'Strange decision,' he said.

'He must have been down here for days,' said Olgeir. 'Listening to them all outside, trying to get in.'

Hafloí sighed. Olgeir's perennial tolerance of mortal weakness could get wearing. 'At least the hunt wasn't wasted. We can withdraw these datacores. If they picked up anything before the station was taken, we'll have it.'

Olgeir pushed over to the nearest cogitator unit. Faint lights still played across its complicated surface, lost amid a filigree of valves and coolant tubes. Each of the cases whirred and clicked, a constant rhythm in the airless cold.

'Start clearing them out,' he said. 'I'll head back up and vox the Old Dog.'

'And once we're done?'

Olgeir looked back over his shoulder, out past the circular hatch where the bodies of the plague-damned drifted in a soup of blood-spores.

'Burn it,' he said, pushing off again.

Gunnlaugur strode through the halls of the Halicon. Menials, servitors and cherubim scurried to get out of his path. The Cardinal's troops were everywhere, refitting and restoring. Golden altars had been hammered down over the older stone ones the canoness had used. Devotional picts of the Wounded Heart had been removed and placed with icons of the Fiery Tear.

It was good to see the citadel being made strong again, but little else pleased Gunnlaugur. The gold, the incense, the chanting – all of it set his fangs on edge. He went as quickly as he could to the upper levels, shoving his way past any of the robed prelates too slow or clumsy to see him coming.

Njal remained on *Heimdall* with Baldr, and the rest of the Wolves had been assigned to kill-teams operating in the wastes. The entire planet had a breathless air of preparation. All knew they would be back in the void soon, though the destination remained obscure. Only one firm message had come in, typically curt from Jorundur – *Datacores retrieved. On our way.*

Gunnlaugur had tried to find the canoness to consult on strategy, but her aides seemed to have gone missing. Everywhere he went, the servants of the Cardinal seemed to have assumed the functions of governance, displacing men and women who had stood in position before the siege. It was getting hard to find anyone who knew anything about anything.

He reached de Chatelaine's private chambers in the Halicon's eastern wing. The doors were unguarded, which was strange – there should have been two Battle Sisters on duty at all times.

Inside, the chamber was empty. The canoness's desk was piled with papers. Two long glass doors stood open on the external wall, the drapes hanging limply in the afternoon heat. A half-empty goblet of water stood on the arm of a throne.

Gunnlaugur moved over to the desk and looked over the paperwork. All of it was stamped with the Ecclesiarchy icon, and looked like routine business – munitions movements, resupply plans. He wondered about leaving her a sign to contact him.

He was about to turn away, when the doors to the chamber swung open again, and Sister Callia came in. When she caught sight of him, she froze.

'My lord,' she said, recovering herself. 'I was looking for the canoness.'

'As was I,' said Gunnlaugur.

Callia's gaze darted around, as if de Chatelaine might somehow be hidden somewhere in the chamber. 'She is not answering requests for audience.'

'I noticed.'

Callia closed the doors quietly behind her. Gunnlaugur thought she looked hunted. 'They should be locked,' she said, and headed towards the nearest of the glass panels. The open panes led out to a balcony overlooking the upper city, and she slipped out onto it.

Gunnlaugur followed her. The space outside was narrow, barely wide enough to accommodate a single power armoured warrior. As he stood next to her, Callia closed the glass door behind them.

Hjec Aleja ran down away from them steeply. From that vantage, the scale of the reconstruction could clearly be seen. Ecclesiarchy-liveried landers were still coming and going in a steady stream. The streets milled with bodies, most clad in carapace armour or the crimson plate of the Fiery Tear. Out on the plains, Sentinels prowled. The noise of reconstruction hammered out from every corner.

'What is it?' Gunnlaugur asked.

'I have not heard from her in hours. She answers on no channels, not even those private to the Sisterhood.'

'Is she with the Cardinal?'

Callia's expression tightened. 'I have not asked him.'

'Perhaps you should.'

'Where is your Stormcaller?'

'On *Heimdall*.'

'He should come back.'

Gunnlaugur gave her a warning look. 'He doesn't answer to my summons.'

'Then this is...' said Callia, glancing up at him. 'I don't know.'

Gunnlaugur waited for her.

'His *severity*,' said Callia, eventually. 'His methods are not those we are used to. We were faithful, were we not?' Callia's expression was oddly trusting.

'You were,' said Gunnlaugur.

'He has been handing out penance,' said Callia. 'I have tried to see the justice in it. My instinct is to *believe*. It is a strong instinct, but... even so.'

Gunnlaugur sighed. 'This is your business, Sister.'

Callia looked at him intently for a moment, as if deciding whether to say more. 'Why did you wish to see her?'

'I've had word from *Vuokho*. We need to confer.'

Callia nodded. 'When I locate her, I will tell her you're looking for her. She will be pleased. It is what we have all been waiting for.'

'Just tell her where I am.'

Callia paused then. She suddenly reached up to her collar and withdrew a small comms-bead. She handed it to him. 'This is aligned to a secure channel, used by our Sisterhood,' she said. 'It might prove... useful.'

Gunnlaugur looked at it steadily. 'I can use the open vox-net.'

'Please, take it,' said Callia.

Close up, Gunnlaugur saw the hunted look in her eyes again. He took the comms-bead, stowing it securely. 'As you wish.'

'Like I said. It might prove useful.'

Then she pushed the glass door open, and walked back into the chamber. She gave Gunnlaugur a parting bow, and was gone.

Gunnlaugur watched her leave. As he was pondering what to do next, a comm-burst from *Heimdall* came in.

'Njal summons you, jarl,' said Derroth. 'Landers are dispatched.'

'By his will,' Gunnlaugur responded, absently, noting the loc-fix of the incoming shuttle. He took a last look around the empty chamber. De Chatelaine's absence was strange. It was out of character, and it would be good to have her back soon.

Then he left, heading down towards the city's landing stages.

It took many more hours before Hjec Falama was cleansed. Its defenders had nowhere else to go, and so they fought on, grimly clinging to what passed for life.

As the sun set, a boiling ember in the rapidly darkening sky, the deep dark crept across empty, dusty streets. Shadows swayed and flickered against the remains of old walls, made to dance by the bonfires on every corner. Though the heat of the day was fading, Hjec Falama would remain hot well into the night, warmed by the crackle and spit of crisping flesh.

Rigal secured the perimeter, sending his men out in teams to patrol. The storm troopers had evaded joining the Fenrisians in combat, keeping to their own disciplined patterns of attack. Bjargborn's troops had been typically reckless, and Ingvar had hunted with them. Ingvar kept his bolter stowed, using a blade just as the kaerls did. They all killed in the old way – face to face, watching the eyes of the enemy as he died.

After the killing, they fell back to the central courtyard and sat around fires, wholesome ones, and did what the Sons of Russ always did after battle – ate, drank, told stories.

Ingvar watched them, holding their battered ration packs over the flames before devouring the freeze-dried gloop and savouring it as if it were konungur flesh. A raw happiness played across their drawn faces.

They had all lost body mass since their service on *Undrider*, but could still crack a grin.

'So,' Ingvar said, turning to Bjargborn, who sat beside him in the circle of ruddy light. 'Tell your story.'

Bjargborn chewed, nodding. 'Your battle-brother, Jorundur,' he said. 'He ordered us to the saviour pods. I ran down from the bridge as the destroyer hit us.' He shook his head ruefully. 'Everything was on fire. It nearly caught me. By the time I got there, most of the pods had gone. I jumped into the last, pulled the hatch, hit the controls. The explosions hit just before the docking-clamps blew, and I thought my thread was cut. Next thing I know, I'm out, and the planet's swinging round me like an ice-skiff.'

'How many got out with you?'

Bjargborn's expression darkened. 'Half the complement? A lot of us made it down. The pods scattered, half of them stuck out in the deep desert. I don't know if any of those made it. We had no comms, weapons, nothing. I remember kicking the hatch open and thinking the thrusters were still burning. Then I realised how hot it is here.'

Wide smiles around the fire. The kaerls listened, just as they might have listened to a skjald as the ice-wind howled.

'Some of us had come down close to cities,' Bjargborn said. 'At first, we thought we were the lucky ones. Then we found out what lived there. That was nearly the end of me, too.' He looked over at the flames. 'You don't see it coming, not at first. You catch their eyes too late, see that they're not really alive, and then they're all over you.'

'How many are left?'

'Ninety of us, here.' Bjargborn's expression held a flicker of pride, an old stubborn arrogance that didn't retreat easily. 'If they didn't catch you at the start, there were things you could do. They were careless. They could hardly see, and daylight made them slow. Once a few of us made contact, we could organise. At night we hunted for others like us, by day we hunted them. We got hold of guns, armour pieces. There was some food left – old ration packs, water. They didn't touch it.'

'Any others groups like yours?'

'There might be, down past the big manufactories.' He looked at the others, but they didn't meet his gaze. 'But I don't know. Probably not.'

Ingvar nodded. 'Then your wyrd was a lucky one. You evaded the Ecclesiarchy, too, and they've landed thousands.'

'We know. We saw them in action, before you got here.'

'Storm troopers?'

'Yes, and battle engines. They were heading west, going fast.'

'You met them?'

'No, not up close.' Bjargborn looked contemptuous. 'They weren't here to take anything back. They were looking for something. By the time we'd worked out what was going on, they were gone, leaving us with all the plague-damned they hadn't killed.'

'What were they doing?'

'No idea. They went through some of the old temples. They stripped one out – I saw them carting crates away. Not the big, grand ones. Just one or two, out on the edge of the desert. It was done quickly, then they were gone.'

Ingvar pressed his gauntlets together pensively. 'You didn't see any more than that?'

One of the other kaerls spoke up then. 'I saw them leave,' he said.

'He is Aerold,' said Bjargborn.

'They were led by a man in black robes,' said Aerold. 'A priest. He was overseeing them all, even the Battle Sisters. I couldn't get close, but I don't think he wore any armour. He walked around unshielded, like he feared nothing. Like it was all his.'

Ingvar stared into the fire and smiled wryly. 'Maybe it is,' he said.

The kaerls waited for him to say something more, looking expectant. Ingvar suddenly thought of the halls under the Mountain, the fire-pits in the vaults, the weapons hanging on chains, the bone-breaking cold. He remembered the skjalds and the Priests declaiming the old sagas. He remembered the smell of it – the charred meat, the oil-thick *mjod* swilling.

'You will come back with me,' he said, reaching for more food. 'All of you. The pack has no Aettguard – that needs changing.'

Bjargborn bowed proudly. 'We live to serve. We can still fight.'

'So I can see.'

'We remained *Fenryka*,' said Bjargborn. 'You can't get the ice out of your blood, not even here.'

Ingvar thought on that. He remembered how it had been just after rejoining the pack – a kind of madness. The desire had been there, to go back, to be again what he had been before, but the ability was not. His old self had become foreign to him, almost unintelligible.

We have become mongrels, Callimachus had told him, in what felt like another life. As always, the Ultramarine had been right.

Now, though, it felt different. The more time passed, the more Ingvar felt the half-buried savagery return. The fire-circle, the sharing of tales, the laughter in the shadows, it all slowly came back.

You can't get the ice out of your blood.

'Lord.'

Ingvar stirred to see Bjargborn looking up at him.

'They say the Stormcaller is here,' the kaerl said. 'Forgive me, if this is forbidden, but we wanted to ask. You fought with him?'

'Briefly.'

Bjargborn turned to his comrades, smiling in vindication. 'Then, if it is not too much... If it can be asked for...'

'You want the tale.'

They were hard-bitten soldiers of the Aett, survivors of the horrors of Ras Shakeh and veterans of a hundred battles, but they nodded.

Ingvar unlocked his gauntlets. It had been a long time since he had been called to be skjald, and then only to battle-brothers of the Great Company. Other Chapters would scorn such rituals. He would have done himself, fresh from Onyx with the sarcasm of Jocelyn in his mind.

But the wind had changed. It was fresher now, cleared of the filth that preyed on the soul and made it defensive.

'This is how it was,' he began.

The Chamber of the Annulus was buried in *Heimdall*'s dark heart. It was a mere echo of the original, but still it soared up into the vaults of the starship. Its curved walls were hewn from granite, held aloft by rough pillars crowned with the heads of beasts.

A single stone, six times the height of a man, stood at the heart of it, jutting up from the iron deck. The stone bore age-weathered runes on its rough surface. The hand that had carved those runes was long gone, for the stone had been old even before Russ first came to Fenris. It had been taken from Asaheim and lodged in the heart of a starship, surrounded by the creak and crack of metal rather than the eternal howl of the mountain gales.

Njal stood before the stone. He felt like one of the old gothi of memory, gathered under the lee of ancient rock circles. The quiescent runes in his armour glimmered with fire-reflections.

Others stood around him: Álfar of his retinue, Gunnlaugur of Járnhamar, Fellblade, Long-axe and Bloodhame with their packs. All wore their armour, fresh from the last of the hunts on Ras Shakeh, marked with new kill-tallies. The dust had not yet been cleaned away, though the stink of the planet had been replaced by the harder aroma of hearth-coals and weapon-oil.

'Brothers, our fight on this world is over,' Njal said.

As he spoke, Nightwing preened itself absently. Every so often, the raven's head would lift to stare at one of the warriors, then it would return to its work.

'The Traitor spilled some truths before he died,' Njal went on. 'The Death Guard Legion is here. He mentioned the Traveller – his fell hand will be shown at some point. And he mentioned another: the Mycelite. I do not know this name. Perhaps some champion, perhaps one consumed by maleficarum. The name was repeated more than the rest, so he, if anyone, is master of these forces we have seen so far. And there is a ship: the *Festerax*.'

'Where?' asked Gunnlaugur.

'The datacores your warriors brought back have been studied. We compared void-markers with those in the annals of the damned. Some were unknown, others too small to pose a threat. Then we found a match. The *Festerax* is known to the Imperium, and appears on the augur-logs. It is a legend of darkness, sighted on a hundred worlds across nine thousand years. Now we know where it is headed.'

Njal raised his gauntlet, and a spinning star of energy formed in front of him. The nimbus resolved into a collection of star-system runes, glowing into a slowly rotating lattice. Carving its way through the heart of the network was a green slick – a jagged spear of lurid light-points. As it progressed, the slick split up, spreading out across the volume of the void and angling towards unconquered worlds ahead.

'They are moving faster now,' said Njal. 'They know we are here. Half the subsector veers on the edge of desolation – if enough worlds are infected there will be nothing left to save.'

Njal gestured, and the schematic zoomed out. Neighbouring star-systems swept into view, each identified with floating rune-markings.

'That is their aim,' Njal said. 'To scour these worlds. This takes strength away from fortresses closer to the real target.'

The star-map kept zooming out. The fringes began to glow with curls of red matter, like licking flames at the edge of parchment.

'The Eye,' said Njal with grim finality. 'Below the Cadian Gate. If they succeed in driving ruin this far, it will be one more wound to absorb on the flanks of the Praeses.'

'They're clearing the tribute subsectors,' muttered Fellblade. 'The ones that supply the front line.'

Njal nodded. 'They are.'

Gunnlaugur studied the schematic. 'Are these positions accurate?'

'As much as anything is.'

'We can't run them all down,' Gunnlaugur said. 'We don't have the ships.'

'No. We have to make choices.'

The star-map zoomed in again, cycling through subsectors, narrowing down to a single vector of the enemy incursion. The rune-markers spread wider and slipped off the edge of the projection. Soon only one remained.

'Kefa Primaris,' said Njal. 'Hive world, significant forge capability, situated at the nexus of several warp-lanes. Take it, and the subsector is torn open. Hold it, and you have some chance of salvaging a remnant. They know this, and they know we're on their trail, so they've sent forces ahead. Once they break that world, it's over.'

Njal watched the slowly spinning system-figure float into focus – a lone planet orbiting a giant red star.

'Speed is not the issue,' said Njal. 'Only the *Festerax* itself is in range of Kefa Primaris, and both *Heimdall* and *Vindicatus* can overtake it. If this were a standard battleship, there might be little issue – Kefa is not undefended, and we have our own weapons – but the *Festerax* is not a standard battleship.'

The projection narrowed down to a single ship – a vast, hunched, bloated ball of amalgamated hulls and prows, jumbled together like a gobbet of molten slag.

'It is a hulk. A living hulk. Its origins are unknown, though they are ancient, maybe even pre-dating the Betrayal. It has been engaged by the Imperial Navy on seventeen occasions, each time destroying its attackers or evading capture. Its gunnery is meagre, but it can take immense amounts of damage. Seven hundred years ago, it was engaged by the *Bellicosa Extremis*, an Emperor-class battleship. The engagement lasted for seven days, during which *Bellicosa* hurled everything it had at it. By the end, its torpedo tubes were empty, its void shields burned away, and the *Festerax* had slipped into the aether.'

Njal closed his fist, and the projection rippled out. 'This is what heads for Kefa Primaris. This is what we must bring down.'

Gunnlaugur let slip a low whistle. 'A fine target.'

Bloodhame laughed. 'So it is. We are boarding, then?'

Njal nodded. 'If *Bellicosa* could not crack it, then nothing we have here will either. But we've seen monsters like this before, and we know how to slay them. Get into the heart of it, into the drive-halls, lock thermal charges. When enough of those go off, every methane chamber in the hulk will ignite.'

The Wolves around nodded appreciatively. A low, barely audible growl ran around the chamber – pack-wide kill-urge taking root. It was all they ever asked for. A target.

'We will need the Cardinal,' said Njal. 'The *Festerax* will have escorts, and his ships can take those on long enough to give us a way in. *Heimdall* will support. Apart from that, we will be on our own.'

Fellblade snorted. 'He's busy scourging the planet below.'

'He will see reason. But remember this: he loathes us. His creatures loathe us. They will provoke, they will protest. For now, it is up to us to keep the peace.' Njal swept his gaze across them all, as dark as the vaults over the stone. 'Do nothing to break faith with them. *Nothing.*'

One by one, the Wolves bowed in submission.

Nightwing cawed then, a thin sound like mocking laughter. Njal looked up, and extended his wrist. The psyber-raven flapped down from the chamber's heights, landing heavily, its metal-pinned wings extended.

'So we have our prey, brothers,' Njal said, fangs exposed as he bared them in the old threat-gesture. Every spirit in the chamber kindled, quickening like flame on oil. 'The wait is over. Now we take the fight to the enemy.'

Chapter Ten

Gunnlaugur left the Annulus Chamber as the others did. The atmosphere of *Heimdall* did him good. It smelt *right*, like a starship should, with its ritual skulls and rune-wards engraved on every panel. Still, he could feel himself on edge, unable to give in fully to the impending battle-joy.

There was much to prove. He had failed against Thorslax. He had managed Ingvar badly. The pack under his watch was not the fluent weapon it had been under Hjortur. He knew it, and his brothers did, too.

More than that, though, were the uncertainties. Was Ingvar's suspicion founded on truth? Where was de Chatelaine? And, most of all, what was the judgement on Baldr, the one he had chosen to preserve, knowing the risks?

'Vaerangi,' came Njal's voice from behind him.

Gunnlaugur felt a chill run through him. He turned and bowed. 'Something else, jarl?'

'Come with me,' said the Rune Priest, stalking off down the corridor.

The two of them set off, heading up towards the next level. Njal's boots clanged heavily as they hit the deck, weighed down by his thick Terminator plate.

'How runs your pack?' asked Njal gruffly, his staff-heel thudding as he walked.

133

'They're prepared,' said Gunnlaugur.

'But you had trouble.'

Gunnlaugur bristled. 'Nothing I couldn't master.'

Njal looked at him sidelong. 'There's no shame in it. You lead warriors. Some bad blood will flow.' His cracked lips twisted in a thin smile. 'On the ice, the warrior-kings were killed by their flag-bearers. That's the world we come from. Nothing changes,' he said, tapping his chest. 'Not under here.'

Gunnlaugur kept his mouth shut, wondering where this was going.

'I spoke to Baldr,' Njal said.

Again, the chill.

'I found nothing,' said Njal. 'He will return to you, but be watchful. The first sign of any change, tell me. We have all lived too long to be unwary.'

Gunnlaugur bowed his head, hoping the relief flooding over him wasn't obvious. 'I'm glad,' he said, gruffly. 'He was a good warrior.'

'He *is* a good warrior. He will need to be, as I want him on this hunt.'

'He's ready?'

'We will need every blade we have,' said Njal. 'More than that, I want him *close*. I want him back among us again.' He shot Gunnlaugur a cynical look. 'I want him away from this world, and I want him away from the Cardinal.'

Gunnlaugur nodded. 'By your will.'

'This is what he was bred for, Skullhewer. His speed will come back once he's got blade in hand.'

The two of them kept going, clanking up a shallow metal stairway. Kaerls saluted as they passed, averting their eyes and clenching their fists against their chests.

'So, can it be done?' asked Gunnlaugur as they reached the next deck up.

'The hulk?' Njal exhaled a bleak laugh. 'We'll see.'

'They killed my blademaster,' growled Gunnlaugur. 'I've not yet slain enough to avenge him.'

'You won't be short of skulls to crack. Not in there.'

They passed along a long, open gantry, flanked by crew-cells and refectory chambers. The life of the ship hummed around them, raucous and echoing.

'The Cardinal is the key,' said Njal. 'We cannot break into that hulk without him, and he knows this. He's powerful in his own kingdom, but powerful enough to refuse a request from a Lord of the Adeptus Astartes? In his theology, we are the Angels of the Emperor.' Njal shook his head, mystified. 'If he practises what he preaches, he will not refuse.'

They left the crew quarters behind and moved into a broad thorough-fare leading up to the flight decks. The smell of promethium and engine lubricants spiced the air.

Njal paused before a barred iron door at the end of the passageway, its lintel carved with an elaborate knotwork bestiary of winged sky-wyrms. 'I could choose to go to him in strength,' he said. 'But that would send the wrong message, so it will be just the two of us. You understand this?'

Gunnlaugur nodded. 'Perfectly.'

Njal raised a finger and the doors slid open. Beyond them stood the antechamber to *Heimdall*'s primary shuttle hangar. Servitors clattered to and fro across a rockcrete deck. Through armourglass viewports Gunnlaugur could see into the cavernous shuttle-bay beyond, where a fleet lifter in slate-grey stood on the apron, surrounded by refuelling cables, its thrusters venting.

'We don't have much time,' Njal said. 'Let us make this as quick as we can.'

Gunnlaugur followed him, reaching for his own helm as the blast-doors ahead started to grind open.

'No argument from me,' he said.

Vindicatus was an immense vessel, only surpassed in void-displacement by the line battleships of the Imperial Navy. Its hull was ancient, laid down as an Exorcist-pattern Grand Cruiser millennia ago. Perhaps it had originally been intended for use in Navy patrols, taking its place alongside the thousands of war-vessels in the standing Imperial fleet. At some point, though, it had shifted purpose and found its way into the service of the Ecclesiarchy, who had taken it and changed it.

Its exterior armour was covered in gold, from the jutting prow to the ranks of slab-sided weapon housings along the flanks. A mighty skull-device, a hundred metres across, had been carved into the hull, grinning out into the void and lit with a circlet of blood-red flood-lumens. The whole vessel hung in the well of space like a gaudy, opulent altarpiece, glinting from the light of Ras Shakeh's vigorous star.

Gunnlaugur peered out of the shuttle's viewports on the way over, watching the baroque flanks slide closer, wondering just how much blood and treasure had been squandered to give the cruiser its skin.

The interior of the cruiser was no less extravagant. The two Wolves were greeted by an honour guard of Battle Sisters, led tersely by the half-bionic Sister Nuriyah. They passed through halls of polished mirrors and crystalflex domes, all filled with devotional items encased in golden reliquaries and guarded by white-masked gun-drones. Heavy fabric drapes hung from ceilings fifty metres up, dusted by the meandering flights of incense-cherubim. The air was thick with cloying fragrance. Unlike on *Heimdall*, there were no mortal voices raised in laughter or cursing. The entire interior echoed to the low drone of endless chanting, piped through vox-emitters hung from gothic arches like battle-trophies.

Delvaux received them in his private audience chamber, which was large enough to house an entire Guard company. He wore thick crimson robes lined with ermine, and his pudgy fingers were studded with jewelled rings. A lone column of gold-tinged light shone down on him from a lumen-cluster directly above his throne; otherwise the room was heavy with darkness. On either side of the dais stood two huge Penitent Engines, their motors idling and their smokestacks fouling the drapes around them. Stranger creatures flitted around in the gloom – servo-skulls dragging litanies of duty with them, cowled priests muttering benedictions and supplications, penitents shuffling on bleeding knees amid the velvety splendour.

'My lord Rune Priest,' said the Cardinal, lounging casually.

'Lord Cardinal,' replied Njal.

'So there is a hulk. The *Festerax*. You think it possible to destroy it.'

'That is so.'

'You are mistaken.' Delvaux shifted slightly on his cushions, lifting a thick arm and hitching up the sleeve. 'We analysed the data you sent, and that hulk cannot be destroyed, not by the power we have here.'

'Not by our ships,' agreed Njal. 'But I command thirty-seven warriors. Get us close enough, and we can disable it from the inside. Its skin is thick, but its heart is rotten.'

'Very bold,' said Delvaux. 'But there is a thin line between boldness and delusion. There is a better way.'

Gunnlaugur studied the surroundings silently as the two conversed. The chamber was soaked in hostility, as if the sanctified stones themselves protested over the boots that trod on them.

'We know what they are doing,' Delvaux went on. 'They infect worlds with mass spore landings, causing waves of contagion that turn defenders into plague-bearers. On a hive world, that canker will spread even faster than it did here. If a hulk that size releases its spores, there will soon be nothing left to fight over. Better to starve the beast.' He placed his hands together on his lap, pressing the fingers together as if in contemplation.

'This vessel is equipped with nucleonic torpedoes. We can overtake the *Festerax* and wreath Kefa Primaris in holy fire. The sacrifice will buy us time, and deprive the damned of the prize they seek.'

Njal said nothing for a moment, taken aback. When he next spoke, it sounded as if he were struggling to process the suggestion. 'You're serious?'

'Very,' said Delvaux. 'They are here for recruits. Once the contagion latches onto Kefa Primaris, they will add billions to their army. We can prevent that.'

'The planet can be saved,' insisted Njal. 'We can destroy the hulk before it makes orbit.'

'And if you fail?'

'It will be done.'

'Well, yes. So you say. But you would, wouldn't you?'

In the face of such studious sarcasm, Njal remained implacable. 'What you propose is forbidden. Only the Inquisition may launch Exterminatus, and even they wouldn't try it with us around.'

Delvaux smiled tolerantly. 'Give it a different name, if that makes you feel better. *Quarantine*, perhaps.' His expression became serious. 'My lord, you have seen what is at stake here. Ras Shakeh is one thing – a world we cherish, but home to fewer than a million souls. A core planet is another. It must not be allowed to be claimed.'

'Billions will die,' said Njal, softly. 'All able to take up arms. All healthy.' His eyes held the Cardinal's. 'I will not allow it.'

The Cardinal's face did not flicker. 'This is not a question of *allow*. We are discussing options. Or did you come to my ship to give me orders?'

'All we need is the firepower to get us in,' said Njal. 'The hulk will be shielded. This ship, working with mine, can crack those shields, just for an instant. We can do the rest. That is all I ask.'

Delvaux smiled coldly. 'I never thought I would live to see it – the Wolves of Fenris asking for help. That is what you are doing, is it not? Tell me, just so I am sure.'

Gunnlaugur tensed, feeling Njal's frustration emanating like kill-pheromone from his armour. When the Rune Priest replied, his voice was like a rusty axe-edge being dragged across stone.

'I am asking for your help.'

Delvaux left the words hanging, enjoying them. 'Well, then,' he murmured. 'We must accommodate what we can. Here is my proposal. We will intercept the hulk together, just as you suggest. Our weapons will be used with yours to break the shields, and we will get you on board the vessel.' He spoke casually, as if setting out the orders of promotion in a Cathedral. 'But the price for my agreement is this. My ship will overtake the *Festerax* once Kefa Primaris comes into strike-range. If the hulk reaches orbit, even if on the edge of destruction, I shall launch my quarantine. I will give you all the time necessary, but no more. This is the condition of my assistance.'

Having said his piece, Delvaux placed his hands back on the armrests of his throne. His face took on a satisfied, almost beatific glow.

Njal waited a long time before replying. 'I have your word?' he asked eventually. 'No deployment of your payload before the hulk reaches orbit.'

'If it makes you feel better, yes, you have my word,' said Delvaux, amused. 'Saints, I am a cardinal of the Emperor's Holy Ministorum. I will swear on the relics of the saints in our keeping, if that will seal things for you.'

'Your word is enough,' said Njal, weighing the words deliberately. 'On Fenris, the oathbreaker is lower than a beast. He is hunted unto the ends of the world.'

'How charming.' Delvaux leaned back. 'Then we have an agreement. Time is pressing, if your augur-scans are to be trusted. My ships will be ready to break for warp within the hour. Yours?'

'*Heimdall* is prepared. My warriors on the surface are being recalled.'

'Good,' said Delvaux. 'I will leave a garrison from the Fiery Tear on Hjec Aleja. They can carry out the work of restoration in our absence.'

'What of the canoness?' asked Gunnlaugur.

Delvaux turned to him, surprised that he had spoken. 'The canoness comes under my jurisdiction, Wolf Guard. Her part in this does not concern you.'

'She fought with me,' said Gunnlaugur. 'She wished to form part of the crusade. I would welcome fighting alongside her again – she was a fine warrior.'

'You thought so?' Another wintry smile flickered across Delvaux's lips. 'But see, we have a rigid code in the Ecclesiarchy. De Chatelaine knew it, just as all the Sisters in my service know it. There are prices to be paid for failure, and her leadership was found wanting on Ras Shakeh. I have made arrangements. The Order of the Wounded Heart will be folded into the Order of the Fiery Tear. The rites can be completed once we are in the warp. A change of leadership will do this world good. A new governor will be found, one more amenable to taking the hard decisions necessary in a fallen galaxy.'

The hairs on the back of Gunnlaugur's neck rose. 'Then the canoness is on this ship?'

'She is.'

'I would speak with her,' he said. Then, from grudging lips, 'If you allowed it.'

Delvaux spread his hands magnanimously. 'Of course. You may speak to her whenever you like. Though whether she will able to reply to your satisfaction is another question.'

He clapped his hands together. One of the Penitent Engines behind the throne hissed, sending gouts of steam from its reverse-jointed legs, then lurched into the pool of light. Its massive feet clanged on the marble floor, and it towered over the two Wolves at the centre of the lumen-beam.

Gunnlaugur looked up to see a woman's body suspended amid the gears and electro-shackles. Her head was covered with a white cloth, obscuring her features. Two muscled arms had been clamped wide, locked into the mechanisms of the Engine's giant weapon-limbs. The rest of her body was half lost in a tangle of implants and cables, the tendrils swaddling more bloodstained robes. From under the cloth drape, the soundless howl of a permanent scream could be made out, imprinted on the fabric.

Gunnlaugur's hand swept to his hammer. He unlocked it in a single movement, activating the crackle of the energy field.

'You *dare*...' he began.

He didn't get anything else out. His limbs locked, his jaw froze. He stood, half poised to strike, raging against inertia.

Only then did he realise the situation. Njal had lifted his staff, pulling him back, enclosing him in a vice of power.

Delvaux looked on, unsettled and unamused. 'This is my place, Space Wolf. Raise a weapon in here again and I will end you.'

Gunnlaugur felt his muscles straining against Njal's bonds, and a ball of agonised frustration rose up in his gorge.

+Stand down,+ came the Rune Priest's voice in his mind. +Strike him, and I will slay you myself.+

The vice lifted. Gunnlaugur staggered, catching himself before falling. The Penitent Engine stood over him, its infernal machinery ticking over. He looked up at it, his thunder hammer growling. If de Chatelaine retained anything of her self, she was not capable of responding to him any longer.

Gunnlaugur swept a heavy-lidded gaze up towards Delvaux, keeping his hammer raised. He took no step towards him, made no threatening move, but the Cardinal still blenched.

'Deactivate your weapon,' Delvaux said, a little quickly, his voice rising.

Slowly, deliberately, Gunnlaugur clicked the energy field off. Then he withdrew, keeping his black-pinned eyes fixed on the Cardinal the whole time. Delvaux shifted agitatedly in his seat.

'Is this what we can expect from your warriors, my lord Rune Priest?' Delvaux asked, rearranging his robes in a pretence at nonchalance.

'It is,' said Njal, his voice stony. 'That is why I remain proud to be one.' The Rune Priest looked up at the Penitent Engine, sharing Gunnlaugur's disgust. 'We have said all we came to. I will send word when we are ready to make for the veil.'

'I shall wait with eagerness.'

Without saying more, Njal turned on his heel and stalked down the chamber's central aisle. Gunnlaugur relocked his thunder hammer, never releasing Delvaux from his stare as he did so, before doing likewise. The two Wolves strode down the length of the audience chamber, their footfalls echoing.

'He is mad,' voxed Gunnlaugur as they cleared the threshold.

'Not mad,' replied Njal, sweeping through the glistening finery.

'She did not deserve–'

Njal whirled on him, grabbing him by the throat. Even for one of the Rout, the movement was incredibly quick. '*Never* lose control like that again,' he hissed. 'Did *nothing* I said register in your mind?'

Gunnlaugur clenched his fists instinctively, shocked by the sudden move. 'I recognise my failing,' he said.

Njal released him, but remained furious. 'Let him run rampant,' he voxed, 'and he will do to whole sectors what he has done here. We must tie him to *our* will.'

Gunnlaugur nodded, humbled. 'I see it.'

'She did not deserve it,' Njal said, his voice quieter. 'None do, who end up in those things, but put your wrath aside. There will be targets for it soon enough.'

'But when this is over–' Gunnlaugur began.

'Hel, when this is *over*,' said Njal, starting to walk again, his staff-heel striking the floor harder than it had done, 'I will hand you the hammer myself. Until then, keep it locked.'

Gunnlaugur bowed. The stink of the incense felt even more repugnant in his nostrils, and the chanting even more offensive. As he walked, he couldn't get the image of de Chatelaine's agonised face out of his mind. His hearts felt sick.

She did not deserve it.

That she didn't. For the time being, though, Gunnlaugur swallowed his fury, kept his fists closed, and followed his master back to the shuttle-bays.

Once the order was given, things moved quickly. Those wolf-packs still on the surface were brought back to *Heimdall* by a succession of lifters and gunships. Ingvar had already made contact, passing on the news of the recovered units of kaerls, and a series of shuttles was sent down under Álfar's supervision. It took some persuasion before Bjargborn's troops were accepted – all were aware of the possibility of contagion, a lesson that had been learned the hard way at Hjec Aleja. In the end, quarantine chambers were isolated on *Heimdall* and medicae-sealed shuttles were allowed to head off-world with them. They were Sons of Fenris, and had fought for too long to be abandoned.

Ingvar came up with them. As the planet's rust-orange landscape fell away in a hail of dust, the sky intensified into a deep blue, and the desert dropped down into the haze of distance. As the shuttle rose higher and the colours bled away to darkness, the trails of other voidcraft scored the starfield. Most bore the red livery of the Ecclesiarchy, some with the Fiery Tear on their hulls, others with the skull device of Delvaux's diocesan command. Ingvar watched a cluster of vapour-lines arcing out from the deep wasteland, and remembered what the kaerls had told him of black-robed officials moving out from temple to temple.

Then the shuttle rolled over, angling for the docking run. The slate-dagger profile of *Heimdall* swooped closer. The Wolves' ship was far smaller than the majestic *Vindicatus*. Its towers were close-clustered, its lone forward lance nestled sharply amid jowls of ice-white armour-plate. Though nominally Gladius-pattern, *Heimdall* was substantially larger than most ships of that class, and had an old and proud pedigree. It was fast, and tough, and brutally aggressive, just as it should be for the transport of the Stormcaller.

Once docked, the kaerls were greeted by armed medicae teams in environment suits and led away to their observation cells. Ingvar headed down to his assigned quarters, pulling his helm off and freeing his ash-blond hair, rubbing the last of the oil from it as he went.

The whole ship was in the throes of pre-launch activity. Kaerls ran down the corridors, seemingly chasing the klaxons that burst into life at every intersection. Bulkheads were pulled closed, hatches hammered down. Sub-warp engines were keyed up, sending growls juddering from the lower levels. Battle-brothers of the Rout passed him on the way to their own musters and he saluted them, clasping his fist to his chest.

He reached his destination, and pulled open a heavy blast-door. The rest of them were waiting for him, standing in a loose circle in the chamber beyond. Jorundur somehow looked hunched even in his bat-tleplate. His hollow eyes lifted as Ingvar entered. Haflói acknowledged awkwardly; Olgeir was effusive.

'We send Gyrfalkon to the desert and he returns with kaerls,' the big warrior said, chuckling. 'Give him longer, and he'd find Russ.'

Ingvar smiled. 'Good void-hunting, Heavy-hand?'

Olgeir shrugged nonchalantly. 'It proved useful.'

Ingvar turned to Gunnlaugur and bowed in acknowledgement. 'Vaerangi,' he said.

'Gyrfalkon,' said the Wolf Guard, looking amused. 'Last back, as ever.'

'Wouldn't want to disappoint.'

It was then that Baldr moved into the light of the lumen. He looked drawn, his armour bulky around a thinned-out body. His eyes still had deep black rings under them, and his lips were grey. For all that, he moved much as he used to – compact, economical. His face had lost some of the tightness it had carried on the last warp jump. If anything, he looked… healthier.

Ingvar regarded him warmly. 'So you can hold an axe again, brother?'

'Pretty well,' said Baldr.

'And Njal pulled your mind apart?'

'Feels like it.'

Gunnlaugur looked at them all, one by one. 'Reunited.' He bared his fangs in a savage smile. 'As it should be.'

The smile was infectious. From that point the savagery would only grow, building up over the short warp-stage as they trained and sparred and drove themselves into the full pitch of combat readiness.

'Our course is set, our prey is marked,' Gunnlaugur went on, setting up for the briefing to come. 'Now. Here's what he wants us to do.'

Two hours after the pack's war-council, with *Heimdall* running deep in the warp, Ingvar and Gunnlaugur met on their own in a chamber down in the darkened lower decks. Gunnlaugur stalked over to the dormant fire-pit at the centre of the chamber and poked at the coals. Ingvar hauled the hatch closed behind them and sealed it.

'What did you find?' asked Gunnlaugur, getting a weak flame to shiver over the embers.

'They were active on the surface,' Ingvar said. 'At least three teams, all led by the Cardinal's man, Klaive.'

'Active. What does that mean?'

'They went ahead of the main purge-squads, striking into enemy territory before it was cleansed. They were hunting for something – targeting the temples, then moving on.'

Gunnlaugur grunted. 'And you think?'

'Datacores, just like the ones in the Cathedral.'

'You didn't find any?'

'They worked fast.'

Gunnlaugur kicked his boot through the coals again, raking up a guttering tremor of fire. 'I'd like to rip their *throats* out,' he snarled. 'I'd like to gut them all, one by one, and hang the corpses from their own spires. De Chatelaine's been put in to an Engine. You know that? If he can do that, he can do anything, and he *wants* to burn that planet. I could see the look in his eyes. Give him a cause, and–' He took a deep breath. 'Njal isn't stupid. The Cardinal's word means nothing. He wants to send Olgeir ahead of the battle-group, to the planet, just in case. There's a system-runner docked in *Heimdall*'s berths. There's no time to evacuate the entire world, but the Guard regiments at least must be saved.'

Ingvar looked doubtful. 'I'd rather have *sigrún* with us on the hulk.'

'As would I, but the ruling's been made. I'll speak to Heavy-hand – he'll understand.'

Ingvar thought for a moment. 'We could use this,' he said. 'Klaive remains on the cruiser. He is the one we seek.'

'Brother, you told me I did not need to worry...'

'And you do not. We will follow our orders, but if the oath is broken...' Ingvar held Gunnlaugur's gaze steadily. 'Then we take Klaive.'

Gunnlaugur resumed pacing, prowling the narrow chamber like a caged animal. 'Njal already watches us. He watches Baldr. If we slip the leash, he'll have our eyes. We need good kills, brother. We should have done better at Hjec Aleja.'

'We did what we could.'

'It wasn't *enough*.' Gunnlaugur stared moodily at the embers, grinding his fangs as his mind worked. 'I'd have welcomed fighting with her again. Skítja, these allies are poorer.'

Ingvar couldn't disagree. 'We'll be rid of them soon enough. I feel the old rages – they're coming back. We have Njal with us now, a whole hunting-pack at our shoulder.' He grinned. 'What is better? What more is there?'

Gunnlaugur nodded. Ingvar's enthusiasm was infectious.

'Nothing, brother,' he said, thinking ahead to the slaughter and feeling acid saliva quicken in his mouth. 'There is *nothing* better.'

11. THE MYCELITE

Chapter Eleven

Four hours before *Heimdall* broke the veil, the Wolves gathered in the ship's main assembly hall. Ancient war-banners of the Chapter hung from the distant ceiling, each one charred at the edges. Columns of alabaster and granite soared up into the smoky heights, banded with iron and studded with red-tinged lumen-beads.

Njal stood on a stone platform at the far end, flanked by the two Wolf Guards Álfar and Gunnlaugur. A fire burned behind them, mounted on a granite altar and sending a column of thick soot twisting up at his back. The symbol of the Priesthood – a wolf-skull against an angular lightning bolt – had been graven into the far wall and lined with bronze.

The rest of the warriors, Járnhamar included, stood facing the platform. The fighting force was divided into four packs, all Grey Hunters. Only Járnhamar had the distinction of fighting with a Wolf Guard at the helm; the other three pack leaders – Fellblade, Long-axe and Bloodhame – carried the same silver-and-black pauldron devices of their brothers.

'So we come to it,' announced Njal, his harsh voice ringing through the hall. 'All of you know void-work. All of you know your craft.'

As he spoke, a glowing representation of the plague-hulk, drawn from the Chapter datacores, spun into existence in front of the watching warriors. The profile was ugly and bulbous. Long, jagged stalactites of fused metal hung underneath it, jutting beneath scarred carapace edges and tangling as they speared into the void. The semi-intact hulls of a hundred space-vessels protruded from its back, rusted and deformed as they were slowly interred within the heart of the corrupted giant.

'We know the spoor of this from the records of those who fought it before,' said Njal. 'Maleficarum has birthed taint in the hulk's innards. It will treat us like a wound treats infection. We will be its disease.'

The glittering hololith zoomed in.

'The skin of the hulk will endure our ships' weapons, and it has void shields. The best we can hope for is a narrow strike, taking out enough to send boarding torpedoes into the underbelly. From there our only path is to destroy the furnace at its centre. The hulk's atmosphere is methane rich, stinking like an auroch's gut-line. We will set off charges in the enginarium core and the blast will eviscerate the entire vessel. It will test us, but it can be done.'

The assembled warriors took in the schematics quickly, scanning the lithcast, orientating themselves and committing the profile to memory.

'Getting out will be fun,' grunted one of them – a scarred, bionic-eyed veteran from Bloodhame's pack called Aesgrek.

'We will have to kill fast,' agreed Njal. 'We won't have long.'

Some of the others snarled under their breath. The danger of it appealed – if any of them got out again, it would be worth a saga back at the Aett.

'Who is on the ship?' asked Fellblade. 'We know that?'

'We have names,' said Njal. 'There will be mutants in their thousands. Remember, though, it is not a battleship – it is a weapon, a vessel for the plague-spores in its belly. That is its only task – to disperse them into the atmosphere.'

'So it'll have fleet escorts,' said Hauki.

'It will. *Heimdall* and *Vindicatus* will keep them busy. We have three Thunderhawk gunships also, but we will need every ranged gun for the hull-breach.'

Gunnlaugur stole a glance at Jorundur, and caught the Old Dog's satisfied expression. He'd be in command of *Vuokho* again, out on his own, just how he liked it.

'We keep together when we are inside,' said Njal. 'We keep moving. This is about *speed* – if we get slowed down inside then we will never get out.' The Rune Priest stared at the hololith, his expression eager. 'This is the filth we were bred to cleanse. Sharpen your blades. Ready your claws.

No greater prize for us exists in this war.'

He bared his fangs in a challenge-gesture, and glared at them all.

'But it is *ours* now. We have marked it. Its fate is fixed.'

Two hours before *Heimdall* broke the veil, the six members of Járnhamar assembled on the deck of one of the ship's five hangar bays. A sleek system-runner stood on the rockcrete. It was less than ninety metres long, with a crew complement of just a few dozen mortals. A hawk-sharp prow jutted towards the distant external doors, dwarfed by the collection of oversized drives clustering along its ventral hull-edges. Njal's device had been painted on its nearside flank, just under the icon of the Chapter. Steam vented from a dozen thruster-housings as the last checks were made on the sub-warp drives. A few loader-bay hatches were still open, swarming with masked menials and loader-gurneys.

'How is it named?' asked Gunnlaugur, looking at it doubtfully.

'*Hlaupnir*,' said Olgeir, casting his own expert eye along the ship's length. 'Njal says it's fast.'

'I can believe it,' said Jorundur, nodding in appreciation. 'They laid these down on Ryza. Not a touch of Mars on them. You don't see many.'

'You will miss the hunt,' said Ingvar to Olgeir.

Olgeir shrugged. 'Njal gives the orders.'

'You won't have long enough,' muttered Hafloí. 'What does he expect you to do?'

'What I can,' said Olgeir. As he spoke, the loaders began to trundle away from *Hlaupnir*'s undercarriage. 'I don't mind it. If this goes to skítna, I'd rather die among mortals than those fanatics.'

Jorundur grunted in agreement.

The last of the fuel-cables clunked empty and detached from the runner's hull, carried away reverently by tech-servitors. The kaerl crew members clambered up the open ramps and into their stations. Warning horns began to blare, and the hangar cleared of support staff.

'Go with Russ, brother,' said Baldr to Olgeir. His voice was stronger than it had been.

'And you,' said Olgeir, cautiously. 'You'll remember how it feels, once the axe whirls again.'

Then he saluted the rest of the pack, turned on his heels and strode towards the ship. As he neared the ramp he started to call out orders. Between now and the entry into the Kefa Primaris system there was still much to do to get it ready for its mission.

Gunnlaugur looked at the others. 'This is it, then,' he said.

They turned and marched away from the apron and towards the corridor that would take them down to *Heimdall*'s torpedo chambers. As they reached the blast-doors, Jorundur peeled off towards *Vuokho*'s berth.

'Keep the pack-vox open, brother,' called Gunnlaugur after him. 'Stay close to the hulk.'

Jorundur rolled his eyes. 'Where else am I going to be?'

'You have Callia's device? The one I gave you?'

'You need it, I'll find it.'

Then Jorundur was gone, stomping down the narrow corridors towards the Thunderhawk hangars. That left the four of them – Baldr, Ingvar, Haflói and Gunnlaugur.

The lumens in the corridors switched to red combat lighting. The drum of running boots and slamming bulkheads swelled up through the ship's innards. Far above them, the cruiser's weaponry was being rolled out and powered up.

'I want us at the *forefront*,' insisted Gunnlaugur, his gait now rolling, assuming the belligerent swagger that the kill-urge kindled. 'I want the axes of Járnhamar at the edge. This is *our* war.'

The others matched his pace and mien. Each of them was primed now. Their bodies were restored, their minds refreshed, their spirits keen. Ingvar drew his blade, looking down the length of it and seeing how the red light caught the edge of the runes.

It thirsted again, just as he did.

With a burst of ionised energy, the veil broke. *Heimdall* was first through, tearing into real space through an expanding corona of torn aether-energies. Its sub-warp drives exploded into life a second later, ricocheting it into the icy vacuum as if hurled from a slingshot.

Vindicatus crashed through a second later. Its impact wave was far bigger – a violent splash-pattern of torn reality, resolving almost instantly into the fire-wreathed profile of a jagged Grand Cruiser of the Ecclesiarchy. Its real space drives thundered into life, throbbing crimson like burst veins. As it surged forwards, its turrets and spires left streamers of flickering luminescence behind them, guttering away as the wound in the universe snapped closed.

The inky starfield of the Kefa Primaris system sprawled away from them. The planet itself was still out of visual range, only barely detectable on the high-gain forward augurs.

Both ships had speared into reality with precision. Dead ahead, already visible through the armourglass real-view blisters, burned the *Festerax*.

Its bulk was staggering – a vast, fist-shaped tumour of dark metal, underpinned with knife-sharp stalactites and crowned with ridges of the ship-hulls that had been drawn into its necrotic embrace. Its bulk blotted out the stars beyond, casting a shroud of ruin across the void. It was surrounded by its own petty fleet of lesser craft – gunships and assault boats, shepherded by two Infidel-pattern raiders.

Both Imperial vessels powered up to intercept speed. *Heimdall* was faster, and pulled away from its counterpart in a blaze of neon-white thrusters. Before its void shields snapped fully into place, it disgorged four craft from its launch bays. The first, *Hlaupnir*, broke away immediately, spiralling down out of the battle-plane and igniting its engines to full burn. It was soon powering clear, locked on to the coordinates for the planet far ahead. A few of the enemy escorts started in pursuit, but as soon as it became clear it was heading away from the combat-sphere they pulled back.

That left the Thunderhawks – *Vuokho*, *Kjarlskar* and *Grimund*. They stayed in close formation with *Heimdall*, powering alongside it but not straying far from the cover of its mighty gun-ranks.

By then *Vindicatus* was catching up. It released its own squadrons of escorts – Fury-class interceptors in the blood-red livery of the Ecclesiarchy. They spun out of the launch bays and streaked towards the enemy escort-cordon, outpacing the Thunderhawks and pulling into the vanguard. Twenty-four of them dropped into formation, arranged in six squadrons of four.

The Infidel raiders were the biggest threat – savage assault vessels with serrated jawline prows, macrocannon batteries and prow-mounted torpedo launchers. Both took up position over the hulk's anterior zone and opened up with a flickering barrage of shells. The Furies evaded the worst of it, ducking under the fire-lanes and angling upwards at the more lumbering enemy assault craft. Tracer-lights sparked silently into the void, creating a sphere of crackling energy around the hulk's retreating profile.

The vast plague-ship itself did not pick up speed. It maintained course, barrelling through space with a fearsome, implacable momentum, unconcerned by the gnat-like movements of the lesser ships in its wake. Its array of engines glowed dully under the segmented layers of outer hull, flecked with angry snarls of plasma-discharge.

Still out of range of the hulk's massive broadsides, the Imperial flotilla closed in on the escort ships. Once within gun-range, *Vindicatus* stood off, rolling starboard to present its twin-ranked rows of broadside cannons. The Fury squadrons, acting as part of the prearranged plan, pushed clear of the front wave of enemy assault craft and dropped low to the battle-sphere's nadir.

The Cruiser's guns opened up, and a blinding flash of light ripped across the void. Enemy escorts caught in the withering assault exploded in sequence, their shields overloaded and their engines detonated.

Even before the corpses of the destroyed had spiralled out of contact, *Heimdall* hove into view, sweeping down from its vantage above *Vindicatus*'s fire position. It loosed torpedoes, each one already primed for the enemy raider coordinates. They tore off towards the targets – six trails of flame, three for each target.

The enemy flotilla, still forming up, raced to fend off the barrage. One of the Raiders was caught amidships by *Heimdall*'s torpedoes and fell out of the defensive pattern, venting heavily. The other one was saved by a suicidal squadron of enemy craft, interposing themselves in a scatter of tight explosions. Three assault craft were destroyed outright, winnowing their numbers down further.

By then the Furies and Thunderhawks had re-engaged, swooping up through the broadside-cleared approaches and opening fire. The three Wolves gunships barrelled up the centre of the engagement, letting loose with battle-cannons and linked lascannons. The Furies angled and twisted in their wake, adding thickets of las-fire to the intense bursts spearing out from the gunships.

The combination was intensely destructive. An entire wing of enemy fighters was immolated, caught in a bow-wave of combined fire. A dozen survivors pulled clear of the engagement, heading for the doubtful cover of the lone Infidel.

By then, the engagement-zone had drifted into range of the hulk itself. As the distance narrowed, the true scale of the monster became apparent. It soared away into the endless void-night like a cliff-face, gouged, scarred and ancient. Its sheer flanks dwarfed even *Vindicatus*, casting a heavy shadow across the Grand Cruiser as it passed between it and Kefa Primaris's sun. The crushed outlines of impacted starships, each one a colossal void-goer in its own right, twisted and jutted across a landscape of ruined immensity.

With a shudder, the plague-ship loosed a volley of ship-killing energies. The barrage was as misshapen as the vessel was – a combination of las-arcs, cannon-shells, torpedo trails and plasma bolts. Some gun-trails came from the dozens of wrecks accreted to the hull, others from deep within the corrupted structure itself, launched from forges and fire-halls lodged in the beast's unfathomably ancient core.

The impact was punishing. *Vindicatus* strayed too close, and took a scything run of lascannon beams along its golden flanks. Its void shields flexed and crackled, stressed to near-breaking by the collisions. Several Furies were caught up in a wave of solid-round fire and exploded into clouds of fast-moving shrapnel.

Emboldened by the carnage, the remaining Infidel escort spearheaded a counter-offensive, burning in hard at the exposed Imperial craft and sending a wave of fighters ahead of it.

By then, though, *Vindicatus* was able to launch its second broadside. Despite the damage sustained by the hulk's attack, the rejoinder was even more ferocious than the first. The battle-sphere blazed white again as every cannon on *Vindicatus*'s nearside flank opened up. A wave of solid, dense destruction flew out at the approaching assault craft. The Infidel was caught up in the radius – it held out for a few seconds, firing all the while, before its shields overloaded and it blew apart.

The Thunderhawks and remaining Furies closed in on what remained, taking out the ragged wings of enemy assault craft. The void clogged with glowing scraps of metal as the wreckage swirled out from the kill-zones, bouncing from speeding hulls amid the criss-cross of lascannon beams.

Amid all of it, *Heimdall* drew in closer to the *Festerax* itself, braving the ferocious torrent of incoming fire to position itself under the hull's shadow. The plague-hulk's trailing underside stalactites hung close, glinting in the flashes of las-fire, each one as immense and crustaceous as a hive spire.

Green-edged beams arced out at *Heimdall*, striking it across its snarl-prow and knocking it out of line. Torpedo trails curled out and sped towards it, but *Heimdall* remained in position, firing back from all points along its facing flank. Soon the reason for its positioning became clear – a dozen Caestus assault rams blazed out from the outward-facing hull-edge and swept round under *Heimdall*'s keel. The Wolves cruiser pulled away immediately, firing hard to cover the attack run of the boarding craft.

The assault rams' boosters ignited in unison, sending them hurtling, arrow-straight, towards the looming edge of the *Festerax*. One was taken out by a snarled lattice of incoming fire, another slammed off-course by a torpedo hit, but the remaining ten made it into range and loosed missiles against the hulk's tangle of outer plating.

At the same time, the retreating *Heimdall* and *Vindicatus* loosed a coordinated barrage from all available weaponry. The move had been prearranged – thick columns of coruscation lanced in at the same point, just under the curve of the *Festerax*'s hull where the underhanging spires jutted. Every cannon on the two ships, every remaining torpedo tube and plasma launcher, every las-barrage and missile station, was aimed at the same zone. The repeated volleys smashed against the hulk's void-coverage, cracking against it with a scream of nova-hot energies.

Just as the first of the assault rams neared the designated impact zone, *Heimdall* finally loosed its main bombardment cannon, and *Vindicatus* followed suit with its ventral lances. The Grand Cruiser's gunners found their range, and the combined maelstrom slammed in amid a hurricane of blazing, spitting energies.

Under such an immense hammerblow of mingled fire, the plague-hulk's void shields guttered out in a blaze of static, exposing a narrow section of mottled hull beneath. Just as the barrier ripped away, the assault rams scythed clear through the rent's flame-edged maw, plunging into the heart of the newly carved rent. It was a tiny gap in the void-umbrella, but just enough.

As they screamed towards the *Festerax*'s flanks, the assault rams loosed their fore-mounted melta weapons. Glittering wreaths of vivid orange fire shot out, slamming directly into the fast-closing hull. The impact was crushing, driving in thick layers of adamantium plating, burning through it and dissolving the struts beyond.

Then the assault rams hit, one after the other in a ragged line of head-on collisions. A rip, hundreds of metres wide, was cut into the flank of the *Festerax* as the reinforced prows of the rams plunged deep into its hide. Secondary explosions went off, rippling along the plating as the rams burrowed in further.

By then, though, the volume of return fire had become apocalyptic. The *Festerax* opened up with a vast array of arcane weaponry, vomiting las-spears, spiked incendiary shells and sensor-disrupting clouds of green-blooming gases. *Heimdall* took a series of heavy impacts as it tried to roll clear, tearing up its ventral plating and forcing it to disengage. *Vindicatus*, which had remained further out during the combined assault, endured a similar battering, and lost a whole ridge of gun-towers when the shielding above them overloaded.

The *Festerax* seemed to have an infinite number of guns, and unleashed them all. With its escorts burning or fleeing, it was free to open up with everything left in its offensive arsenal. The void around it shimmered with the rolling barrage, and both Imperial ships were bludgeoned further out of range. The remaining gunships and interceptors hared for cover, aiming to dock with the larger craft before being overcome by the tidal wave of destruction.

Heimdall and *Vindicatus* finally pulled clear, ravaged and broken. They gained position just beyond the edge of the hulk's main range, absorbing a reduced level of punishment just to remain in contact. *Heimdall*, having run closest, was in the worst shape, and it was all it could do to maintain position. *Vindicatus* was able to launch a few retaliatory strikes, but did little more than pepper the *Festerax*'s immense profile with glancing hits.

Contemptuous of such threats, the plague-hulk maintained trajectory towards Kefa Primaris, its escorts destroyed but its integrity almost perfectly intact. The contagion-spores still survived, locked in the launchers deep in its core. Its weaponry remained potent, and the only real damage done to it was restricted to a tiny pocket on the immense tracts of its lower hull, the product of all the Imperial forces' combined might in arms.

It was a minor wound, no more than an insect bite in the hide of a sauroid. Within that wound, though, bodies stirred, blades were drawn and oaths were sworn.

Deep in the darkness, the Wolves were already moving.

Chapter Twelve

The impact of the assault ram hitting was all-consuming – a tearing, burning, juddering collision that threw its occupants hard in their pistoned restraint mechanisms. Ingvar's mind immediately shot back to the assault on the plague-destroyer over Ras Shakeh. The hit was greater this time, though – the hulk's outer hull-plate was far older, and far thicker.

The rams drove and ground their way far inside, crunching onwards through walls of solid metal as the melta-tipped prow burned. Ingvar gripped on just like the others, thrown around by the immense shocks striking the ram's exterior.

The speed, the roar of the engines, the tortured scream of shearing adamantium – it made him want to *roar*. Even as the thunder-rain of jolts juddered down the shock absorber columns, he found himself straining at his bonds, desperate for the crew bay doors to slam open.

Baldr was shackled ahead of him, swaying jerkily.

'Ready for this, brother?' Ingvar voxed over the crashing echoes.

Baldr laughed eagerly. *'Craving* it.'

Every time Baldr spoke, he was more like the old warrior he'd been. The dryness, the cracking, was going.

The assault ram's momentum finally slowed. The shrieks and cracks fell away, replaced by a howl of escaping air and a thunder of flame.

They had lodged deep, wedged at an acute angle. Bolts and brace-rods slid back from Ingvar's armour, freeing him up to move again. With a wrench of tortured ironwork, the doors at the front end of the assault ram crashed down. A caldera-hot wave rushed over them, flecked with spinning motes of ash and rust, followed immediately by the echoing roar of racing atmosphere.

Gunnlaugur was first out, shouldering through a tangle of twisted support struts. Baldr followed him, then the rest, spilling from the melta-hazed prow of the assault ram and levelling bolters.

A ruined chamber stretched away from them, partially lit by flickering green lumens. It was ink-dark and stinking. The assault ram had demolished the inner wall it had come through and was now wedged amid a heap of smouldering wreckage. Fire still ran across its back, catching on the white-hot edges of seared metalwork.

Gunnlaugur took point, hefting *skulbrotsjór* and activating the hammer's energy field. Electric light spilled from it, picking out the gloomy surroundings. Baldr and Hafloí took up bolters, Ingvar his power sword. Four other warriors burst from the ram's second crew-berth, all marked with the insignia of Bloodhame's pack.

Ingvar activated his helm's proximity sensor. It was dotted with rune-locators from other ingress points. Some were just a few dozen metres away – a deck up, or across. Others had come in far out of position. He saw Njal's signal several levels up and fixed on it.

Gunnlaugur moved out. The pack fanned across the chamber behind him, keeping close on his heels, scanning as they went. Eight pairs of glowing red helm-lenses pierced the shadows.

The chamber ran for ten metres before terminating in a heavy-set wall of iron. Every surface was thick with glistening slime, pooled over rusting pressed-metal panels. It could have been in the hold of any Imperial vessel in the fleet, only given over to the ravages of corrosion in a way that no ship of the line would ever be. Blooms of rust spread everywhere, gnarled and pocked and glinting in the faint light of the Wolves' power weapons. The glare from their blades illuminated pools of oily water on the decking, rippled from the howling wind and streaked like blood-splatters.

From far below them came the dull rumble of weapons-fire. The hulk's ordnance was still active, sending recoil judders through the entire structure.

Gunnlaugur reached the door and pressed himself against it, listening.

Then he pulled the hammer round, smashed the bolt-lock, and pushed through the splintered gap.

The corridor beyond was narrow and clogged with filth. The Wolves jogged down it, heading for Njal's marker signal. As Ingvar moved, he caught glimpses of old Imperial iconography on the walls. They had broken into one of the old ships that made up the *Festerax*'s hull – it might have been a Navy frigate by the pattern of aquilae on the roof, though impossible to tell through all the grime and corrosion.

'Target,' reported one of Bloodhame's warriors.

Ingvar picked it up a fraction later – a cluster of runes on his helm-display, closing fast. He ran his tongue over his fangs.

'Here they come,' he breathed, almost to himself.

The eight of them broke into an iron-walled octagonal chamber lined with moisture-slick chains. Other corridors led off in the four cardinal directions, and a deep well-shaft ran down from the centre.

Gunnlaugur looked up. The chamber was roofless – the base of a larger shaft that seemed to run up for at least several decks. The chains swayed down from unseen heights, clanking together and dripping with liquid.

'We climb,' he said, seizing two chain-lengths and hauling upwards. The steel links took his weight, and he kicked off, climbing fast. Bracing against the walls, each warrior followed suit, grabbing a handful of chain-lengths and ascending quickly.

Just as they did so, a cluster of bodies broke into the chamber below – the first inhabitants of the hulk they'd seen. Ingvar was barely a few metres up when he saw them. They were full-helmed, mortal fighters, clad in rags and carrying drum-barrelled projectile weapons.

'Mine,' voxed Ingvar, letting go of the chains and plummeting back to the chamber floor.

He took two of them out as he landed, kicking out with his armoured boots and crushing them against the chamber wall. *Dausvjer* whipped around in a lashing arc, spraying blood across the grimy decking.

Something heavy crunched down next to him, and he whirled to face it.

It was Baldr. He opened fire, and a storm of bolt-rounds surged off into the darkness, punching into the press of bodies. Baldr then aimed up at the lintel and destroyed the metal housing, bringing the corridor ceiling down in a crash of heavy panels. There were a few high-pitched screams, then the debris settled, silencing the defenders and sealing the ingress point.

Ingvar grinned under his helm. Baldr fought just as he always had – calm, clean, effective. Ingvar leapt back up for the chains and started to climb, slamming his boots against the shaft's inner wall for purchase.

'So you *are* ready,' he voxed.

'Just the start, brother,' Baldr replied, following him up.

Jorundur brought *Vuokho* up and out of a potentially ruinous spiral, gunning the engines hard and boosting clear of danger. All around him, space was filled with the tumbling carcasses of destroyed assault craft, most of them bearing enemy insignia on their ripped-up hull plating. A few had survived the inferno and were harrying the bigger warships, so his hands remained full. Keeping alive during the initial assault had been the hardest task, but he wasn't out of the woods yet.

'Shut that down,' he snapped to his co-pilot, a female mortal from Njal's retinue named Morven. She was good – as good as any mortal – but it was irritating not to have fellow Sky Warriors handling the support functions of void-combat.

Morven nodded smartly, working to close the fuel-loop to the gunship's damaged spine section. They were still leaking promethium into the void – a perilous thing to be doing when half of the space around them seemed to consist of plasma explosions.

The two other crew, also mortals, worked furiously at their stations. Beor was a competent enough navigator and had kept them out of the most obviously suicidal points on the battle-sphere, and Terrag, the gunner, already had a brace of kills against his name.

'Incoming enemy, *fyf-un* vertical,' reported Beor.

Jorundur pushed the gunship harder into its climb, wondering how long it would be before *Heimdall*'s guns came back online. He caught sight of the incoming ships – two skinny-looking interceptors with missile-underslung wings, thrusting clear of the Fury squadrons and heading up after *Vuokho*.

'We can outrun them,' said Morven, still working hard to plug the leak.

'Of course we can,' snapped Jorundur, calculating angles. He punched a series of coordinates into the cogitator. 'Gunner, you can handle that?'

'Affirmative,' said Terrag, running his fingers over the firing mechanism.

The Thunderhawk abruptly lost momentum, falling back towards the approaching interceptors. Seeing that they were going to overshoot and stumble into *Vuokho*'s fire-angle, the interceptors spun away to starboard, using their agility to pull out of the attack.

As they did so, though, Jorundur kicked the drives back to full power and swung the gunship hard about, swinging neatly onto a parallel course and opening up a shot for the starboard heavy bolters.

Terrag performed ably, working both mounts at once and sending twin lines of armour-shredding shells lancing out into the void. One of the interceptors took heavy damage to the rear engine quarters. Its fuel tanks were punched open, after which the igniting bolts detonated the promethium stores and destroyed the ship in a cloud of spinning metal. The second took hits all along the facing flank, forcing it to climb rapidly in an attempt to break away.

Jorundur calmly hauled *Vuokho*'s prow after it, keying up the lascannons as he did so. 'There you go,' he voxed to Terrag. 'All lined up for you.'

Terrag punched the controls and the lascannons cut the interceptor cleanly in two.

Vuokho sailed through the wreckage, smashing the fragments apart and driving back up to full battle-speed.

Jorundur stole a glance out of the cockpit armourglass, looking up to where the curve of the plague-hulk's hull filled his visual field.

It was almost like atmospheric combat, fighting so close to such a massive object. The detail on its surface was clear enough – a forest of interlocked and embedded ship-corpses, tied together by strands of ossified matter. Tiny lights glowed like marsh-gas amid the arcane tangle of gothic buttresses and ancient hangar bays. Somewhere under all of that accumulated carnage was the original structure, the forgotten battleship that had started the whole millennial process, now buried under kilometres of detritus.

'Power spikes detected, all along underside batteries,' reported Beor.

Jorundur switched his attention back to the near-range augurs. 'They're gearing up to fire again,' he growled, judging distances and feeding more power to the main thrusters. 'Run for *Heimdall* – those lances will end us.'

The crew got to work – calmly, coolly, obeying his orders without a second thought. *Vuokho* swung around, pitching through a glowing debris-zone and boosting down away from the range of the hulk's fearsome guns.

Work quickly, brothers, Jorundur thought, already spying his next targets and working the controls hard. *This grows difficult.*

Gunnlaugur reached the lip of the shaft and hauled himself over the edge, emerging into a vast open chamber lined with iron pillars. The thick gloom was oppressive and dank – a near-perfect dark, broken only sporadically by flickering lamps or faulty strip-lumens. The environment was hot and close: a heavy cocktail of methane and carbon dioxide with an aftertaste of more exotic chems.

He loped across the chamber floor, his boot-falls echoing with dull clangs. Behind him came his brothers, spilling out of the shaft, their helm-lenses glowing. Njal's location-beacon glowed on all their helm-displays – still several levels up and already moving deeper into the heart of the hulk.

An archway towered up ahead, thirty metres high and ten across. The lintel was engraved with old Gothic, now worn away and unreadable in the murk. He picked up echoing booms, just on the edge of hearing, like distant detonations in the deeps. Either the hulk was still firing, or something was stirring in its labyrinthine innards.

Then he heard it for the first time.

Scuttling.

'Getting that?' voxed Ingvar, going swiftly, his head low as he ghosted through the archway.

'They are gathering,' growled Gunnlaugur, watching proximity points on his helm-scanner converge. 'Make your kills swift.'

As Gunnlaugur ran, he had to duck under a collapsed bulkhead before powering onwards, his shoulders hunched low, his hammer held two-handed. Blooms of gas hissed from shattered pipework, gusting across the tortured floor panels in luminous snarls. The spaces constricted into tight, claustrophobic capillary tunnels.

Then he caught sight of the first mutants, up ahead where the ways grew even more confined. Their eyes glowed in the dark – many eyes, like insects. They surged towards him, scrambling on four limbs over every surface, scampering along the walls, the decks, hanging from the sagging tunnel roof on hooked hands.

The tunnel filled with the whoosh of bolt-shells, followed an instant later by the dull crack of explosions. The mutants were blasted from their perches and sent spinning across the width of the passages.

Then Gunnlaugur was among them. He lashed out with his thunder hammer, crushing the head of one and sending it slamming into a knife-sharp wall section. The backswing caught another, sweeping it up at the roof where its spine severed with a wet snap. He ploughed on, tearing through the horde of defenders, driving into them with hard, swift strokes.

The rest kept pace. Ingvar remained at his shoulder, working his blade with ferocious speed. Bodily fluids slapped and sprayed across the narrow passageway, bringing with them the screams of the dying. The pack-members kept close together, forming a wave of grey-edged steel that tore down the twisting tunnels, never dropping speed, never pausing.

Eventually they burst out into the open again, and the tunnel walls gave way entirely to a new set of surroundings – bone-white matter. The new terrain curved away from them in sinuous arcs, glimmering softly in the deep night of the hulk's interior. A vast plain extended into the gloom, studded with sculptural undulations like some frozen sea.

Gunnlaugur nearly slipped as he ran. The mutants were everywhere, spilling out of crevices like blowflies clustered on rotten meat.

'This is… unusual,' he muttered, pivoting on one foot to send the head of *skulbrotsjór* into the midriff of a mutant. The screams echoed strangely, rebounding from the immense void above them. It felt like they'd stumbled into some bizarre hololith world.

A distant roof soared away from them, towering like the sheer flanks of the hive spire. More ivory matter curled and twisted in a mesh of buttresses. It all glittered softly, as if studded with tiny crystals.

'Xenos,' said Ingvar coldly.

As soon as Ingvar said it, Gunnlaugur saw the truth of it. He'd fought the eldar before and should have recognised their architectural excess. He'd never been inside one of their warships, though. The colossal chamber had the stench of ages on it, as if it had been incorporated into the hulk's warped menagerie an unimaginably long time ago.

He checked the tactical map – Njal was close now, and above them. More mutants emerged from the tangle of eldritch spires and walkways, defiling the ground over which they scurried like rats.

'I do not know what is worse,' snarled Gunnlaugur. 'This filth, or the ones that built this.'

'I do,' said Ingvar grimly, following him into battle again.

Hlaupnir was nearly as fast as Njal's boasts – a long, lean system-runner that wouldn't have looked out of place in a Naval formation. Olgeir liked it. It had a good smell, like charred stone, and its engines burned hard and clean.

He sat in the command throne. The hewn-stone chair was set at the rear of the bridge atop a low metal platform. Ahead of him, the main sensor station ran in semicircular ranks, interspersed with servitor pits and bulging logic engines. A large iron-framed portal, elliptical like a stained-glass eye, formed the main real-viewer, and took up nearly the entire forward wall of the bridge chamber. The crew worked at their positions, clad in Fenrisian grey, bent over pict screens or sensor tubes.

Olgeir checked the augurs, seeing how far the *Festerax* had already fallen behind. None of its escorts had come after them, which was something of a disappointment – it would have been good to exercise *Hlaupnir*'s guns a little before breaking for the planet.

'How long, Hanek?' Olgeir asked.

The sensorium officer – a burly kaerl with an unruly beard – pulled up the figures.

'Entering extreme augur-range now, lord,' he reported. 'I'm getting some ghosting on the fore array – either we're picking up some static from the battle, or they've seen us.'

'Broadcast our position marker. Sooner we make ourselves known, the better.'

Kefa Primaris was still some distance from visual range. Ahead of *Hlaupnir* ran an empty-looking starfield. Its lingering sub-warp trail-signatures were perfectly standard for the planet's grade – plenty of bulk carriers, a few light cargo freighters, the odd military patrol. All those ships had plied the incoming space-lanes to the planet recently, their spoor hanging in the vacuum like animal scent.

No doubt they were hanging in orbit over Kefa Primaris now, surrounded by clusters of unloading barges, refuelling and refitting after the warp-stage. Reaching those berths would seem like reaching sanctuary, with prayers of thanksgiving to be offered to the Emperor and the saints after the turmoil of the aether. They could have no idea what was heading their way.

'We need more speed,' Olgeir said.

Thraid, the navigation officer, looked up at him. 'We're already operating at far beyond–' He saw Olgeir's expression, and shook his head resignedly. 'I'll see what I can do.'

Olgeir grunted in satisfaction, resting his gauntlets on the armrests of the throne.

'You do that,' he said. 'Stormcaller wanted us on Kefa twelve hours ahead of the hulk.' He smiled broadly at Thraid, enjoying the challenge. 'Make it sixteen.'

Ingvar climbed fast, speeding up the smooth curves of the terrain around him. His boots crunched into a brittle surface, cracking it in tiny patterns.

He grabbed at trailing lengths of it, hauling himself higher, immersing himself ever further in tangled trails of alien psycho-substance.

It was like being immersed in a vast, static cataract. All around him, dirty white matter stretched upwards in twisting trunks sweeping towards the cavern roof. The Wolves raced up it, grabbing on to outcrops for handholds and wedging their boots into intersecting forks and platforms.

Ingvar had encountered wraithbone first during Onyx's raid on Craftworld Nyo-Fae. Halliafiore had taken care to brief the squad on its properties.

'Harder than ceramite,' the inquisitor had told them, hefting a piece, 'yet lighter than honeycomb. And it's saturated with the warp. Break it open, if you can, and for an instant you're staring into raw aether.'

The wraithbone on the *Festerax* was different – it was dull, lifeless, riddled with cancerous pocks and patched with mould growths. On Nyo-Fae it had been magnificent, swirling into arches of such purity that it hurt the eye to look on them; here, it had no more lustre than the scattered bones of a decaying mortuary.

The eldar warship had paid a heavy price for being dragged into the heart of the hulk. Nothing could survive millennia inside such a ruin-ark and not succumb eventually, and he felt the fragility of it all around him, like desiccated flesh stretched too long under a beating sun.

The creatures that screamed at them were no eldar, though. They were the same plague-zombies as before – human in origin but now twisted and distorted into grey-fleshed monsters. Ingvar caught scant glimpses of their faces in the dark before he killed them – jaws pulled wide, eyes staring from bloodshot rims, cadaverous flesh glistening clammily. They burst out of the wraithbone like roaches and scuttled down the long fronds, throwing themselves at the climbing Wolves in a disparate tide.

They were not hard to kill, not for warriors of the Rout, but every wave of defenders slowed them down. Just like all his brothers', Ingvar's helm displayed a ticking chrono on his inner lens, incessantly reminding him of the shrinking window for completion.

'Faster!' roared Gunnlaugur from up ahead of him, smashing aside four shrieking mutants with one vicious hammer-blow, dislodging them from their precarious handholds and sending them sailing into the emptiness.

The pack fought its way high above the surface of the wraithbone plain, racing up dozens of undulating pillars and cross-spans. The threading walkways led ever upwards, rising towards a single oval orifice at the summit of the chamber. Gunnlaugur made the lip of the passageway, leaping

from a wraithbone platform to land on its rim. Three ragged mutants
sprang at him, and Gunnlaugur punched them aside, cracking their backs
and sending them tumbling over the edge.

Then he was through, charging into the dark. Ingvar raced up after
him, stamping aside the snagging fingers of a half-buried zombie before
clearing the last of the wraithbone fronds. A thin frame of pale stone ran
around the orifice, lined with flowing runes in the xenos tongue, much
of it faded and mutilated.

Ingvar plunged through it, and into a second wraithbone chamber. The
previous one had been big; this one was colossal. Vast wraithbone sculp-
tures rose up into smog-streaked gloom, each one pitted and worn with
age. Sweeping columns soared up towards an obscured and distant roof.
The chamber's floor-level ran away from him, strewn with the broken
eddies of some arcane, flowing design. Empty-eyed, lissom statues lined
a series of avenues running into the darkness, blank-faced and passive.

The whole place already rang with the noise of battle – a jarring, per-
cussive hammer of boltguns and projectile weapons, underpinned by the
roar of hundreds of voices in overlapping, distorted waves.

A few hundred metres ahead of him, more than twenty Wolves had
taken position. They crouched behind the cover of broken statuary, firing
steadily out into the shadows. Beyond the defensive line, everything was
shrouded in murk.

Ingvar spied Gunnlaugur's marker. He ran up the front line and skidded
into cover, stowing *dausvjer* and pulling his bolt pistol from its holster.
Next to him, the Wolf Guard was firing short, deliberate volleys into the
smog.

'Why do we not run at them?' Ingvar hissed, taking aim himself.

'Njal is here,' Gunnlaugur voxed, firing steadily all the while. 'He has
sensed something.'

Ingvar picked his targets, and opened fire. More Wolves emerged from
adjoining chambers to join them, racing up to add their firepower to the
fragile defensive perimeter. Ingvar spied Njal's own contingent fifty metres
to the left, clustered around the base of one the hall's gigantic supporting
pillars. Further down the line, Bloodhame's squad were already creeping
slowly up the left extremity, taking position for flanking fire.

Just then, Njal suddenly broke from cover himself, surrounded by warriors of Fellblade's pack. He lifted his rune staff high and cried out words of
power. A clap like thunder boomed out, filling the entire hall, making the
miasma shudder. Howling winds spiralled out of nothingness, shearing

away the oppressive heat and pushing back the roiling banks of smog. Harsh light suddenly leapt up the faces of the pillars, illuminating for a moment the intricate carvings still visible on their surfaces.

That was not all it illuminated. Njal's lightburst flooded out across the emptiness, dazzling the hordes of approaching mutants. Beyond them, several hundred metres out, rose a further pair of columns, each one as wide as a Titan. Beyond those columns lay a chasm running transverse across the full width of the chamber. A single span crossed the divide, gently curved.

Something massive was crossing that bridge. Huge, cloven feet cracked against the dusty floor, crushing the lesser creatures beneath it. Gangling legs shot up, bulging in xenos-tainted curves. Long, grasping arms hung down from armoured shoulders, almost human in scale, but deformed by eldritch slenderness. A curved blade of dull, black metal swung rhythmically, balanced by a segmented fan-shaped shield on the opposite arm. A tapered, faceless head swept back and forth, lolling as if intoxicated.

It was fully fifteen metres tall – a giant of xenos tech-witchery, towering far above even Njal's Terminator bulk. Every heavy stride brought it several metres closer. The mutants around it yelled and goaded, lost in terror and awe, oblivious to those of their number it killed with every crunching footfall.

Ingvar narrowed his eyes. He had seen such sorcerous engines before. Imperial strategos had given them a name fitting their spectral appearance: wraithknight. Under normal circumstances the war machines were shimmering, elusive monsters of combat, sweeping across battlefields, glittering brightly from the energies coiled deep within their ghostly cores.

The thing before them was different. It strode clumsily, as if blind or maimed. Its curved shield was corroded and punched with black-edged holes where projectile fire had once stabbed through. Muddy-green fluid leaked from plated joints and cavities, dribbling across pitted wraithbone. The pregnant swell of its head-unit was fractured and smashed open, revealing intestinal growths spilling out of what had once been the pilot-chamber.

The wraithknight was true xenos no longer: just a shell over a deeper corruption. The black blood now boiling through its artificial veins had once hummed with esoteric harmonics. The Ruinous Powers had turned it into a tool of their own, slaved to the very powers it had been built to fight.

'Hel's teeth,' breathed Gunnlaugur.

By then, Njal was already moving. Heedless of the ravening hordes tearing across the emptiness, he strode out into the preternatural dark, his staff blazing with light and fire. Mutants raced towards the searing light, dying even as their addled eyes caught sight of it.

'To *me*, brothers!' Stormcaller cried, his old voice choked with kill-urge. 'In the name of Russ – *bring it down!*'

Chapter Thirteen

The crystalflex viewer still filled with intermittent light, dazzling from discharged lances, though the mortal danger had passed. *Vindicatus* had pulled back to agreed coordinates, holding position parallel to the plague-hulk and remaining just on the edge of its mainline gun-range. The cruiser's shields fizzed and guttered as the tech-adepts struggled to restore them, but otherwise damage had been containable – just a few hundred casualties along the macrocannon-ranks; nothing to lose sleep over.

The Cardinal's throne dominated the centre of the bridge. Its seat was high-backed, ridged with gold and lined with blood-red leather. A domed silk canopy hung over him, held up by the grunting efforts of twelve skull-faced cherubs. Incense filtered out through grilles in the throne's side-panels, dribbling across the marble dais in filmy swirls.

Hundreds of bodies moved in the spaces under the gaze of the throne. Most wore the crimson livery of the Grand Cruiser's bridge crew, their faces tattooed with the Cardinal's emblem and their tabards draped in devotional screeds. Others were tech-priests, spared the most egregious symbols of the Ministorum and given a wide berth by their superstitious counterparts. A few were of Sister Nuriyah's battalion, towering over the non-power armoured, their cloaks swishing softly as they strutted.

The crowds moved with a purpose, tracing pathways across the enormous bridge expanse. Data-slates were passed from hand to hand and orders were conveyed in soft whispers. *Vindicatus*'s command stations echoed with the hum of earnest tactical consultations. With its towering columns of bronze and its glassy seas of polished marble, the bridge looked a little like one of the great cathedral precincts of Holy Terra, and that was not entirely accidental.

Delvaux rested his elbows on his lap, and considered the situation. He hardly noticed any of the finery. He had hardly noticed it for many years – opulence was the water in which he swam, as transparent as the seas around a shark. His gaze fixed on the floor-to-roof observation panels at the far end of the bridge. Immense facets of armourglass, framed by curved metal fixings in the shape of angels' wings, gave a superlative view of the void outside. Ocular implants in his left eye superimposed fleet markers over the polished surface, delineating the patterns of combat still taking place in the vacuum.

He gloomily watched the surviving wings of his interceptors taking their chances against the last dregs of the plague-hulk's escort. He watched *Heimdall* stay riskily close to the enemy ship's lance range, continuing to loose its weapons with reckless defiance. He watched the three slate-grey gunships wheel and dive, shadowing the hulk like raptors harrying prey too big for them.

For a long time he did not stir, lost in his thoughts, knowing none of his servants would so much as dare to look up at him.

None but one.

'What do you make of it?' asked Klaive.

Delvaux twitched, and looked down. He hadn't heard the confessor approach. Klaive was out of armour, wearing his favoured black robes, velvet stole and soft slippers. The man's ivory skin shone under the bridge's intense light, and his wet gaze was unsettlingly unblinking, just as ever.

'Make of what?' Delvaux asked.

'The attempt,' said Klaive, coming to stand just below Delvaux's left armrest. 'Can you detect the Wolves?'

'Intermittently. The deeper they go, the harder it gets.'

Klaive nodded. 'Let us hope they are preserved. Such *fighters*.'

Delvaux shot him a scornful look. 'You admire them.'

'Of course.'

'I detest them.'

'For shame. They are the Emperor's instruments.'

'Preach at me here, confessor, and I'll stuff your tracts down your throat.' Delvaux felt the urge to reach for more snuff, and resisted. He was getting bad at resisting things. There had been a time, long ago, when he'd not needed stimulants to get through the diurnal cycle, when he'd fervently believed the things he was required to say. It was hard to remember that, now.

Klaive examined a broken nail. 'How long do they have?'

'Seventeen hours.'

'And you're going to give them that long?'

'That was the agreement.'

'Was it? You were generous.'

Delvaux turned to glare at Klaive. Something about the man had always made him angry. Perhaps it was the calm, otherworldliness of him, like the saints were always supposed to be. Klaive never got angry, never raised his voice. That was unnatural.

'Did you find what you were looking for on the surface?' Delvaux asked.

'Some of it. The rest will turn up.'

'Anything of interest?'

'Not really. Wasted effort, for the most part, I'm afraid to say.'

Delvaux studied his face carefully. 'Archives, you told me.'

'That is right.'

'A lot of trouble you went to. For archives.'

Klaive smiled thinly. 'Such things are important, lord. Records, transactions, documents of succession. When this war is over, they will be needed. Ras Shakeh was a small outpost of your diocese, but not an unimportant one.'

'It was a blasted rock,' Delvaux muttered. 'I still cannot quite believe you persuaded me to take it back in such force.'

'It was but a detour, lord. The real prize lies ahead.'

With that, at least, Delvaux could agree. Kefa Primaris was a colossal world, one harbouring billions of souls. To send it to the flames – that would be an act of supreme commitment. It would send a message, not just to the enemy, but to those who had begun to doubt his zeal.

The Ministorum had its own games of power, ones that cardinals were compelled to play just like everyone else.

'And what of you?' Delvaux asked. 'What odds would you give them?'

Klaive pondered the question. 'I am not sure that is the right question, lord,' he said. 'The true question is this: can we risk giving them time for the attempt?'

'I have made my judgement,' snapped Delvaux. 'Their Rune Priest knows my limits.'

'He is out of contact, at least for the moment. You are an honourable man, my lord, but do not lose sight of the danger.' Klaive's eyes flickered around the bridge. 'A whole world given over to ruin. Billions of new souls for the faithless. Once that is started–'

'Say no more. I know the consequences.'

But Klaive's speech nagged at him. He could already envisage the torpedoes being launched. It would not be hard to outpace the *Festerax*, to thunder into range ahead of it, gain optimal orbital position, deploy the life-eating virus-bombs. By the time the hulk made orbit, Kefa Primaris could be a scoured rock, as barren as the void itself.

No one would blame him. On the contrary, he would be commended. What were a few billion lives compared to the security of the entire subsector? These were the calculations a *statesman* made, one with the nerve to rise to the very top.

'I have made my judgement,' Delvaux repeated coldly. Beyond the armourglass viewers, the void-battle raged on silently. 'Let that be an end to it.'

Klaive bowed, though his faint smile lingered a little longer, hanging on his face like the reflection of gold on glass.

'As you will it, lord,' he said.

The xenos engine soared up into the gloom, huge and corroded. Njal could sense the heart of corruption beating within it. Something, just a sliver, of the pilot remained buried inside, wretched and agonised, locked in millennial torment and bound to the machine it had once commanded.

The machine sensed him, too – whatever gestalt mind still functioned within its eldritch body could respond to the power of the runes. Its shattered head swung towards him and it took a heavy stride clear of the bridge. Its curved blade glowed with a dull green light, sick as poison gas, and it swung low across the horde at its feet like a reaper.

At that moment, Bloodhame's pack opened up with a barrage of long-range bolter-fire, scything in from the left flank. A rain of shells smashed across the wraithknight's body in a shower of explosions, rocking it and making it stumble. Tracer-lines speared out in the flickering dark, cutting through billowing smog. Raw flame-bursts spread across the xenos's torso, washing over the curving breastplate and shoulder-arches.

The xenos engine wasn't hard to hit – it moved slowly, its joints leaking gas and fluid with every staccato movement – but physical rounds wouldn't be enough.

Njal whipped his staff around, building up a whirl of speed. Rune-energy lashed around him, snaking up to his clenched fists and rippling along the length of his skull-staff. The bone-totems tied to his weapon-belt clanked and jolted as the storm ramped up. He extended his staff, aiming the skull-head directly at the xenos engine. Vast arcs of lightning crackled out, snapping against the pillars.

'*Heidur Rus!*' he roared, and the echo of the war-cry rang from the pillars around him.

The wind suddenly flared into a full-blown gale. The temperature in the hall plummeted, collapsing into extreme, bone-breaking cold. Ice-crystals surged up the edges of the columns, fracturing and freezing.

Njal's Wolves streaked out ahead of him, carving a bloody path through the half-blinded mobs of mutants standing between them and the bridge. Glowing blades hacked and danced in the shadows, all locked in a cacophony of snarling, roaring and tearing. Bloodhame's pack secured the left flank, piling on more long-range ordnance. Long-axe's warriors fought their way up to a shallow stairway on the right flank and held position there, lancing fire in hard at the wraithknight. Gunnlaugur and Fellblade drove up the centre, their packs gouging a path of ruin into the heart of the enemy.

Njal spoke again, and gusts of the searing wind surged across the battlefield. Mutants froze in agony, their skin instantly blackening in frostbite. Their weapons shattered, their muscles seized up. Knife-hard blasts ripped through them, throwing them from their feet and sending them spinning and slamming into ice-rimed columns.

The xenos engine limped towards Njal, its carapace already glittering with a thickening coating of hoarfrost. It *shrieked*, a sound like metal shearing from its fastenings. Its shoulder-mounted weaponry spun around and opened fire. The Wolves in its path leapt and pounced from danger, veering and darting around the impacts before charging back into the fray.

Njal laughed out loud, as wild and brutal as a gothi of the old ice. Tethered skulls cracked against his armour, snapping and writhing like serpents. The storm-gale intensified, ripping wraithbone from stone and sending it flying into a vortex of whirling debris. The aether-ice gripped fast, cracking everything it coated. The Wolves fought on, in their own savage element, while the hordes of the damned were shriven into submission by the void-cold maelstrom.

Only the wraithknight weathered the storm, absorbing wave after wave of impacts. Its shoulder-weapons were blasted from its hide, its greaves driven in, and its faceplate cracked further, exposing a brain-like mass of glossy folds underneath. Throughout it all, it kept lumbering towards the Rune Priest, swinging its immense blade as it came. A single sword strike ripped through Fellblade's pack. Another swipe scattered Hauki's. None of the Wolves got close to the creature.

'Face *me*, then!' roared Njal, feeling his whole body blaze with elemental forces. A kind of ecstasy of power thundered out, making the runes on his armour burn with a furious, cold coruscation.

The ice-wind became ruinous. Massive chunks of the hall's wraithbone structure dislodged, crashing to the ground and sending up great clouds of dust. The wraithknight staggered, hammered by ball-lightning strikes and ravaged by the frigid gales. It stretched out a clawed hand, as black as coal amid the sheeting ice. Its tortured head emerged once more, surrounded by gouts of steam. It tried to take another stride towards the Rune Priest, to grasp at him.

'Your body is *broken!*' bellowed Njal. 'Your soul is *shriven!*'

Njal swung around, his staff whistling through the air as it churned up yet more power. The hurricane overflowed from him, bleeding from the joints in his ornate armour. The air roared, thundered and sped, chilling and cracking, as irresistible as glacier-grind. Nightwing, riding the squalls high in the vaults, shrieked defiance at the monster below.

'I name you *xenos!*' Njal boomed, grasping his staff two-handed, planting his feet, and jutting the skull-tip at the creature's head. The wraithknight towered over him, surrounded by the spinning cloud-patterns of the aether-whirlwind. 'By the will of the Allfather, you are *ended!*'

Storm-fury lashed out, crashing into the monster's midriff with an echoing explosion of multi-hued lightning and spinning ice-shards. Radial shockwaves shuddered outwards, ripping away in the deafening wail of the tempest. Every loose object in the chamber spiralled wildly around the icy vortex, dragged into the heart of the Stormcaller's summoned devastation.

The wraithknight, reeling in the eye of the gale, tried to get a sword strike away, and hauled its massive blade upwards. The dark metal surface, latticed with thick hoarfrost, glinted amid a blizzard of driving sleet, then swooped down. The wickedly curved edge tore towards Njal, swift as the raven's flight, perfectly aimed and weighted with massive kinetic force.

Njal swung his staff to meet it, bracing himself for the impact. The sword hit, and he was driven down into the cracking wraithbone underfoot. He felt his arms jar, his vision go black with stars. Around him, the blast-wave crashed out, flooring any mutants still standing.

Njal gritted his fangs, pushing back against the colossal pressure, feeling his staff flex as the strain took. Sweat burst out across his brow, veins throbbed in his bulging neck. The crushing power of xenos tech-sorcery came up against the bottomless well of Fenris's world-soul, and the epicentre raged like the heart of a star.

Amid all the ice and spiralling magicks, Njal looked up at the monster. It towered over him, vast and corrupted, bleeding raw pain and madness. Every surface was coated in a thick rime, as tight and frigid as the grasp of Helwinter. The diamond-bright carapace glowed with a harsh white light, and crackles of lightning flickered across the face of it.

The frost was lethal. It was spun from utter desolation, drawn from the airless chill of Fenris's utmost unforgiving heights, and no power, be it mortal or divine, could withstand its gnawing power forever.

At the end, it only took one word. As Njal uttered it, gasping through a clenched jawline, he even managed a grim smile.

'Shatter.'

The creature's sword burst apart, smashed into a thousand flying shards. The wraithknight stumbled, caught by the pull of gravity. The hoarfrost coating it contracted viciously, cracking wraithbone and driving deep. Wraithbone spars shattered, blown apart as cracks raced up the creature's armour plates.

The wraithknight screamed a final time, frozen in its death-lunge, bludgeoned by the ice-wind and racked by the clinging frost.

Then it exploded, flinging shards across the entire hall. The gales whipped up the debris and hurled it into the heights. A crack of released warp-essence rushed out, shaking the columns and making the floor tremble. The wraithknight's body disintegrated entirely, lost in a flailing tempest of crackling lightning and tearing ice-winds. Its meagre remains, harrowed by the ice into nothing more than withered scraps of flesh and metal, crashed to the ground in steaming chunks.

Njal pulled his head back, spread his arms, and howled. His warriors howled with him, charging with fresh savagery into the remaining hordes of mutant footsoldiers.

'Gothi!' they roared, en masse, and the sound of it made the chamber shake anew. '*Stormurstjórn!* Hjá, gothi!'

Buoyed by the surging hurricane, the Wolves cut through the cowering surviving mutants in a frenzy of unfettered bloodlust. Blades whirled in blurs of sliver-edged speed, cutting deep into the reeling masses of the damned.

Njal's whole body still rang with storm-magic. Every muscle blazed with pain from where he'd met the creature's blade, but his blood still ran fast with hyperadrenaline. The last forks of lightning still sparked across his amour, vital and dagger-sharp.

He kicked free of the wraithknight's downed corpse and started to move again. The chasm's edge drew nigh. On the far side, Njal could see the wraithbone architecture give out, replaced by a vast wall of rusting iron. Grotesque gargoyles, huge and crusted with the patina of ruin, glared out over the chasm amid riveted panels the colour of dried blood. A high portal gaped open, its interior velvety dark. Across the gate's lintel were carved words of ruin in a language that no mortal had ever spoken.

As he gazed at the portal, Njal felt the aura of absolute decay wafting out through the gateway. It was like a portal into the maw of Hel.

'To the bridge!' he commanded, his voice raw, striding out into the sea of bodies.

The Wolves surged forwards alongside him, driving the mutants over the chasm's edge. Bloodhame's pack came in from the flanks, with Long-axe's not far behind. The squads went swiftly now, unhindered, killing freely.

'First test passed,' Njal gasped, under his breath, before joining them in the slaughter.

Kefa Primaris filled *Hlaupnir*'s forward scopes. The globe was dirty grey and striated with lines of earth-brown cloudbanks. Even from the extremes of the orbital approaches, the massive urban coverage was clearly visible – vast geometric patterns of transit clusters and ground-level shield patterns. On full magnification, augurs showed up the core spire zones, the tracts of power-gen stations, the furrowed wastelands seething with chem-effluent.

Lights glinted in the shadow of the solar terminator – trillions of them, sparkling in the void with a beauty of abundance.

Olgeir left his throne and walked up to the railing around the command platform, gazing intently at the armourglass portals. 'Signals, Hanek,' he said.

'Standard system traffic,' the sensorium officer replied, scouring his pict-feed assiduously. 'Several hundred carriers in high orbit. No military-grade warp-capable vessels. We're not... Oh, we are. We're being intercepted.'

As Hanek spoke, Olgeir saw it for himself – six fighters burning towards them in formation. They were smaller than Imperial Navy Furies, with what looked like lone prow-mounted lascannons and limited missile tubes. Each had navy-blue livery on angular wings marked with a white hawk's head.

'Calm them down,' said Olgeir.

Hanek broadcast the standard approach codes as Thraid pulled the *Hlaupnir* two points away from an intercept course and dipped the cockpit towards Kefa Primaris's orbital holding zones.

'Unauthorised vessel,' came a tinny order over the ship-vox. 'Stand down or be disabled.'

Olgeir glanced at Hanek, raising an eyebrow. 'Are they serious?'

'They're powering up, lord.'

Olgeir shook his head in irritation. 'Get me a visual link.'

Hanek's fingers ran across his console. 'Shunting to your throne now.'

Olgeir went back to his command throne and sat heavily in it, clicking a rune on the armrest panel. A thin translucent screen spun out from the holocast projector revealing a pict-feed of a helmeted pilot in a cramped cockpit.

'Can you see me?' Olgeir asked, addressing the image.

There was a brief delay, a visual freeze, and the transmission juddered into life again.

'I... Yes. Getting a signal.' The pilot rapped the side of his helmet, as if checking to make sure his view was genuine. 'Lord,' he added hastily.

'Good. Then you know what I am, you have our codes, and you know what I will do to you if you fail to power down and fall into escort formation.'

The pilot looked briefly uncertain. 'I have orders–'

'Here are your new orders. You will escort us to the zone above the capital spires. You will send ahead orders for a lander to bring me to the governor. You will make sure he is ready for me on arrival.'

'It will be done, lord. It is... I mean she is...'

Olgeir sighed. Mortals were no use when they let their awe get the better of them. 'Do it now.'

He cut the link. Out in the void, the fighters pulled out of their attack run and split into two groups. They turned expertly and took up flanking position around the *Hlaupnir*.

'We have our coordinates,' reported Hanek. 'They're guiding us in.'

Olgeir leaned back in the throne, watching the arc of the planet swell in the forward viewers. He already knew how it would be – hyper-urban, towering habs, thick layers of industrial smog, crammed with worker-souls like insects in their nests. They were the greater part of the Imperium's teeming quadrillions. They were the backbone, the template, the standard pattern of human existence in the galaxy.

It was a depressing thought.

'Take us in,' said Olgeir, grimly.

Baldr ran with the pack across the bridge, glancing up at the towering cliff-face ahead. Bolt-rounds still fizzed out from the chasm's edge, but fewer than before. All blades were bloody now, caked with the thick residue of mortal fodder. He was still exhilarated from witnessing Njal's true power. The spectacle had been magnificent, though all of them knew sterner tests would lie ahead. The most powerful denizens of the plague-hulk would be stirring now, uncurling from whatever dark pits they were spawned in, slowly reacting to the intruders within the vessel's vast body.

We will be its disease.

Njal's words still echoed in Baldr's mind. He hadn't liked hearing them the first time – too close for comfort. He could feel the collar chafing at his neck as he ran, jostled by the cables running up the inside of his gorget. At times, the circlet felt hot, at others, rough, like uncured hide. He could never quite forget that he wore it, no matter how close the fighting became.

The portal loomed above him. Already the vanguard had fought through it, hurling frag grenades into the dark before racing after them to clear out the corridors beyond. Baldr was part of the second wave across, close on Álfar's heels, just ahead of Ingvar and Gunnlaugur.

He could hear his breathing echoing harshly inside his helm. He was pushing himself hard, just as he had planned to do, all to show his brothers that he was back to full fight-potential. Only in combat could he truly shake off the sense of shame that marked him, just as the torc marked him. There could be no shame in the rush of the hunt, and so he hurled himself into it, caught up in the bloody-mawed embrace of his heritage.

Once through the portal, the air instantly changed. The musty atmosphere of the eldar warship gave way to a close, hot, humid bloom of gaseous vapours. The tunnel closed down around him quickly, collapsing in on itself until barely more than head height. The dark shadows of his battle-brothers charged up ahead, forging a path into the eternal gloom. Ahead, the iron-ribbed lengths of twisting tunnel walls grew ever tighter.

'More targets,' reported Álfar from up ahead.

A second later, Baldr received the same data. Runes blinked into life on his helm-display, homing in from all directions. It was near impossible to gauge distance and orientation – the paths twisted quickly into sweeping curves, before branching off into dozens of alternative routes. The metal outlines of the walls dissolved into what looked like pus-coloured layers of fleshy matter. Baldr saw bulbous polyps throbbing amid the slime, glowing softly, and his boots sunk deep into gurgling pools of liquid that splashed up against his greaves as he ran.

He risked a look over his shoulder. The bulky outline of Ingvar's power armour was visible a long way further back. Beyond that, nothing. Locator runes for the rest of the packs seemed caught in some kind of lag, and didn't report true.

The tunnel snaked around to the right, angling sharply. Long trails of saliva-like ooze ran from the low ceiling. False colour patterns imposed by his helm did nothing to disguise the essential darkness, the claustrophobia, the foulness.

Then he heard bolter-fire from up ahead, followed by Fenrisian curses coming over the pack-vox.

'Flamers!' came a furious order – Baldr couldn't tell from whom.

The tunnel around him shuddered, rocked as if by a quake. Baldr nearly plunged headlong into the filth at his feet, and skidded to a halt. He saw Álfar up ahead; he had stopped running.

'Something just... shifted,' the shieldbearer said.

A sucking sound ran along the tunnel walls, like skin being ripped from flesh.

'Keep moving,' Baldr voxed, breaking back into a run, scanning the tunnels around him as he went.

Álfar joined him, and the two of them raced through the narrow, switchback tubes. The second time the shuddering came, there could be no doubt – the flesh-like covering of the walls had come loose. About ten metres ahead, a tumbling mound of translucent skin detached, slipping down like an eyelid drooping.

Álfar fired instantly, punching two holes in the barrier, but the bolts popped harmlessly within the thick curtains of glutinous matter. With a rip and a splurt, the ceiling started to sag. Thick walls on either side of them sucked closed, sealing them off in both directions.

Baldr joined up with Álfar in what space remained. Both of them mag-locked bolters and took up blades. Álfar punched his longsword into the quivering bulk ahead, drenching himself in watery pink fluids. Baldr joined him, hacking into the thick blubber and pulling the edges apart. The first cut revealed a brief glimpse of the tunnel beyond, but it was quickly obscured by more folds of glistening fat.

'Grenades,' voxed Baldr, reaching for a krak charge from his belt.

Before he'd had time to prime it, a shattering explosion burst out from behind him, filling the narrow bubble with flying, gore-splattered debris. Baldr was thrown hard to the tunnel's far side, impacting with a wet crack of ceramite against iron. Álfar was hurled further back, his armour charred from the blast.

Baldr struggled to his knees, reaching for his bolter again. One entire side of the tunnel wall had been driven in and stood in a tangled ruin of metal struts. As smoke boiled from the molten ruins, six power armoured figures emerged out of the smog, their eye-lenses glowing pale green.

Álfar was the quickest. With a growl of aggression, he leapt at the lead warrior. He got his axe-blade up into its face, hacking into the bul-bous helm and biting deep. The two of them crunched together, trading hammer-blows that tore shards from their battleplate.

Baldr opened fire, striking one of the intruders and sending him stag-gering. Then the bolt-rounds came in. Álfar was smashed back against the tunnel walls again, his armour pitted and cracked. Baldr was hit before he could get another shot away. One bolt crunched into his shoulder, spinning him around, then another exploded into his side.

He scrambled away, firing back, keeping the shots low, aiming to topple one of the advancing Traitors. One of his shots must have connected, as he heard a throaty grunt of pain and the wet snap of corrupted ceramite breaking.

That was drowned by a strangled bellow of pain from Álfar – he'd felled his first adversary, but a second had closed him down. The Traitor plunged a power maul into Álfar's bolter-ravaged torso, driving through the armour with an explosive burst of disruptor energy. Álfar fought on, hacking out wildly, but the maul lashed round, striking him in the throat and nearly severing his head entirely.

Baldr charged at the closest enemy, his bolter kicking in his grip, his sword crackling with energy. He lashed out, driving his blade into a pockmarked chest and twisting it. The Traitor collapsed, and more of his shots drove home, fragmenting armour and sending another to his knees.

Then he took a direct hit, this time to the helm, blinding him. Another hit exploded against his breastplate, sending ceramite fragments spinning. He tried to rise, to get another shot away, but a power scythe hit him hard, whistling in at chest height and driving him down onto his back. He felt a heavy boot clamp on his neck, and the agony of a blade-edge pushing through his cracked breastplate. His wrist was stamped down, his sword ripped away from him.

For just an instant, he caught the smeared outline of a Plague Marine helm hovering above him, expressionless and splattered with blood. He saw a power fist clench up, crackling with worm-like energy, and could do nothing to evade it.

'The one,' he heard, filtered through a rust-laced vox-grille.

Then the fist beat down, smashing into his damaged helm, shattering the lenses and pushing the faceplate inwards, and he knew no more.

Chapter Fourteen

Heimdall's structure shook as the impacts ran along it. Deep inside, confined to the medicae observation cell, Bjargborn could do nothing but listen.

'We're not thralls,' said Aerold, bitterly.

'There's a reason for it,' said Bjargborn.

'We deserve more.'

Bjargborn turned on him. 'Deserve? What are you talking about?'

The rest of the retrieved kaerls sat or lay about them. All ninety-two had been crammed into the same cell, one that had been built to accommodate a little over half that number. There was food, water, medicae supplies, and not much else. Overhead lumens flickered every time the cruiser took a hit.

'We never stopped fighting,' muttered Aerold.

'We didn't.' Bjargborn ripped a piece of reconstituted meat-stick from its packing and chewed. 'Too stupid to do anything else.'

Aerold looked at him darkly. His beard was straggly, his flesh still unwashed since the lifter from Ras Shakeh. They all still bore the mark of the desert on them, and the stink was oppressive.

'Then why don't they let us?' Aerold asked.

'Because they know what happened down there,' said Bjargborn, working his jaw methodically. It felt good to eat proper rations again – the
food, at least, had improved. 'So do you.'

Aerold pulled the sleeve of his tunic up to the elbow and brandished
his arm. 'See any signs?' he asked. He pulled his collar down and bared
his neck. 'Any sores?'

Bjargborn shrugged. 'You'd need a full scan. We were lucky they didn't
leave us behind.'

'Lucky.'

'Yes, lucky.' He leaned closer to Aerold, lowering his voice. 'This is a
lucky wyrd. Fate smiles on us.'

Aerold didn't look convinced. 'I wish to *fight*. They're short-handed.'

'*You* know you're healthy. I know you are. They don't. They can't. Rest
up. When they come for us again, you'll remember this as a good dream.'

Other kaerls looked over at them. Some had the same belligerent
expressions as Aerold. They'd taken it hard, being accused of carrying
plague after fighting for as long as they had.

Bjargborn glared back at them all. 'You heard me! What are you going
to do? Forget your vows?' He shook his head in disgust. 'Remember
who you are.'

They turned away again. They were a long way from revolt – they were
sons of Fenris, committed by blood and conditioning to fight for the
Sky Warriors until death took them. About the only thing that would
shake that faith was the idea, even the suggestion, that their loyalty had
become somehow questionable.

Whatever he said to the troops to keep them in line, Bjargborn could
understand their resentment. Despite himself, a fragment of it burned
away inside him. When he'd seen the Grey Hunter emerge from the
haze, he'd imagined battle would call again soon, this time alongside
the masters.

Instead they had confinement, suspicion, followed no doubt by the
gruelling examination of the apothecarion once the void-battle was
over.

He ripped another slice of meat from the pack and rolled it up in his
fist. The walls of the confinement chamber shuddered again, either from
Heimdall's macrocannon batteries firing or from taking another hit.

It would have been better to be out there, manning a gun-station or
a tactical console.

That wasn't going to happen. The only choice now was to wait it out, to sit idly until the chance to prove themselves came again.

'A good dream,' he said to himself, and started to eat again.

Gunnlaugur raged at the bio-matter around him. The walls had come sucking in on him just as they had all across the capillary tunnels. His hammer ripped through the screens of flesh, driving them back against the rotten metal substructures that underpinned them. The decking underfoot pulled at his boots, the sluice of fluids ran down his helm. Everything dragged at him, weighing him down, tying up his arms, wrenching him deeper into the fleshy entrails.

'*Fenrys!*' he bellowed, lashing out double-handed. His hammerhead flew wildly, eventually breaking through a final tattered skirt of pulsating blood-vessels. Staggering from released momentum, he burst into the open again, dripping with bloody residue.

A gruesome chamber opened up ahead of him – a stomach-shaped bowl of bile-flecked effluent. The walls themselves were contorted into organic nodes and folds, each one popping with fluids. Further chambers could be glimpsed beyond, each one similarly draped in pulpy bio-residue. Flamers roared in the dark, illuminating the flesh-sheets with flares of crimson.

Others had broken through ahead of him – he saw Fellblade, and Hafloí and Hauki, all hacking at the retreating walls of blubber and torching what remained. More emerged at every moment, crashing through the retreating flesh-piles from a dozen different orifices. The sudden contraction of bio-matter had caught them off-guard, but the application of blade and flame was driving it back with ruthless efficiency.

Njal stalked through the chamber, his huge armour-shell coated in the burned remnants of tunnel-bile. He looked furious.

'Too *slow!*' he thundered at the warriors around him. 'We cut it out, then we *move!*'

Gunnlaugur came up to him. 'Losses?' he asked.

'Three to the xenos-construct, three in here,' Njal snarled, the numbers clearly angering him. 'Six is too many. They're wearing us down.'

Gunnlaugur looked up, to see Ingvar emerged from the next chamber along, his blade-edge still running with semi-cooked phlegm-gobbets. 'Eight, jarl,' he reported flatly. 'Baldr is gone, as is Álfar.'

The word *Baldr* hit Gunnlaugur like a blow. For a moment, the news seemed to rock even Njal. The Rune Priest stared back, and in that instant, for all his immense power and bulk, he looked wounded.

Then Njal lifted his head, and drew in a deep, rasping breath. 'Enough. We keep moving.'

Ingvar remained where he was. 'Was he ready, jarl?' he asked.

Gunnlaugur couldn't believe it. It seemed the Gyrfalkon had not changed as much as he'd hoped.

Njal turned his red-lensed gaze back to Ingvar slowly, astonished that his decision would be so much as commented on, let alone questioned. Ingvar glared back up at the huge Rune Priest, holding his ground.

'You play with danger, Grey Hunter,' Njal growled, his old, deep voice grating with an instinctual threat-note. 'You are here to fight. Now, *move on*.'

For a moment, Gunnlaugur feared Ingvar would not comply. He could feel the rage emanating from his pack-mate. He knew how hard Ingvar had worked to keep Baldr alive on Ras Shakeh, and how dark and strange his fervour could be.

Then, slowly, Ingvar backed down. 'I recognise my error,' he said, bowing stiffly.

Nightwing, mounted on Njal's shoulder, extended its pinions and screeched out denunciation. Njal turned away from him, shaking his head in disgust. 'There is ironwork ahead,' he said to Gunnlaugur. 'Multiple tunnels, all leading down.'

As he spoke, the rest of the Wolves fell into their pack formations again, clustering in the blood-streaked chamber.

'Then we are getting close,' Njal announced. 'I sense the core. We press deeper.'

Njal shot a brief glance at Ingvar before turning his death mask helm back to the path ahead.

'And no more delays,' he snarled.

It had been hard for Callia to ensure she remained stationed on *Vindicatus*'s bridge. Since taking on duties as part of the Order of the Fiery Tear, she had been pressurised into assuming a more junior position elsewhere in the warship's lower reaches. Nuriyah didn't trust her, and nor did the other Sisters of the Cardinal's entourage.

Once battle broke out, though, there had been no time to let the issue come to a head, and even Nuriyah could not argue with her combat-rank and experience. In the end Callia's presence was tolerated on the command level, perhaps out of a lingering sense of unease over what had happened to de Chatelaine, perhaps for more pragmatic reasons.

Once the void-strike had got under way, Callia had glanced up at the huge Penitent Engine as little as possible. The last time she'd walked under its shadow she'd risked a proper look, daring to hope that somewhere amid the gears and pain-nodes and cabling the canoness might still be able to respond to stimuli.

Yet Callia had seen nothing but that frozen scream, hidden under a sheet of pure white linen. De Chatelaine, for all her loyalty and valour, had ceased to exist. What remained was a mechanical thing, a bringer and an endurer of pain.

Delvaux kept the Penitent Engine close to him at all times, perhaps as some kind of trophy. Together with its counterpart, it stood guard behind his throne. Every so often, servitors would shuffle up to the two Engines and apply some sacred oil to their joints or whisper some prayer for the continued shriving of the souls at their hearts.

Callia maintained her distance after that, attending to the many small duties that her position gave her. The plague-hulk loomed on *Vindicatus*'s forward viewers, just as staggeringly vast as ever. The volume of exchanged fire had fallen away sharply since the Cardinal had given the withdrawal order. With the last of the escorts destroyed, *Heimdall* still risked attack runs, but the shared task now was a limited one – keep in watching range, ready for when the Wolves gave the signal to re-engage.

Callia wondered how likely it was that they'd ever receive that signal. She yearned to see it appear on the consoles, vindicating boldness over pragmatism, remembering Gunnlaugur's almost casual bravado towards the task at hand.

She looked over her shoulder, back up towards Delvaux's throne. As her eyes alighted on his corpulent robed form, an involuntary spike of hatred rippled through her, quickly pushed down again.

That is unworthy. He is still the Cardinal.

She walked over to a cluster of navigation stations just below the throne platform. As she did so, she heard Klaive enter the bridge. Huge slide-doors at the rear of the bridge chamber hissed closed, and the confessor padded up to the Cardinal's throne.

Callia lowered her head, making a show of studying the pict screen closest to her, listening carefully.

'Back again,' remarked Delvaux to Klaive, unenthusiastically.

From the corner of her eye, Callia watched Klaive make himself comfortable on the steps leading up to Delvaux's seat. The Engine that had once been de Chatelaine stood silently over him. She could have crushed him with a single stride, if any of her will remained.

'We have had communications,' said Klaive. 'From… Well, you know.'

Callia always found Klaive's tone with Delvaux surprising. It was over-familiar, not tinged with the fawning attention to precedence that coloured all the others' dealings with the Cardinal. If there was a reason for that, she'd not discovered it yet.

'And?' asked Delvaux.

'They judge the Wolves' ambition overreaches itself. I told them of your proposal. They approved.'

Delvaux pursed his lips, causing his jowls to wobble. 'Did they, then?' He looked out through the forward viewportals. *Heimdall* was just visible, far out into the void, holding station as close to the hulk as it dared. 'But they are not here. I am.'

'Their views are hardly insignificant.'

'Of course not.'

'And there is the question of reputation.'

'So you have often reminded me.'

'Such things are important.'

Delvaux smiled at him coldly. 'Enough. You can save the arguments you came to make. The matter is already decided, so your presence here comes after the event.'

Callia tensed. Klaive raised an eyebrow. They both waited.

'Then you have–' Klaive started.

'What did you think, that I'd let them burrow away until the End Times? This is madness. I have changed my mind.'

Klaive bowed, unusually respectfully. 'You have come to the right decision, lord,' he said. 'Though the Stormcaller…'

'You think I *fear* him?' Delvaux's lips curled in outrage. 'You think I fear the bone-rattler and his entourage? He can howl as much as he likes – it will change nothing.' His cheeks reddened. 'I have given them long enough. The Throne knows I have. Let this be an end to the madness.'

Klaive folded his arms, satisfied. 'Then shall I pass on the order?'

'You do not give the orders. You never have. Just watch, and keep your counsel to yourself.'

Callia turned away, looking back at the pict-feed before her. Already coordinates were scrolling down the lens aperture, updating a matrix of movement vectors for the enginarium to act on.

As she saw them, her heart sank. He was really going to do it.

'Can we still outpace the plague-hulk?' she heard Klaive ask Delvaux.

'Of course. The margins have been calculated.' She heard Delvaux sniff. 'By the time the vessel reaches orbit, the last flames over Kefa Primaris will already have died down.'

'A noble sacrifice,' said Klaive, softly, as if awed by it.

'A necessary one,' said Delvaux.

Callia felt the bridge deck vibrate as the engines powered up. Lights flickered on all across the tactical stations, warning of imminent course change.

Somewhere down below, she knew, the life-eater canisters would be being shunted into torpedo casings. The priests would already be reading benedictions over their deadly cargo.

On another mission, she might have swallowed her unease at that. She had performed many difficult tasks during her service, not least the destruction of plague-bearers on Ras Shakeh, and it was part of her conditioning to obey.

But loyalty worked both ways. She glanced up at the Engines again, seeing de Chatelaine's frozen scream impacted on the linen.

She moved smoothly away from the navigation station, keeping her demeanour natural. Silently, she activated the comm-bead at her collar. Once out of earshot of the throne, she opened the secure channel she'd given Gunnlaugur access to.

'Grey Hunter,' she voxed quietly, noting the successful connection. 'I think we need to talk.'

The primary urban cluster on Kefa Primaris was called Kallian Hellax. It contained two billion inhabitants divided between twenty major hive spires and a heavily built-up hinterland of sprawling hab-units and communal manufactory clusters. The city core had existed for seven thousand years, having been added to and augmented dramatically during nine separate expansionary phases.

As big as it was, Hellax was only the largest of many such hive complexes arranged across the planet's temperate zones. No one had ever been able to survey accurately just how many workers lived in the full tally of towers – even the logic engines of the Mechanicus had their limits. However, it could be ascertained with reasonable certainty that the figure ran into the trillions, a factor commensurate with the sizeable levy the planet contributed to the Imperium in both tithes and manpower.

All of these things Olgeir knew due to the databursts sent over by his escorts on their way down through the upper atmosphere. The statistics were impressive enough, but the actual sight of the hyper-cities emerging through the bands of cloud underwrote the cold facts.

Hellax was wreathed in night-shadow. Great spikes of adamantium and rockcrete thrust out from the planet's surface like blades, glittering with electric light and surrounded by a halo of moving aircraft. The entire pattern glowed with activity – furnaces, industrial venting, neon display-patterns on spire-summits, transit-spans carrying closely packed megatrains and bulk cargo streams.

Hlaupnir had been left behind, hanging far above them in a stationary orbit and still flanked by the same void-fighters that had ushered it in from the outer limits. Olgeir now piloted an atmospheric lander down to the landing stages. Thraid had come with him, leaving Hanek in command of the system-runner.

As they plummeted, military aircraft in royal blue livery soared up to meet them, dipping their wings in salute as they approached. The escort operation was slick and well organised, just as their orbital encounter had been once credentials had been established. Kefa Primaris, it seemed, was well governed enough.

'Lord, if it pleases you,' came a pilot's voice over the lander's comm, 'follow the course-markers being sent to your ship's cogitator. The governor has been informed of your arrival and awaits you in her chambers.'

The governor: Praesidia Magisterial Lujia Annarovea, two hundred Terran years old, the Imperial authority on Kefa Primaris for seventy-nine. Olgeir studied the data on his pict screen carefully. It was hard to gauge much from the brief bio-note attached to the planet's propaganda material, but he liked the way she looked in her image – stern, clear-eyed, standing tall in a military uniform of black trimmed with the same royal blue her fighters carried.

'Lead on,' he replied over the comm, easing the lander downwards and following the angled flight of the fighter wing.

The tips of immense spires loomed under him, their outlines luminescent with heavy shielding. Olgeir's lander glided towards a docking platform near the summit of the largest, situated on a narrow rockcrete apron just below a tall copper dome. An imposing Imperial aquila decorated the dome's facing surface, picked out in golden lumens. Rain bounced and whipped across the exposed apron, where an honour guard of sixty Guard troopers in leather greatcoats waited.

The lander touched down, hissing gently as shock absorbers contracted. Thraid activated the door-release mechanism.

'Remain here,' Olgeir told him, extracting himself from the pilot's seat. 'No one touches this vessel, no one moves it.'

Thraid bowed. 'By your will.'

Gull-wing cockpit doors cracked open, easing down on long pistons. Olgeir clanged down the ramp, mag-locking an axe to his armour as he emerged into the elements.

At the end of the twin rows of honour guards, a lone figure waited for him. She looked much as she had done in her pict – silver hair cropped severely short, a thin face, straight shoulders. She wasn't wearing the ceremonial uniform of her calling and carried no aquila devices on her jacket, but was dressed in some kind of long gown of shimmering pearl-silver.

Olgeir walked up to her. 'Governor,' he said.

Annarovea bowed in acknowledgement. 'Lord,' she said. A slight tightening of her jawline gave away her tension. 'This is an unexpected honour.' Olgeir glanced at her gown, and she caught the look. 'You'll forgive the dress. Ceremonial dinner for the One Hundred and Forty-Fifth Regiment Kafjian Lanciers.'

'Sorry to call you away.'

'It wasn't you,' said Annarovea. 'They pulled me out three hours ago to monitor long-range augur signals. Something's inbound. Something worrying. I can only assume your appearance is in connection with it.'

'We need to talk, somewhere secure.'

'I had a chamber prepared as soon as I received notice of your arrival. Please, come with me.'

Her voice was calm and business-like. Olgeir decided he liked this governor.

'That's good,' said Olgeir, walking with Annarovea out of the rain and under the cover of the dome. 'Though I warn you, you're not going to like what I have to say.'

Vuokho powered smoothly under the vast shadow of *Heimdall*'s starboard flank. Jorundur worked the controls, readying the gunship to dock. The two other Thunderhawks, *Grimund* and *Kjarlskar*, had already gone in, their work done and their damage taken.

Jorundur looked out at the cruiser's edge, noting the heavy damage sustained all along the facing hull-line. The flickering void shield coverage looked close to ripping away. Intermittent bursts of las-fire still belched out from the distant plague-hulk to test it, but *Heimdall* had finally pulled out to long range and was spared the full intensity of the vessel's firepower.

'We have clearance?' Jorundur asked, watching the marker lights blink on along *Heimdall*'s hangar edges.

'We do,' said Beor.

Jorundur grunted. He'd hung in the void for as long as possible, reluctant to give up the freedom of his own craft in exchange for the corridors and fire-pits of *Heimdall*. All there was to do on Njal's ship was wait for news or fresh orders, neither of which appealed.

'Then we–' he started, then broke off. The comm-bead Gunnlaugur had given him suddenly signalled an incoming feed.

'Lord, do you wish to make preparations?' asked Beor.

Jorundur waved the question away, feeding the bead's input to his helm system.

'Grey Hunter,' came a message, crackling with distance and interference. 'I think we need to talk.'

Jorundur sat back, surprised. 'Sister,' he replied. 'There are easier ways of getting in touch.'

'None so secure. You need to know this – the Cardinal is making his move.'

'He can't be. We are far from orbit.'

'Klaive convinced him. You need to warn your brothers.'

'*Skithof!*'

'Be in no doubt, he will do it,' said Callia.

Jorundur quieted the comm and leaned towards Terrag's station. 'Run a scan on *Vindicatus*. Tell me if you detect course change.' Then he reactivated the link. 'Why are you telling me this, Sister?'

There was a static burst – perhaps the germ of a bitter laugh. 'My service is to the Imperium and the Order. One has gone mad. You are what is left of the other.' Her voice lowered. 'He is set on this. It must be stopped.'

Jorundur checked the augur readings on his console. The Cardinal's huge warship still occupied its allotted position, holding a parallel vector to the hulk at a similar distance to *Heimdall*.

'He wouldn't break an oath to the Stormcaller,' he muttered. 'He's not that stupid.'

'It's already happening,' said Callia. 'Once we're under full thrust and out of lance-range, you will not be able to overhaul us.'

Terrag looked up from his station. 'Detecting power build-up in *Vindicatus*'s sub-warp drives, lord. It'll be moving soon.'

Jorundur exhaled in disbelief. 'Can you do anything to hold this up?' he asked Callia.

'There's only a few of us left. Nuriyah controls the ship, so it won't be much. If you want to stop this thing, you'll–'

'Yes, yes.' Jorundur balled his gauntlets, assessing options. 'I'll do what I can. Sister, you have…' He swallowed. It was difficult, even then, to force the words out. 'My thanks.'

He cut the link and turned to Terrag again. 'Can you reach Njal?'

Terrag shook his head. 'Not at this range.'

Jorundur smiled thinly. 'Thought not.'

Beor turned to him. 'We're cleared to dock, lord.'

'We're not going in,' said Jorundur, running a careful eye over *Vuokho*'s vital signs. As ever, the gunship looked half ready to fall apart. Every time the thing was patched up, it was sent right back into the warzone.

Just like the rest of us.

'Signal *Heimdall*,' he said, preparing to plot in a new vector. 'Tell them to shadow *Vindicatus* and not let it out of range. Then run a course back for the hulk.'

Beor hesitated. 'The hulk?' he asked.

Jorundur nodded grimly. 'Aye,' he said. 'Njal needs to hear this, so we need to close in again.'

Morven cleared her throat. 'Lord, just so you know, I'm required to inform you that we're in no shape to go back out there.'

'And?'

'Just doing my duty.'

'So you should,' growled Jorundur, pulling the control column round and dipping *Vuokho*'s cockpit below *Heimdall*'s keel. 'Now get ready to do some flying.'

Chapter Fifteen

Ingvar could feel Gunnlaugur's gaze on him. He kept his head down and ran along the corridor with the rest of them, not wanting to have it out with him now.

Gunnlaugur had other ideas. He caught Ingvar's shoulder, just as they were about to break back into the next intersection.

'What was that?' he hissed.

Ingvar shook off Gunnlaugur's gauntlet. 'Baldr should have remained on the ship,' he said, using Járnhamar's closed channel. 'I know it, you know it.'

'He's gone, brother. We still have the hunt.'

Ingvar knew the truth of that, but it still burned at him. Whatever canker had overtaken Baldr's body and mind had been *beaten*: to see all that progress snuffed out, so soon, filled him with a fury born of both pain and frustration.

An octagonal hub intersection loomed, now populated by the jostling of warriors as they assembled before the push into the core.

'We are shield-brothers,' Ingvar said, angrily, just before crossing the threshold into the chamber.

'You *were*,' growled the Wolf Guard. 'All there is now is vengeance – fix on that.'

Then he pushed past, into the chamber beyond, and Ingvar followed. Njal already stood at the centre of it, his huge battleplate streaked with blood. The Rune Priest was barely lit by the clusters of red helm-lenses glowing around him.

'We are close,' Njal said, turning his head up to the low ceiling, as if sniffing out a scent. 'From now, keep locked on the main energy spike – that is the target. Gunnlaugur, Fellblade – your packs run with me. We will break through the centre. Bloodhame – stay back and hold the core gate. Long-axe – spread wide through the side-tunnels, sow fear in those that come at us.' His severe glare swept back to them. 'They know we are here. Now, more than ever, *keep moving.*'

There were low growls of assent from the assembled warriors. They shook the bile from their weapon-edges, keying themselves up for a plunge deeper into the dark. Just as Njal looked ready to lead them in, a crackle of static burst out across the pack-wide vox.

'Stormcaller,' came Jorundur's voice over the link, thick with white noise and barely audible. 'Do I reach you?'

Njal halted. 'Speak.'

'Signals from *Vindicatus*. The Cardinal has broken his oath. His ship is powering up. Ordering pursuit.'

Njal swore. 'He has moved yet?'

'Still in position. *Heimdall*'s preparing intercept.'

'What is *Heimdall*'s status?'

'Heavy damage. It can fight. Just.'

Njal's whole body bristled with anger. 'Bring him *down*,' he ordered. 'Full sanction.'

'Do you need extraction, lord?' Jorundur asked.

Njal looked torn for a second. If *Heimdall* was drawn too far away or was destroyed, their chances of getting off the hulk were zero. In any case, the Wolves frigate was a poor match for the massive *Vindicatus*, even without the extra damage it had taken.

'Negative,' he snarled. 'We are finishing this.'

'Understood,' came Jorundur's reply. 'The Hand of Russ be with you.' Then the feed crackled out.

'This thing is not over,' snarled Njal, turning back to the packs. His staff flickered with slithers of lightning, as if his own rage were spilling out of the dark shaft. 'We will *destroy* this place. We will tear it apart from the inside and cast the fragments to the void. *Then* we will destroy the oathbreaker. He cannot run forever.' He lowered his staff tip towards the archway, and the skull-head burst into flame. 'The hunt must be completed.'

With Njal at their head, the packs loped into the dark, pelts swirling, heads low.

Ingvar, though, held back.

'Brother,' warned Gunnlaugur wearily, seeing the hesitation. 'No more of this.'

'We can't let him go,' Ingvar said.

'What do you mean?'

'Klaive is on that ship. We lose him now, the scent dies.'

'*Now?*'

Ingvar backed away, inching towards the chamber exit. 'There is still time. Jorundur is in close. I can get to him.'

'They will tear you apart.'

The last of the hunting packs slipped into the tunnels, leaving Gunnlaugur and Ingvar alone.

'We have to do this,' said Ingvar. 'You know why.'

For a heartbeat, Ingvar thought the Wolf Guard would reach for his thunder hammer and drag him to heel. Gunnlaugur, though, did not move.

'Njal will not forgive,' the Wolf Guard said.

'You lead the pack, not him,' said Ingvar. 'You asked for a name. Klaive can give us one.'

Gunnlaugur remained poised to strike – poised to haul him away and shove him back into the fray. Then, slowly, he relaxed. The need for vengeance had never been questioned, only the means of obtaining it. 'You are actually serious,' he said.

'Njal will need you,' urged Ingvar. 'Hafloí, too. But let me go.'

The distant roar of battle echoed up from the tunnels ahead, growing in volume, capped by the stark bellow of Njal's kill-rage. Gunnlaugur's helm twisted away, angled towards the battlefront, over to where he belonged.

He glanced back at Ingvar. 'Go, then,' he said. 'Hunt him.'

Ingvar bowed. '*Vaerengi*, I will not forget.'

'*Succeed*. That is all.'

Gunnlaugur clamped his fist against his breastplate in salute, then followed the rest of the pack down into the darkness. As he ran down into the tunnel, he unlocked his hammer, its head kindling with energy as he disappeared into the endless shadow.

With Gunnlaugur's passing, Ingvar felt a final spasm of doubt – a flicker, as ephemeral as the curls of lightning running across the Stormcaller's staff. There would be no way back from this, nor forgiveness for it.

This will damn me.

He drew his sword. Its edge glowed keenly in the dark.

So be it.

He broke into a run of his own, heading the other way. Already he could hear fresh movement in the cloying dark – remnants of the hordes they'd battled through, coming together for the lone, mad soul they could sense heading back towards them.

'Old Dog,' Ingvar voxed. 'In range?'

Another hiss of static, then the link burst back into fractured life. 'Gyrfalcon?' came Jorundur's irritated voice. 'Not for long. We are being flayed out here.'

'Hold position,' said Ingvar, picking up his pace. 'Lock on to my signal – I am coming out.'

'Skítja. Coming *out*? You know what you're asking?'

Ingvar's helm-lenses were already giving him targets – runes in the dark, zeroing in on hunched shapes in the shadows. He didn't break stride.

'Surely, brother,' he said, picking up speed, angling *dausvjer* for the first strike. 'This is but the start.'

The Cardinal hunched in his throne. He had an almost unbearable urge to gnaw on his fingernails. The habit had been with him ever since infancy, and even after so long occupying the high offices of his order, it had never quite been banished.

There were many other things that ought to have been banished. He should have put aside his appetites for food and drink, for the pleasures of his sensor-shielded bedchambers, for the daily influx of narcotics that stimulated his nerves and dulled his mind. All these things should have been limited, freeing up the time for him to do what his followers expected of him – to be a *leader*. A prophet. A Prince of the Church.

The problem was, of course, that since rising to the highest offices of the Ministorum there had been no external pressures on his conduct. None of his retinue would dare to so much as query any foible, much less question an order. He could click his bejewelled fingers and Nuriyah would bring him a fresh platter of cortex-snuff, or a salver of hydroponic-grown grapes, or a wide-eyed youth fresh off the tithe-shuttles. She would never say a word. Ever.

Who, save a saint, could have resisted that kind of indulgence for long?

But that, of course, was the point. He was supposed to *be* a saint, or something like one. His billions of followers revered him as such, fed by a ceaseless propaganda missionaria and desperate for hope in a darkening galaxy.

He had told himself for so long now that the reform would come soon – that he would cast off the ephemeral trappings of luxury. He would undertake penance. The petty flashes of vindictiveness would cease, and he would lead a *real* crusade. In the higher echelons of the Ministorum there were, he knew, voices raised against him. Stories of excess had filtered their way back to Terra and Ophelia VII. He needed to prove himself. He needed a grand gesture, something to still those wagging tongues.

His mournful gaze flickered up to the great crystal viewscreen. The planet was out there somewhere ahead, unsuspecting, unprotected.

It was a high price to pay to restore his position, but there were other justifications, ones that the Wolves would never accept. Klaive had always been right – even the *risk* of letting the world fall to the Ruinous Powers was not worth entertaining.

So it was not all about him, not just about his faltering vocation. There were reasons. Good ones.

He sniffed. The temptation to chew on his nails became overwhelming.

'Lord Cardinal.'

Delvaux stirred out his reverie. Harryat, *Vindicatus's* bridge-captain, stood at the base of the throne's dais, bowing. He was a broad-chested, square-jawed man in a trim crimson uniform – the best of the Ecclesiarchy's officer cadre.

'What is it, captain?' asked Delvaux, placing both hands in his lap and curling them into fists.

'Communication from *Heimdall*. They're asking for confirmation that we intend to hold position.'

Delvaux felt a twinge of panic. *So quick. How do they know?*

'How soon before we're ready to move off?' he asked.

'The engines took some damage,' said Harryat. 'We're working on restoring full power. It will not be long. An hour, no more.'

Delvaux drew in a frustrated breath. 'An hour is not good enough. I gave the order. I expect it to be complied with.'

Harryat didn't flinch. Unlike most of the others, he could look Delvaux in the eye while giving bad news. 'If we ignite the main drives now for a full burn, the damage will be permanent. The work can be done swiftly – I have three hundred crew working on it.'

'Thirty minutes,' said Delvaux. 'That is all I will give you.'

Harryat looked like he was going to protest, but then his gaze shifted up to the two Penitent Engines standing behind Delvaux's throne, and he changed his mind. 'We will do what we can,' he said.

'No, captain,' said Delvaux, fixing him with a heavy stare. 'You will do what I tell you. In thirty minutes this ship will be headed for Kefa Primaris, at full burn.'

'And the Wolves?'

'Tell them the agreement stands. Tell them they've detected rogue energy spikes while we repair the main power system.' Delvaux rolled his eyes. 'Love of the Throne, tell them whatever you want – just keep them quiet. They should be concentrating their efforts on the hulk.'

Harryat nodded brusquely, but for an instant his face gave away a flash of what he really thought.

He wishes to stay, to fight alongside them.

'And do not forget, captain,' said Delvaux, his voice darkening, 'where your loyalty lies. The beasts can howl at shadows all they wish, but our task is the safeguarding of souls from corruption. Better to die in the flames than succumb to damnation, is that not so?'

Harryat drew in a curt breath. 'It is just as you say, my lord.'

'Now go,' said Delvaux, dismissing him with a wave, 'and do not return until you have given me what I need to destroy that world.'

Baldr's eyes flickered open. He tensed immediately, going for his weapon, but his limbs did not obey him. He tried to move, to struggle against whatever force held him in place, but he remained stubbornly immobile.

His mind felt cloudy. Pain – hard, unyielding – throbbed all over him. Sluggishly, he realised that he was not wearing his helm. The rest of his armour was intact, but he was breathing the unfiltered air of the hulk's interior. It was foul, like ingesting faeces, and he felt the gag-reflex at the back of his throat kick in.

The space around him was jet-black and as hot as blood. Without the aid of his helm-lenses, it took a while for his eyes to adjust – even his occulobe-enhanced optics struggled without any kind of light source to latch on to.

He blinked heavily, staring out into the utter blackness. He made out the faintest hint of darker edges in the gloom. The sound of something gurgling thickly echoed close by. He tried to move again, pushing hard against his bonds, and failed.

Then, a long way ahead of him, a soft green light bled out of the darkness. It was the first chance Baldr had to orientate himself – he was upright, suspended less than a metre above the floor of some narrow, low-roofed chamber. His arms and legs appeared to have been absorbed into the walls around him – thick knots of organic material clamped him in place, twisting over his body like tree roots.

The light continued to grow. The floor was illuminated by its creeping progress, exposing fungoid nodules clustered tightly together. They thronged like a carpet of spores, thick and bulbous, glistening faintly as the crepuscular light-shafts slipped through the murk. Long, stringy tendrils hung in loops from vaults above, each one swollen with trembling pustules.

Baldr tensed his arms, pushing against the bonds that held him in place. Whatever the roots were made of, they were incredibly strong – he forced one of them to flex, just by a few millimetres, before having to relax his muscles again in exhaustion.

By then, the greenish tinge had sunk across the whole chamber. A shadowy figure clarified at its far end, slowly hobbling. Baldr heard wheezing breath. He smelt a fustiness, like long-mouldered bread. He saw cloven hooves treading down the fungus, sinking into the deep layer of milky softness underfoot.

Slowly, the outline of a Plague Marine appeared. Unlike any uncorrupted Adeptus Astartes, he hunched over almost double. His shoulders bulged with growths. His ancient armour, pitted with jagged holes, hung from a warped frame, and flesh as pale and grey as Baldr's own livery protruded from the gaps.

The Plague Marine carried a staff – a gnarled thing, knotted like a vine. The green light came from a hollowed-out human skull at its tip. The creature's own head was helmless and withered. Vaguely human features competed with knots of tumours. Two deep-set, heavy-lined eyes looked up rheumily at Baldr.

'Welcome, Son of the Wolf King,' said the creature.

The voice was quiet, and old. There was a kindness to it, as if the speaker knew what suffering had been caused to bring him there and regretted it. Nothing about that voice suggested the speaker had once been a Space Marine, and yet the armour was there to prove it – dull grey-green, still bearing the forbidden marks of Mortarion's old Legion under a thick layer of rust and dirt.

Baldr felt the ancient hatreds kindle quickly. It was automatic, primed by a lifetime of gothi warnings and augmented by decades of psycho-conditioning.

Traitor.

Baldr bared his fangs instinctively. The hunched Plague Marine moved close enough, so he spat, tasting acid on his curved teeth as he sent it into the grey-skinned face before him.

The spittle sprayed across the Plague Marine, fizzing as it impacted. The stooped figure wiped it away with a hooked, arthritic finger. He sucked on the fingertip, musingly.

'A long time,' he muttered. 'A long time since one of you got close enough to spit.'

Baldr raged again at his bonds, straining to get a weapon-hand free.

'Rest,' the Plague Marine urged. 'Please. You will only damage yourself. Do you think we would have placed you in bonds you could break?'

Baldr's amber eyes narrowed. 'Know this,' he snarled. 'I will die before I give you anything you value.'

'No doubt you would, if that were an option.' The creature smiled sadly. His voice remained soft, almost melodically so. Two moist eyes shone in the dark, peering out from a ruined, sepulchral face. 'But I do not wish to hurt you, Space Wolf. On the contrary.'

Baldr's eyes roved across his surroundings, looking for something – anything – that he might use to extricate himself. There were always features of an environment that could be used. The Archenemy were powerful, but also capricious, and their desire to prolong agony rather than go for the swift kill was a weakness he had used before.

'What are you?' Baldr asked.

The Plague Marine raised a scab-covered eyebrow. 'That is a question,' he wheezed. He limped over to a natural outgrowth in the chamber's walls – a rock shelf in a fungus-filled grotto – and painfully sat down. The experience of watching him move was unsettling, for he carried himself like a decrepit old man, his breath rattling, his hands shaking. After seating himself, he slumped, letting the curve of his spine drag his head down even further. He kept hold of the skull-staff, though.

'What answer would satisfy you?' he asked. 'You would not believe much that I tell you. It will all be the truth, of course. Those of my Legion rarely tell lies. An old habit. We left the lying to others.' He chuckled dryly. 'What use is a lie? It gains you a little advantage, but this is the Eternal War, and eternals have no use for little advantages.'

Without meaning to, Baldr found himself listening, and cursed himself inwardly. The Plague Marine's voice remained quiet, almost tremulous. There was no threat in it at all – no bombast, no defiance. It wasn't even resigned.

'My name was Jeshua Ben Gur. I was born ten thousand, two hundred and sixty-nine years ago, by the reckoning of Terra. I grew up in sight of the Imperial Palace. That is more than you can boast, scion of the ice. I do not remember much of it, though – they took me for the Legion when I was eight, even before the primarch had been found. Younger than you were when they came for you, I expect.' He drew in a tremulous breath. 'I recall golden spires. I never saw them again, not even when the Siege came and we ran at the Gates in a world of fire. Sometimes I dream of those spires, and those flames. I no longer know if my memory of them is even reliable. Who knows? They are long gone now, and there is no going back to check.'

He coughed, bringing up a lumpy gobbet of phlegm. He spat it out and it landed, bloodily, on the chamber floor.

'After that I was called many things. I have lived a long time. Not, of course, for ten thousand years – the Eye melds time in strange ways – but long enough. When Calas brought the change with him, I changed too. I learned new things and forgot old ones. I learned that every situation brings its opportunities. I became a *gardener*. Do you believe that? A cultivator of forgotten things. I discovered that some lives will flourish in the dark. Some harbour their own light, inside themselves, cradled in phosphor, needing no sun or starlight to warm them.'

Baldr couldn't stop listening. A warning voice in his head screamed at him to plug his ears, to recite some litany against corruption, but he was unable to comply. He felt his muscles relax in their bonds. Even his wounds, which had been angrily painful, felt numb.

'There are organisms that thrive on decay, Son of Russ. There are creatures that lap up the matter of the dying and transform it to sustain themselves. Do they have no place in the galaxy? Do they have no beauty of their own?' He chuckled sadly. 'They need their champions, too. It cannot all be ice and iron, talon and tooth.'

The Traitor looked up directly at Baldr, and the light from the staff fell across his face. His skin was impossibly lined, like a reptile. Glossy sores bunched around dry lips, swollen with dark blood.

'The name I took in the Garden was the Mycelite. I lived for a long time there. I sat at the feet of the caged goddess and listened to her weeping. That taught me pity. I determined that striving against the inevitable was a peculiar kind of cruelty. It has to be ended. The War, everything, the whole meandering story – it has to be ended. And it will be, thankfully. It has started at last, and the whole carnival will finally pass into the long night again. Everything – all the striving, all the contests, they'll all slide away. It'll start at Cadia – you know that? The threads are pulling together there.'

The Mycelite's speech flitted from subject to subject, but as Baldr listened to the sibilant tones in the warm dark, he felt as if there were some truth there, ready to be grasped if only he could glimpse it. Nothing he heard made him angry any more – only curious.

'Is that why you are here?' Baldr asked, surprising himself as he heard the words leave his mouth.

The Mycelite shook his head. Every gesture he made had a kind of sorrowful benevolence to it, like a weary grandfather gently correcting the errors of a wayward protégé.

'Matters have gone awry,' he said. 'You responded swiftly, and your Rune Priest already burns his way towards the heart of my kingdom. Perhaps he will halt my spores landing, perhaps not. I have sent my servants to hinder him, but it no longer much matters to me, truth be told. The Traveller will be here soon, and then the tide will be rising faster than even your rune-witches can handle.'

He got to his feet once more, leaning heavily on the staff. Rasping from the effort, he limped up to Baldr again.

'But surprises can still be found – flowers amid the filth. That is another thing I learned.'

The Mycelite extended a withered hand and ran it down Baldr's cheek – gently, like a caress.

'*You* are here,' he breathed, as tenderly as a father. 'And, amid all the ruin, I could not have asked for more than that.'

For a long time, Hafloí had doubted the sagas recounted by the Grey Hunters around the fire-pits. He had fought well with his old pack of Blood Claws, charging recklessly into the oncoming storm alongside his battle-brothers, whooping and howling as his bolt pistol kicked and his axe whirled. He'd existed for nothing else. Combat had been a rush, thumping in his temples, fuelling the white-hot furnace at his warrior's core. His brothers had all been the same – flame-haired, hot-blooded, short-fanged and short-tempered.

They were called Blood Claws for a reason. At times, it seemed that his gauntlets were never free of it. He revelled in the killing, each time testing himself a little further, seeing just how far he could push the immense gifts he had been given. There was nothing finer, nothing purer – to be young, and vital, and given the power of a demigod to use in the cause of humanity.

The summons to leave that existence and join Járnhamar had been a shock, and an unwelcome one. Packs of young bloods were expected to fight together, to grow older and tougher together until their locks greyed and their fangs curved. After taking the Helix, that is what he'd been told would happen.

'You will be shield-brothers until death takes you,' the old Wolf Priest, Aesde, had told him, his ancient yellow eyes glowing in the firelight of the Aett. 'Mark the names. They shall stand with you at the End Times when fire consumes the galaxy and Russ comes again.'

It had been difficult to leave after that – to be joined to an older, colder band of brothers. Grey Hunters were tempered and harrowed by time. Each one of them had been beaten into something tougher and harder, and the flames within them had shrunk with it. From the beginning, they had looked down on him, and he had looked down on them. The two of them might as well have been different breeds.

If times had not been so straitened, if the entire Chapter were not stretched as thin as throttle-cord by the Long War, then it would never have happened. Ragnar had told him as much when he'd delivered the order. He'd done it in person, at least. That ought to have been a rare honour, but the tidings were too bad for him to see it.

'Everything is changing,' Ragnar had said, back on Fenris. 'The old order is eroding. You will have to learn faster than those you leave. Your new pack will test you, and you will rage against them.' Ragnar had gazed down at him impassively, giving nothing away. 'But you can learn from this. If you weather the storm, you will rise even faster than I did.' A wary smile. 'And I never fought as a Hunter. So we are both misfits.'

At the time, Hafloí had listened in silence, part awed by the Wolf Lord standing before him, part sullen from the news. Now he saw what Ragnar had been trying to tell him. If he had not been so thick-headed, so stuffed with rage and kill-urge, he might have appreciated it at the time.

Járnhamar fought so differently. Each one of them, taken individually, was far stronger than him – far wilier, far more experienced and far more adaptable. He'd seen it on Ras Shakeh, on the plague destroyer, and now within the hulk itself. For all he'd boasted of his Traitor kill on Hjec Aleja, he'd always known he needed to overachieve just to keep up with his taciturn, grim-faced brothers. He could boast, and they would indulge him, but every one of his new brothers had kill-tallies far in excess of his.

So it was that, as Hafloí sprinted through the arteries of horror in the depths of the plague-hulk, his breathing was ragged, his heart-rate was dangerously high, and his muscles were shrieking with pain. The packs had been fighting non-stop for hours, lost in the swirling hordes of mutated enemy soldiers. Since the passage of the bridge, they had been attacked constantly. The mutants never stopped coming. At times they burst from the walls like larvae from pupae, scattering into the open with embryonic fluids still trailing from their diseased flesh. There was never room to properly *fight*, only to hack and kick and claw them back into submission before treading their remains into the knee-thick filth.

Throughout, the Hunters around him fought on with undiminished fervour. Their endurance was phenomenal. Hafloí stayed close to Gunnlaugur for most of the descent, and for the first time he truly saw what it took to become vaerangi. The Wolf Guard hewed with undiminished heft and purpose, roaring out his defiance even as the air around him hummed with heat and hatred. The raw fires of the underworld could have rippled across him and he would have shouldered them aside. He was immense – unbowed, furious, unstoppable.

The rest of the pack-brothers were scarcely less formidable. They entered combat low and fast, swinging and pivoting to bring their blades to bear. They smashed heads, ripped open torsos, punched through spines. Even before their fists had stopped moving they were pouncing onto their next prey. Their armour ran with trails of gore, slapping around them like flails as they moved.

Hafloí laboured to keep up. He drove his axe with as much speed as his burning arms could muster. He fired his bolt pistol into the dark as accurately as his mind would allow. He leapt to the aid of his brothers on the rare occasions when their guard was broken, just as they kept watch over him when his judgement faltered.

Once, during the long, horrific fight down from the hub towards the hulk's core, he'd spotted the desperate lunge of an eyeless terror as it pounced towards one of Fellblade's pack. Hafloí got to it first, sending it tumbling with a pistol-shot before eviscerating it with two crosswise swipes of his axe.

The warrior he'd saved, a grizzled old fighter named Eir, nodded at him, once, before loping off after fresh prey.

By then Hafloí was sprinting again, never resting, always heading further down. The bodies of his battle-brothers loomed around him in the dark. He could smell their acrid hunt-scent – sweat, armour-coolant, the sharp tang of overloaded disruptor fields. The humidity was incredible, bearing down on him like a vice.

You will have to learn faster.

His breath became rapid. His vision clouded at the edges. His axe strikes became erratic from weariness, but still he kept his feet, maintained the pace, ran with his brothers in the very maws of Hel. All that was left was to *keep going.*

'Maintain speed,' came Njal's vox-command again from up ahead, somewhere in the clogged mass of twisting tunnels. 'The core approaches.'

Hafloí kept his head down and his legs pumping hard. A bloated mutant swung down at him from the sagging tunnel ceiling and he lashed out with his axe, severing it diagonally. Another loomed up out of the murk from the left, grasping at his waist with tentacled arms, and he sent a lone bolt-round into its scabrous torso.

Down they ran, further down, and the environment became even more febrile. Echoing screams ran up the tunnels, the sound of whole crowds of blood-maddened damned roaring up to meet them.

When the break came, when they burst through into the open once more, Hafloí barely noticed the change. The shrieks echoed differently, but for a few moments nothing else altered – it remained corpse-dark, fever-hot and stinking.

Then Njal's staff lit up. Hafloí saw that they had charged into a vast space again. Actinic light lashed up into the void, rebounding from soaring walls of iron. As the storm-lightning kindled, green-tinged flames thundered into life ahead of them, surging out from deep pits in the floor.

For a fraction of a second before his conditioning kicked in, Hafloí didn't exhale. The sheer scale of it was hard to get a grip on. Ranks of obsidian columns soared into the high roof. The pits between the walkways boiled and seethed with unholy fires, sending smoke roiling up in thick pillars. At the far end of the chamber, half lost in a miasma of drifting soot, was the target – the impossibly huge engines that powered the entire hulk. Each one was cast in bronze and iron, towering up in terraces of twisted pipework and organ-like heat exchangers. Dull red flames growled away behind thick metal grilles the size of Reaver-class Titans. Colossal, eyeless, multi-limbed statues stood sentry about the drive units, hewn from granite and depicting obese and foul deities of ruin.

Huge arcs of energy snapped and snaked across the surface of the enginarium chambers, briefly throwing flares of putrid green light across the fiery shafts. Enormous wheels turned slowly in the depths, driven by linked-iron chains and shackled to hab-sized gearing mechanisms of beaten adamantium.

Every surface glistened with corruption. Every metal component was thick with rust, and every exhaust vent belched toxic sludge. The whole edifice looked liable to collapse in on itself at any moment, driven apart by the incomprehensible levels of power thrumming through its cancerous structure.

In that split-second moment, just as he looked up at the full extent of the drive chamber, Haflói realised for the first time just how potent its destruction would be. His armour-readings of the power contained in the coils and fusion chambers were off the scale – if its shell could be cracked, the blast would be world-endingly huge.

But the enemy knew it, too, and had pulled all of its strength back towards the ship's ancient heart. The space between the Wolves and the engine gates swarmed with legions of mutants. Among them strode greater horrors – figures twice the height of a mortal man with clawed fists and elongated, muscle-bunched arms. Demented vermin scuttled and shrieked across every surface, their eyes shining in the fire-flecked dark. Traitor tech-priests stalked among the hosts, their tattered robes exposing bizarre biomechanics of contaminated flesh and bolted augmetics.

But beyond them all, by far the most potent of all the terror troops assembled in that cathedral of ruin, were the Traitor Marines. Their armour swelled and cracked as they stood sentinel, massive and unmoving, under the engine gates themselves. They carried power scythes and snub-nosed boltguns. Some wore armour from forgotten ages, with angular vox-grilles and heavy ceramite plating. Others stood in Mark V or VI variants plundered from more recent campaigns, slung with skulls and surmounted by blunt spikes. In every case, their helm-lenses glowed pale green, glimmering spectrally as the hordes of Chaos howled before them.

They would wait there. They would let the filth before them absorb the brunt of the attack before taking the field themselves. Only when the packs had waded through the deranged masses at their feet would the scythes be taken up. Then the real test would come – equally matched, equally potent, each driven by an equal hatred nurtured over ten thousand years of endless war.

Haflói wasn't blind to the extent of the test. All things being equal, this chamber would see the death of all of them. Even the fury of the massed packs had little chance of penetrating such deep and eternal corruption.

But things were not equal. One factor tipped the balance.

Njal strode into the open, his outline already shimmering with storm-energies. His heavy Terminator tread cracked against the stone, his staff lifted high. Lightning spilled from the runes on his battleplate, fierce and eye-watering. A chill, steel-hard wave of intimidation radiated out from him, as pitiless as Helwinter. When facing the xenos-construct his rage had been wild and free, the exuberance of the hunter. Now, with the deaths of Álfar and Baldr, it had become a thing of pure, distilled hatred, and even Hafloí was taken aback by its intensity.

'Heidur Rus!' roared Njal Stormcaller, summoning the storm-wind once more. His cloak snapped and billowed, and silver forks of lightning blazed from his staff's tip. His runes flared, and he stood, inviolate and immense, a pure shard of defiance against the limitless nightmarish hordes.

'Gothi!' the Wolves roared in unison, thrusting their blades high into the flame-edged dark. 'Stormurstjórn!'

Hafloí roared his soul out with them, forgetting fatigue, revelling in the raw potency of the battle-challenge. Flames flared up again, greater than before, rippling like walls of plasma. The mutated denizens of the engine core yelled and bawled their defiance, and surged across the cavern floor towards the thin line of steel-grey. The Wolves thundered out raw death-oaths, levelling their axes just as the tribes of the iron seas had done since the age of legend, choosing those whom they would slay in the name of the Stormcaller, the Allfather and the Wolf King.

Then they charged.

Chapter Sixteen

'We have ships. They are already prepared for launch. Let us fight it.'

Annarovea's tone was defiant. She sat in a high-backed chair at the head of a long table. The walls of the narrow room around her were black and glossy. The table was black. The floor was black. Every surface reflected dully from the few low-power sodium lamps set into the ceiling.

Olgeir faced her at the opposite end of the table. Annarovea's staff sat along both sides: General Galx Favel, the commander of the Joint Guard Regiments; Marshal Brejial Hagh, controller of the orbital defence forces; Lord Commissar Selucius Morfol; Hamoda al-Yeshiv, Mistress of Astropaths; Salvia Verdello, Senior Judge of the Adeptus Arbites.

They had all had their say, and had all voiced similar sentiments. Hagh estimated he could have twelve of the planet's void-fighter wings out of their orbital hangars within ten minutes. Eight more wings could be called from reserve within three hours. Favel judged he could mobilise six armoured divisions for the main spire zone, thirteen more for the rest of the planet's urban territories. They could, he claimed, hold out for weeks. Morfol agreed – Kefa Primaris was a well-defended world, a linchpin system: it had reserves, munitions, supplies. It had raised nine Guard regiments, six of which had garrisons in-system.

Olgeir admired the sentiments. As the mortals spoke, he tried not to show impatience, even though the chrono in his armour-collar kept ticking down steadily. If he had been in their position, he would have argued the same way. They were cogent, measured, defiant.

'You have heard all this, lord,' concluded Annarovea. 'Only hours remain. We must give the order now.'

Olgeir still liked her.

'No order will be given,' Olgeir said. 'You're getting off the planet. Guard only, no civilians. You can't defend against this. As many as you can, all into deep void.'

His words stunned the chamber into silence. Commissar Morfol, who had welcomed Olgeir effusively on arrival as a fellow zealot for combat, looked as if he'd been kicked in the stomach.

Annarovea's jawline dropped a little, only to be swiftly clamped shut again.

'Is this some jest, lord?' she asked.

Olgeir shook his head. 'I wouldn't insult you.' He leaned forwards, resting his arms heavily on the tabletop. 'You can't stop it. Line battle cruisers would not stop it now. It'll make orbit whether you launch your fighters or not. It's already mauled ships with more firepower than your entire defence grid. Once it comes into range, it'll launch contagion spores. Millions of them. You'll take a hundred out, but when the rest hit, they'll burn through your cities. A few of you will be able to take refuge, the rest will be infected. They'll begin to change. They'll look sick, but they'll be far stronger than your best warriors. They'll overrun every defence-line you have. They'll keep coming. You'll empty ammo-dumps at them, and they'll keep coming. Your own troops will begin to change. You won't be able to kill them fast enough.'

Olgeir looked at Favel. 'Hold out for weeks? Not against this. You'll have a few days. Once the spores are in the atmosphere, it's over. The infected don't die. They'll take any voidcraft you have and they'll launch for other worlds. More plague-ships will come here once your defences are down and they'll pick up more. The army will swell, getting bigger with every conquest. This place will be the source, then. It'll be the *incubator*.'

He returned his gaze to Annarovea.

'You wish to serve?' he asked. 'Get off-world. Every battalion you can pull out of the system is another battalion that will fight again. That's the truth, governor. There are no other choices now.'

For a moment, no one spoke. The lamps burned away in their brackets;

the air-filters hummed behind mesh grilles. Olgeir remained where he was, letting the news sink in. It was a strange thing, being a diplomat rather than a killer. In other circumstances he might have enjoyed the challenge. As it was, the words he was forced to speak made him feel hollow.

Morfol was the first to respond. 'I had *dreamed* of meeting one of you,' the commissar said, holding his emotion in with difficulty. 'And now, you come here, and tell us...' His voice trembled with fervour. 'We have ships. Guns, fighters. What kind of... *cowardice* is it that–'

'Enough, Morfol.' Annarovea's voice – calm but steely – cut him dead. Her cool grey eyes remained fixed on Olgeir's, as if trying to work out whether he was some kind of horrific fraud. 'This cannot be right, my lord. We have the resources of an entire world ready to deploy. There must be something we can do.'

'Nothing you have would get close to it,' said Olgeir, flatly. As he spoke, he felt a dull ache run through his body. Morfol was right – it felt like betrayal. 'This thing is no ordinary ship. Such vessels leave the warp once in a thousand years, and even a full Navy battle-group would struggle to halt it. It is your misfortune that it came here, but something can yet be saved. There will be other battles, and your guns will be needed for those.'

Annarovea's eyes never left his. Her defiance slowly gave way to understanding. She took it in, absorbing the bitter truth.

'Is there nothing, then?' she asked.

'My brothers have already boarded it,' Olgeir said. 'They fight towards its heart. A Rune Priest is with them, as well as more than thirty warriors of my order. That is the last hope for this world. They will kill it or they will die in the attempt.'

Hagh perked up immediately – before that, he had been slumped in a kind of mute state of denial. 'Then it is not all lost,' he said.

Olgeir made no mention of Delvaux. There was no reason to – it would not help their resolve to know that if the Wolves failed to destroy the hulk then the Ecclesiarchy stood ready to immolate the planet instead.

'Not yet,' Olgeir said. 'But it will be soon.' He flexed his gauntlets, ruefully wishing they clutched at an axe-shaft rather than air. 'So, then. This is the situation. We need to stop talking, and you need to start moving. I have your word of command?'

The disillusionment in Annarovea's face was still heavy. A lesser soul might have been crushed by it. Slowly, though, the hardness of her features reasserted itself.

'If there is no other way,' she said slowly, sitting erect in her chair, her back straight in defeat, 'then there is no time to lose.'

She turned to her staff.

'Begin the evacuation.'

Jorundur had flown gunships for longer than most mortals had been alive. He felt their every tremor, their every yaw and shudder, and knew just what they meant. At times he could almost imagine the machine-spirits whispering in his ear, summoned up from the coils and logic-boards buried deep in the sacred heart of the vessels.

To fly a Thunderhawk was a privilege and a joy – the only true joy he felt any more. The heavy vibration of the engines thundering away at full blast, the immense power of the main cannon, the surprising manoeuvrability of such a huge and cumbersome object – they were the things that stirred his withered soul.

To take such a thing into the edge of annihilation, then, was a test of nerve. He held no fear for himself, nor for the mortals around him who struggled stoically to keep the machine in one piece. His fear was reserved for the thing of beauty that would depart the universe forever should the near-infinite gunnery of the plague-hulk catch up with it.

His rage at Hafloí for nearly destroying it on Ras Shakeh had not been feigned. To see it cut apart by the guns of some plague-addled starbehemoth would infuriate him far more than the likely prospect of his own demise.

'Are you getting him yet?' he snapped, pulling *Vuokho* out of a steep plummet, just in time to evade a ship-killing brace of las-beams.

The hulk's impossibly gigantic hull soared away from them, a cliff-edge in space, scarred and tangled with the patina of the warp. *Vuokho* danced and shot across the ruinous vista, darting among the lines of incoming fire. There was no point in firing back – nothing the gunship carried would so much as scratch the hulk's surface. All they had to keep them alive was speed and guile.

'Negative,' said Beor. The faintest note of accusation hung in his voice. The attempt was becoming more than suicidal, and even the loyalty of Fenrisian kaerls had its limits.

'Coming round again,' said Jorundur, working the controls as deftly as he'd ever done. Projectiles and energy-lines shot silently past the gunship as it corkscrewed and thrust. So far they'd only taken glancing hits. That couldn't last.

'If we maintain course–' began Terrag.

'We'll run into those macrocannons,' finished Jorundur, well aware of the make-up of the hulk's nearside weapon arrays. 'Keep monitoring for signals. We can give it one more pass.'

As he pushed the Thunderhawk's tortured frame harder and faster, he glanced at the close augur readings. *Heimdall* was already crawling towards *Vindicatus*, but slowly. The frigate looked badly mauled, and its engines were bleeding into the void. On its own it wouldn't last much longer against *Vindicatus* than *Vuokho* would against the *Festerax*. The Cardinal's flagship was still stationary, but its main drives were demonstrably keying up. Time was fast running out.

Jorundur coaxed an iota more power from *Vuokho*'s straining drive-train, sending the gunship skimming across the face of the plague-hulk. More fire scythed in at them, launched from the hundreds of emplacements embedded in the *Festerax*'s grotesque underbelly.

Jorundur checked back out of a dive, rolled hard, and pushed up towards the hulk's nearest stalactitic vane before shoving mercilessly down back into the void. The gunship's structure cracked and shrieked, causing red warning runes to flood across the cockpit consoles like bloodstreams.

We are the prey here. An unfamiliar sensation.

'Are you getting anything?' he demanded again, working the control columns hard.

'Nothing,' reported Beor flatly.

Jorundur cursed, and prepared for another hard dive.

Just as he did so, something hit *Vuokho*'s ventral plating. Hard.

The gunship slewed violently, tilting away and losing speed. A warning klaxon sounded, and tiny stress-fractures spidered out across the armour-glass viewscreens.

'Hull breach below,' reported Morven calmly. 'Losing pressurisation.'

'Clamp it down,' snapped Jorundur, fighting with the controls. *Vuokho* locked into a steep plummet, driven by blazing engines that no longer responded. The trajectory took them straight at the vast face of the nearest descender vane.

'Control system's gone,' growled Terrag, reaching up for a lever and yanking hard. 'Switching to backup.' As he pulled down, a hard clank rang out from the gunship's innards, followed by an explosion of sparks across the cockpit's right-hand side.

It did the trick, though – *Vuokho* immediately responded, pulling high and gaining power again. Projectile rounds followed them, peppering the dorsal armour and making the whole craft spin and buck.

'Leak plugged,' said Morven. 'For now.'

'Good,' snarled Jorundur, still wrestling to keep the racing gunship from tearing itself apart. 'Keep it that way.'

A shimmering criss-cross of las-fire streaked out into the void ahead of them. Jorundur hauled on the control columns, pushing *Vuokho*'s nose up and out of their path, but it wasn't quick enough. A brace of beams impacted, burning through the multi-layered hull-plates and spearing through the far side. *Vuokho* reeled again, its lower crew bay carved open and venting freely.

'We can't stay in this, lord,' said Beor, quietly.

Jorundur rounded on him, ready to tell him what to do with his advice, but the words died in his throat. More dire metrics ran across the consoles, heralding a fresh barrage from the hulk. The void was filled with energies, snarling and spearing across the dark in a dense web of destruction.

'You're right,' Jorundur snarled, checking *Heimdall*'s position and calculating whether they could race back to its shadow before destruction overcame them.

Beor twisted in his seat, as if wanting to be sure. 'Did you–'

'You heard me,' Jorundur said, pulling *Vuokho*'s trajectory away from the incoming storm and back out towards the deep void. 'We're getting out of this.' He glanced back at the retreating hulk-face, feeling the sting of failure.

'You left it too late, brother,' he breathed, watching the immense slab-side of twisted metal flash and swing in the light of macrocannon discharge. 'You're on your own now.'

'Tell me of your childhood.'

Baldr struggled not to respond. He willed his mouth not to move, to remain clenched shut in defiant silence, but, just as before, the muscles relaxed before he knew it.

The Mycelite's power was in his voice. It was soft, almost mournful. The ruined Traitor Marine looked as fragile as a hollowed-out tree-bole, but Baldr could feel his strength burning away, filling the air, heating it and making it thicken.

Njal could have resisted that voice. Gunnlaugur, too, perhaps. Any of his brothers with greater strength of will would have remembered their vows and stayed quiet.

Why could he not?

'What do you want to know?' Baldr replied.

'Your life on Fenris. I have heard many stories of your wild planet. Who in the galaxy has not? I am genuinely curious.'

The words spilled from Baldr's lips like blood from a wound. Once he started talking, it became harder and harder to stop.

'I was born on the ice,' he said. 'I only remember the later days, just before they took me.'

'They watch your combat, taking the valiant. Is that so? That is what I heard.'

'The Wolf Priests do. They draw the dead from the red ice. They re-knit their bodies and remake their flesh.'

'And you were among the dead.'

'A long time ago.'

'They take you into the Mountain,' said the Mycelite, his eyes rapt with fascination. As he sat, hunched like some vast toad in his squalor, dull rolls of noise rose up from the depths. Baldr knew those noises meant something, but it had become hard to even conceive of a world outside that dark chamber. 'They test you there, yes? They make you pure before they give you an axe.'

Baldr remembered what Njal had told him, back on *Heimdall*.

We were looking for a sign – any sign – of aptitude. None was found.

'What does "pure" even mean to you?' Baldr countered, dredging up some scorn from somewhere.

The Mycelite smiled wryly. 'Something different to your Priests, I admit.' He stirred himself, extending the staff and making its skull-tip loom closer. 'Let me tell you something. You won't believe me, but I will tell you anyway.'

He pushed his battered body from its seat and got to his feet. The effort made his breath scrape and whine.

'You are remarkable, you Sons of Russ,' he said. 'Every other Legion has faced the truth. One by one, they have all acknowledged the way of the universe. They have accepted that the warp runs through them, boiling in their blood, turning them into the thing that they hate. They can ring it with wards, they can bind it with rituals, but still it is *there*, the reminder of their failure. Every time a Librarian closes his eyes, it's grinning back at him.'

He lost his smile. 'The warp,' he croaked, as if the word pained him. 'We must perforce use the tools of our own damnation. The irony was not lost on your Imperium's architects. They tried to excise the whole charade, once, but by then greater forces were already in play, and Nikaea was always doomed.'

The Mycelite shook his head in wry wonder. 'After that, we all had to swallow the bitter taste of truth, sooner or later, but you – the attack dogs of Fenris – never did. You told yourself stories about your home world, and its storms, and the magick of the runes, and convinced yourself that you, and *only you* among the Eighteen, had no need to use witches on the battlefield.' He laughed hoarsely. 'Ha! Such story-weavers. The best in the galaxy, even if you told your tales only to yourselves.'

Baldr listened, unable not to. Some of what the creature said made no sense to him. The events he referred to were thousands of years ago and lost in the fog of legend. 'I have seen runecraft,' he said, maintaining at least the veneer of resistance. 'It draws from the world-soul. What you do is... different.'

The Mycelite nodded wearily. 'No doubt you truly believe that.' He shuffled closer to Baldr, and extended a withered hand. The gauntlet that had enclosed it had long gone, revealing atrophied flesh stretched over a network of bone. 'You see this? It was once as firm as your skin, and just as strong.' He turned his hand in the gloomy half-light, watching the lines and wrinkles move. 'You would hardly know we were forged from the same gene-coding, yet we have your Corpse-Emperor's trickery embedded within us both. That's the thing, Baldr Fjolnir: we *look* different, but that's all on the surface.'

He withdrew the hand, moving stiffly, as if, despite himself, some part of him was still capable of registering shame.

'Runecraft *looks* different. It *sounds* different. You can tell yourself as many stories as you like about how it *is* different. I admire you for doing so. But, deep down, even your Stormcaller knows it's all lies. He knows that he drags his power up from the same place we all do. He can call himself a Priest if he wants – I've heard worse titles for our kind.' He shuffled close again, lifting his reptilian face up to Baldr's. '*Our* kind. You, me, him. We are all locked in the same prison. Some of us are a little more honest about where the walls are.'

Baldr stared down at the creature before him. 'You have made this place a living Hel,' he said, quietly, fixing the Mycelite with a mask of contempt. 'We are nothing like each other. The *Fenryka* chose to keep our oaths.'

The Mycelite snorted. 'Chose? *Chose?* What did you *choose*, young hunter? You were not even allowed to *die* on your own.' He spat on the floor. 'This is the only time you have truly had a choice to make in your life, and I am the one to give it to you.'

Baldr watched him carefully. 'You can give me nothing.'

'So sure, for one so merely on the cusp of knowledge.' The Mycelite reached up with his staff, resting the tip of it on Baldr's breastplate. The skull clinked against the ceramite. 'I sense the collar you wear,' he said. 'Your mentor knows his art. To remove it would kill you. Possibly me, as well. While it remains in place, I can only show you a fraction of what I had hoped to.'

Baldr tensed, feeling heat building up before him.

'As I said, you cannot–'

'Hush,' whispered the Mycelite, closing his eyes. 'No more words.'

Baldr tried to speak again, to defy the order, but the two empty eye-sockets before him suddenly flared into green-edged life. He felt a huge pressure bearing down on him, as if he'd been plunged deep underwater, and the dim light around him snuffed out. For an instant, it was as if the entire universe had been erased, replaced by a black, muffled wall of infinite weight and density, but then the crushing mass ripped away.

He realised he had closed his own eyes, and carefully opened them.

'Where am I?' he asked, too lost in surprise to remember any defiance.

The Mycelite's voice still rang in his mind – just as soft, just as seductive.

'Everywhere,' said the creature, chuckling as he spoke. 'Do you see it? You are *everywhere*.'

Ingvar ran.

He strained with every sinew and burned every muscle, forcing his body into new extremities of raw speed. In the foetid plague-hulk, everything was tight, clogged and enclosed – rammed with screaming, jostling armies of the damned. They emerged in droves from crevices and cracks, shrieking and blind, thirsting only to lay scab-encrusted hands on him and bite into healthy flesh. The only response was to keep ahead of them, to keep his limbs driving and the sword-edge dancing. As the enemy came after him, time and again, the runes on *dausvjer*'s edge ran black with clots of blood and bile.

Ingvar sprinted back through the halls of the eldar starship, fighting his way across the bridge and past the stricken outline of the downed wraithknight. He hewed his way across the wraithbone plains, and he fought his way, stride by bloody stride, back into the outer core where the impacted voidcraft lay thickly atop and within one another.

As he neared the surface levels, weariness began to slow him at last. His genhanced arms burned, his chest spiked with pain. Sweat ran down the inside of his armour, trickling down the back of his neck and pooling around the carapace nodes in his spine. They got closer with every attack, scrabbling at his armour with their talons before he could kick or swipe them away. They launched themselves from hidden roof-vaults, they burst up from compartments in the floor, they spilled out of void-dark culverts and air-cycling tubes. They were like locusts, covering every pressed-metal floor panel and grease-streaked wall section, scuttling and skittering and hissing in the penumbral gloom.

After a final, blood-drenched push, Ingvar broke out into a high-roofed hall, gothic-arched and encrusted with defiled Imperial iconography. At the far end rose a soaring gateway marked with old rune-identifiers for fighter hangars. It was as good a destination as any – one of the thousands of void-facing apertures that would give him a chance to make contact with Jorundur.

The mutants knew well enough what he was doing, and came after him with even greater frenzy. Hundreds surged into the hall behind him, all thirsting to pull him down and back within the hulk's dark embrace. Ingvar felt a clawed hand grab his arm, and wrenched its owner from its feet. Three more dropped down from the vaults above, wailing as they plummeted. Ingvar punched out as they fell, still running, breaking their bones as they thudded and bounced from his armour.

The impact made him stagger. If he lost his footing now, they would be on him, dozens of them, then more, piling on so fast he'd be buried alive. He forced his limbs to keep pumping, to keeping powering on through the fatigue.

The hangar entrances rose over him, vast enough to accommodate Valkyrie gunships being lifted on claw-rails. He gained the launch-zones beyond and raced across them, his boots finally striking rockcrete again. Ranked launch bays stretched off on either side, empty of the craft that had once lined them. Up ahead, two hundred metres off, void-entrance gates glittered from the exposed starfield beyond.

He was close, now – desperately close.

'Jorundur!' he voxed. 'Fix to my loc.'

No reply – the comm-link hissed with static. Ingvar tore onwards, sprinting towards the closest of the void-gates, and the mob followed him like a breaking wave. One clamped a fist around his trailing leg, another nearly speared his shoulder with a heavily thrown blade.

'Jorundur,' voxed Ingvar again, seeing nothing on his armour's scanners. 'Are you getting this?'

He neared the far edge of the launch bay. There was nowhere else to go.

With a cold lurch in the pit of his stomach, Ingvar contemplated, for the first time, the possibility that Jorundur had not been equal to the firepower of the hulk's outer guns. Perhaps even the Old Dog, the finest pilot Ingvar had ever fought alongside, had succumbed to the barrage.

As the lip of the hangar approached, Ingvar let out an echoing roar of rage, skidded around and faced his pursuers.

They careered into him, carried into contact by the huge momentum of the crowd. Ingvar ripped into them, hurling bodies clear in all directions. He hewed and blocked with ferocious, blinding speed, carpeting the apron in fresh gore. He lashed out in the baresark way, worked his blade two-handed, blurring the edge with velocity even as they pushed him back towards the edge of the void.

'For *Russ!*' he roared, time and again. 'For the honour of the Wolf King!'

Not since leaving Fenris for the Deathwatch had he fought like it. There were no Blood Angel strokes in his hammering display, no Dark Angel tricks or Ultramarine restraint. The mutants died in swathes, thrown against the glittering arcs of his vengeful blade and broken asunder by its wrath.

In the face of such limitless ferocity, even those hordes fell back. They scrambled and clawed to get away from the blue-edged sword.

The hangar fell silent. Ingvar stood on the very extremity, the open starfield at his back, panting heavily, his armour red from the gore that covered it, his head low.

There were still hundreds of them. More streamed into the halls with every passing second. Ingvar's blood still boiled with the war-fury, but it could not last forever. It was only a matter of time before they summoned the courage to rush him again, and this time there would be no victory.

Gunnlaugur had been right. It had been a foolish effort, one born of overweening pride. He would die on the hulk, alone, with Klaive's secrets still hidden in the depths of *Vindicatus*.

Ingvar smiled wryly under his battered helm. Callimachus would never have approved.

But I am a true Wolf again, he thought. *That, at least, has been proved.*

He angled his blade at the face of the nearest mutant, feeling the energy field spit with relish.

'Who will be first, then?' he cried, challenging them all. 'Who will have the honour of this scalp?'

At that, the spell broke, and the front rank of mutants rushed him again, stumbling in their haste and panic, driven by the swell of the hundreds pushing behind.

Ingvar bellowed a fresh war-cry, tensing for the almighty impact.

The row of mutants before him exploded in a sequential line of blasted flesh and armour-shards, blowing up as columns of bolt-rounds thudded into them. A thunder of thrusters filled the hangar space as something huge and furnace-hot broke the atmosphere seal over the hangar's exit.

Ingvar looked up to see *Vuokho* labouring hard to maintain loft. Its entire underside had been ripped to pieces, and it looked like the heavy bolters were about the only thing that still functioned on its entire chassis. It turned on a thick downdraught, laying into the hordes of plague-damned as it circled about.

'Gyrfalkon,' came Jorundur's furious voice over the pack-comm. 'You have two seconds.'

Ingvar grinned, and leapt up to grasp the mangled remains of the lower crew bay door.

'What kept you, brother?' he asked, hauling himself clear of the hangar floor.

'I changed my mind,' said Jorundur, sounding very angry about it.

Then Jorundur wheeled the Thunderhawk around and pointed its charred muzzle back towards the void outside. The engines fired, and both gunship and passenger tore free of the *Festerax*'s interior, back out into the las-beam-crossed storm beyond. Ingvar hung on, clambering up into the crew-bay even as the Thunderhawk powered into the void.

Behind them, the screams of the damned lingered – furious, rabid, but impotent.

Chapter Seventeen

Gunnlaugur felt the blood in his throat. Every time he roared out a fresh battle-cry, the pain flared up. He ignored it, and kept bellowing. His armour made his voice swell out across the entire space, filling the fire-hot hall with the sound of his wrath.

His brothers did the same, howling raw fury at the enemy. The combined effect was electrifying – it made his hearts surge and his mind sing. Even in the midst of almost infinite ruin, the cries of the Wolves were chilling. Deep in the depths of the plague-hulk, a fragment of immortal Fenris had lodged, and with every stride it worked its way further into the flesh of its prey, ice-cold, steel-hard.

Gunnlaugur and Hafloí had spearheaded the charge on the right flank of Njal's advance. With Fellblade's surviving warriors, they carved a bloody trail out across the pit surface. Bloodhame held the left flank, while Njal pushed up the centre, bolstered by his own retinue and Hauki's fighters.

The warband cut a diminished aspect from the numbers that had broken into the hulk on the assault rams, and now fewer than thirty remained. Set beside the forces ranged against them, those numbers were pitiful. Laughable.

Yet no one laughed. The mutant tides yelled and bawled their defiance.

223

Monsters in their midst lumbered into contact, their minds slushed by pain-amplifiers and thick layers of disease. At the rear of the horde, the bloated Plague Marines waited patiently, immobile and inscrutable.

'*Russvangam!*' thundered Gunnlaugur, decapitating the mutant closest to him with a broad sweep of his hammer. He lurched back into the counter-swing, punching the crackling weapon-head through the bodies of another two.

Ahead, half shrouded by drifting smoke-lines, loomed a greater test. It might have once been an ogryn, a grotesque abhuman many times the size and strength of an unaugmented mortal. Its swell-veined muscles bulged unnaturally, bursting out from under ramshackle plates of beaten iron. As it came on, it laid about itself with a crackling power maul. Its roars of challenge were nearly the equal of Gunnlaugur's own, though thickened by madness into a bestial, slurring mess.

Gunnlaugur barged his way through a squad of lesser fighters to get to it. The plague-ogryn saw him coming and ploughed its way straight at him. As Gunnlaugur crashed and bludgeoned his way closer, he saw the metal tubes punched through the monster's corpse-white skin, each one gurgling with combat-stimms. Lodged among the overlapping armour plates were vials of sludgy bile, fizzing from some toxic combination of battle-poisons.

Then the two of them collided, and the impact was shuddering.

Skulbrotsjór scythed, smashing against the jangling gourds and sending them clattering. The ogryn slammed its power maul down, aiming to crack Gunnlaugur's trailing pauldron. Gunnlaugur evaded the blow, then launched another crushing hammer strike at the creature's midriff.

The smashes came in thick and fast after that – heavy, driving blows that dented ceramite and tore up iron plating. Gunnlaugur was faster, hauling his hammer around him in speed-blurred arcs, but the tainted ogryn was taller, bulkier and immeasurably strong. Both of them took bone-breaking impacts. Gunnlaugur's plastron was nearly sheared in two from a sharp maul swing, while the ogryn's right leg was virtually cloven open by a sharp switchback from the thunder hammer. Blood, both post-human and abhuman, spiralled out from the epicentre of the combat.

The plague-ogryn worked to shut the Space Wolf down, bearing over him and cracking the maul down two-handed. Gunnlaugur responded instantly, ducking low and thrusting up under the creature's guard. As he did so, he fed a sliver of extra power to *skulbrotsjór*'s energy field, making it roar like a voidship's thrusters.

The impact was explosive, lifting the colossal mutant from its feet and sending its power maul flying. The wounded ogryn tumbled away, disorientated and nearly disembowelled. Gunnlaugur pounced after it.

'For Russ!' he roared, leaping high, then smashing the hammerhead down on the ogryn's forehead.

The creature's skull blew apart, drenching both of them in cranial slime. The ogryn tottered, headless, for a few moments more, its fists still clenched and its legs braced, before crashing backwards.

Gunnlaugur thrust his thunder hammer high and howled his triumph out.

'Heidur Rus!'

His every pore streamed with sweat, his muscles screamed from the effort of wielding his great weapon, both his hearts raced to keep his genhanced systems from overloading, but still his spirit raged and his eyes blazed.

This was what he had been desperate for. Around him, his battle-brothers raced forward, echoing his howl of triumph with savage whoops of their own. He was where he had always been destined to be – at the heart of the tempest, slaying freely for the Allfather and the primarch.

As the last echoes of his kill-cry rang across the chamber, Gunnlaugur burst into movement once more. Over to his left, Njal was striding out, wreathed in snapping wyrd-lightning. The warriors of the Rout tore into the hordes like the predators they were, leaping across the pits to get at the enemy, driving in low and forging gore-soaked paths through whole knots of mutated troops.

Step by step, blade-swipe by blade-swipe, they were cutting their way towards the objective. The colossal heat-exchanger towers loomed closer.

It was then that the Traitor Marines began to move, hefting their scythes and striding down from the portals. Gunnlaugur detected twelve of them.

Back on Ras Shakeh, right at the thickest of the fighting, the Plague Marine champion had bested him. Now he latched on to the greatest of those who marched under the fires of the enginarium, and bellowed out his challenge.

'You!' he thundered, and his hoarse voice cut through the mass of screams and roars to reach its target – a huge monster with a lone-eyed helm, bearing an armour-fixed scythe blade in each hand. 'I claim *you!*'

For a moment, Gunnlaugur could not be sure that the Plague Marine had heard him. Then the Traitor paused. His corroded helm swept the battlefield, and his gaze alighted on him. The two of them stared at one another – twin titans of slaughter, separated by a raging sea of lesser warriors.

Then the Traitor nodded, acknowledging the contest, and strode out to meet him.

Gunnlaugur grinned under his helm, licking hot blood from his fangs, and broke into the charge.

Challenge accepted.

Dawn broke over Kallian Hellax. The sunlight was weak, and struggled to push through thick banks of violet-tinged cloud. The vast sprawl of the spire complex rose up through layers of mist like islands in a milky sea, drear and immense.

On the far northern rim of the conurbation, landers came and went like clouds of metal insects. Requisition orders had streamed out of the command centre during the night, rousing divisional commanders and stirring them into action. Regimental barracks were given red-alert warnings, and whole battalions now marched into the waiting maws of orbital lifters. Huge troop-carrying craft squatted obesely on rockcrete aprons, their hulls open and glowing with red-tinged light.

It all looked orderly enough – long lines of marching men in uniform disgorging from ground transports and heading for the cavernous craft interiors. Every ten minutes, one of the big lifters would haul its doors closed, prime its engines and take off in a blaze of smoke and thruster-fire, swaying heavily up into the gathering dawn sky. Every time a space was cleared on the landing stages, another troop carrier would emerge from the clouds above and take its place on the grid, ready to absorb another detachment of living cargo.

'You have done well, governor,' said Olgeir, watching the progress from a balcony high on the southern edge of the compound. He'd taken a skimmer over to the complex with Annarovea an hour ago.

He hadn't slept. None of the planet's high command had done so. Organising a lift involving such vast numbers of soldiers was no easy task, even more so in the time they had been given. Some orders, inevitably, had been mangled. One regiment, stationed in the equatorial city of Bennafela, had somehow decided that the planet was in revolt and had taken over the local levels of control. Others had wasted precious time querying the orders and demanding to know under whose authorisation the evacuation was being enacted.

But they were the exceptions. The bulk of Kefa Primaris's many millions of registered Guardsmen were now being lined up for redeployment, drummed into shape by their commanders and commissars and prepped for orbital lift. Every voidcraft in the planet's orbital zone had been pressed into service, giving them a huge potential capacity.

Annarovea, standing beside Olgeir, smiled resignedly. 'I am glad you approve.'

'This is just the start, you realise. News will get out.'

'Verdello is very thorough.'

'Even so. Talk will have started. Your people are waking up.'

Annarovea ran a tired hand across her face, massaging the skin. 'It is in hand. All the compounds are guarded, and enforcers are deployed.'

'Do they know why this is happening?'

Annarovea gave him a dry look. 'Of course not.'

'Good,' Olgeir said.

Throughout, the governor had performed with calm competence. All of her staff had done so. As far as any of them could tell, panic had yet to hit the hive spires. Even if those being evacuated guessed the true reason for the orders, loose talk had not yet penetrated far out of the confines of the regiments. Keeping control of information was a specialism of Imperial command cadres, one of the very few things they had improved upon in ten thousand years of planetary administration.

Annarovea leaned heavily against the balcony railing. Half a kilometre away, shrouded in mist and steam, another lifter took off and lurched up into the sky, trailing columns of smog like tentacles.

'I don't enjoy watching this,' she said. 'My world, stripping itself bare.' She looked back at him. 'Would you have done this on Fenris?'

Olgeir's mind instantly went back to the Fang. He envisioned the immense fortress carved out of the solid matter of the planet's core, the ranks of ship-killer batteries on the flanks of the Asaheim peaks, the orbital fleets, the Great Companies stationed in the halls of the Mountain, the beasts that dwelled in the shadows, the Revered Fallen sleeping in the deepest holds.

It felt ludicrous even to consider the proposition of evacuation *there* – Fenris was one of the most heavily defended worlds in the Imperium. For all that, the *Festerax* was a truly unique threat, one spawned from the nightmares of the Eye itself. Could even the Chapter's massed warships have stopped it out in the void? If not, and it somehow made orbit, would the brutal logic that governed Kefa's fate also have extended to the home world of the Wolf King?

'They are different worlds,' he said, eventually.

Annarovea pushed free of the balcony and started to walk, back and forth, getting some circulation going in night-stiff limbs. She'd long discarded her ceremonial gown and now wore gilt body armour shrouded in a royal blue cloak.

'You know we can pick it up on the long-range augurs now?' she asked.

Olgeir nodded.

'Soon other stations will detect it,' she said. 'The comm-chatter will begin. We won't be able to keep the truth to ourselves.'

Olgeir turned to her. 'You trust your staff?'

'I do.'

'All of them?'

'I picked them myself.'

Olgeir grunted, and turned back to the view. Another bloat-bellied leviathan was coming into land, replacing the carrier that had last taken off. More smoke spilled across the rockcrete, thick and oil-black as it mingled with strands of drifting mist.

'Morfol, your commissar,' he said. 'He wants to fight. Every part of his training demands it, and he is a fine example of his breed. We have six more hours. He could cause problems.'

'Ah, but that is why you're here, is it not? To keep us in line.' A trace of bitterness entered Annarovea's clipped voice. 'Forgive me, lord, but it won't matter to you much longer. As soon as you have our regiments safely pulled away, you'll be back into the void.'

Olgeir regarded her again, surprised. 'Will you leave, then?' he asked. 'You could take any ship you want.'

Annarovea lifted her chin proudly. 'In six hours, I'll be on my command throne. If the spore-clouds come, I'll marshal what remains of my armies and we'll burn them wherever they land. I'll fight the changelings every step of the way when they come for us. The last thing they'll see, when they break into the command spire, is an Imperial aquila standing guard over an uncorrupted, duly appointed leader. Then I'll set off the hive-atomics, and take as many of the bastards down with me as I can.'

Olgeir suppressed an approving smile. He didn't wish to insult her with condescension.

'A fine strategy,' he said. 'I will be there with you.'

Annarovea looked at him disbelievingly. 'You? Why?'

'I am not leaving, governor. My task is not done, and I do not leave until it is.' He drew in a long breath of Kefa's acrid air. 'Believe me, I am not here to goad you on, governor. I am here to protect you. This is my fate now – caught up with yours.'

'*Protect* me?'

'The news will be out by now.' As Olgeir spoke, the mist boiled away from the vista before him. The hazy outlines of spires grew firmer amid the drifting clouds. 'My Wolf Guard tells me the prospect of death does strange things to mortal minds. Perhaps you can trust your staff, perhaps not. In case not, I am here.'

Annarovea stared at him. For a moment it looked like she might burst out laughing, or perhaps flare into anger. In the end, she just shook her head.

'Twenty-four hours ago,' she said, 'I was planning an inspection mission of the ore refineries in the south. The prospect bored me immensely – seven days of touring industrial facilities in the company of tithe officials. Up until then, this world had never known a major assault by the Archenemy. It had never even been visited by one of the Adeptus Astartes. Boredom was the worst I had to fear.' She smiled grimly. 'And now I have a Wolf of Fenris as a chaperone, and a nightmare – a *real* nightmare – is about to be unleashed upon us all. Things change quickly.'

'They do. You regret that?'

Annarovea rolled her shoulders. Every move she made was tight with stress, but she was keeping herself together.

Out on the apron, more lifters came and went, transporting their precious contents into the temporary safety of the void.

The sunlight continued to grow stronger. The chronos kept ticking over.

'Ask me in six hours,' she said.

Vuokho shuddered, struck hard by more las-beams, and ducked down towards the nadir of the battle-sphere. More cracks shot across the armourglass of the cockpit, and the engines began to labour.

'Maintain power for main thrust,' snarled Jorundur, pulling the gunship away from a ruinous thicket of incoming projectile fire. 'Blood of Russ, if you keep anything going, keep the drives going.'

The flight crew worked as hard as ever. Once aboard, Ingvar had taken the co-pilot's chair alongside Jorundur, with the mortals placed further back at the gunner's and navigator's stations. The metal cage around them rattled and screamed, flexing every time another impact came in.

'We're coming out,' said Ingvar calmly, running forward scans on the vessel's augur array. His armour was still caked in slowly drying fluids, making him look like some butcher's remnant amid all the naked steel.

The *Festerax*'s profile fell away behind them, though it still swelled in the rear viewers like some grotesque planetoid. Ahead of them, the void boiled with the lattice and turmoil of discharged weapons-fire.

Heimdall could be detected over to starboard-zenith, though it was moving chronically slowly. Its thrusters glowed black-red, looking more like wounds than drives, and the evidence of the beating it had taken was painfully obvious. Ahead glittered the opulent profile of *Vindicatus*, its own drives flaring up for launch.

'I need more speed, brother,' murmured Ingvar, watching the Grand Cruiser complete its pre-burn cycle. Any moment now the main thrusters would ignite, beginning the acceleration that would take it far out of range. *Heimdall* wouldn't catch it then, not in its half-crippled state.

'You find it, then,' hissed Jorundur, pulling out of another dive just as a phalanx of torpedoes scythed past ahead of them. The volume of fire was diminishing with every kilometre they put between them and the hulk's edge, but the hulk was still more than capable of knocking them out of the void with a full hit.

Ingvar ran another scan. *Vindicatus* was getting under way – grindingly slowly, but its momentum would soon pick up.

'Get me the link,' he said.

'What link?' grunted Jorundur, fully occupied with keeping *Vuokho* out of the many paths of destruction.

'Callia.'

Jorundur snatched the comm-bead from the socket in his gorget and threw it at Ingvar before hauling on the control column again.

Ingvar caught the bead, implanted it, and activated the channel.

'You are moving, Sister,' he voxed as the connection crackled into life.

'Nothing I can do about that,' came Callia's voice. 'Aiming to board? You don't have long – the shields are compromised in zone forty-five. You can detect that?'

Ingvar checked the readings. There was a window – a small one. 'It will be difficult,' he said.

'I might be able to mask your approach. They are all scanning *Heimdall*.'

'Do what you can.'

Ingvar cut the link, just as the gunship slewed violently in a patch of projectile fire. The whole structure rattled as the ship was flung around further. As Jorundur worked to right it again, *Vindicatus* picked up speed, its engines suddenly blazing like stars.

'Full burn, brother,' insisted Ingvar, watching as the prize began to escape.

Jorundur looked up at the real-view portals, made a quick calculation, and pulled out a whole raft of levers.

'It'll shake us apart,' he warned.

'We will not get another chance.'

Jorundur fed the last sliver of power to the main drives, and *Vuokho* kicked into attack speed.

All manoeuvring subtlety disappeared as the gunship shot directly for its target. *Vindicatus*'s hull raced towards them, its fearsome macrocannon-studded flanks looming rapidly into sharp detail.

'You have Callia's coordinates?' asked Ingvar, gripping the sides of his command throne. Jorundur was right – the whole cockpit felt like it was splitting open.

'The target is *moving*,' muttered Jorundur, nudging the muzzle a fraction to the left. 'This is *complicated*.'

Two-thirds of the way along the ventral flank, a docking bay was opening. Gusts of venting atmosphere glistened as the doors slid apart, sparking as they interfered with the ragged edges of the void shields on either side.

'Like a needle through leather,' grunted Jorundur, fighting with the controls.

Vuokho was coming in too low, driven down by the final barrage from the plague-hulk's wall of las-fire. Jorundur pulled the nose up, though the momentum of the thrust still carried them in on the edge of destruction.

Ingvar felt a rush of endorphins, like combat-fervour. He leaned forwards in the throne, staring at the speed-blurred edges of the Grand Cruiser.

'They are not firing,' he said.

'By the time they have a fix,' said Jorundur with some satisfaction, twisting the gunship up for the final thrust, 'we'll be inside the shields.'

Vuokho gave a last judder before the engines delivered what was needed. Clean as a thrown spear, the gunship blasted into the shadow of *Vindicatus*. Callia was as good as her word, and they streaked through the gap in the void shields towards the opening launch bay.

'Hard landing coming,' warned Jorundur, suddenly kicking in reverse thrust.

Ingvar was thrown forward against his throne restraints. Terminal-sounding clangs resounded from deep within the Thunderhawk's tortured frame, and a thin snap echoed out from above the cockpit. He got a blurred impression of bulkheads rushing to meet them, picked out in crimson and bronze, before *Vuokho* slewed through the gap.

Jorundur aimed the gunship as well as he had ever done. By rights, an entry at that speed, in those conditions, carrying that much damage, should have smeared them across the side of *Vindicatus* in a thousand glowing shards of adamantium. Somehow, though, he managed to hit the aperture without clipping the edge, fast enough to evade sentry guns tracking them but with just enough room to brake once inside the atmosphere bubble.

'Skítja,' Jorundur muttered, physically wrestling with the last responsive sections of the command console.

Vuokho skidded round sharply, nearly tumbling over on its axis before righting drunkenly. *Vindicatus's* gravity field clamped down strongly, slamming the gunship's twisted undercarriage hard against the flight deck. A soaring roof and colonnaded walls enclosed them, all picked out in smog-blackened gold leaf.

The rear wall of the hangar raced towards them, half obscured by the cloud of sparks and smoke kicked out by *Vuokho's* driving progress. It looked very, very solid.

'Brother...' began Ingvar.

'I *see it*,' snapped Jorundur, activating the air-brakes and diverting all remaining power to the retro-thrusters. Huge gouts of flame surged out, arresting the suicidal momentum. The Thunderhawk's undercarriage gouged long trails into the hangar floor, though even that only partslowed the charge.

They hit the wall with a heavy crack of ceramite breaking. Power lines shorted across the roof, sparking like fountains, and the thrones rocked on their mounts.

The main drives whined down, clanking eerily as broken components rattled around in their casings. The entire structure steamed, and smoke rose from the console, coupled with the acrid smell of metal burning.

For a moment, no one said anything. Then Jorundur turned to Ingvar.

'So I got us in,' he said. 'Now what?'

Ingvar reached for his bolter.

'You and me,' he said. 'To the bridge.'

'Tell me what you see,' said the Mycelite.

Baldr tried to twist around, to determine where the voice came from. Nothing happened. He didn't move. He had no neck left to move, nor a head to swivel. The visual field before him was like nothing he'd ever experienced. He saw a shimmering wall of colour, moving in clots and streaks across a deeper well of luminous cloud. Motes of darkness skated over that tapestry – hard, sharp things that violated the beauty of the spectacle.

He found himself wanting to remove those motes, to restore the vista to unbroken splendour.

'I do not know,' he said.

His voice was just an echo. He had no lips to move, no tongue to form the words. They spun in existence like thoughts, and yet they were not just mental figments – they were words, spoken to another intelligence.

'You do,' said the Mycelite, his voice echoing in his mind. 'Use your eyes. Think. Tell me what you see.'

Baldr tried to relax. A feeling of astonishing power coursed through his veins. Except he had no veins – just the vague after-image of a body, like a faint echo still ringing in his consciousness.

He tried to move again, and this time something changed. His gaze altered, adjusting, zooming in a little. The tapestry flexed and bent, though the motes remained in place. There were three of them – three dark little clots of movement. If he had arms, he would have reached out to swipe them clear.

'I see the universe,' he said, not knowing where the words came from.

'Just so,' said the Mycelite, 'and you see the depths beneath it.'

Baldr recognised the truth of that immediately. He saw the relatedness of it all – the swirls of colour and the bluffs and wells of light. It was end-lessly moving, turning like water, stretching and changing.

It was infinite. It was compelling.

'The *warp*,' he said, the word catching in his mind.

'You see it better than I,' said the Mycelite, delighted. 'You are something truly new, Baldr Fjolnir. How could your Priests have tested for this taint? It did not exist, not until now. But these are the Times of Accomplish-ment, and all is changing. Doors are unlocking that have remained shut since before the Corpse-Lord took us into the stars. You are just the *start*. Thousands will follow. Though will many be as powerful? I doubt it'

Baldr hardly listened. His gaze roved across the tapestry, then alighted on the three motes of darkness. Two of them were much larger than the third. As he watched, the tiny speck made its way towards the largest, and disappeared into it. Without knowing how, he began to realise what he was seeing.

'Ships,' he said. 'I am seeing the void.'

'They are the ships that besiege the *Festerax*. Tiny things, are they not?'

'Where is the hulk?'

'The *hulk?*' came the Mycelite's voice, amused. 'A poor name for this magnificent thing. You can guess, I think.'

Baldr's mind probed further into the tapestry. He saw the outlines of the other ships, blurred as if by heat. They swam amid the glory and the infinitude, fragmentary and insubstantial. It felt as if he could reach out, just extend an arm, and pluck them from the void.

'I *am* the hulk,' he said, once again letting the truth come to him. 'I am this ship.'

The Mycelite sounded pleased. 'That is it. You are the ship. Flex your muscles. Use your gift.'

Baldr began to see how things were ordered. His perspective was from the core of the great vessel. He could feel the torpedo tubes as if they were his arteries, the fuel cells as if they were his hearts. The universe surrounded him, cold and vacuous, but also rich and magnificent. He floated on the face of the deep, conscious, immense, eternal.

At the back of his mind, like an old memory, he felt other things stirring. Aside from the Mycelite, he half heard different voices whispering. They were oddly familiar – the words made a kind of sense to him.

God-marked.

'How are you... doing this?' Baldr asked, unable to fight back against the sensations flooding through him but not quite overwhelmed by them. 'I have a–'

'Yes, your collar. It holds you back. You feel that? If we could break it, then the link would be complete.'

'It will not break.'

'Give it time.'

Baldr felt a sudden pang. He was talking to the Mycelite like he might talk to any of his brothers. The fury had gone, the contempt had gone. He knew he ought to feel both those things, but somehow the will to defy had dissipated.

Part of that was sorcery, he knew. He could still taste the stink of it, hanging like vomit at the back of his throat. But only a part. Something else called to him.

He was being shown another way of being. He began to remember the dreams he'd had on Ras Shakeh while his body repaired.

He remembered the Dark Garden. He'd walked among those twilight groves, breathing in the spores and the poisons.

He had seen the goddess there, locked in her cage of iron. Her eyes had been rimmed with tears, her pale skin running with fever.

He had wanted to reach out, to press a cooling hand against her brow.

'You were *unlocked* by us, Baldr,' said the Mycelite, as if able to sense what he was thinking. 'You were fertile soil, but you still needed the seed. We gave it to you.' Just as before, his voice had an edge of tenderness to it. 'You are *home* now.'

Baldr ought to have recoiled at that, just as he had done when the Mycelite had run his diseased hand down his cheek.

But he didn't.

'I can control this,' Baldr said, feeling the thousands upon thousands of interlocking ship-systems unfolding in his mind. 'I can make it move. I can keep it alive.'

'Not quite,' warned the Mycelite. 'The collar was well made. It holds us back, but you will learn. There is time.'

Baldr felt a tremor of unease then. The *Festerax* was not as it should be. The vast structure was riddled with infections, but that was its natural state – the contagions made it stronger.

We will be its disease.

He couldn't remember who had said that. He couldn't even remember why he had ever come to the *Festerax*. But something wasn't right. There was a presence at the heart of the vessel, at *his* heart.

'There are intruders,' he said. 'To be purged.'

The Mycelite agreed. 'There are,' he said. 'Do you know what must be done to purge them?'

Baldr thought on that. He had no idea how to exert his will over the ship. There were huge structures within it – he could feel them. They could be made to move, to crush, to stifle, but only with the correct command.

'I do not,' he said, slowly. His mind moved in a fog, as if emerging from sleep. Ahead of him, he could see the glorious void glow and shimmer.

'But… I can learn.'

Chapter Eighteen

The engine-gates loomed, now less than thirty metres away. The fires set before them roared into new and terrible shapes, throwing lurid light across a battlefield of swinging shadows. The enemy had been driven back, but their numbers remained. There was no end to them – they poured out from hidden arches, the vaults above and the pits beneath, an infinite tide of corrupted humanity.

Njal wasted none of his power on them. Fatigue was beginning to weigh on his arms, driving like lead through his veins. His throat was bloody and raw from the death-oaths he swore, his arms flared with pain from the effort of hurling storm-fire at the endless tides of ruin. He could feel the psychic tsunami of hatred crashing against him, surging against his own will and seeking to hammer it down.

The foul breath of the Dark Wolf lapped across his shoulder, as close as it had ever been. He could sense the purring growls behind him, catching up. Every exercise of runecraft summoned it closer, the avatar of his own destruction.

I sense you, now. You are on my heels.

They could have no understanding of this, those who did not walk the path of the runes. For outsiders, the power he wielded was nothing but dabbling in the shallows of the warp, just like any trickster or fallen sorcerer. Njal had heard the arguments a thousand times, and had read the same in a hundred proscribed manuscripts.

You are no different. You are warp-weavers, just as we are. All rivers meet at the same source, and our damnations are the same.

They were wrong. The whispers were wrong. Njal had seen the world-soul, raging in the heart of darkness. He had heard the low growls in the netherworld, and seen the pairs of eyes glowing in the afterdark. He had felt the power that would consume him in the end, dissipating his soul into the raging tempest that would break at the galaxy's end.

The power he wielded was of a different order, one tempered and purified by the mystical symmetries of the hunt and the wild. Those who had never known Fenris could disbelieve it all they liked. It changed nothing.

Somewhere deep in the soul of the storm, the Dark Wolf's fangs bared, as yellow and decayed as the bones of the earth.

'*Fenrys!*' Njal thundered, feeling his own fangs bare in symmetry.

He thrust his staff forward, and wild-edged coruscation surged around him once more, lighting up the eternal night in blood-edged silver. Storm-wind rushed to his aid, swirling about him in accelerating eddies. Flames bloomed out, catching on the backs of the hordes before him and flaring into roaring life. Fork-shaped gouts of fire leapt from his staff tip, lashing into the smog-shrouded vaults above. Great cracks opened at his feet, zigzagging across the pitted deck before spewing torrents of magma. His Terminator plate glowed deep red, thick as blood-clots, and the runes seared the dark like brands.

Fenris was a world of ice, but it was also a world of fire. Through sheer force of will, Njal had dragged the Summer of Flame into the enginarium chamber, and the devastation was as complete there as it was on his violent home world.

Ranks of mutant soldiers were hurled from their feet by the squalls and thrown, aflame, into the pits, where the forge-fires leapt up to welcome them. More were impaled by the sheets of red lightning rippling across the battlefield. The whole chamber swelled with the rip and tear of the racing winds, and fires latched on to the bare metal, making the fevered atmosphere shake.

Njal strode forth, his staff held high and his pelts snapping in the rune-summoned gales. The mortal enemy fell back before him, cowering and scrambling. Even to look on him in such an unleashed state was enough to burst corrupted eyeballs and tear open tainted flesh.

The engine-gates drew near, towering over all else and lit by their own vast furnaces. Njal felt the magma-heat thundering away before him, hot as a brand against his skin.

There was little in the enemy host capable of standing before him then, let alone fighting him. In his wake came the Wolves, swift and brutal in vengeance, already reaching for the thermal charges that would be hurled into the depths of the fusion reactors.

But between them stood the last line of defence – the Traitor Marines. Dragged into the combat at last as their minions withered away, the bloated leviathans strode down from their portals, each one carrying scythes or hefting massive organ-guns with carved daemon-head muzzles. Nightwing, circling high above the combat, ran scans on each and filtered the results back to Njal's armour systems. The Plague Marines were riddled with corrosion, their ancient bodies fused and integrated into a bizarre mix of tumescent organs and semi-bionic components. By rights, none of them should have been able to draw breath, let alone fight, but Njal knew well enough how utterly deadly they were.

The Plague Marines converged on Njal, advancing fearlessly into the inferno even as the flames whipped and curled around them. Njal's bodyguard raced to intercept them, and the two forces crashed together. The fighting became truly vicious then, with no quarter given on either side – Traitors were hammered into the burning iron floor; Wolves were crushed under cloven boots, their hearts ripped out on the curve of Hel-forged blades.

Three huge scythe-bearers broke the cordon of Njal's bodyguards, eviscerating the Wolves in their path before lumbering on at him. The warriors' scythes glowed pale green, bleeding corpse-light into the fervid air. They were fearsome things, forged on some long-damned plague world and tempered with the malice of daemonic metalwrights.

Njal smiled savagely, and opened his fist.

Forks of blood-red lightning leapt out, slamming into their prey and spraying magma like the maw of a volcano. The flaming rune-magic blazed wildly as it came into contact with the fell metals, but it gripped tight, wrapping around the blade-edges in tight snarls.

The scythes exploded, sending circular blast-waves shuddering out. The Plague Marines weathered the rain of magma, reaching for bolters and meltaguns. They opened fire, loosing a volley of bolts and atomised energy straight at him. Njal felt searing heat as the molecular tech gnawed into the ceramite, stripping away the outer layers in a haze of fizzing smoke, followed by the hammering rain of shells exploding across his tortured armour. A second volley impacted hard, smashing him back several paces and ripping into his already battered plate.

Njal spat out a curse, and drew on fresh power. He spun around, whirling hard and driving the fire-winds into a vortex of speed. The Traitor Marines kept firing, but now their shells were sucked into the whirlwind and sprayed out wildly. Still surrounded by the flame-edged gale, Njal advanced again, gripping his staff two-handed and preparing the next blast.

The Plague Marines met the onslaught defiantly. The meltagunner opened fire again. His comrades kept up the barrage of bolter shots, shouldering into the fury of the gales.

Njal angled his staff at the leader, and poured all his battle-fury into a single word.

'Skemmdarvargur.'

His staff erupted. The space before him disappeared into a furnace of bestial energies, snarling and tearing at the bit like a leashed pack of hunting dogs. Somewhere buried in all the rampaging light and noise, the vague shapes of jaws could be half made out, latching on to the enemy and biting down. Arched backs plunged, powered by spectral, thick-pelted limbs. In a tornado of roars and snarls, the galloping predator-shapes surged ahead, sweeping aside any resistance. The three Plague Marines were swept away, deluged by the roiling fire-tide and slammed back into the pits whence they had come.

Panting with exhaustion, Njal let the furnace burn out. The winds, the flames, the lightning-shards, all of it ripped away and howled off into oblivion.

In front of him, a gorge of pure scorched devastation stretched off towards the gates. The bodies of the Plague Marines had been ripped apart, now little more than scraps of necrotic flesh and burning armour-pieces. Dozens more bodies were twisted and contorted all along the length of the carved-out furrow, still racked by the last sparks and flickers of the lightning that had killed them.

They can disbelieve it all they like, thought Njal grimly, surveying the ruin. It changes nothing.

Then he strode out, crushing the remnants of his enemies under his boots. Around him, surviving Grey Hunters regrouped and followed him back into battle. The toll had been horrendous, but enough still fought to gain the gate. The hordes screamed, and pushed back, but there was panic lacing their hatred now.

Step by step, stride by bloody stride, the Wolves were closing on the target.

On Kefa Primaris, word had got out. It had been impossible to hide the movements of so many ships, and attempts by the high command to shut down the city-wide comm-channels had been only partially successful.

Once the data from short-range planetary augurs came in, panic began to spread. Whispers ran from hab to hab, speaking of Guard officers summoned from their cells in the middle of the night, and of an enemy fleet making its way into orbit above them. The story got about that Annarovea had already left the planet, and that every voidcraft in-system was primed to leave, stranding the planet to the mercy of whatever ravening force was heading for the drop-zones.

Not all the details were correct, but the gist was close enough. The people of Kefa Primaris knew something terrible was about to happen, and they could see that their rulers were abandoning them to it.

In the face of all that, no amount of deference would hold them back. They took to the comm-stations, demanding action. They marched out of the manufactories, massing in crowds at the main hive intersections. They besieged the Adeptus Arbites control points in the core spire, unperturbed by the frequent vox-casts warning them to return to their assigned zones and get back to work.

As the morning wore on and the official response continued to be muted, the levels of disorder grew. Broadcast reassurances that all was in hand had no effect – they could see the data from unofficial augur screeds, and they could see with their own eyes the long trail of off-world traffic from the Guard garrisons.

With three hours until the *Festerax* was due to reach orbit, the crowds began to reinforce one another, pooling into larger groups and marching up from the lower levels. Most were menial workers from the big production lines, hardened by a lifetime of labour in the manufactory levels. Their overseers needed to be brutal to keep them in line at the best of times; now, as often as not, they marched alongside them.

Olgeir watched the incoming datafeeds from the vantage of the governor's private chambers. Annarovea's domain was a slender tower jutting from the northern flank of the main command spire, set just below the landing stages and astropathic pylons at the very summit. The entire tower had been cordoned off, and was guarded by the last remnants of her personal protective unit – blue-armoured soldiers wearing blank, reflective helms and carrying heavy-calibre autoguns.

The governor herself sat in her throne, surrounded by mobile pict units and shuffling attendants. The incoming tide of data brought no reassuring messages. The plague-hulk's speed had not diminished. Time was running out to get the last of the big troop carriers away, and many regiments were struggling to get to their launch-points in time. Low-level disorder was becoming widespread, with transport arteries blocked and convoys slowed. Shots had been fired over at the Bedelo training yards in order to secure the base perimeter, something that had only inflamed passions further.

Olgeir said nothing. Annarovea had a hundred other demands on her limited time, and he had no wish to add to them.

He turned his attention to the spire schematics. The intricate network of corridors and levels rotated slowly before him, picked out in the glowing lines of a hololith. Flashpoints were marked with a skull-rune, based on reports from the hard-pressed enforcers down in the depths. Slowly, the markers were creeping up the height of the spire.

He accessed pict-feeds from the upper-spire security net. The scenes were much the same wherever he looked – mobs running down transit lanes, looting or storming control points. The pict-feed had no audio track, and so he watched the eerily silent images of a world collapsing under the weight of mass hysteria.

He switched to the hab-levels immediately below the command dome. In one scene, he saw enforcers being driven back by a huge crowd. In another, he saw spire Guard units opt not to fire on a similarly massive mob, abandoning their barricades as the rabble charged them.

The tide of disorder was getting perilously close. As Olgeir studied the various incoming strands, he noticed how well organised they were. Their movements were coordinated expertly, flanking command points before taking them, isolating bottlenecks until they could be overwhelmed with force of numbers.

He scanned over to a different bank of pict screens. The story was the same everywhere – enforcers abandoning their posts or being overrun. As he pored over the feed, Olgeir noticed a familiar face at the forefront of the closest disturbances.

He zoomed in, correcting the image for distortion. Slowly, the features clarified.

Morfol.

Olgeir reached for his bolter, turning it to check the ammo-counter.

'You are not thinking of using that, I hope?' came Annarovea's concerned voice from the throne. She had seen the same thing.

Olgeir turned to face her. 'Your commissar seems to have forgotten his vows,' he said.

'Or is he the only one who remembers them?'

Annarovea looked fragile, yet defiant. Imperial governors were taught that their greatest and final duty was to fight and die to defend their worlds, and Olgeir knew that every sinew of Annarovea's body strained to call the Guard units back.

'You gave the order, governor,' said Olgeir quietly. 'You cannot take it back now. He must be stopped.'

'He is a good man.'

'He could be a saint. That means nothing.'

The populace were acting just as herd animals did when panicked – stampeding for an exit, any exit. It had been bound to happen, sooner or later, but Morfol had stirred them too soon. The commissar could not be allowed to jeopardise the void-lift – there were still three hours. A lot of carriers could be got away in that time, but only if anarchy were postponed for a little longer.

'I'm going down,' Olgeir said, walking over to the doors leading to the main hive transit shafts.

'My troops can handle him,' said Annarovea. The protest was weak – she had more than enough on her mind without worrying about trying to rein in a Space Wolf.

'Evidently not,' said Olgeir, reaching the gates and gesturing for the guards to let him pass.

'No slaughter, though,' called out the governor. 'Not unless you have to.'

Olgeir turned to face her. He was aware, as always, of how he looked – the scraggly beard, the metal studs in his tattooed flesh, the grim panoply of kill-markers and bone-totems covering his heavy battleplate.

Annarovea's face was drawn with anxiety. It was not for herself – it was for the world she had built, patiently and faithfully, and which now teetered on the edge of annihilation.

There was nothing he could say to that. He was *built* for slaughter. It was his only function, and the sole reason he had stayed on Kefa. If the enforcers could not stop Morfol, then that left only one option.

So he said nothing, but strode through the blast-doors and into the antechamber beyond.

From below, far below, he could already detect weapons-fire.

Vindicatus was racing. Once fully powered, the Grand Cruiser had phenomenal motive power, and Delvaux was happy to push it as hard as he could.

With the ignition of the main drives, the plague-hulk fell swiftly away aft. The *Festerax* was now barely a figment of the sensor-net, and it felt good to be out of its shadow. *Heimdall* had stayed in pursuit for a little while, before falling back again, its engines glowing over-hot. The Wolves' early bravery had cost them dear, and their teeth had been drawn.

Delvaux relaxed a little in his throne. He'd tensed up after the order was given, desperate to pull away before the decision reached the ears of Stormcaller. While the crew struggled to key up the sub-warp engines, he'd drummed his fingers impatiently, gnawed at by the fear that they would come for him.

On Fenris, the oathbreaker is lower than a beast.

Now, at last, they had ripped clear. Stormcaller would either die on the plague-hulk or remain too far behind to impede him. *Vindicatus* would arrive at Kefa Primaris well ahead of the deadly spore-pods, ready to immolate the planet and deprive the enemy of the army it sought.

It had been determined. There was no turning back. A great victory was at hand, a decisive stroke, and forever his name would be associated with it.

Not all men would have had the stomach to give the order. Those who did so were the elect, the chosen, the ones for whom greatness beckoned.

'Do we have the planet on our forward scopes yet?' he asked, trying to take his mind off the thought – even hypothetically – of pursuit.

'Not visual, lord,' replied Harryat, standing down below the throne dais, on a platform just above the sensor pits. Officers of his command staff came and went, handing him data-slate after data-slate to sign off on. 'You may inspect the augur schematic, if you wish.'

Delvaux narrowed his eyes. Was Harryat being curt with him? Was that disrespect in his voice? It was hard to tell. The captain spoke in an officious manner that gave nothing away.

Delvaux's eyes scanned across the expanse of the command bridge.

Battle Sisters of Nuriyah's command were stationed at all the strategic points. The crew, from servitor up to tech-priest, were busy at their work. The low hum of conversation and data-exchange was just as it ever was.

Still, the nerves were there. There were thousands on the ship. Some of them could be plotting against him. Many of them could. Perhaps he should order Klaive to run a purge, once the business was over. You could never be too careful.

'Yes, I will take a look,' Delvaux said, adjusting his robes.

Harryat gestured to one of the sensorium operators, and a moment later a translucent schematic shimmered into existence at Delvaux's eye level. The *Festerax* was indicated with a red rune, and glowed softly to the right of his visual field. Kefa Primaris was marked out by a large blue circle, and stood on the very left. Between them, bisecting a long curved trajectory-line, was *Vindicatus*, approximately a third of the way between the two bodies. Even as Delvaux watched, the glyph blinked a little further along the line.

'And we are travelling at maximum speed?' he demanded.

'We are, lord.'

Delvaux grunted. He'd have liked to see the distances shrinking faster. He could feel his stomach beginning to knot. Tension always made his innards flare.

He was about to order the hololith away, when a warning rune lit up on the arm of his throne. He gazed down at it for a moment, unsure what it referred to.

'Do we have a problem?' he asked, almost to himself.

Harryat went over to a console, and consulted a bank of optical pict screens. 'Are you sure?' the captain muttered, speaking to the operator.

'Sure of what?' asked Delvaux. 'Captain, you will address your queries to me.'

Harryat ignored him, absorbed in what he was seeing, and ran another test. Just as he did so, more runes lit up on Delvaux's throne.

He knew what those ones meant.

'Nuriyah,' Delvaux voxed, trying to keep his voice steady.

The Battle Sister was already on the move, striding over from her station and calling a squad to her side. Her flamer-arm cast off its ceremonial drapery, and the feeder-nozzle kindled with a spurt of blue.

Harryat looked up at the throne. 'No response from checkpoints in outer security zone,' he reported. 'Weapons discharge in antechambers sixty-six and seventy-one.'

By then, Delvaux could see the results for himself, transmitted to his personal retinal implant. Something was heading towards the bridge, and it was moving very fast.

He is hunted unto the ends of the world.

How had they got on board?

Delvaux twisted around in his seat, growing alarmed. Squads of Battle Sisters were running now, heading for the entry points to lock them down. Sister Callia, one of those who had been taken from de Chatelaine's old force, was jogging towards one of the side entrances along with eight of her warriors, their bolters already drawn.

'Where is Klaive?' Delvaux blurted, speaking to no one in particular, running an increasingly panicked gaze over the command bridge. The black-robed confessor was nowhere to be seen.

A warning klaxon sounded. The faint sound of bolter explosions was now audible, growing louder with each moment.

'Seal the bridge!' cried Harryat, striding up from his position at the sensor station. He pulled a slim projectile pistol from the holster at his waist and released the safety. 'Do it now – full lock-down.'

There were many entrances and exits into the command space – at least eight visible from the throne dais. Immediately, all of them were shuttered by thick blast-doors that slammed down from their housings. The power supply switched to a separate generator, making the lights fade to a dull red. Proximity scanners whined into life, sending out faint bleeps as the augur equipment probed the spaces behind the sealed doors.

Delvaux felt his heart thumping hard, and swallowed thickly. The bridge contained over fifty Battle Sisters in full armour. They stood before each barred entrance, their weapons trained on the blast-doors. Several hundred armed guards in Ecclesiarchy body armour backed them up or stood sentry on the high terraces. The two Penitent Engines behind his throne were fully primed and armed, and each one of those was surely a match for a whole pack of Space Wolves.

In the distance, the sound of muffled bolt crashes grew louder. He thought he could hear, just on the edge of detection, something like snarling, and the hairs on the back of his arms rose.

'How soon before we reach Kefa?' he demanded.

Harryat looked up at him. That time, it was unmistakable – a faint blush of contempt. When this was over, the man would have to go.

'One hour, nineteen minutes,' Harryat replied.

'You can keep us secure for that long?'

'Depends who's trying to get in.'

'Do you venerate the soul of the Immortal Emperor?' snapped Delvaux. 'Do you love His Church with all your being? Do you wish to see the will of the Holy Ministorum enacted here?'

Harryat fixed Delvaux with his practised look of stony forbearance. 'I do, lord.'

'Then do your duty. Increase velocity two points beyond safety margins. We will not be derailed. We will not be deflected.'

Delvaux's thick lips pressed into a determined grimace.

'That world *will* burn.'

Chapter Nineteen

Ingvar raced through the final chamber before reaching *Vindicatus*'s bridge. Jorundur loped alongside him, axe in hand. The two of them had made it up twenty levels and two kilometres in, killing silently and swiftly, before the alarm had been raised. After that, the fighting had escalated quickly. Ecclesiarchy-trained guards were well equipped and fanatically loyal, and the ship had a whole series of automatic defence mechanisms that had kicked into life once their progress had been discovered.

The Battle Sisters, though, were the real problem. On Ras Shakeh, Ingvar had observed how well the ones under de Chatelaine had fought. Those on the Cardinal's ship were no different, and once they had responded to the warning klaxons screaming out on every level, things had slowed up.

'I can't enjoy it,' voxed Jorundur, panting as he ran.

'What?'

'Killing them. I'd started to see them…' Jorundur snorted sourly, as if disgusted with himself, 'as allies.'

'Some still are,' said Ingvar, just as the doorway loomed before them.

The chamber around them was dark, lit only by devotional lumens that floated somewhere high in incense-clouded arches. Vast graven images of saints and primarchs stood in two files all along the main processional corridor, draped in shadow and wearing sombre, dull-eyed expressions. Ingvar hadn't been able to resist a grim smile when passing Russ's likeness. The Imperial sculptor had made him tall, noble, clean-shaven.

Perhaps he was, Ingvar had thought.

Just as they reached the ornate doorway leading to the bridge, bolt-ignitions whooshed out. Ingvar instantly dived over to his left, Jorundur to the right. The rounds pumped through the air where they'd just been.

Ingvar found the cover of a statue's plinth and spun around, rising to one knee to fire back, but his pursuers were already moving, darting into the cover of the statues ten metres back. He caught a faint glimpse of crimson power armour before the darkness swallowed them.

'Nuriyah's,' he voxed. 'Bring them down.'

By then Jorundur had reached cover of his own. He stowed his axe, unlocked his bolter, and began to creep forwards.

Ingvar ran a scan, but something in the ship's counter-offensive systems was dampening his helm-systems. He shut the proximity detector down and used his own hunt-sense.

Four of them. No, five. Spread out, moving behind the cover of the statues. Three this side, two the other.

Just as if he'd been stalking live prey on Fenris, he put himself in the mind of the enemy.

They'll break from Jorundur's side – fast and low. They need to draw us out.

He slunk forwards, still in the plinth's shadow. Every second that passed gave the Cardinal more time to prepare, to summon more defenders, but impatience could not be allowed to ruin this – Adepta Sororitas were serious opponents.

'Brother,' he voxed to Jorundur, 'stay in cover.'

'You are serious?'

'Stay in cover.'

Ingvar waited another two heartbeats, still in the shadows, his hyper-acute eyesight peering into the gloom ahead. He had to judge it to perfection.

Now.

He burst into movement just before they did. If he'd gone any earlier, they would have had a clear shot. As it was, two of them broke cover ahead of him, hampering the sight-lines of those behind.

Ingvar pounced on the foremost, loosing rounds from his bolter even as he swung *dausvjer*. His snarling blade lashed into the stomach of the lead

Sister, cracking open her power armour and doubling her over.

The second made it into combat, wielding a chainsword two-handed and screaming devotional screeds. She was fast, and dragged the whining blades into Ingvar's side before he could bring his own blade to parry. He resisted the instinct to pull away, and let his armour take the damage. Staying close, he punched out heavily with his sword arm. The Sister's helm snapped back, her neck nearly broken, and she staggered away. Ingvar stumbled as he went after her, feeling hot blood running down from the wound where the chainsword had bitten.

Jorundur tore past him then, using Ingvar's fight to shield him as he ran down the remaining Battle Sisters. He sprayed a thick wall of bolts before him that blasted into the statues' bases and blew them apart. In a hail of spinning stone fragments, the Sisters were flushed out, firing back steadily and trying to retreat back down the long chamber.

Jorundur downed one of them, but was hit by return fire. More bolt-shells thudded in, exploding across his amour in a wave of sparks, and he lost his footing.

By then Ingvar had finished off the stricken Sister with a sharp stab to the throat and was adding his own volleys to Jorundur's. He sprinted at the two final adversaries, crashing into them both and forcing them to switch to close combat.

They were quick enough, but it did them little good. Ingvar's greater speed and bulk swept them aside – one beheaded with a savage slash from his power sword, the other run through with the same blade. The final Battle Sister jerked and twitched on the sword as the energy field ran through her body, gurgling with trapped blood in her helm, before going limp.

Ingvar hurled the corpse aside before going to Jorundur. The old warrior got to his feet. His whole body bristled with irritation.

'Lucky shots,' he muttered.

Ingvar checked the data scrolling down his retinal feed. He'd taken a deep hit, but the blood was clotting and the skin already closing over.

'We are out of time,' Ingvar said, drawing out a krak grenade and heading for the blast-doors.

Jorundur joined him. 'Kraks won't dent those doors,' he said.

Ingvar primed the charge. 'Any better ideas?'

Jorundur activated the comm-bead. 'In position, Sister,' he voxed.

'Location noted,' came Callia's voice. 'The bridge is locked down – you'll need to come in fighting.'

'How many are with you?'

'Eight. More once the bolts are flying.' She paused. 'There are two Engines here, and a lot of guards.'

'It won't help him,' growled Jorundur. He glanced at Ingvar, who slammed a fresh magazine into the bolter and nodded. 'Open the doors.'

'Emperor be with you,' said Callia, and cut the link.

Ingvar and Jorundur pulled back to the walls on either side of the door, bolters held ready.

Ingvar could feel his wounds flaring painfully. Jorundur didn't look in much better shape – his armour was pocked and scored from shell-impacts.

This will be interesting.

Then, with a squeal and grind of metal on metal, the doors began to slide apart.

Gunnlaugur hardly noticed Njal forging his way towards the engine-gates. The lightning storm roared ahead, devouring and annihilating, and it barely registered. His every thought was consumed by the fight he'd initiated – he was locked into it, his mind fixed in total concentration.

No one else got close. The severity of the combat was so complete, so total, that even the most rabid of the mutants shied away. Three weapons swung and twisted in double-helix counter-movements, each pattern locked with the other. Gunnlaugur wielded his thunder hammer heavily, knowing how hard the hits needed to be in order to register with such an enemy. The Plague Marine champion responded equally savagely, slicing and slamming with the twin scythes embedded in his arms. For one of his Legion, he was swift, and the scythes danced a deadly series of sweeping figures.

The impacts, when they came, were crushing. Gunnlaugur was nearly floored by a sudden backhand lunge, barely keeping his feet before pushing back. The champion struggled to match the Wolf Guard's brutal skill with *skulbrotsjór*, and both his shoulder-guards were cracked nearly open. Whenever the addled ceramite took a hit, though, it closed over like scabrous flesh, morphing instantly into a hard defensive carapace. The Traitor's body absorbed punishment by sucking the force out of every blow. It felt like punching into water – the energy of the strike would just dissipate, spreading out across the creature's fleshy, yielding torso.

Broken slivers of battleplate were smashed clear. The last of Gunnlaugur's pelts was ripped away, hacked from his back by the scythes. The Death Guard's feeder-tubes and toxin-vials were shattered, spraying noxious fluids in blood-spattered streaks across both combatants.

Gunnlaugur whirled around, using the hammer to build up momentum, and sent a thundering blow ringing from the Death Guard's right
arm. Ceramite cracked, cobwebbing out from the strike and rippling
like crude oil. The Traitor withdrew steadily, wheezing through a dented
rebreather, before pushing back. His left-hand scythe shot out, driving
deep into Gunnlaugur's opposing arm. The blade entered at the elbow,
severing armour cables and biting deep into the flesh.

Gunnlaugur roared again – this time from pain – and he lost his grip
on the hammer. The huge weapon clanged to the ground, rolling to the
edge of a smoke-laced pit and teetering on the edge.

The Traitor champion pressed his advantage immediately, rushing at
Gunnlaugur with both blades aimed at his hearts. The long curved edges
ran with shimmering green energies, poised to hammer clean through
his ravaged breastplate.

Gunnlaugur surged forwards, both hands extended, eluding the twin
blades as they came for him and seizing the champion by his throat. Hit
hard, the Death Guard's balance went, and he stumbled back. Gunnlaugur followed up, squeezing up through the creature's gorget and driving
the ceramite collar into the skin beneath.

The Death Guard hacked at him, choking, desperate to loosen the grip.
The scythes rose and fell, slicing more chunks from Gunnlaugur's armour-
plate. The Wolf Guard took more wounds – a deep laceration across his
left shoulder, a savage chop at his right flank – but he kept up the pressure.

The pain became excruciating. More blows came in, increasingly frantic,
trying to deflect him, to knock him off-balance, to send him slamming to
the ground. Gunnlaugur exerted all his remaining power into the twin-
handed choke-hold, feeling the Traitor weaken at last. The scythe strikes
grew more desperate, but the strength behind them ebbed.

Gunnlaugur gasped, tasting blood on his fangs as his armoured fingers
twisted deeper. Cords severed, muscles ripped. With an agonised choke,
the Traitor champion went limp at last. Gunnlaugur released the pressure,
and the huge body thudded heavily onto its back, scythe-arms splayed. By
then, the Plague Marine's neck was nothing more than a bloody, mucus-
slick swamp.

Gunnlaugur sunk to his knees, exhausted. His entire body felt harrowed. His right arm fountained blood. He drew in deep breaths, fighting
the well of dizziness that threatened to overcome him.

All around him, the enemy was in full retreat. Mutants were being driven like cattle, screaming as they were herded into the fire-shafts. He heard Hafloí's whoops of triumph, cutting like clear ice through the tumult.

The enemy was broken. Njal had forged far ahead and secured the portals into the fusion chambers. The last of the Plague Marines were fighting a rearguard action, but the remaining Wolves had the initiative, and were not about to release it.

He grasped his elbow with his left fist. The bloodflow was slowing at last as clotting agents flooded the wound. His right hand felt numb and heavy, and he could no longer flex his fingers.

Grunting, he clambered to his feet again and retrieved his hammer. Hefting it in his good hand, he limped after his brothers. Up ahead, the gates towered over him. Blasphemous scripts ran around the iron frames.

Hafloí staggered up to him. He was bloody and battered, but his raw exuberance still radiated in his every movement. He was exhausted, just as they all were, but the savage spirit had not been extinguished yet.

'Good hunting, vaerangi!' he said, brandishing the severed helm of a Plague Marine in one fist.

Gunnlaugur grunted wearily. He had done well. They had all performed mighty feats – worthy of a song around firelight if they ever made it out again.

'That it is,' he growled, recovering some of his poise. With every second, the miracle of his genhanced physiology countered the heavy wounds he'd taken. 'And not over yet.'

At the vanguard, Njal was forcing the passage of the gates. The Rune Priest was still enveloped in a corona of raw flame. Lightning flickered around him, licking and twisting up against the frame of the central portal. Beyond the dark outlines of blackened iron, the air was raw-red. The heat was incredible, bleeding out of grilles the size of Titans. Vast exchangers hung on chains from the heights, thundering away as power coursed through them.

Hafloí and Gunnlaugur limped up to Njal's position, joining all the surviving Wolves at the portals – fifteen Hunters. The diminished warband assembled around Njal. Before them rose the main fusion reactor shell. Pillars of adamantium sheathed a heart of boiling liquid flames. The glowing innards of the reactor flared brighter, throwing bars of garnet-red light across the heart of the enginarium.

'Charges,' ordered Njal, drawing a spherical device from his belt.

Gunnlaugur, Hafloí and the others did likewise. They had all brought a heavily shielded thermal charge, each one capable of setting off a ruinous chain reaction if deployed within the heart of something as massive and plasma-rich as a starship engine.

Njal levelled his staff at the engine housing, and sent a bolt leaping towards it. The metal casing buckled, cracked, and melted, leaving a ragged-edged hole. From within, all that could be made out was the shimmer and blur of extreme energies.

'One hour,' ordered Njal, setting his chrono.

Gunnlaugur followed suit, just as they all did. It briefly crossed his mind that an hour was a ludicrously short time for them to get back to the Caestus assault rams – it had taken longer than that to fight their way in – but the mission demanded it, and there was no time to spare if the hulk were to be destroyed before reaching Kefa.

Njal turned to them all, sweeping his ice-blue gaze across the assembled warriors. Already the howls of fresh defenders could be heard from the depths, ready to surge back out from whatever temporary holes they had found to shelter in.

Njal held his thermal charge up. Behind him, the swell and spit of the reactor silhouetted his armoured bulk.

'This is what we came for,' he said. 'Russ guide their path.'

Then he turned, and with an almighty heave, sent the first charge spinning into the depths of the reactor.

The voices were growing louder. Some of them seemed to welcome Baldr's presence in their midst, some of them were hostile. For all that, he could not catch the words properly. They sounded familiar, with inflections he thought he ought to recognise, but the chatter was just too diffuse to latch on to.

As more time went on, it became harder to distinguish his own thoughts from the babble around him. Even the Mycelite's soft tones half blended into the morass, just one more part of the *Festerax*'s gestalt consciousness.

'They are invaders,' the Mycelite assured him. 'You can drive them out.'

For a moment, Baldr wondered why *he* was needed to do this. The Mycelite was a powerful sorcerer – could he not do this himself? Were there not a thousand corrupted souls on board the plague-hulk who could have taken his place? What was so unique, and precious, about him?

That troubling thought, though, was soon buried, and replaced with desire. Baldr found that he *wanted* to act. The interlopers felt like a wound lodged deep in his own flesh, barbed and hooked. The pain of their presence was a real, physical pain. If he had been a mortal, he would have drawn a blade and excised them.

But he was no longer a mortal. He was the *Festerax*, the majestic scion of the Plaguefather, just a part of the infinite tide that would sweep away the rotten Imperium and bring an end to the fruitless striving, the endless scheming, the millennial violence.

It had been going on too long. The universe needed *rest*, repose from the struggle. It needed to slip back into the wet embrace of decay and gracefully slide into obsolescence. That was its fate anyway – to resist it further was, as the Mycelite had taught him, to usher needless pain into a reality already ringing with it.

'You know what to do,' came the Mycelite's voice again, half buried in the psychic hubbub.

'I do not,' replied Baldr. His senses were foggy, much as they had been before the attack in the gorge on Ras Shakeh. He felt, deep down, as if something were terribly, horribly wrong, but it was impossible to remember just what it was. All he could sense with any certainty was the matter of the ship around him – its vast spars, its thousands of interlocking chambers, its immense weapons arrays and its gargantuan engines, all swelling with nigh-on infinite power. His mind stretched out through it all, creeping like a cancer into every part.

'You do,' insisted the Mycelite. 'Use your gifts. Search for the source of the pain.'

Baldr did as he was asked. He withdrew into himself, blocking out the spectral chatter from the *Festerax* as best he could, delving into the network of sensor readings and physical sensations that constituted his new nervous system.

His mind swept through it all, running down twisting passageways and abyssal transit shafts. He moved through the colossal birthing chambers where new mutations were spawned from rows of cylindrical pods. He soared across forge-chambers where munitions were hammered into being on endless segmented conveyor belts. He ghosted amid the rendering plants where the flesh of a million conquered subjects was boiled down in greasy tanks, ready to be piped to the stomachs of limitless armies. He lingered in the spore vaults where thousands upon thousands of torpedoes waited to be sent out into the void, ready to start the cycle of death and rebirth all over again.

The pain was in none of those places. Only when he reached the ship's ancient core, where the reactors belched and roared, did he feel the sharp stab return.

They were *there* – the parasites, clawing their way towards his innards. He heard their voices raised in fury and triumph, and felt the bite of tiny weapons stabbing at his flesh.

For a moment, something made him hesitate. One of the voices made his hearts stop – it brought the terror rushing back, and for a moment he could almost grasp at the source of his doubts.

'Good,' said the Mycelite, soothingly. 'You have found them. Now flex your muscles.'

The doubt faded. Baldr realised he could do it. He felt a burning sensation, and remembered the collar he had once worn about his neck, but it was not enough to prevent him. A well of astonishing, exhilarating power surged up, frothing and surging. He directed his mind towards the interlopers, suddenly seeing how they could be destroyed.

If he had had lips, he would have smiled. As it was, the entirety of the *Festerax* seemed to shake with renewed energy.

From somewhere, he knew the word.

'*Skemmdarvargur*,' he breathed, and the rune-curse was echoed by a thousand new voices in his mind.

The last charge had just been flung into the furnace when it happened. Green-tinged energies suddenly lanced down from the enginarium roof, far out of visual range and lost in swirling clouds of soot.

Spears of warp-matter slammed down among the Wolves, whipping and virulent. Arik, one of Fellblade's pack, was impaled on the shimmering shafts. He jerked, prone, for a few moments, before his body exploded outwards, showering the engine chamber with armour-chunked gore.

Two more warriors were caught in secondary tendrils of aetheric power, their breastplates smashed in a bloody stab of warp-kinetics. The rest of the warband fell back, aiming bolters up at the hidden source of the deluge. Only Njal remained in place, still burning with stormlight. The Rune Priest met the incoming warp-spears with fires of his own, and the engine chamber rang and spat with the messy impacts of rival wyrd-work.

Gunnlaugur drew back with the others, unable to fight whatever power had been unleashed. They need to *move* – to finish the task and get off the hulk before it ripped itself apart. He tensed, ready to race to Njal's position.

'Stay back!' warned Njal, fighting the rain of esoteric fire. More aether-lances crashed down around him, spraying madly as they hit his protective aegis. The heat, already febrile, ramped up further, making his outline blur.

Njal launched a counter-attack, throwing twisting columns of razor-edged lightning high into the heights. Huge explosions rang out, bringing down arch-sections in crashing clouds. The two rival energies surged against one another, filling the entire chamber with a lurid mix of silver and green. The matched spheres of energy pushed against one another, swelling, flickering and striving. Njal was driven to his knees. Gunnlaugur and the others could only watch, their weapons held ready but with no living foe to take on.

Eventually, grindingly, Njal's spirit asserted itself. His neon-white pillars of storm-fire punctured the blooms of corruption, tearing clear shafts through the raging storm. He stood again, one fist raised in defiance, the other holding the skull-staff. With a resounding clap, he summoned a roll of thunder and sent it sweeping up into the distant roof. The whole structure shuddered, shaken to its rotten foundations. The rain of corruption roared and raged, and more debris showered down over the growling enginarium machines.

Finally, the rain of tainted power guttered out, as if shoved bodily back into the warp. Great clangs rose up from the depths, and the howl of ancient winds echoed for a few heartbeats more before sinking back into silence.

Njal sank to one knee again, breathing heavily. Gunnlaugur rushed over to him. The Rune Priest's grizzled face was haggard from effort.

'The ship,' Njal rasped.

'What of it?' asked Gunnlaugur, crouching beside him.

'It is the *ship*.'

Gunnlaugur didn't understand. 'We can–' he began, but Njal cut him short.

'You will do nothing,' said the Rune Priest. 'I know where it is. I *felt* it.' He looked up, his grey eyes searching into the infinite darkness above them. Dimly, the outlines of great buttresses and stairwells could be made out, twisting into shadow. 'It will crush us all.'

Gunnlaugur looked over his shoulder. Twelve Wolves stood around them, all of them battle-ravaged. Beyond their slender defensive line, the sound of mutant activity was already beginning to creep back into aural range. The enemy had been blooded, its champions slaughtered, but its near-limitless numbers had only been curtailed.

'Go,' said Njal. 'The assault rams can be reached. We have done what we came for.'

'The hunt is not complete.'

Njal smiled grimly. 'You fight like the Slayer, vaerangi, but you cannot fight this, so save your hammer for another dawn.' The smile disappeared. '*Go*. I will not order it again.'

'How will you get out?' Gunnlaugur asked.

'You have less than an hour,' growled Njal, summoning Nightwing to his shoulder.

Giving in to the inevitable, Gunnlaugur saluted Njal, fist-on-chest in the Fenrisian way. Then he turned, gathered the survivors together and shook the gore from *skulbrotsjór*. He was the only pack-leader left alive, and the rest of the Hunters, their armour scored and their blades cracked, looked close to exhaustion.

'To me, then,' he snarled, already focusing on the road ahead. It would be a bloody path. 'To the Caestus.'

Chapter Twenty

Olgeir raced down nine spire-levels, picking up support from those of Ann-arovea's security staff still at their stations as he went. He was obliged to silence a knot of half-hearted agitators up in the exclusive protected zone, but the real disorder was still in the ranks below, drawn from the hab-units that sheltered the skilled worker cadres.

He eventually reached a wide assembly chamber just below the main portals to the upper spire. It was a natural defensive position, with wide fire-lanes opening up across a huge semicircular auditorium. Dozens of entrances opened out into the lower levels of the auditorium, but only one gate-cluster guarded the summit, where the turbo-shafts leading up into the higher spire had been sited. Crowds had assembled at the base of the audi-torium, and they were already moving up the aisles towards the summit.

Olgeir emerged from the upper portal, flanked by a dozen blue-armoured spire guards. They had their weapons drawn, but for the time being he kept his own bolter lowered. Thus far, his presence alone had been enough to deter even the most desperate of rioters, and he had no appetite for killing more than necessary.

'Do not fire unless I give the word,' he ordered his escort, taking up posi-tion under the upper gate's lintel.

The guards crouched into firing positions around him, training their projectile weapons on the crowd below. The mob kept approaching, more slowly now, clambering up over the rows of empty seating with their eyes fixed on the prize ahead.

Olgeir watched them come. There must have been thousands assembled, with many more filtering into the auditorium from the low-level entrances. The closest were less than fifty metres away, though the sight of a Space Wolf standing guard above them slowed them down.

'That is *enough!*' roared Olgeir, his helm-enhanced voice echoing across the vast space. The crowd's progress halted. 'Go back. Leave this place. You will not be allowed to travel higher.'

Olgeir looked across the front ranks of the mob. They were not soldiers. Their faces were uncovered, exposing fearful, desperate expressions. They had never been given any reason but fear and duty to serve their masters in the elite spire heights, and once a greater fear had penetrated their minds, that coercive force lost much of its deadening power.

Olgeir saw hab-workers, menials, minor Administratum officials, medicae field staff and pedagogues among them. They all wore the same panicky pallor. The jet-black armour of Adeptus Arbites enforcers could be made out further back in the press of bodies. That was surprising – they had a reputation for incorruptibility. Then again, when the entire world was teetering on the brink of annihilation, perhaps even their heavy conditioning could be suborned.

'Do not listen to him,' came a new voice.

Olgeir's eyes snapped onto the source. All around him, a dozen weapons trained on the same point.

A lone figure strode up from the lower levels of the auditorium. He advanced up the long central aisle, and the crowds parted to allow him passage.

Morfol.

The lord commissar was wearing what looked like some kind of carapace armour draped in robes of oily black and bearing the death mask emblem of the Imperium. He was accompanied by a retinue of heavily armed enforcers together with a small cadre of Guard soldiers. More armed troops, marching in disciplined ranks, followed behind.

'Come no closer, commissar,' warned Olgeir, resisting the urge to aim his bolter.

Morfol halted at the forefront of his ramshackle army. The light of certainty burned in his eyes. Olgeir had seen that light in a hundred other commissars on a hundred other worlds, and had always admired it.

'Or you will do what to me, Angel of the Emperor?' Morfol asked. His words carried to all corners of the huge space, broadcast by vox-emitters in his armoured collar. 'You will end me? You think I fear that?' He turned to address his followers. 'There is nothing to fear in death. There is *everything* to fear in cowardice.' Morfol knew his craft, and the crowd began to shuffle forwards once more. 'An enemy is coming. We see it on the augurs. The Emperor – as He must ever will it – demands that we *fight*. If the governor will not do it, if her newfound bodyguard will not, then *we* must.'

The lord commissar's words were infectious. As Olgeir watched, the front rank began to move again, climbing up over the rows of seats. Fear still shone in their wide eyes, but there was something else there, too – a dogged, desperate determination.

Morfol was a powerful orator. He was courageous, too, and marched with them, drawing a chainblade as he came.

Olgeir knew he could take Morfol out with a single shot, but that would enrage the others and vindicate his words. He knew he could hold the high gate virtually indefinitely against such opposition, but that would provoke huge bloodshed and tie up the spire completely.

As he hesitated, Annarovea's comm-signal blinked into life.

'My lord, a ship approaches orbital range,' said the governor, her voice reproachful.

Olgeir's grip on his bolter tightened by a fraction. 'Impossible,' he replied, glancing at his retinal chrono. 'Too soon.'

'It's not the one we've been tracking – it is a Grand Cruiser, it doesn't respond to hails, and it's ignoring the troop carriers in orbit. Its shields are raised.'

Olgeir backed up towards the high gate, keeping his weapon trained on the advancing Morfol. The lord commissar pushed on fearlessly.

'That ship is not here to help,' Olgeir warned.

'Does it not have Navy-level ordnance?' Annarovea's voice was tight with suspicion.

'It is a Ministorum ship, governor. They will not speak to you.'

'I can recall the Guard regiments. We have been hasty – we gave up on defence too soon.'

'Do *not* do it,' Olgeir felt his frustration rising. The mob was inching closer, climbing towards the gate with ever-more determined steps. 'Listen. Even if they could stop this thing, they will not. I say it again: they are not here to help.'

When Annarovea replied, her exasperation was evident. 'Then why *are* they here?'

Olgeir immediately imagined the life-eater torpedoes being readied for launch. It would be a quicker death, but just as agonisingly pointless as the plague. What had happened? Had Njal sanctioned Delvaux to run ahead? Or had the mission already failed?

By then, Morfol was less than twenty metres away from him, shouting out encouragement to his followers and waving his chainblade to beckon them on. Every movement he made exemplified that damned Commissariat certainty.

'I will return as soon as I can, governor,' voxed Olgeir. 'Until then, maintain the troop-lift. Do nothing to slow it.'

He cut off the comm-link, and burst into motion, charging down from the gate and leaping at Morfol. The commissar had no time to react – he tried to get his chainblade into position, but Olgeir swatted it aside. Then the Space Wolf's gauntlet was clamped around Morfol's neck, lifting him into the air one-handed.

Morfol glared back, still defiant, mastering his fear. 'Like I... said,' he gasped, his hands scrabbling uselessly against Olgeir's grip, 'I do not fear... death. Kill me here, and there are... thousands more.'

The crowd had fallen back when Olgeir charged, but now they edged forwards again, caught between fear, uncertainty and their lingering sense of outrage.

'Kill you?' hissed Olgeir, his eyes boring into the mortal's own. 'I could kill you with a twist of my fingers. I could kill every soul in this room and not one blade would come close to touching me. But why would I? You are *irrelevant*. You talk of duty, but I have already told you what you must do. If you will not listen, then you damn yourself.'

Morfol was struggling for breath by then, and Olgeir released his grip by a fraction. The mob around them kept its position, held rapt by the scene before it.

'If those spores land on this world,' Olgeir went on, 'you will have all the fighting you could ever wish for. Believe me, I would fight alongside you then. Do not be fooled, there can be no victory. Unlike some of my brothers, the prospect of a glorious death for no purpose does not fill my hearts with joy, but I would fight until the last breath nonetheless.'

Morfol was listening. His eyes bulged, his forehead was shiny with sweat, but he listened.

'Until then, there is only *one* duty – to get as many living souls off this world as we can. Your governor understands this, your generals understand it. You are charged with discipline on this world, lord commissar. Why do you not understand?'

For a few seconds longer, Morfol remained defiant. Then his bloodshot eyes ran across Olgeir's war-plate. He saw the tokens of a dozen campaigns, and the marks made by an extended lifetime of unbroken service. He saw the bloodstains, still uncleared from the fighting on the comm-station, and the heavy marks of use on his weapons.

The resolve went out of him. Olgeir released him, and Morfol fell to his knees, heaving in deep breaths.

Olgeir turned to the crowd. 'I told you to leave,' he growled.

Those closest fell back, cowed by the low threat-note in his voice. Bereft of Morfol's leadership, their will became fragile. Some looked to the commissar, but he longer met their gaze. Instead, Morfol stared up at Olgeir, a mix of humiliation and resolve on his bruised face.

'How long have we got?' he asked.

'Less than three hours,' said Olgeir. 'Use the time wisely. It might be all you have left.'

Then he turned on his heel, and strode back to the upper gate where his escort still waited. Their guns remained trained on the crowds below, but Olgeir doubted they would be needed now.

As he walked, he made a record of Morfol's locator-ident. If the spores started to fall, he would track him down again. He had a sense the commissar might be a good man to fight alongside when all the other barricades had fallen.

That done, he reopened the comm-link to Annarovea.

'The spire is secure, governor,' he voxed, reaching the gate. 'I am coming back up.'

Baldr shuddered, and drew in a painful breath. It was air – real air. He was using his lungs again, and the body that housed them was his own.

The Mycelite's foetid grotto surrounded him once more, as dark and clammy as it had been before. The Plague Marine gazed up at him, and his withered features were twisted into a smile.

'Well done,' he said.

As soon as he heard the words, Baldr realised what he had done. The horror of it cut him to the core, and he raged against his bonds, thrashing and kicking out. The glutinous matter around him flexed by a finger's width, cracking where his right leg pushed against it.

The Mycelite remained calm, watching him with the keen interest of a guardian watching a child.

'It will do you no good to fight it,' the Plague Marine told him, shuffling back over to where he had been seated. 'Memory will fade again. You will become the ship, the ship will become you.' His smile drifted away. 'Imagine it – mightier than any of your brothers, mightier than any of mine. You will be something new.'

The fog of deception felt weaker now. Baldr's hatred was stronger, driving his body against its bonds. 'I will not do that again,' he swore.

'Evidence tends to the contrary.'

'I will fight you.'

The Mycelite shrugged. 'You cannot sustain your resistance.' He ran his withered hands up the length of his staff. 'The *collar*, though. The remaining obstacle. We must find some way to circumvent that.'

'I felt them reach the target,' said Baldr, clinging to the one sliver of hope. 'They have planted their charges. That ends the game.'

The Mycelite looked equivocal. 'Nothing in this vessel is beyond you. Your mind can travel down communications conduits and drift through cogitator wafers. You can manipulate matter, divert energies. Eliminating a few thermal devices from your fusion cores will be trivial.'

Baldr pushed against the material around him once again. It didn't shift at all.

'I will not do it,' Baldr said again.

'You will.'

'You are exhausted. You cannot force me again.'

The Mycelite looked up at him with an expression of genuine affection on his etiolated face. 'Ah, but the Grandfather has been kind. To even *witness* you – that would have been enough, but to be the guide to your ascension… That is more than I know how to compass.' He got to his feet again and hobbled up to Baldr, leaning on the staff two-handed. The Mycelite's breath was sweet with corruption.

'Perhaps you wonder why you are so important,' the Mycelite said. 'Perhaps it has occurred to you that I myself am a sorcerer, and that there are many others on this vessel who are touched by the Eye's gifts. Perhaps, you are telling yourself, this whole thing is a deception, and it is not *you* who is important at all. Perhaps that gives you some hope.'

Baldr regarded him scornfully. 'I will not do it,' he said for a third time, issuing the words like a litany against destruction.

'But I cannot command this vessel like you do,' the Mycelite went on.

'No one can. The talent you command is not something any of my Legion could ever match. Shall I tell you why, nightjar? We are interlopers, that is why, merely passengers. You, on the other hand, are where you belong.'

Baldr spat at him again, trying not to listen.

'You call this ship the *Festerax*,' said the Mycelite, sounding amused. 'I've always liked the name, but I did not give it.'

As the Mycelite spoke, cracks of blue light began to run down the inner walls of the grotto. Clumps of fungus fell away, plopping wetly on the floor. A great sigh ran across the chamber's roof, as if huge and rusty metal beams were being hauled into new formations.

'All things are corrupted by time. Thoughts, deeds, words. They all twist in the aether, mutating as the whim of the gods demands.'

Whole sections of the grotto's roof suddenly lifted away, pulled clear by massive cantilevers. A chill blue light flooded in, exposing swathes of pale fungi trembling in the dark. The temperature plummeted. Baldr narrowed his eyes against the sudden glare. The Mycelite's chamber was just a part of a larger structure, one that was being revealed as the shell around them unravelled.

'*Festerax* is a forgivable slip,' the Mycelite went on, 'a melding of similar sounds. It was merely luck, or perhaps fate, that made it possible.'

The last of the chamber's roof swung away, pulled clear on vast chain lengths. The chill illumination exposed Baldr's position for the first time – he was bound by stone-hard lengths of organic matter, as tough as oak and covered in veinous growths. The binding roots that supported him had engulfed a platform of stone.

A towering ceiling soared away above him, half lost in a miasma of pale blue fog. Thick-boled columns of granite supported ranks of gothic arches, all of which enclosed a teardrop-shaped platform of dusty marble. There were terraces beyond that, rows of sensor stations. In the seamy distance soared an armourglass viewing portal.

It was a command bridge.

'The *Festerax* is truly massive,' said the Mycelite, looking up in appreciation as the last vestiges of his fungus chamber unfolded themselves. In the cold light, he was hunched and diminished. 'But its core, as such hulks always are, is a single vessel. Wrecks and void-corpses were added to it, piling atop one another and bound by the will of gods and daemons, and so the original was lost, buried amid the vastness of what had been accumulated by time.'

Baldr recognised the things around him. He saw runes carved into the

granite, thick with dust. He saw iron-rimmed doorways running around
the chamber's edge, gaping blindly into nothingness. He saw command
stations, each one manned by skeletal figures in pearl-grey fatigues. The
crew were long dead, and their eyeless, skinless cadavers slumped motion-
lessly in their seats.

'You know these things?' asked the Mycelite, hobbling across the filth-
strewn marble towards the closest corpse. 'Perhaps you recognise their
voices? They were speaking to you, Baldr. You recognised the language,
even if you could not hear all the words. They have been here for nine
thousand years.' He chuckled mournfully, and pulled the corpse's chair
around. A dust-dry skull wobbled on a bony neck. 'I am afraid they are
all quite mad. It is a long time to be locked in here, never quite being
allowed to die.'

Baldr looked on grimly. The bodies all bore the age-faded livery of
kaerls. Some of them seemed to have fused with their old machines,
locked together in a desiccated embrace of entropy. All wore expressions
of terror on their frozen faces.

'So that is why *you* must be the one to command the *Festerax*,' said the
Mycelite, shuffling back over to him. 'You are on the command throne.
The bound souls will only listen to you. This *ship* will only listen to you.
If you learn to hear them, they will tell you why. They will tell you that
only a Son of Russ could ever pilot this vessel, and not just any Son of
Russ, but one marked out by the bounteous masters of the warp. They
will tell you that *this* is the core, the heart of it all.'

He drew closer, wheezing as he leaned on his staff.

'They will tell you the ship's name was never *Festerax*, but *Frostaxe*, and
that it last plied the void unsullied when the primarchs lived among men.'
The Mycelite shot Baldr a wry smile. 'Perhaps you now also see the truth
of what I was telling you: we are all the *same*, Baldr Fjolnir. We draw from
the same source, we are prey to the same corruptions.'

He laughed – a foul sound, dredged up from a withered throat.

'You are home,' he said. 'The voices will drag you back in, and you will
learn to listen. This has always been your home, and it has always been
calling you.'

With a wrench of hollow insight, Baldr felt the truth of it then. He *had*
heard the voices. He could still hear them, like after-echoes of a recited
saga. They would whisper to him until his mind cracked and he joined
them in eternal confinement, buried alive at the core of the plague-
raddled Hel-ship.

He would give in. The Mycelite's deceptions would spin their veils of decay again, and his mind would once more join the choir of those locked forever in the *Frostaxe*'s tomb-cold soul. It could not be resisted, not forever.

'Time is short,' the Mycelite whispered, gazing into Baldr's eyes with an intense, almost infatuated, look. 'Soon we will go in again, you and I. You will purge the disease from your glorious, eternal body. After that, you will destroy the last of your brothers. You will not need to emerge. You will never need to emerge.'

His soft eyes glistened in the dark.

'Then we will be alone again, you and I, and with all the time in creation.'

Ingvar and Jorundur charged straight into a hail of las-fire and bolter-rounds. Callia and her squad of Battle Sisters were on either side of the doorway, hunkered down behind overturned cogitator stands and firing steadily ahead.

The two Wolves joined them. Ingvar crashed down beside Callia, his bolter kicking in his right hand as he added his own barrage to hers.

'My thanks, Sister,' he voxed.

'Bring him down,' she replied stonily. 'I need no more than that.'

The Cardinal's enormous throne was more than sixty metres away. Once clear of the piles of half-demolished cogitator units, the route to it had almost no cover. Though taken by surprise by Callia's rapid change of allegiance, the rest of the command bridge's defenders were rallying, laying down disciplined walls of suppressive fire while others advanced through the maze of sensor pits beyond the throne. Ingvar could see Sisters of Nuriyah's retinue among them, accompanied by more Ecclesiarchy troops. There must have been dozens of them, all told. Once they brought all their guns to bear, there would be few hiding places across the expanse of the bridge.

Ingvar glanced up towards the throne. Delvaux cowered there, his outline blurred by a personal shield-generator. He seemed to be shouting something, and Ingvar caught the familiar outline of his jowly face trembling.

Before he could see any more, though, the view was obscured by the two Penitent Engines striding into range. One was still on the far side of the throne, turning clumsily amid a squeal and roar of gears. The other lurched into range, venting flames from both extended weapon-arms. Circular saws mounted on either fist accelerated into whirls of adamantium, sending sparks spinning through the gouts of crimson.

'We do this quick, or not at all,' said Ingvar, gauging the distance to the throne. A rapid sprint would bring him into strike-range of Delvaux's throat within seconds, but he'd have to survive a punishing amount of fire.

Callia nodded. 'We'll break left, laying down covering fire. You can do the rest?'

Ingvar glanced over at Jorundur, who was hunched behind the broken remains of a sensor-unit and firing two-handed. The Old Dog nodded towards him. 'Say the word.'

'Then now,' Ingvar ordered.

Callia and the rest of the Battle Sisters leapt clear of their cover and advanced over towards the left flank of the battlefield, running hard and firing all the while. One Sister was hit while out in the open, going down in a whirl of smashed armour and blood-spray, but the rest made it to the doubtful security of a comm-station – a semicircular array of battered machinery rising from the bridge's polished floor. As the Battle Sisters ran, they drew whole swathes of tracer fire towards their position.

A few seconds later, Ingvar and Jorundur burst out, heading straight out into the open. Ingvar fired one-handed, laying down a withering rain of bolt-shells. Jorundur stayed on his shoulder, adding to the hail of rounds. Exposed Ecclesiarchy troops were blown away, lost in the tumbling haze of blasted marble and exploding rockcrete.

Ingvar sprinted low and fast, relying as before on hunt-sense rather than armour-sensors. He swerved unconsciously around an incoming blast from a heavy projectile weapon and powered onwards, never breaking stride.

'I'll take the Engine,' voxed Jorundur, racing towards the first lumbering war machine.

Ingvar nodded, and raced directly for the throne. He veered away from the worst of the incoming fire, but a shell ricocheted off his shoulder-guard, nearly sending him sprawling. He fired back, suppressing the worst of the barrage, and then the throne loomed up ahead, half screened by the whirl of blown dust and debris.

To his right, he was dimly aware of Jorundur taking on the Penitent Engine – he could hear the roars of fury and the sharp clash of metal on metal. He sensed the incoming presence of Nuriyah and the main body of Delvaux's defenders. In a few more heartbeats they'd be on him, and then things would get difficult.

He pounced away from a line of solid-round projectiles and leapt up at the throne's dais. Clouds of dust ripped away, and for an instant he saw Delvaux's fat face glaring down at him in terror. Shielding still glittered between them, but that would never be enough to keep the Gyrfalkon from his prey.

Ingvar bounded up the steps, firing at the shield cover to rip it clear while activating *dausvjer* with his free hand. The blade-edge flared with energy, sensing an imminent kill.

Then, just as he was about to leap, hidden compartments on the throne's base swivelled open, revealing twin lines of autogun-barrels.

Too late, Ingvar tried to arrest his ascent and dive away. The guns opened up with an echoing volley, blasting him from the dais and sending him skidding across the pocked marble floor. He spun around, his vision blurry and flecked with red, before returning fire, strafing the throne's base and silencing the concealed batteries.

By then, though, time had run out. He felt a shadow fall across him, and looked up, twisting to avoid the hammer of incoming fire.

The second Penitent Engine towered over him, its flamers active and its saws whirling. There was no escape, and no room to move – before he could so much as raise his blade the war machine had extended its arms, raising them like some savage champion of pagan worlds, before plunging them down.

Gunnlaugur ran from the enemy.

He wanted to turn. Every fibre of his being yearned to stop the headlong race to the assault rams, swivel on his heel and bring his hammer to bear again. It had felt good, to be unleashed once more. He had remembered what it was like to command again – free of doubt, free of dissension.

And now he was haring through the endless gloom as if fear meant something to him.

He could have laughed, though the sound would have been bitter.

We race for the landing stages like whipped curs.

Every second that passed brought the thermal charges closer to ignition. The amount of destructive potential now laid in the churning heart of the hulk was chilling to contemplate – those charges would crack the enginarium's shell as easily as Gunnlaugur's fists might crack a skull.

The pack remained close on his heels. He could hear their strained, throaty breathing even through their armour. They were near the end of their strength, driven to extremity by the long, punishing, non-stop combat.

'*Faster!*' he thundered, giving them no quarter.

And they responded. They squeezed a morsel more energy from burning muscles, and their ragged breaths grew even more strained. They did not run because they feared what was on their heels. They did it because *he* had ordered it, and because their pride was now to live up to his demands.

I am vaerengi *again*, thought Gunnlaugur, and, despite everything, that kindled a spark of pride within him.

More corridors wound away ahead, cloaked deep in eternal night, twisting like entrails through the unimaginable vastness. Already he could sense fresh filth scurrying to cut them off – to clog the narrow ways with their own dead, to claw at them and lock them within the ship that would soon be their death-byre.

He checked the chrono. It ticked down mercilessly. He could no longer detect Njal. He did not know if Ingvar and Jorundur still lived. He did not know whether Olgeir had made it to Kefa, and if anything had been salvaged from that world. All he knew for certain was what he could *smell* – frantic hatred from the ship around him, grim determination from his brothers behind him.

From somewhere, from some place lodged deep within his warrior's soul, he dredged up a sliver of additional energy. His strides lengthened by a fraction, his hammer swung further, his wounds cried at him more intensely.

'For the oathbreaker!' he bellowed. 'We will *live*, if for no other cause than to rip his faithless heart out!'

And amid the dark, running hard to keep up with the Wolf Guard's furious progress, his brothers roared the same vow, using it to fuel them, to drive them onwards in hatred.

For the oathbreaker.

The pain was phenomenal. It did not merely strike at his body – it raked across his soul, chilling it, scraping it into near-oblivion. Each time Njal delved into the source, the frigid grasp of agony became more acute, as if he were being shoved beneath pack-ice and held down there. Actinic fire rippled across him, caught and twisted by the elemental power unleashed within. He was racing, hurtling up through the heart of darkness, propelled by will alone in defiance of the law of the universe.

There was no possibility of withdrawal. There was no time left to use his mortal body as the others did. He had been forced to haul on the deepest fragments of runecraft, to turn his very body into an instrument, to send it soaring just as Nightwing did.

The raven cawed and circled around him, pushing higher, spiralling up through the myriad levels that constituted the *Festerax*'s upper reaches.

Njal followed it. He was already far above the enginarium and still climbing fast. Lightning flared and snapped, buoying him like a rising flood. He streaked upwards, tearing along vertical shafts gouged through the vessel's core, and the rune-storm boomed in his wake, roiling with soul-summoned thunder.

Decks passed by like dreams, lost in shadows. He caught only glimpses of their interiors. There were colossal arches leading to unknowable regions of utter darkness, unimaginably vast pillars holding up grotesque halls of plague-devices, pulsing energy fields throwing lurid green light across the gaping chasms. Some of those chambers might have lain undisturbed for millennia. Secrets might have been set down in those foetid halls, secrets that could change the course of the war, or summon back a golden age for humanity, or expose the forbidden secrets of the ten-thousand-year Imperium.

Or there might be nothing – nothing but ruin and disease, festering forever amid shadows that never lifted and air that never stirred.

Njal surged up through it all, his totems clattering against his armour, his staff-skulls rippling in the headwind. He was drawing near to the source. He could *feel* it, lodged like a canker in his mind.

I have faced this thing before.

Even amid his pain, the thought intrigued him. No mortal had ever set foot in this hulk and lived. There was no enemy within it that he could have met in combat before.

And yet. Something about the spears of warp-power that had eviscerated his warriors had borne the tang of dreadful familiarity. He swooped past a lattice of intersecting buttresses, ascending more rapidly now as momentum built. The air became less furiously hot. He saw moisture glistening on the surfaces of the iron and stone around him. Growths, shaggy like beards of moss, hung from every spar and brace-beam.

Nightwing called out, now just a few dozen metres above him. The raven had flown unerringly towards the target.

Njal drew deep on the runes, and thundered after it. He raced up a long well of iron, a narrow shaft that closed down nigh to the width of his armour-plate, before bursting out into a vast spherical chamber above.

The sphere was kilometres in diameter, half drowned in abyssal shadows and dank with nebulae of drifting spores. Arcs of green-tinged fulguration cracked and shivered across the cyclopean gulf. Above him, suspended on hundreds of bone-like spars and tendrils, hung a warship. It was part melded to the concave walls around it, lodged like a thrown blade in a wound. Enormous conduits connected the warship's hull to the greater mass of the *Festerax* around it, many throbbing with electrical currents or swelling with seething liquids.

Njal immediately recognised the profile. Despite millennia of decay and damage, he saw the gunmetal-grey of the armour plates. He saw the knotwork icons etched above the ventral gunwales, and the vessel's name picked out in gold-edge runes.

Frostaxe.

Nightwing screamed at the obscenity of it, pinning its wings back and tearing towards the starship's mottled hull. Njal followed the raven up, and the shadow of the starship's hull fell across him. He saw many ways in, gaping holes in the once-proud exterior. Even as he did so, he sensed the malign force cradling within it, as old and maleficent as the gods of ruin.

And I am already weakened.

The Dark Wolf growled then, stirred by the enormous discharge of rune-power keeping Njal aloft. The Rune Priest thrust upwards towards the nearest breach, and grasped the shredded adamantium with both hands.

For a moment he hung above the gulf, his muscles flaring with pain. The chrono inside his helm ticked down, marking the shrinking window before the charges ignited. He looked down, seeing his boots suspended over the yawning void.

Enough.

He dragged himself up and into the carcass of the warship. Hauling his bulk onto the ironwork structure, he reached intact decking and stood once again on firm ground. He unlocked his staff and kindled the skull-tip with silver light.

Nightwing had already flown ahead, twisting up through the decks towards its target. Njal saw what it saw, and so the way was marked out like a trail of twine through the labyrinth.

'So be it,' snarled Njal, setting off into the shadows. 'To the core.'

Chapter Twenty-One

Ingvar stared up at the Penitent Engine. There was no time to do anything but get his sword into the path of the spinning fist-blades, but he knew he would not be able to stop them. He glared up towards the agonised pilot of the machine, determined at least to face death head on.

The machine's linen-shrouded face gazed down at him, the features hidden but for a static scream marked on the fabric. It was de Chatelaine. The circular saws continued to whirr and the muzzles of the flame-cannons gouted pre-burst smoke.

Then it turned aside.

Ingvar watched the massive Engine sweep its weapons away from him and take a stride towards the throne. He heard Delvaux screaming for it to halt. Bolter-fire sparked and ricocheted from de Chatelaine's metal exoskeleton, but it was far too sporadic to halt her.

Ingvar leapt to his feet, opening up with his own bolter. Battle Sisters advancing behind the cover of the Penitent Engine were mown down, struck by his shells as they turned their fire on their own war machine.

'Withdraw!' shrieked Delvaux, his voice shrill with panic. All his corpulent self-assurance vanished, replaced by a frantic, wide-eyed terror. 'I *command* you – withdraw!'

By then de Chatelaine had reached her target. Her flamethrower arms opened up, flooding the throne with crimson immolation. Delvaux cried out in pain, thrashing about on his seat while still trying to clamber out of harm's way.

But there would be no salvation for him. De Chatelaine plunged both chainfists down on the Cardinal's flabby form, shredding his body into a whirl of flying gore and flesh-scraps. The screaming only lasted seconds before Delvaux's torso was torn into strips, spraying the marble and gold-leaf in a curtain of thick, lumpy red.

Ingvar mounted the dais steps again, firing all the while. The bridge's defenders hesitated, shocked by the death of the Cardinal. The rain of bolter-shells faltered for a moment, and the battle suddenly hung in the balance.

'Take down the remaining Engine,' Ingvar voxed Callia. Jorundur was still fighting it, and the duel was an unequal one.

Then Ingvar set off, sprinting out from the throne and towards the shocked figure of Nuriyah. She stood motionless, her flamer-arm held limp, staring at the ruins of the throne.

It was all the time Ingvar needed. He streaked across the bridge deck, his blade lashing with energy, and threw himself through the air towards her. By the time she saw him come at her, the chance to defend herself was gone. She spun round, lifting the blackened muzzle of her pyromaniac augmetic, but Ingvar had already whipped *dausvjer* round at her neck.

The blade sliced clean through, cutting precisely between gorget and helm. With a snap of released disruptor-essence, Nuriyah's head flew through the air, tracing a line of blood in its toppling wake, before thudding heavily to the marble and rocking to a standstill.

Ingvar hit the ground hard, cracking the deck beneath his feet before whirling to face the remaining defenders.

'Enough!' shouted Callia over the bridge-wide vox.

The balance of power had shifted. De Chatelaine's Penitent Engine was still busy smashing the last pieces of Delvaux's throne into molten scrap. The other Engine had been disabled by Jorundur with the assistance of Callia's squad. The rest of the Battle Sisters were now leaderless and divided, since many had come over to Callia's side already.

The last of the incoming fire faded away in a series of banging echoes. The bridge's defenders began to emerge from behind devastated sections of cover, hands raised.

'This is still an Ecclesiarchy vessel,' announced Callia, taking control with all the resolve she had displayed in Hjec Aleja. 'Resume your stations, remove the bridge lock-down. Transmit messages to all decks that Cardinal Delvaux has been relieved of command and *Vindicatus* is now under the control of the Fiery...' Callia glanced over at de Chatelaine's rampaging Engine. 'Of the Wounded Heart.'

Ingvar looked over at Jorundur. The Old Dog gave him a weary nod from amid the ruins of the second Penitent Engine. He looked as battered as Ingvar had ever seen him, with his armour carved half open by the war machine's chainfists, but he still stood and still held a weapon.

That only left de Chatelaine. Her movements were becoming increasingly jerky. Delvaux's throne was now nothing more than a pile of bloody fragments, and still she hammered away at it. Her mechanisms, damaged by bolter-fire, began to overheat. The cantilevered arms flailed wildly. Something like a howl issued from her clamped-open lips, and the whole edifice of her iron exoskeleton began to totter.

Ingvar raced over to her just as the Engine fell, crashing onto its back amid the ruin of the throne dais. Columns of spark-filled exhaust twined up from her awkwardly twisted limbs. Her mortal body, shackled to the instruments of agony, twitched and bucked in its bonds.

Ingvar crouched beside her and pulled back the scrap of linen that covered her face. De Chatelaine's everlasting scream stared back at him. Blood ran from her eyes across scourged cheeks – the machine was pumping pain-amplifier chemicals into her body at a wildly punitive rate.

She was somehow defying it. With self-command bordering on the superhuman, de Chatelaine had overridden the dreadful straitjacket of the Penitent Engine's psychosis-inducing mechanisms. She had resisted the entire battery of control devices implanted into her shriven body, and, almost impossibly, turned the tools of the Ecclesiarchy against its own representative.

In a lifetime of combat across a thousand worlds, Ingvar had never seen mental strength quite that acute. Even now, as her body arched with pain, de Chatelaine was still fighting.

If Ingvar could have saved what remained of her, he would have done, but there was no living extraction from an Ecclesiarchy machine. He rested his bolter gently against her sweat-streaked temple.

'Be at rest, battle-sister,' he said. 'Your saga shall be sung in the Halls of Fenris.'

De Chatelaine's face remained contorted in agony, but something like understanding flashed momentarily in her eyes. For a second, gratitude mingled with the pain.

Then Ingvar fired. The spasms ceased immediately. The nerve-impulse units in the Penitent Engine registered the death of the host, and the last of its generators sputtered out. The chainfists wound down, the flame-throwers coughed out.

Ingvar stood up slowly, gazing down at de Chatelaine's body.

Callia walked up to him, followed closely by a limping Jorundur. Ahead of them all, glimpsed through the immense forward viewscreen, Kefa Primaris could now clearly be seen.

'The plague-hulk is on the augurs,' she said, checking her chrono. 'It is less than an hour away. Can your brothers–'

'They will kill it,' said Ingvar, turning away from the carnage over the throne. 'Have faith.'

'What of the life-eaters?' asked Jorundur.

'I have already given the order,' said Callia, moving to the sensor station just below the dais. She ran her fingers over the console. 'The torpedoes have been withdrawn. They will soon–'

She broke off again. Ingvar and Jorundur joined her at the console. Runes glowed across a cracked screen.

'This is impossible,' she said, glancing up at the curve of Kefa Primaris in the forward real-view portal.

Ingvar scanned the runes. 'They are still primed to fire.'

'I shut them down!' cried Callia.

Jorundur hefted his axe with fresh purpose. 'Is there an override? Some way to control them directly?'

'I don't know,' said Callia. 'Where's the ship's commander?'

Harryat was already dragging himself towards the console, clutching at a bloody patch over his shoulder and wincing from the pain. 'Ordnance control,' he said through gritted teeth. 'You can override from there, but you'd need full clearance. The Cardinal has gone. He couldn't–'

Ingvar looked at Jorundur, and the same thought flashed through their minds.

'Klaive,' he said. 'Give me a location.'

'Three levels down – I can shunt the coordinates to your armour. But you'll never reach it.'

'Do what you can from here,' growled Ingvar, already moving. 'Pull the ship out of orbit.'

Jorundur came with him, and the two Wolves broke into a run.

'He's the one you came for, isn't he?' Jorundur voxed as they sprinted back towards the bridge exits.

'He is the target,' confirmed Ingvar, picking up speed. 'But I want him alive.'

'That might be difficult.'

'*Alive.*'

Jorundur didn't reply immediately. When he did, his voice was dark. 'We'll see,' was all he said.

'You are afraid,' said Baldr.

The Mycelite looked up at him. 'Why do you say so?'

'Time runs out for you. Njal is still on the ship, and he hunts for you.'

The Mycelite would not be goaded. Everything about him remained as it had been – sad, stooped, drenched in soporific heaviness. 'He can destroy this ship,' he said. 'He can destroy me. It will only drag out the agony.'

He reached for his staff, and his fingers wrapped around the gnarled wood.

'I show you *mercy*,' he said. 'You understand this? Your Apothecaries administer battle-rites, do they not? To end the pain of your fallen? This is the same thing.'

Baldr examined the Plague Marine. The sorcerer's voice was weaker than it had been. Perhaps the effort of subduing Baldr's will had beaten the strength out of it. He could still feel the collar around his neck, biting into his flesh. When Njal had placed it on him, it had felt like a humiliation. Now it felt like a token of fate – a fragment of galactic luck, just as the skull-totem had been on Ras Shakeh.

'No more,' snapped the Mycelite. He reached out his clawed hand and rested it on Baldr's forehead. 'We do this again.'

The *Frostaxe*'s bridge shuddered away, and Baldr's mind immediately fell into the pit of darkness. For an instant, he felt the clammy touch of the Mycelite's skin on his, then nothing at all.

Colours swam out of the void, vivid and swirling. He sensed the movement of souls within his colossal body – the ship's body – running hard for the outer skin. He felt their desperation, not to survive, but to make their sacrifice worth something.

He felt the burning presence of the Stormcaller raging up through the chambers below, and wondered if the Mycelite knew that he was now very close.

Then Baldr felt the pricks of pain at his heart – the cluster of charges buried in the fusion reactor cores, ticking down within their shielded shells, poised to rip him apart in a supernova of destruction.

'Destroy them,' the Mycelite commanded, his voice floating in his mind – urgent now, persuasive.

Baldr knew that he could. Just as he had summoned fire to purge the interlopers from the inner enginarium, he knew he could douse the incipient inferno buried in those chambers of plasma. He could take each one in turn and shift them all into the void, where they would explode in silent puffs.

He wanted to do it. The instinct was as natural as plucking a thorn from one's flesh.

He reached out with his mind, delving into the plasma chambers. He saw the irritants, swimming in a luminescent mass – little dark spheres, glittering with heat shielding and ready to ignite. The urge to absorb them, to gather them up and fling them clear of danger, was virtually overwhelming. He cupped the closest of them in a ghostly hand, watching as the plasma around it slipped and slopped from invisible fingers.

'No,' he said.

He felt the power in Mycelite's voice immediately. 'You are the ship.'

It was difficult not to obey. It was crushingly, agonisingly hard.

But he could do it.

'No,' he said again, fighting to break free of the visions. He heard the other voices murmuring in half-aware fury, all of them struggling to drag him in with them, to consign him to the same incorporeal life they endured. They *were* mad, locked in debates of which they had no understanding.

Amid the struggle, the Mycelite's voice softened further.

'This gift is unique,' he said. 'It is new. Think on that. In ten thousand years there has been no one like you. The stars fade, and still such magnificence is created. Do not spurn this. You will be a god. You were always marked out for it, right from birth. The daemons of your ice-world knew it. They could feel it. You could feel it.'

Baldr remembered the wolf, the one that had stood before him in the dark, dripping wood. He remembered the amber eyes.

Why doesn't it move? Why doesn't it pounce?

He wavered. He felt the soul of the ship assert itself, surging up to swallow his own. He felt dizzy. Nausea piled in, welling up from the nigh-infinite volume of matter pressing down around him.

He reached for the charges again. He grasped them, enclosing them in an aura of suppression. All he had to do now was cast them away, scattering them into the void like a child throwing stones into the waves.

'Do it,' urged the Mycelite.

He would have done. The Mycelite's words had performed their work, and the last strands of Baldr's resistance flaked away. Given a free hand then, he would have nullified the threat from the devices before turning his wrath to those of his brothers still fleeing from the reach of his multifaceted mind. It would have been over, and all within the blink of an amber eye.

But then, just as Baldr's thoughts crystallised, the Mycelite's hold broke.

Baldr came around, snapped roughly back into reality. His eyes flickered open, watering from the harsh light. The *Frostaxe*'s darkened bridge danced with corposant, stirring up the dust of aeons and making the corpses shiver. Baldr shook his head, blinking hard and trying to shake off a crippling wave of nausea.

Bodies were moving ahead of him – huge bodies, wreathed in light and swaying amid a blur of torn reality. For a second Baldr thought he might have somehow died, and that his soul had been translated into an afterlife of insubstantial wraiths and spectral energy-flows.

Then his vision compensated, focus returned, and he saw the truth of it. The Mycelite had turned away from him, suddenly distracted by a new threat. Beyond the stooped and twisted form of the Plague Marine, Njal Stormcaller loomed dark and tall, his staff crackling and his armour-runes blazing.

'Ready your soul for damnation, Traitor,' Njal growled, summoning rune-fire to himself in iridescent streaks. 'Hel is upon you now.'

The impact sites flickered up on Gunnlaugur's helm-display. He gave the order, and the packs peeled away, each one heading for the loc-reading of a different Caestus assault ram. They had been forced to make calculations on the run, seeking out strong signals from undamaged vessels.

Given their losses, only three of the Caestus rams were needed. Gunnlaugur had run scans as the outer rim approached, and five had responded with live signals – four of them reporting battle-readiness. Each was sealed and locked down, their heavy ceramite armour protecting them from the predations of all but the most well-equipped and determined enemy.

Two packs of five split off, haring down the plunging tunnels towards the signals. The remaining four came with him, pressing ahead to the most distant of the loc-readings.

The target was almost open to the void – lodged in a vertical gouge in the hulk's flank the length of a starship comm-vane.

Gunnlaugur checked the chrono as he sprinted.

Sixteen minutes, and still ticking down. This was too close.

Hafloí's voice crackled over the comm, breathless and panting. 'Targets incoming.'

Gunnlaugur blinked to tactical, and watched the proximity markers crowd across his forward scan-field.

'Skítja,' he breathed. They were already clogging the tunnels ahead. Gunnlaugur's helm worked to give him numbers – two hundred, three hundred...

'*Break* them!' he voxed, slamming a fresh magazine into his bolter. It was his last.

The corridor echoed with the snap, thud and slide of ammo being replenished. Power weapons crackled into full-burn, sending neon flickers out across the dark.

Ten metres.

He spied the first pair of enemy eyes, glowing marsh-green.

'Allfather!' he roared, whirling his thunder hammer in one hand as the bolter kicked out shells with the other.

His brothers thundered their own battle-cries, tearing along in a tight knot of grey steel and ceramite. Then they crashed as one into the barricades, and the tunnel dissolved into fire and annihilation.

Olgeir burst into Annarovea's chambers. The governor turned to face him, her face flushed with anger.

'You *knew*,' she accused. 'It wasn't just you – there were other ships.'

Olgeir looked wearily around the chamber. The rest of the governor's staff glared back at him with censorious expressions – as far as they dared.

This mission was proving impossible to balance. There was no one to fight with honour, and no story to spin that would convince doubting souls.

'Nothing has changed,' he said.

'We cannot speak to the Ministorum vessel,' Annarovea said. 'Why is that?'

'You have a location fix?'

Annarovea pushed clear of her throne and strode over to a sensor station.

Olgeir followed her. A glassy pict lens showed a rune-filled depiction of the immediate orbital zone. Troop-carriers making slow progress out of the system, hauling the precious human cargo beyond destruction's reach.

And then there was the Cardinal's ship. It was approaching deployment range, skirting the limit beyond which life-eater torpedoes would become unstoppable.

'Scan it,' he said.

Annarovea nodded towards an aide, who directed an augur-sweep towards *Vindicatus*.

'What do you see?' asked Olgeir.

'Extensive surface damage,' reported the aide. 'Its course is erratic. Engines seem slow to correct.'

'That ship took on the plague-hulk,' Olgeir told Annarovea. 'You can see the results. If it tries to do so again, it will be destroyed.' He studied the data scrolling across the pict screen. 'Run a weapons analysis.'

The aide adjusted the scope of the scan. 'There is a power build-up along the lower hull. Sporadic, but growing.'

Olgeir nodded grimly. 'Torpedo batteries.' He turned to Annarovea. 'The commander of that ship has the power to erase all life on this world. He will do it if he sees the plague-hulk reaching deployment range. Better to strip a planet of life than risk it supplying soldiers to the enemy. That's the calculation.'

Annarovea went pale. 'I do not–'

'There is *no help*, governor. Launch your fighters at it, if it will make you feel any better, but that is an Ecclesiarchy Grand Cruiser, so do not fool yourself they will do more than scratch its shields.'

Annarovea seemed to shrink in her armour. Fatigue, and hopelessness, were catching up with her, and she struggled to find a reply.

Just then, an alarm sounded from one of the watch-stations on the far side of the chamber. An officer leapt up.

'First signal, lords,' he reported.

'Put it through,' said Annarovea.

The pict screen updated. A new icon appeared on the extreme edge of orbital space, moving slowly but purposively. Unlike the troop carriers and *Vindicatus*, it had no standard fleet-identifier.

'So that is the hulk,' said Annarovea, quietly.

Olgeir nodded.

'What do we do?' she asked. Her self-possession had left her. She was no longer angry, no longer defiant. In the space of a single day, her armouries had been stripped bare, her citizens were rioting, and two vessels with the power to destroy every living thing on the planet were powering steadily into strike positions.

Olgeir drew in a long breath. 'How many regiments did you evacuate?' he asked.

'Four. Five, perhaps, if those carriers clear orbit in time.'

Olgeir forced a smile. Despite everything, Annarovea had done well. Kefa Primaris had done well. The forces already void-lifted were worth having – an Imperial commander could make use of such numbers.

'Then we've done all we were asked to,' he said.

'There's nothing else?' Her voice betrayed quiet desperation. 'Nothing at all?'

Olgeir crossed his arms, and watched the icons tick across the visual field. He thought of Gunnlaugur, and Ingvar, and the rest of the pack, and how much he would have preferred to be fighting alongside them. If they still fought, that was.

'Nothing, governor,' he confirmed. 'Now all we have to do is wait.'

Chapter Twenty-Two

Ingvar and Jorundur raced to the location shunted to them by Harryat, streaking through chambers thick with incense and fogged in confusion. Ecclesiarchy officers stared at them as they passed, paralysed by shock. Callia's orders had been issued, but still a few looked ready to fight them, as if the whole thing were some kind of elaborate sham.

Ingvar ignored them. The two Wolves tore down transit shafts and barrelled along corridors. As they went, warning lumens kicked in, heralding the imminent launch of the life-eater missiles. The entire structure around them shuddered as, somewhere below them, vast void-doors opened up ready to expose the launching tubes inside.

Ingvar swung around a right-angle corner. Twenty metres ahead stood two thick blast-doors chevroned in yellow and black.

'Krak charges,' voxed Ingvar, pulling two from his belt while still running. 'Zero delay.'

Jorundur did the same, and they hurled the four grenades directly at the doors. The charges went off as they hit, exploding in a hail of splinters, doing just enough to weaken the structure. Ingvar and Jorundur smashed into it, travelling at full tilt.

The door's centre-line crashed open, sending both panels barrelling inwards. The control chamber was small – about fifteen metres across – and octagonal. Each wall was lined with cogitator equipment and towering pict screens glowing with pre-launch runes.

Klaive spun round to face them, his face even paler than usual. He reached for the lever that would complete the launch protocol.

By mortal standards, his movements were quick.

Jorundur's bolt-round hit him on the shoulder, sending him slamming into the far wall. Jorundur followed up quickly, reaching for a knife. He grabbed Klaive's tumbling body and plunged the knife down, pinning the confessor to the floor with the blade.

Klaive screamed, twisting like a fish out of water. Ingvar made for the control panels. He shut down the launch orders one by one, restoring the safety protocols and issuing the commands to close the launch tubes.

'This is the Emperor's holy work!' shrieked Klaive, his features twisted by anger rather than pain. 'The Cardinal ordained it! You will burn for this!'

'Certainly,' muttered Ingvar, closing down the last of the launch systems and walking over to where Klaive lay prone.

The confessor's face showed nothing but fury. His red-lined eyes bulged, and he strained against the pin of the dagger, robes darkening with the stain of his blood.

Then the noise of running boots echoed down the corridor outside. The *Vindicatus*'s crew was catching up, and a dozen soldiers in crimson carapace armour formed up beyond the wreckage of the blast-doors.

Jorundur pulled his dagger free of Klaive's shoulder and walked slowly back towards the exit. As he did so, he hefted his bolter casually in the other hand. 'Get back,' he warned the guards, his voice catching with a low threat-note.

'They won't let you kill me,' spat Klaive, gazing up at Ingvar with perfect contempt. 'You can't take on the entire ship.'

Ingvar grabbed him by the throat and hauled him to his feet. 'You really think that?'

Jorundur activated the private channel to Callia, still functioning despite all the damage his armour had taken. 'Sister. Your life-eaters are disabled.'

'Good,' Callia replied, her voice distracted, as if uneasy about what she had to say. 'Then you will return to the bridge.'

Jorundur looked at Ingvar. 'The bridge?'

Ingvar checked his chrono, and suddenly understood. 'The *Festerax*,' he said.

'Lords, your place is here,' Callia went on. 'I shall look forward to your presence beside me as we end this.'

'They have detected the plague-hulk,' repeated Ingvar. 'It still lives. If we leave this chamber, they will rearm the life-eaters.'

Outside the doors, the Ecclesiarchy troops waited. More were joining them each second, unclamping weapons as they took up position along the length of the corridor.

'It is the *only way*,' urged Klaive, whispering into Ingvar's earpiece as if he could be swayed by rhetoric. 'You know it, and Callia knows it. The Stormcaller has failed. Loose vengeance on the world below! Better to burn than be damned.'

Jorundur cut the link to Callia, then took up position standing across the broken doorway. He emitted a low growl, vox-augmented, making the Ecclesiarchy troops back away a few paces.

But they didn't withdraw. They kept their weapons lowered, and held position.

Ingvar ran through the options. If the *Festerax* still burned through the void, if the Wolves kill-team had been destroyed, then Callia was right. Delvaux had broken the oath by disengaging early, but the fate of Kefa still hung by a thread.

'Don't even think of it, brother,' warned Jorundur, facing outwards at the gathering squads of crimson-armoured troops. 'Olgeir is down there.'

Klaive began to chuckle softly.

'You won't hold out forever. They'll break in eventu–'

Ingvar punched Klaive, breaking his nose and knocking him out cold. The confessor slumped in his grasp.

Ingvar hadn't been plagued by visions of the Deathwatch for a long time, but he remembered Callimachus then. He remembered the agonies they had unleashed to strip worlds of life in the face of the oncoming hive-fleets. He remembered when the order had come in, and how long he had struggled over it.

Back then he couldn't have prevented it even if he'd wanted to. It had been their mission, the one they'd sworn to execute. It was abhorrent, and even the Ultramarine had blenched, but it had been the *mission*.

This was different. Ingvar had seen what happened to those on Ras Shakeh. The Ministorum, for all Delvaux's sadism, was right about Kefa Primaris – the world could not be allowed to incubate an army of trillions.

Jorundur looked over his shoulder. 'Gyrfalkon?'

Ingvar shoved Klaive to the floor, placing him well back. Then he unlocked his bolter.

'Njal will do it yet,' he said, defiantly, joining Jorundur in standing guard over the doorway. 'Until then, this chamber is ours.'

'Good,' Jorundur said, checking his ammo-counter. 'For a moment there, brother, you had me worried.'

For the first time since Baldr had awoken, he witnessed surprise on the face of the Mycelite. The Plague Marine's shock was quickly followed by an elated smile, as if he had got used to a nigh-eternal life of utter certainty and was now pleased to find that some unexpected events were still possible.

Njal's expression was unreadable under his helm. The Rune Priest's armour was dark with burned-on blood and slime. The heavy covering of animal skins had been ripped away, and the skulls hanging from chains at his waist were black with the patina of war.

Baldr could hear Njal breathing heavily through his vox-grille. His psyber-raven still accompanied him, hovering accusingly over his shoulder-guards in what looked like an oddly protective formation.

How had he fought his way to this place? What hunt-sense had he used to navigate through the endless dark of the hulk? From his mind-excursions through the plague-ship's interior, Baldr knew better than perhaps anyone just how huge and labyrinthine the *Festerax* was.

Then he remembered his forced actions at the enginarium, and guessed the cold truth.

'The Priest,' remarked the Mycelite, backing away slowly, clutching his staff two-handed as if it were some kind of shield. 'You have been gnawing through my ship like a cancer, and now you're here.'

Njal circled the sorcerer warily. His gaze flickered up at Baldr briefly, and the movement halted.

'You no longer have any claim on him,' the Mycelite said. 'You waste what you do not understand.'

Njal gripped his staff more tightly. Baldr felt the build-up of storm-power, making the air thicken and shudder.

'This ends now,' said Njal.

The Mycelite lost his smile. 'You are weakened, Priest. You have poured your soul out in my kingdoms, and now you have nothing left.'

Njal's gaze moved to Baldr a second time, as if trying to fathom whose side he was on, before the staff rose higher.

'We shall see,' Njal snarled.

The chamber suddenly filled with the hard clap and grind of thunder. Wind howled through the command bridge, sweeping away the withered fungus that coated the walls. Shards of silver leapt out from the metal underneath, snaking and lashing around Njal's staff.

The Mycelite buckled down, crouching low to weather the storm. His own staff surged with a sick green light, and a stench like vomit flared up in the shimmering air.

Baldr raged at his bonds, desperate to shake free of the shackles that bound him to the throne. Njal angled his staff at the Mycelite, and a corona of neon-white energy slammed into the sorcerer's hunched body. The light smashed crazily away from him, flaring and bouncing across the bridge's ruined expanse.

The Mycelite reeled from the impact, muttering half-heard words as he retreated. Njal advanced after him, and the fusty atmosphere curdled with more electric discharge.

The Rune Priest was about to launch another bolt when he suddenly stumbled. He whirled around, blazing with magnesium-bright coruscation, to see a grey-skinned cadaver clawing at his armour. Njal slammed the staff down, and his assailant exploded in a spinning cloud of dust and stone-dry flesh.

By then, the crew of the *Frostaxe* were moving. They dragged themselves up from their seats and skittered across the bridge decking. They made no sound save for the shuffle of bone on metal, and their milky eyes revealed nothing but a faint sheen of pale green.

Njal snarled, and hurled fresh bolts of rune-fire into their midst. The corpses burst open in droves, sending severed limbs cartwheeling across the empty thrones. The cadavers kept coming, clustering at the Rune Priest. They clambered up service hatches and dragged themselves through intersection orifices. Soon the bridge was full of them, swarming like bacilli on a plate.

Baldr kept tearing at his bonds. Powerless, he watched the tide of the dead rear up, clawing at the Rune Priest and threatening to overwhelm him. Njal reaped a swathe with his glittering staff tip, crying out words of power, shattering bones and bursting atrophied lungs.

As the corpses piled in, the Mycelite summoned up a fresh vortex of foul, green-laced energy. He let loose, slamming a clot of boiling warp-essence into Njal's breastplate.

The Rune Priest was hurled backwards through the knots of living dead, crashing into a command station and smashing the ancient cogitator units. The Mycelite's energy bolt clamped on to him like a slick of oil, worming its way into the cracks of his Terminator plate.

Nightwing plummeted, going for the sorcerer's eyes. The Mycelite screamed at it, flailing his staff wildly. The skull-tip connected, sending the psyber-raven careening across the bridge.

Njal righted himself, sending more crushed corpses cracking into the deck, but his armour was now covered in a writhing cloak of green-black mucus. It smeared across the ceramite, dragging him down, extending slobbering tendrils into every joint. The putrid warp-essence boiled and seethed, growing like a living thing, bubbling and multiplying into a cascade of soul-draining, matter-burning filth.

The Mycelite hobbled towards Njal, all the time whispering words of ruin. Spectral figures shimmered into life around him, their faces glowing with an unhealthy, ravening pallor. The ghosts launched themselves at Njal, still besieged by clusters of undead and bogged down by the dragging weight of the sorcerer's noxious bile. They were monstrous and misshapen – every phantasm that had ever haunted the *Frostaxe*'s corrupted bridge, from the echoes of daemon-kin to the plague-infested troops who had first stormed the Wolves' ancient defences. They shrieked as they swooped, reaching out for the Rune Priest with translucent arms. Njal's staff banished them into glassy fragments, but every time they impacted, he weakened further. His enormous shoulders bowed, he dropped to one knee, and his cries of defiance cracked into hoarseness.

The Mycelite hobbled up to him, his gnarled staff now burning freely with fell energies. Fresh waves of the phosphorescent mucus crashed across the Rune Priest, blistering as the armour corroded beneath it. The undead kept on coming, clawing and tearing, fixed on Njal like predators on a stricken prey-beast.

Baldr felt his hearts hammer with rage. His bonds fixed him tight, forcing him to watch powerlessly as the Stormcaller was beaten down. His mind strained at its bonds, desperate to do *something*, and he felt a sudden kick of power unlocking deep within him. The sensation burned furiously, surging into his limbs and locking them rigid in their bonds.

His collar suddenly flared white-hot, and the pain became agonising. Baldr roared out, and spurs of lightning escaped from between his fangs. Power ramped up within him, out of control, swelling into a pain-filled nightmare.

He felt a dark presence unravel within his soul – a wolf, black-coated with yellow eyes, vast and silent. He saw its jaws open, and curved fangs glint wetly.

Why doesn't it move? Why doesn't it pounce?

'The collar!' Baldr cried, forcing the words out as his body was seized by uncontrollable spasms.

Njal looked up then. His red helm-lenses shone fiercely, staring at Baldr from beneath a swirling tempest of warp-energies. He was stricken, hammered down by the Mycelite's art and prone for the killing blow.

The withered plague-sorcerer loomed over him, his staff held high, and a vortex of lurid green aether-matter crackled into life. The emerald plasma leaked pure *sickness* as it spiralled around the skull-tip, ready to finish what the undead had started.

'The scalp of the Stormcaller,' murmured the Mycelite, a strain of pure malice entering his soft voice for the first time.

Njal's staff-fires, doused by torrents of corroding warp-oil, guttered away. The last of the storm-lightning crackled out across his runic armour. He stared up at the Mycelite, still on his knees.

He only issued one word.

'*Shatter*,' he rasped.

And with an eye-burning snap, Baldr's collar broke in two.

Hafloí could hardly see from fatigue. His limbs worked mechanically, chopping and hacking with automatic, nerve-conditioned skill. He'd long since run out of ammo and so had switched to his axe. If the enemy had been any more potent than the mutant filth that swilled around every bilge of the vast ship, he might have been in trouble. As it was, the killing had become a test of pure endurance.

He could feel both his hearts hammering at an insane speed. His helm-display listed a whole plethora of red warning-indicators, each one of them screaming for him to slacken his rate of movement. With a grim smile, Hafloí realised the truth – he was fighting himself to death.

The Grey Hunters around him were in scarce better shape. All carried wounds from the ferocious battle at the enginarium. Two more had been lost, dragged down as they tried to cut their way free of the mutant mobs. Such deaths were the worst of all, slain by foes unworthy of anything but contempt.

Hafloí set his jaw, ignoring the blood running down the inside of his battered helm, and dug deeper. Somehow, his limbs kept working, driven down solely by excess hyperadrenaline and combat-stimms.

The Caestus was less than thirty metres away, though it might as well have been on the far side of the solar system – the space between was crammed with swarms of plague-damned, whose only remaining task was to keep the intruders from escaping the Hel they had created.

Hafloí was so absorbed in the fighting, was so intent on staying on his feet, that he barely heard the first explosion. It was low – right on the edge of his enhanced auditory range, and far, far away.

The mutants heard it, though. Whether because they were used to the myriad creaks and clangs of the *Festerax*, or through some warp-bound sixth sense, they responded immediately. What little formation they had broke. Some started screaming, not with their usual battle-rage, but with a frantic fear.

A second boom rocked the chamber, far louder this time, like the distant grind of thunderheads in the Asaheim peaks. Every structure around them – the corkscrew pillars, the sagging roofline, the rockcrete floor – trembled as if shaken by a giant hand.

The mutants began to scatter. Some fought on, but many started to scamper for cover, as if there were anywhere to hide from what was to come.

Hafloí, exhausted, checked his chrono.

It read zero. Down in the reactor cores, in the heart of the boiling inferno in the enginarium depths, the charges were going off. The fire would be racing after them, boiling up through the infinite shafts and kindling the methane. In his mind's eye, Hafloí saw the colossal wave of pure destruction welling up towards them, churning and destroying as it came. It would take mere moments to reach them.

His exhausted head lifted. Urgent energy stirred in his ravaged body once more. He could see the target now – half lost amid the melted panels of the chamber wall and skewed at a steep angle.

He kicked out, breaking the spine of a mutant who was too mind-addled to retreat, then joined his brothers in the race.

As the two halves of the collar fell away, Baldr's power erupted into life. Fulguration screamed out from him, roaring like an unleashed avalanche. The throne exploded around him, breaking into a thousand pieces. His bonds were hurled aside, burning with silver-edged fire. He rose into the air, his arms outstretched, surrounded by a halo of pure, devastating power.

Baldr swept his gaze across the horde of undead. He clenched his fists, and they blew apart in a rippling wave of torn flesh and bone. The ghosts screamed out of existence, howling as they were banished back to the underverse.

He surged then towards the Mycelite, who was already backing away. Baldr opened up his clenched gauntlet, and a column of raging silver coruscation lanced out, slamming into the sorcerer and hurling him across the bridge. The Mycelite tried to respond, to fight back against the deluge, but Baldr's fury was unstoppable. The power flooded out of him, wild and feral, vomiting out of his soul from where it had been confined for too long. The fires broke open the Mycelite's armour, revealing a hunchbacked, milk-fleshed body beneath. The sorcerer screamed, locked in the thundering aegis of silver fire, and his staff shattered.

Baldr swooped down on him, both fists blazing. The Mycelite cowered. Gouts of black smoke roiled up his broken armour as the exposed skin was consumed in the fire.

Baldr drew his right fist back, coiling up yet more power in his clenched gauntlet. The Mycelite tried to raise his arms in some kind of defence, but Baldr punched straight through them, breaking the creature's wrists and driving the bone-fragments deep into his age-withered face.

He kept on punching, pouring out his wrath on the one who had imprisoned him. He remembered killing his own kind while lost in the warp-dream, and his cry of anguish echoed around the bridge. The blows rained down, smashing and cracking in a hail of anger-driven strikes.

With a wet snap, the Mycelite's neck broke. A huge explosion boomed out, and the entire chamber was consumed in a driving wind, flickering with ghoulish lights like the flashing eyes of the dead.

Then the tempest died. Baldr's own fires went out, leaving him standing on the decking amid the last echoes of the horrific outpouring. He swayed on his feet, suddenly feeling hollow. Black stars crowded his vision, and he felt his awareness sliding away.

Njal, his armour still coated in the last of the foul warp-bile, staggered to his feet. The remains of the Mycelite lay before them both, a blackened husk of scorched flesh. For a moment, it was all Baldr could do just to look on it. The hatred did not diminish. He felt *sick*, dragged back into the corruption he had worked so hard to fight off.

The two pieces of his null-collar lay behind him, lifeless and inert. With dreadful realisation, Baldr saw how completely he had damned himself. There could be no doubt now.

I am awakened, he thought, just as the wave of blackness rose up to engulf him.

The deck rippled like a wave, breaking open into fire-edged plates. A flash of deep red flame briefly surged up, swiftly doused. More booms rang out from a long way down, growing far louder. Hafloí heard secondary sounds follow in their wake – a sustained roar, like the tide coming in.

The pack tore through the remaining resistance and reached the Caestus. Embarkation ramps slammed down, whining on impact-stressed pistons. Gunnlaugur clanged up the interior towards the cockpit.

'Five seconds,' he ordered.

Hafloí was the last one in before the ramp pulled closed again. It bolted shut and the brace-clamps slotted into place. From outside, a great, sighing snap heralded the bifurcation of the chamber's structural underpinning, followed by a rain of dislodged rubble from the roof.

The Caestus pushed off clumsily, buoyed by a surge from its retro-thrusters. Metal debris slewed from its outer hull as it turned on a cushion of superheated exhaust. A supporting column collapsed close by, shattering as it hit the undulating floor.

Then the main engines kicked in. Hafloí had barely reached for the restraint harness when the motive force hit, throwing him hard against the vessel's metal interior. A booming growl of thruster-fire filled the space, and the assault ram powered for the open void again.

By instinct, Hafloí routed his helm-feed to the craft's anterior real-viewer. At first, the feed showed nothing but fire and static. Then, as the Caestus picked up speed and raced beyond the hull perimeter, the colours and shapes fell into cohesion.

He saw the flanks of the *Festerax* rear up behind them, stretching away in every direction. The outer shell had been dark and mottled on the way in, like a clenched fist of rotten iron. Now it burned and flared like the surface of a star.

As he watched, whole sections of fused starship-carcasses were consumed by vast, silent explosions. Rivers of magma spontaneously burst from cracks in the plague-hulk's flanks. The vista reeled, collapsing and expanding as colossal reservoirs of toxic gases at the ship's heart ignited. Voidships that had remained lodged tight for centuries were suddenly blasted loose, before disintegrating in spiralling orgies of destruction.

Hafloí watched it in silence, slumped against the shuddering sides of the Caestus. He watched the *Festerax* slowly shrink in the viewers as the

Caestus shot away from the impact site. He watched the chain reactions pick up force, blasting massive chunks of matter out into the void. He registered the phenomenal build-up of heat and pressure within the heart of the hulk.

The *Festerax* was dying, carved apart by the insanely rapid reactions boiling away in its bowels. A vessel of such magnitude would still take a while to die, but die it would, condemned by its own internal, infernal chemistry.

'*Heimdall,*' came Gunnlaugur's voice over the pack-comm. 'Hunt is complete. We are out, running hot. Loc-reading needed.'

There was a crackle, and then the link solidified. 'We detect two Caestus rams outbound, lord. Can you confirm?'

A pause. 'Scan for a third. Hulk void-weapons are disabled. Come in and get us.'

'Understood, lord. Do you have the Stormcaller among you?'

Another pause. 'No. You detect his loc-reading?'

'Negative.'

Haflói heard Gunnlaugur's curse over the shared comm-loop. It sounded bone-weary, as if all his strength had been left behind on the battlefield.

'Keep scanning,' he ordered.

Then the link cut.

Njal limped over to Baldr, catching him before he crashed to the deck. The Hunter's face was as pale as death, his eyes rimmed with blood. The destruction of the collar had left a bloody weal around his neck.

Baldr looked blearily around him. The command bridge was shaking, rocked by titanic movements. The sound of vast, echoing booms roiled up from below them.

'The charges...' he rasped.

Njal dragged him back to his feet. A badly damaged Nightwing flapped heavily on to his shoulder.

'*Heimdall,*' the Rune Priest said, running rapid checks on his Terminator teleport homer.

'Too... far,' gasped Baldr.

More echoing crashes sounded. Cracks suddenly jagged across the bridge decking, opening up flame-filled fissures. The remnants of ancient armourglass shattered, sending crystal rain showering across the dust.

'You forget who you are with,' growled Njal, preparing his mind for the trial.

More spars fell from the roof of the grotto, disintegrating into heaps of glowing ash as they hit the floor.

A gout of pure magma suddenly shot up through the ruined decking, less than a metre away, foaming and raging. More booms resounded, making the whole chamber shake.

Njal activated the teleport mechanism. A sphere of warp-frosted silver burned out, enclosing them both in a perfect orb of glittering iridescence.

The floor of the *Frostaxe*'s bridge gave way entirely, dissolving into a steaming, frothing sea of molten plasma. More magma-streamers jutted upwards, crashing into the chamber's roof and slicing clean through it. The entire bridge tottered, slewed, then imploded, buoyed up only by the glowing swell of liquid energy beneath.

For a few seconds, the ruined body of the Mycelite was the only thing to resist it, remaining intact amid the orange tide like a cork bobbing on the waves. Flames scorched across the ancient ceramite, stripped clear the layers of filth that a lifetime of corruption had generated. The emblem of Mortarion's proud Legion flashed clean again – a death's head enclosed in a dark star-pattern.

Then the sweep of destruction overtook it all, subsuming the chamber in molten ruin. The residual fungus crackled and crisped. The ancient corpses blazed like torches, accompanied by the impotent screams of their maddened souls.

Then the last of the superstructure fell away, the brace-beams cut free of the shaft's walls, and the Mycelite's domain was finally overcome by the fiery death of the *Festerax*.

Chapter Twenty-Three

Ingvar held his ground. From beyond the broken blast-doors, the Ecclesiarchy troops held theirs. He could sense their unwillingness to open fire, but neither were they going anywhere.

Jorundur radiated steady belligerence. The earlier combat seemed to have provoked the darker side of his nature, and Ingvar knew he would have no qualms about laying into any mortals daring to cross the threshold.

Ingvar could smell Klaive's blood in the air. The confessor was still unconscious, his body stretched out on the deck. There were so many questions. What had he been doing on Ras Shakeh? What secrets had he swept up with him, lifting them into the sanctuary of *Vindicatus* and away from prying eyes? Surely he'd taken any sensitive material with him, the kind of thing Bajola had warned him about. Klaive was the link – the reason the Ecclesiarchy had come to the isolated world in such numbers.

He needed to get him away, a place where he could ask the questions directly and without fear of interruption.

Do you know the name Hjortur Bloodfang?

Why was he killed?

And the most pressing:

What is the Fulcrum?

Every second they waited there, locked in a stalemate of mutual suspicion, the window for action shrunk a little further. And yet, if the two of them forced their way out, the Ministorum would respond and Delvaux's last order would be enacted.

The fate of an entire world, versus the truth of a lone murder. Not much of a choice.

Ingvar turned to Jorundur. 'Any signal?'

'Nothing.'

'We are wasting time.'

'Nothing's wasted.'

Jorundur wasn't going to move. Ingvar envied his certainties. 'Hand me the comm-bead,' he said. 'I want to speak to her.'

Jorundur unclipped the device from his gorget and passed it over. As Ingvar held it in his hand, it snapped into life.

'News, my lord,' came Callia's voice. 'Your Rune Priest has done it. The hulk is breaking up.'

Ingvar felt a surge of raw relief. 'My thanks, Sister. And you?'

'We're heading out of orbit. *Heimdall* is moving into range. We detected two boarding craft docking.'

Some survived, then.

'Our place is there, Sister,' he said.

'Your gunship is where you left it, and I have ordered it not to be touched. I remember how... particular your brother is about that.'

Ingvar checked to see if his armour's comm system backed her tidings up. Initially, his helm-display showed nothing. Then, with some distortion, a message flickered up on his retinal feed.

'Hunt complete,' came the burst, bearing *Heimdall*'s security mark. 'All warriors to return to *Heimdall*. Repeat: all warriors to *Heimdall*.'

Ingvar found himself wondering who had authorised that message. Had Gunnlaugur got out alive? Had Njal?

Ahead of them, in the corridor beyond the broken doors, the soldiers stood down, holstering weapons and standing to attention. They looked relieved.

'Can you get *Vuokho* moving again?' Ingvar asked Jorundur.

The Old Dog issued a low warning growl, which was all the answer he was ever going to give, and stomped off.

Ingvar reached for the still unconscious Klaive and hauled him, one-handed, from the deck. As the confessor was dragged up from the floor, his eyes flickered open briefly.

'Best you stay asleep,' hissed Ingvar coldly. 'When you next wake, things will look a lot worse.'

Annarovea was the first to receive the sensor readings. She pored over the pict screen, her face lit green by the runes flickering across it. As she took in the data, her grip on the console edge gradually relaxed. She pushed back in her chair and looked up at Olgeir.

'They're moving off,' she said.

Olgeir studied the readings for himself. *Vindicatus* had changed course, pulling higher. The power build-up along its flanks reduced, indicating that the torpedo launches had been cancelled. Soon the ship would be out of launch-range.

In addition, the hulk's trajectory had slowed radically. It no longer barrelled along on a direct course for the planet, but seemed to have blurred into a whole smear of indistinct sensor-ghosts.

'Can we get a hololith of that?' he asked.

Annarovea gave the order, and a cloud of red wireframes spun into life above the sensor station. The translucent edifice rippled for a while, struggling to latch on to an incoming feed, then started to rotate more surely.

'Throne,' breathed Annarovea, rapt. 'They killed it.'

The hololith showed the *Festerax* breaking into huge chunks. Mighty explosions rippled through the canyons between segments, showing up as patches of grainy white noise amid the glittering lith-lines. As the behemoth tore itself apart, its approach slowed, skewing it off-course. As the process continued, what was left of the ship would be eaten up before it reached orbit. The molten remains would tumble off into the deep void, the residual toxins freezing into inertness.

Annarovea stirred into action. With the threat of immediate annihilation averted, her earlier air of command returned.

'Broadcast this signal on all channels,' she ordered. 'Report that the incoming anomaly has been destroyed before reaching orbit. Reassure all citizens that order will shortly be restored. Repeat earlier commands restricting movement, and remind the populace that any citizens participating in disorder will face the full sanction of emergency law.'

Her officials hurried to comply, and soon the city-wide vox-casters were blaring the message out, accompanied by images of the *Festerax*'s lingering death.

Annarovea turned to face Olgeir. 'Your comrades...'

Olgeir continued staring at the hololith. For a moment, it looked as if the plague-hulk carcass was all that remained.

Then his helm-comm activated. 'Hunt complete. All warriors to return to *Heimdall*. Repeat: all warriors to *Heimdall*.'

As the message completed, the ravaged outline of Stormcaller's ship appeared within the sensor ambit, far behind *Vindicatus* but nonetheless moving under her own power.

Olgeir drew in a deep breath. Something remained to be salvaged, then.

'You may recall your troops now, governor,' he said, closing the comm-link.

'The orders are already sent,' said Annarovea. 'The first carriers will make planetfall in a few hours.'

'That should give you all you need to restore order.'

'It will take a while.'

'That it will.'

'And you?'

'I have my summons.'

Annarovea bowed. 'Very well. You must attend to your duties. But...' She paused, as if struggling to find the words. 'My thanks, lord. When you arrived–'

'Noted, governor,' said Olgeir. He let a smile crack across his scarred face. 'It is good to endure the storm.'

Heimdall's bridge was a mess. Cables hung in loops from the battered roof-arches, many sparking with unstaunched electrics. A whole section of the rear tactical area was in ruins, with both servitors and mortal crew trapped in the rubble. The command throne had survived relatively intact, as had the control stations ahead and below it, though the main forward viewscreen was scored deeply from repeated impacts.

Gunnlaugur stood on the rockcrete platform before the throne, his arms crossed, staring out at the scene before him. The surviving members of the kill-teams surrounded him – just fourteen, including himself, Hafloí and the two Thunderhawk pilots who'd remained on *Heimdall*. There was no sign of Njal.

'Detect anything yet?' he demanded of Derroth, *Heimdall's* shipmaster.

The *Festerax* was gone. Its messy demise was clearly visible from the real-viewers. The burning remains looked like some huge asteroid being ripped apart by blood-red tectonic movements.

'We are working, lord,' said Derroth.

Gunnlaugur's combat-euphoria ebbed slowly. The incoming flight on damaged Caestus rams had been nightmarish, contending with stuttering engines, a mauled landing stage and *Heimdall*'s own erratic movements through space. On reaching safety, Gunnlaugur and the others had made their way straight to the command level.

There was no sign of Stormcaller, and no reliable link to Kefa Primaris. The *Festerax*'s huge burning ruins stood between them and the planet, playing havoc with their surviving systems.

'Then he is lost,' said Gunnlaugur, his voice grim. 'What news from *Vindicatus*?'

'Moving to high anchor,' replied Derroth, running a weary hand across his cropped hair. '*Vuokho* is inbound, and will dock soon.'

Gunnlaugur nodded. Ingvar had survived, so it seemed, and was bring-ing something with him. The Gyrfalkon had sounded animated over the comm, which boded well.

'So be it,' Gunnlaugur said, turning to his battle-brothers. 'We have–'

His words died as soon as the first stab of warp-energy snaked out across the centre of the bridge decking.

Gunnlaugur backed away from it. The bridge crew cleared a wide space around the empty command throne, opening it up as the air shook and shimmered.

Worm-like slivers of actinic matter snaked across the marble, joining up and twisting into slithering whips of power. The temperature suddenly plummeted, sending a fractured skin of hoarfrost shooting across exposed metalwork. There was a hard, echoing bang, the stench of ozone, then a vivid flash of magnesium-white.

When the blast cleared, two figures stood at its heart. One was Njal, the other was Baldr. Both were covered from head to boot in a thin layer of steaming ice, and residual warp-energies danced across their armour. Njal's battleplate had brutal rents in the ceramite, as if mauled by some huge beast.

'Stormcaller!' cried one of the crew, his voice filled with a savage, unlooked-for joy.

Gunnlaugur had no time to react. His shock at seeing Njal on the bridge was only matched by that at seeing Baldr again. No teleport signal had been detected, and no locus had been issued. The Rune Priest had guided himself, somehow fighting through the vagaries of the warp to emerge, with pinpoint accuracy, back in the world of matter.

'Did we kill it?' growled Njal, his voice thick with effort. 'Does it burn?'

Recovering himself, Gunnlaugur bowed clumsily. 'It burns, lord,' he said.

Out in the void, secondary explosions continued to go off, radiating silently like the birth of new and strange stars.

Njal twisted his helm free, revealing a harrowed, fatigue-hollow face. His blue eyes scrutinised the fallout.

'Deploy the gunships again,' he rasped from a hoarse throat. 'Scan for movement in the wreckage. Any signs of life, notify me. Signal *Vindicatus* and request it remains in contact. Signal the surface and inform the Governor. We cannot relax yet.'

As all eyes were on Njal, Baldr suddenly fell to his knees. His ice-pale face was streaked with blood, and his eyes were glassy.

Before any kaerls could reach him he had crashed to the metal plating, out cold. Haflói hurried to his side, but Njal held up a warning hand.

'No!' he commanded darkly. 'Do not go near him.' The Rune Priest turned to Gunnlaugur. 'The fault is mine. He should never have been taken back.'

Njal stalked over to Baldr's prone body and stooped over him, holding out an open palm, as if scanning for residual corruption.

No one moved. Gunnlaugur waited with the rest of them, powerless to intervene. They all watched the Rune Priest, not daring to interrupt.

Eventually, Njal straightened. His expression was mixed: grim, marked by a weary, duty-driven reluctance.

'He lives?' asked Gunnlaugur, already fearing what the response would be.

'He lives,' said Njal. 'As do I, and that counts for something.'

Nightwing turned its gimlet eye towards Gunnlaugur.

'But there is no doubt now,' Njal went on. 'He invoked the storm. He has the blood of our packs on his claws. I was wrong. I was badly wrong.' The Rune Priest's voice was tight with loathing. 'Suffer not the witch to live,' he said, bitterly. 'There can be no other judgement.'

The words hit Gunnlaugur like blows. Such was the iron law of Fenris, and it was just, and sanctified by millennia, but it made the verdict no less hard to hear.

He bowed his head stiffly.

'As you command it,' Gunnlaugur said, forcing the words out, 'it will be done.'

Vuokho came in hard, skidding across the flight deck apron as the thrusters gave out. Just as it had been since the void-battle over Ras Shakeh, the gunship remained on the verge of destruction, held together seemingly by Jorundur's will and little else.

Gunnlaugur watched it land. The assault ramp slammed down and Ingvar stomped down to deck level.

'Old Dog?' Gunnlaugur asked, as the void-deck crew raced towards the gunship with fire-dousing gear.

'Looking after our guest,' said Ingvar, wryly. 'The confessor, brother. I have him.'

Gunnlaugur raised an eyebrow. 'They let you take him?'

'We did not ask.'

Ingvar radiated zeal – his hunt-sense was palpable. Ever since Bajola's death he'd been obsessed with this quest.

Gunnlaugur couldn't match the euphoria, not any more.

'What is it, brother?' Ingvar asked.

'Come with me,' Gunnlaugur said, turning and walking towards *Heimdall*'s interior. Ingvar fell in alongside him.

'You heard what happened?' Gunnlaugur asked.

'We detected the *Festerax*'s destruction.'

'After that?'

'Nothing. *Vuokho*'s instruments barely function.'

'Baldr lives. Njal retrieved him.'

'He's... How?'

'I do not know. Njal discovered him at the hulk's heart. Baldr used the way of the storm.' Gunnlaugur shot Ingvar a bleak look. 'It happened again.'

Ingvar shook his head furiously. 'He was *recovered*.'

'Obviously not.'

'Did he use sorcery? Was it corruption, like before?'

Gunnlaugur shrugged. 'What does it matter?'

'It means *everything*.' Ingvar stopped walking, and gripped Gunnlaugur's arm. 'We knew he had changed. It was bound to come back, but what was he *like*? Was he corrupted?'

'I know not. Njal has ruled, brother.'

'I do not care what Njal has ruled! Damn you – he is one of *us*. What do *you* rule?'

Gunnlaugur shook his head. The certainties that had flooded back to him in the heart of combat were now dissipated. He knew nothing of the ways of the runes, and that blunted his instincts. 'I do not know.'

'We brought him *back*.' Ingvar's voice rang with certainty. 'We made him whole again. Njal should never have taken him on the hulk. It was too soon, and we both knew it.'

Those words had the ring of truth to them – Baldr *had* recovered. Whatever had been done to him on that ship might have affected any of them.

'Maybe so, but it is over now, brother,' said Gunnlaugur, unwilling to follow the path this was leading down.

'Where is he held?'

'Do not even think that.'

'Just tell me.'

'The apothecarion,' said Gunnlaugur, angrily. 'And when he wakes, judgement will be served. He is guarded.'

'Where is Heavy-hand?'

'Inbound on *Hlaupnir*.'

Ingvar started to walk again, his strides full of purpose. 'We cannot let this go, brother,' he said. 'You brought him back in. He was restored.'

Gunnlaugur went after him. 'There is nothing we can do.'

'You said it yourself: he's one of us. He's Járnhamar.'

'Then *say* it, brother,' said Gunnlaugur, feeling both cornered and shamed by Ingvar's fervour. 'What do you propose?'

Ingvar turned to face him. His grey eyes glittered with fresh purpose.

'Just listen,' he began.

Chapter Twenty-Four

Bjargborn stirred as the locks to the chamber clicked. Others around him looked up, roused from whatever torpor they had sunk into.

For hours there had been no contact. *Heimdall*'s structure had continued to creak and crack, though the worst of the impacts had ceased a long time ago. Bjargborn had been pleased enough just to be alive to hear it – the cruiser had evidently weathered a hard period of void-combat. In the dreary hours that followed, however, when no word came down to them of any change in their status, his spirits had flagged. A dour mood had descended across the chamber as his warriors did their best to keep occupied.

The enforced inactivity was enervating. There must have been things they could have done on the ship – repairs to be made, gun-stations to man. They were all experienced soldiers, many of them drawn from *Undrider*'s specialist ranks, and they were withering away.

But when the lock clicked, Bjargborn snapped back into old habits immediately.

'Prepare,' he ordered, pulling his tunic straight and brushing down his grey fatigues.

By the time the doors opened, the entire space had resumed a semblance

of military order, with troops standing to attention alongside the ranks
of still-warm bunks.

Ingvar entered, and sought out Bjargborn. 'Rivenmaster,' he said. 'You
have been patient.'

Bjargborn bowed. His pulse was racing. He found himself praying for
a combat mission. 'We're needed?' was all he said.

Ingvar closed the door behind him. The Space Marine was as brutally massive as ever, but something about his movements was almost...
furtive.

'You should never have been kept here,' he said, his voice low. 'Forgive
us. The fighting has been hard.'

'Anything,' said Bjargborn. 'We'll do anything. Just say the word.'

'How many of you are primary ship-crew?'

'Most. Between us, there isn't a starship-system we can't cover.'

'A warp-runner will soon be docking in berth two. Its designation
is *Hlaupnir*, and it requires a full crew replacement. It is smaller than
Undrider, but burns well enough through the void. We will be travelling
on it for some time.'

Bjargborn nodded. 'I can organise the work details. How long do we
have?'

'Under an hour,' said Ingvar. 'Work details can wait. I want your troops
armed and combat-ready, then make your way to the hangar straightaway.
We launch as soon as the engines are primed.'

Bjargborn hesitated. 'Of course,' he said. 'Can I ask–'

'Do you trust me?'

Bjargborn thought back to Hjec Falama. He had been raised and trained
to obey the orders of a Sky Warrior without question, and before him stood
the one who had delivered them from a slow death in the plague-wastes.

'It wounds me that you would ask, lord,' he said.

'I need that trust,' Ingvar said. 'You will answer to Járnhamar, just as
before. We are going to be out on our own for a while. There may be
other mortals on *Heimdall* who do not see things the same way. You
understand me?'

Bjargborn did. Such things were, and always had been, the way of the
Fang. Wolf Lords left for hunts, Lone Wolves split from the Great Companies. The *outrider* was a part of the Canis Helix's heritage – the urge
to charge off across the ice alone, splitting from the herd and pursuing
whatever wyrd had fallen upon him.

'I understand you.'

'Olgeir will bring the ship in. Do whatever he commands. We will be loading *Vuokho*. That will be difficult – manpower will be required. Do not attempt the enter the gunship – it contains sanctioned cargo.' Ingvar fixed Bjargborn with a significant look. 'You will be a shipmaster again. That suits you better than...' He looked around him. 'This.'

'By your will,' grinned Bjargborn.

'*Hlaupnir*'s current crew will be discharged. You will replace them. If there is any confusion or resistance, you will end it. No deadly force unless necessary – these are our people. But we *will* leave on that ship.'

'Understood. Weapons?'

'I will see to it the armoury is unlocked within ten minutes. You will do the rest. Take only what is necessary – we are not here to weaken *Heimdall*. Anything else?'

Bjargborn looked at his fellow kaerls. There was nothing but enthusiasm in their expressions, and that was reassuring. They had survived amid a living, boiling nightmare with nothing but saviour-pod rations and a blind faith that their masters would, sooner or later, come looking for them. That faith had been rewarded, cementing a bond of loyalty that was stronger than adamantium.

'Nothing at all, lord,' said Bjargborn, flexing his fingers in anticipation. 'We live to serve.'

Gunnlaugur strode down the corridor towards the apothecarion. The conduits were not busy this far down – most of the crew were engaged in urgent repair work or the recovery of weapon systems. Njal had ordered a quick turnaround prior to entering orbit alongside *Vindicatus*. He had much on his mind: the re-establishment of a working relationship with Ecclesiarchy forces in-system, proper contact with the Guard regiments on Kefa, a restoration of *Heimdall*'s fighting capability.

That was fortunate. If things had been less frenetic, a chance of slipping through the net would never have presented itself.

He rounded the last corner. Arjen, a Hunter of Bloodhame's pack, stood guard outside the doors. He was helmless, but two kaerls in full combat-gear were with him, each bearing an autogun. The doors were locked and braced, cutting off access to the cell beyond.

Gunnlaugur emerged into the open.

'No closer, vaerangi,' said Arjen warily, raising his bolter.

'Does he live still?' asked Gunnlaugur, keeping his hands well away from his weapons.

'No idea. Leave, now. Njal will–'

Gunnlaugur held his ground. 'He is my warrior.'

'Not any more.'

Gunnlaugur took a step closer. 'Just a look, brother. A final word. You would wish for the same, if he were of your pack.'

Arjen aimed straight at Gunnlaugur's chest. 'One more step.'

Gunnlaugur held Arjen's gaze. They had fought together for a long time in the depths of the hulk, but he had no doubt at all that Arjen would fire.

He backed off, slowly, keeping his hands in the open. 'So you say.'

Just then, there was a crash from inside the apothecarion, steel clanging heavily on steel. Arjen's head snapped round. He reached for the door release.

Gunnlaugur responded instantly, whipping his bolter from his belt and opening up. Bolt-rounds hit Arjen's shoulder, throwing him back against the doors with a heavy crash.

The kaerls fired back, and a rain of projectiles pinged and ricocheted from Gunnlaugur's armour.

Arjen recovered quickly, sweeping his own bolter back into a firing angle. Just as he did so, the doors slid open from the far side, revealing Hafloí standing under the lintel with his bolt pistol already aimed.

He fired twice, sending Arjen slamming towards the far corridor wall. Gunnlaugur pounced after him, switching to fists. As the wounded Arjen tried to right himself, Gunnlaugur hammered him hard – once, twice, then a third time.

Still he wouldn't go down. Snarling, Gunnlaugur thumped down both balled fists, nearly taking his head clean off.

That finally did it. Arjen slumped to the floor, his face a mask of blood. By then one of the kaerls had already been immobilised by Hafloí, but the second had managed to flee, running down the corridor, firing behind him erratically.

He ran straight into the emerging grey cliff-face of Ingvar's power armour, and bounced painfully from the unyielding ceramite. Ingvar swung out with a half-strength backhand swipe, throwing the mortal to the deck. He didn't get up.

'Swiftly,' said Gunnlaugur, moving into the apothecarion.

Baldr was restrained on the metal slab, just as on Ras Shakeh, shackled at the ankles, wrists and neck by thick adamantium loops. He was still unconscious, though he showed none of the signs of the Red Dream,

nor of the deep sickness that had plagued him on Ras Shakeh. A rune-
totem hung from the ceiling above him, no doubt left by Njal to stifle
any recurrence of maleficarum, and a new collar had been fitted around
his neck to dampen his innate powers.

A lone ceiling panel rested on the floor where Haflói had dislodged it.
In the hole above, ragged edges of cut metal still glowed red from where
he had used a melta-blade to gain access from the chamber above.

Ingvar followed Gunnlaugur in, drawing *dausvjer* as he came. 'This will
be quickest,' he said, activating the blade's energy field.

Haflói moved to cover the open doorway, keeping his bolter trained on
the corridor outside. Ingvar worked quickly, slicing through the bonds
without cutting into the flesh below. As he did so, Baldr stirred.

'Remain calm, brother,' said Gunnlaugur.

Baldr looked like he barely understood. As Ingvar severed the last of
the shackles, he looked around himself groggily. 'What happened?' he
muttered.

Gunnlaugur grabbed him by the arm and roughly hauled him from the
bunk, righting him to prevent him crashing face-first to the deck. Ingvar
seized his other arm, propping him up. The three of them stumbled back
into the corridor, supporting Baldr's armoured weight between them.

Haflói went ahead, scanning for movement.

'You need to stand,' said Ingvar, trying to right Baldr. 'Can you do that?'

Baldr swayed a little, but kept his feet. 'Where are we going?' he asked,
his speech still slurred.

'Now walk. Our orders are to take you to *Hlaupnir*.'

'Stormcaller...' started Baldr, frowning in confusion.

'They are his orders,' snapped Gunnlaugur. 'We have little time.'

The habit of pack-command kicked in, and Baldr started to shamble
forwards. With every step, a little more fluency returned. By the time
he'd reached the end of the first long corridor, his gait was more or less
normal.

As Gunnlaugur strode along beside him, he reflected on the risk they
were taking. There was no possibility of stealth – they had to brazen it
out, trusting to speed, to the servility of the kaerls, and to the fact that
anyone likely to recognise Baldr's armour markings was either on the
bridge or engaged in fresh combat preparation.

If that assumption proved wrong, punishment would be swift, merci-
less, and unavoidable.

'Keep moving, brother,' he muttered through gritted teeth, resisting the urge to push Baldr along or pick up the pace. 'It is all you have to do. Keep moving.'

Olgeir strode down *Hlaupnir*'s main embarkation ramp and onto the floor of the docking berth.

It was still active with refit-teams and servitors. The turnaround he'd been asked to make had been ludicrously tight, even without the added complication of a full crew-switch. Thraid and the rest of the ship's complement had obeyed without question, of course – they were used to sudden redeployments across the Chapter vessels as the needs of war dictated – but the numbers involved were a challenge.

Bjargborn's detachment were now on board and prepping the ship for launch. *Vuokho* had been lifted into the vessel's lone hangar, fuel had been taken on, the engines given a final, though cursory, check.

They were good to go. For all that, Olgeir remained tense. Gunnlaugur's orders had come with no warning, and though he guessed the reasons for it, that didn't mean he liked them.

This will damn us. There will be no way back from this.

He heard a heavy series of thuds behind him, and turned to see Jorundur heading down the ramp after him.

'You know what's in there, don't you?' Jorundur asked.

Olgeir shook his head.

'The Cardinal's confessor,' said Jorundur. 'That's our cargo.'

'Skítja,' muttered Olgeir.

He checked his chrono again. Any minute now, Thraid would be reporting for duty. He'd be looking up at his superior officer, confused that he wasn't expected. Data-slates would be retrieved, and discrepancies would be noted. Then it would become apparent that he hadn't been ordered to leave *Hlaupnir* at all, and Njal would be alerted.

All it would take would be a lock-command placed over the berth's void-gate.

'Where *are* they?' Olgeir breathed. 'If this doesn't happen soon–'

His comm-bead blinked. The ident-rune was Rasek, *Heimdall*'s void-deck controller, one of many kaerl officers overseeing the movement of the various gunships and landers stowed in the cruiser's hangars.

'What is it?' Olgeir asked.

'Apologies, lord. I have word from Derroth, requesting your presence on the command deck. Did you receive it? The Stormcaller is waiting.'

'I got the message. Tell Derroth we have a problem shutting down the drives on *Hlaupnir*. It will not take long.'

'A problem? Do you have sufficient servitor cover, lord?'

Olgeir could sense the uncertainty in the man's voice. There was no reason for him to oversee any repairs – he was not an obsessive like Jorundur, and there were many more pressing tasks for a Sky Warrior to undertake.

'Tell Derroth five minutes.' He cut the link. 'He will start the process now,' he growled to Jorundur. 'The checks will begin.'

Jorundur chuckled darkly. 'How long have we got?'

'I'm going on board. We need to get those engines fired.'

Jorundur was about to join him when a set of cargo-lift doors in the nearside walls suddenly slid open. Both of them spun around, instinctively going for their weapons.

Ingvar, Gunnlaugur and Baldr emerged, hurrying across the hangar deck.

'Let us *leave*, Heavy-Hand,' Gunnlaugur ordered. '*Now.*'

Njal stood on *Heimdall*'s command bridge. Kefa Primaris hung in the forward viewer, far huger than it had been during the final living hours of the *Festerax*. Its dirty grey surface was clearly visible through the bands of drifting cloud, as were the looming silhouettes of Guard troop carriers steadily making their way back to orbital berth-points.

Wreckage of the destroyed plague-hulk still registered on the augurs. Every chunk was tracked and investigated lest it be carrying some vestige of spoor-matter. Even a tiny amount could still prove ruinous, should it somehow survive the entry into Kefa's atmosphere.

He remembered the final moments aboard the *Frostaxe*. He remembered the horror, the chill grasp around his hearts. He remembered Baldr's fury.

God-marked.

The law was immutable. It was the Chapter's only lasting defence against corruption. It was whispered among the ignorant that no Son of Russ had ever fallen to the service of the Great Enemy, and that the Rout alone retained the purity of the early Imperium in its Helix-strengthened veins.

Njal knew the falsity of that. Wolves had succumbed, whether through lust for battle, or power, or via the cruel arts of the enemy. Njal knew the tally of such lost souls. He knew their names, and what their wyrd had become.

Vigilance had to be eternal, unbending and relentless. Njal had already failed in that regard once.

I recognise my error. Even I am not above that.

His gaze shifted, passing up from the curve of the hive world to where *Vindicatus* hung, magnificent even in the wake of the damage it had taken. Callia, its new commander, was a woman he could work with. They were both warriors, and that bred a certain understanding.

That was well, for the war had only just started. There would be more incursions, more contagion-fleets, each one designed to cripple worlds, to sap the strength from the sector defences, to strip the productive capacity of every system between the Shakeh worlds and the Cadian perimeter. More plague-ships were ploughing through the void, and more Imperial vessels were burning across the warp in response. With a ponderous, uncertain trajectory, the war-sphere was expanding. There was no telling how many more hulks had been roused from the heart of the Eye, or what strength of Death Guard still marched across the sea of stars.

And at the centre of it, somewhere, was the architect. The Traveller. The master of the *Terminus Est*. He was hidden for now, but it would not stay that way forever.

That would be the real test, the one besides which all others would pale.

'My lord,' came Derroth's voice from close by. 'Did you authorise a launch?'

Njal snapped out of his thoughts. 'I did not.'

Derroth was standing amid the semi-functioning wreckage of a sensor station, surrounded by maintenance servitors. The forward scanners were only giving intermittent readings, and for the time being the bridge crew was relying on a range of short-scope real-viewers.

'A docking berth is open. We have an unauthorised departure.' Derroth looked up at him, shocked. '*Hlaupnir*.'

Njal swept down from his vantage and seized a pict-feed. The screen showed a clear departure vector. The ship was already moving fast.

'Who is on that ship?' he asked.

'Unknown. I just tried to raise them.'

Foreboding suddenly kindled. Nightwing flapped agitatedly on its mount. Njal opened a comm-channel to Arjen, and the link seethed emptily.

Njal swore. He turned to Eir, the most senior of the Wolves still on the bridge. 'Go to the apothecarion. Take others with you. If they are still there, pin them and keep them alive until I reach you.'

Eir stalked off. Njal didn't watch him go – he guessed it was already futile. 'Can we target the ship?' he asked.

Derroth was already working on it. 'We've barely any weapons left, lord,' he said, apologetically.

'Find some.'

By then, Njal could see *Hlaupnir* for himself through the main forward real-view portal. It was powering away at full speed, curving back round in the void. He didn't need to run trajectory analysis to know where it was going – straight for the system's Mandeville point.

'I can give you a limited macrocannon burst,' announced Derroth. 'But the window is closing.'

As Njal watched *Hlaupnir* thrusting away from the planet, an incoming transmission came in from *Vindicatus*.

'My lord Stormcaller,' came Callia's voice. 'We are tracking a rapid acceleration from a ship in your flotilla. Is all well?'

It would not do to have the Ecclesiarchy alerted to division within his ranks. Njal indicated to Derroth to stand the macrocannon crews down. *Heimdall* was already running on uncertain power – loosing a broadside at his own craft risked plunging the ship deeper into crisis.

'All is well, Sister,' replied Njal, working hard to keep the fury out of his voice. 'Chasing down a few stray scents.'

'Understood. One other thing: we have received long-range signals from the Ministorum battle-group *Rasumova*. It will be here in two weeks. There are other markers, but the provenance is yet unknown.' Her voice was triumphant, as well it might be, given her rapid elevation. 'Praise the Emperor. His armies gather.'

Njal's eyes remained locked on the diminishing outline of *Hlaupnir*. He knew who was on it.

Their name will be stricken from all sagas.

'So they do,' said Njal. 'We will confer again soon, Sister.'

Njal cut the link. Derroth was still waiting for an order.

'I can divert power for a single strike,' the shipmaster said. 'One shot. I've inlaid targeting coordinates.'

Njal considered that. He envisaged the lone streak of energy, lancing through the void. He saw the explosion, tumbling through space just as the *Festerax* had done.

He almost gave the command.

He closed his eyes.

+Hear this, Fjolnir,+ he sent, casting his mind-voice out after the wake of the fleeing system-runner. +You know the precipice on which you stand. You know the depths to which you can fall.+

He couldn't tell if the message had found its target. Just making the attempt, though, at least gave a channel for his anger to run down.

+I may have been wrong about you. We all may have been wrong. But if we were not, and if you fall – then I will *hunt* you. I will not let my laxity plague the stars.+

His words spilled into the uncaring void.

+If the time comes, if the touch of corruption stirs, you know what to do. You still have that power, even when all others fail. *Use* it.+

The sending finished. All that was left of *Hlaupnir* on the viewer was a brilliant point of light in the far distance.

Njal watched it for a few moments longer. None of the crew dared interrupt him.

Then, finally, Nightwing extended its wings again, and cawed bleakly. That was enough to break the spell. Njal drew in a deep breath.

'Enough of this. They are gone.'

He turned back to the command bridge, still in semi-disarray, and faced the thousand tasks that still awaited him. It would not be long before battle called again, and *Heimdall* would have to be ready.

'Vox the governor,' he said, wearily. 'We have much to discuss.'

Epilogue

Hlaupnir ran smoothly through the warp. Just as they had said, the vessel was fast. Its lines were cleaner than the old *Undrider*, and it rattled and creaked less as the aether-gales thrust it further and further from Kefa Primaris.

Baldr limped towards the ship's rather makeshift Annulus chamber – a cramped space set near the rear of the main structure. His body had made a swift recovery from the exertions on *Heimdall*, though it was hard to shake the images that still crowded his waking thoughts. Every so often, as he moved his head, or when he blinked, the shrivelled visage of the Mycelite would stare back at him. He still saw those dark, sympathetic eyes staring at him in the dark, and felt the clammy fingertips that had traced a line down his cheek.

He still wore the second collar that Njal had fixed on him, and had no wish to remove it. For as long as he wore it, the risk of his power creeping back was dampened. Perhaps, in time, that state would become permanent, allowing him to fight as he had once done – carefree, untrammelled, his mind locked on the physical and untroubled by thoughts of the immaterial.

Perhaps, he thought. *In time.*

Ingvar was waiting for him outside the low doorway to the Annulus chamber.

'Recovered?' the Gyrfalkon asked him.

'You lied,' Baldr said. 'About Njal. I would not have come, if I'd known.'

'Which is why we lied. The others are waiting.'

'Why take the risk, brother?' asked Baldr, staying where he was. 'You have seen what I can do.'

'You are one of us. That is reason enough.' Ingvar pulled the door open, revealing the chamber beyond. 'There will be a cure. The galaxy is full of secrets. I have seen more than any of you – have some faith.'

Ingvar's voice betrayed the clarity of a certain mind. Baldr couldn't share it.

The two of them entered the Annulus chamber. Gunnlaugur, Jorundur, Olgeir and Hafloí were already there, standing in a loose circle around the stones. Fires burned in alcoves behind them, dully illuminating the iron outlines of sacred runes.

'Recovered?' asked Gunnlaugur.

They all asked the same thing. It felt as if they'd been enquiring after his physical state ever since landing on Ras Shakeh. That would have to change – he was a warrior, cast in the image of Russ, not some sickly patient to be chaperoned through what remained of his service.

'I am restored,' Baldr said, taking his place.

The others all looked at him, each giving away his own thoughts as they did so.

Gunnlaugur had his pride back, no doubt earned in the fiery heart of the plague-hulk. He stood taller, adopting the unconscious swagger of a vaerangi, and the danger – that old, unmatchable danger – had returned to his eyes. Ingvar, too, looked more at ease than he had done. His place had been found again, one of the pack, one of the Rout, and the dark temper that had marred his return had retreated. The bad blood boiling away between them had ebbed, and the prospect of their blades being wielded together in unity was a vision for a hunter to salivate over.

Jorundur and Hafloí had changed little. The Old Dog had spent his time since launch in the repair bays, slowly reconstructing *Vuokho* and lamenting the paucity of tools at his disposal. Hafloí had been badly scarred by the fighting on the hulk, though he already looked stronger for it. Like a blade tempered in the fire, he was rapidly growing sharper. A few more battles like that one, and he'd be as battered and hard-beaten as the rest of them.

Olgeir was the only one not to meet his eye. Baldr knew the reason – he had ever counselled against Baldr's return, and for good reason. There was no malice there, just belief in the law of the Chapter. The distrust would just have to be borne, until such time as one of them, Ingvar or Olgeir, was proved right over what had been done.

'So the step has been taken,' said Gunnlaugur, addressing them all. 'We are on our own. Get used to *Hlaupnir.*'

'Where are we headed?' asked Hafloí, his voice giving away his unease. He still had the weakest ties of brotherhood with the others, despite all that had changed since his arrival.

'Klaive will be our guide,' said Ingvar. He extended his hand, turning it palm-up to reveal a small golden cherub's head, less than a finger's-width in diameter. 'Soon we will have names, and locations, and access to the truth.'

'What truth?'

'The truth of the Fulcrum.'

Hafloí didn't look satisfied. He turned to Gunnlaugur, as if the Wolf Guard were likely to order them back, undoing everything and seeking Njal's rare forgiveness. 'We're running from the war,' he said, disapprovingly.

'There are many wars,' said Gunnlaugur. 'We have a new hunt, no less dangerous than the one we had before.'

'This is blood-debt,' said Ingvar. 'We are bound to honour it.'

An uneasy silence fell. Olgeir said nothing. Jorundur, of all of them, seemed the most content. He had always liked running out on the margins.

'It will be *done*, brothers,' Ingvar went on. 'Hjortur's shade cries out for vengeance. It will be restitution. It will be–'

'Absolution,' said Baldr, realising at last what was being proposed. 'A way back.'

'Perhaps,' said Ingvar, defiantly. 'If we take this to completion, then why should we not return?'

Again, silence fell. The only sounds were the faint crackle of burning coals and the low, ever-present grind of the warp engines.

'Then we are resolved,' said Gunnlaugur. 'We hunt across the sea of stars, never resting, never halting, until we claim the head of Hjortur's killer and bring it back to the Fang. I swear my soul to this, and may Morkai take it if I turn aside.'

Gunnlaugur drew his thunder hammer and extended it over the central stone. The others all did likewise, pulling axes or sword-blades from scabbards and joining them in a six-pointed circle. One by one, they swore the vow, binding their souls to the new hunt.

Baldr was the last. With the eyes of his brothers on him, he spoke the words.

'I swear it,' he said, feeling the weight of the other blades resting on his.

The weapons withdrew. The braziers continued to burn, the engines continued to growl. It was almost as if nothing had changed, but they knew, they all knew, that everything had.

Ingvar looked at him. 'This is the beginning, brother,' he said confidently. 'This is the greatest test.'

Baldr nodded, trying to believe it. In his mind, though, Njal's words still rang clear, the ones that he alone had heard, just before *Hlaupnir* had reached the jump-points.

If the time comes, if the touch of corruption stirs, you know what to do. You still have that power, even when all others fail. Use it.

'The beginning,' he replied, forcing a smile.

All around them, the walls of the Annulus trembled slightly as warp-gusts shook the ship. *Hlaupnir* powered onwards, forging a path deeper into the aether, leaving the Kefa system behind.

Ahead of them, vast and unknowable, stood the open void. Somewhere out there lay the object of the hunt.

For now, though, they flew blind – alone, adrift, and guided only by fate.

ABOUT THE AUTHOR

Chris Wraight is the author of the Horus Heresy novel *Scars*, the novella *Brotherhood of Storm* and the audio drama *The Sigillite*. For Warhammer 40,000 he has written the Space Wolves novels *Blood of Asaheim* and *Stormcaller*, and the short story collection *Wolves of Fenris*, as well as the Space Marine Battles novels *Wrath of Iron* and *Battle of the Fang*. Additionally, he has many Warhammer novels to his name, including the Time of Legends novel *Master of Dragons*, which forms part of the War of Vengeance series. Chris lives and works near Bristol, in south-west England.

DATE DUE
